THE
DREADFUL
LEMON
SKY

John D. MacDonald

FAWCETT GOLD MEDAL • NEW YORK

A Fawcett Gold Medal Book
Published by Ballantine Books
Copyright © 1974 by John D. MacDonald Publishing, Inc.

ISBN 0-449-12395-2

First Fawcett Gold Medal Edition: September 1975
First Ballantine Books Edition: July 1982
Second Printing: July 1983

For each true friend of Travis McGee

Life is not a spectacle or a feast:
it is a predicament.

—SANTAYANA

1

I WAS in deep sleep, alone aboard my houseboat, alone in the half acre of bed, alone in a sweaty dream of chase, fear, and monstrous predators. A shot rang off steel bars. Another. I came bursting up out of sleep to hear the secretive sound of the little bell which rings at my bedside when anyone steps aboard *The Busted Flush*. It was almost four in the morning.

It could be some kid prowling the decks for a forgotten camera, portable radio, or bottle of Scotch. Or a friendly drunk. Or a drunken friend. Or trouble. I could not know how long I had slept past the first ting of the bell. I pulled on a pair of shorts and went padding through the blackness, past the head and the galley, through into the lounge to the locked doorway that opens onto the sheltered deck aft. The handgun which I had slipped from its handy recess before I was totally awake felt cold in my grasp.

I heard a small knocking sound, secret and tentative. "Trav?" A husky, half-whispering girl voice. "Trav McGee? Trav, honey?"

I moved over to where I could see through glass at

7

an angle, just enough to make out the girl shape of the small figure huddled close to the door, out of the brightness of the dock lights. She seemed to be quite alone.

I called through the closed door, "Who are you?"

"Trav? Don't turn on any lights, huh? Please!"

"Who is it?"

"It's me! It's Carrie. Carrie Milligan."

I hesitated, then sheathed the revolver under the waistband of the shorts, cold against belly flesh. I unlocked and let her in and locked the door again.

She hooked one arm around me and hugged her small self tightly against me and let out a long breath. "Hey, hello," she said. "No lights. Okay? I don't want to get you involved."

"Lights will get me involved?"

"You know what I mean. If somebody was close, if they knew I came over toward this way and they watched and saw lights go on here, then they'd want to find out."

"So I can black out the captain's quarters."

"Sure. It'll be easier to talk."

I took her by the hand and led her back through the darkness. Just enough light came in so that the lounge furniture made bulky shapes to left and right. When we reached my stateroom I released her and pulled both thicknesses of draperies across the ports. Then I turned on a light, the reading lamp over the bed which makes a bright round pattern on a book and leaves the rest of the room in darkness. It shone on the wrinkled sheets of recent dreams and bounced off, illuminating her in soft light.

She had hugged me with one arm because she held a

package and her purse in the other. The package was the shape of a shoe box, wrapped in brown paper, tied with cord.

"I know, I know," she said, backing away from the light. "I'm not wearing very damn well. I'm not lasting so good. What's it been? Six years. So I was twenty-four, right? And now I look forty."

"How's Ben?"

"I wouldn't have the faintest idea."

"Oh."

"Yes, it's like that. I haven't lived with him in . . . over three years. I threw him the hell out."

"Oh."

"Stop saying 'Oh.' You know, I felt a little pinch when I saw this great old boat. I really did. I didn't know I could feel anything like that, related to Ben. I thought it was all gone. But we were happy aboard this crock. It was the only really happy time, I think. Shiny new marriage, and not a dime in the world, but a great boat to have a honeymoon aboard." She sat in the chair in the corner by the locker, out of the light. In a different voice she said, "I should have settled for you."

"You figured I wouldn't marry anybody," I said. I sat on the bed, facing her.

"I know, I know. What I don't know is why I was so red hot to get married. So I married Ben Milligan. Jesus! Know what he was, really? He was a child bride. His mother spent twenty-five years picking up after him, waiting on him, telling him how great he was, and then she turned him over to me. Whine, whine, whine. He couldn't hold a job. Nobody appreciated him. Bitch, bitch, bitch. He had like fourteen jobs in two years, and the last part of that two years, he didn't even *look.* He stayed home and watched the soaps on TV. He did all that body-building stuff all the time. Muscles on muscles. When I came home from work, I was supposed to cook, or at least stop on the way home and buy pizza or hamburgers. Trav, couldn't you tell what he was like?"

"Sure."

"Couldn't you have said something?"

"And lose an eye?"

"Okay, so I was in love. Thank God for no kids. I think it was him, not me. But he wouldn't go see a doctor about it. He got very grumpy that I could say anything might be wrong with the perfect body. Look, McGee, it was all a long time ago. All forgotten. I didn't come here to talk about my great married life. I was thinking on the way here, I don't *really* know Travis McGee. But you made me feel close to you, way back. I had to find somebody I could trust. I went through an awful lot of names. I came up with you. Then I started thinking, Maybe he's got somebody aboard with him, or somebody lives aboard, or he's away, or he's married. My God, it's six *years.* You know? I stepped aboard and six years were gone. You look great. You know it? Absolutely great. You haven't changed at all. It isn't fair. Look at me!"

It happens to people. They get up to the point of explaining the mission and can't make it, so they go into a talking jag. She needed help. There was a thin edge of anxiety in her tone, and the words came too fast.

So I gave her some help. "What have you got in the box?" I asked.

She exhaled harshly. Almost a gasp. "You get right to it, don't you? What have I got in the box? In this here box, you mean? Once you said you had a safe place for things. Do you still?"

"Yes."

She came over and put the package on the bed beside where I was sitting. She grasped the cord and popped it with a swift sure motion. She stripped the brown paper off. Meyer says whole tracts could be written about character revealed in opening a package.

"What I've got in this box," she said, "is money."

She lifted the lid. It was money. It was packed in tightly. Used bills, some loose, most tied into tidy bricks with string, with adding-machine tape tucked under the string. "I've got here ninety-four thousand two hundred dollars. Plus ten thousand for you, for keeping it until I want it."

"No need for that."

"It's worth that to me. And I'd feel better."

"Can I ask any questions?"

"Hardly any. That's part of the fee."

"Stolen?"

"Like from a bank or payroll or something? No."

"And if you don't come back?"

"I'll be back to get it before . . . what's today?"

"Early early in the morning of May the sixteenth, a Thursday."

"Okay, if I don't come get it before the fifteenth of June, or get some kind of word to you before the fifteenth of June, then I'm not coming at all. So it should go to my sister, Susie. Do you remember my maiden name?"

"Dee. Carrie Dee."

"That was short for Dobrovsky. She uses the whole name. Susie . . . Susan Dobrovsky. You get it to her.

That's part of the fee. And not telling anybody at all about me being here. That's the rest of the way you earn ten."

"Where is your sister?"

"Oh. Sorry. She's in Nutley, New Jersey. She's younger. She teaches nursery school. She's now like about the age I was when I knew you before. Twenty-three? Yes. Two months ago. She's nice, but . . . dumb about things. She doesn't know how things are yet. Wouldn't it be nice if she didn't have to find out? Look, will you put this in a safe place and keep it for me?"

"Yes, of course."

She swayed, took one dizzy step, and turned around abruptly and sat down on my bed beside the box, bouncing it, spilling the bricks of money. She shook her head. "I'm dead for sleep. And I'm dirty, Trav. I've been in these same clothes too long. I can smell myself. These clothes, they ought to be buried. For the ten thousand, dear, could I ask for three more things?"

"Like a bath, a place to sleep, and a change of clothes?"

"I'm a size ten."

After she was throat deep in the big tub, sploshing and sudsing, scrubbing her cropped pale hair along with the rest of her, I located an old surplus ammo box, the kind with the rubber gasket and the flat metal lever that fastens it safely tight. I moved the money, all except the ten thousand, into the ammo box and put that forward in the flooded area between the double hull. I added the ten to my own cache, mentally adding another four or five months to my retirement. I retire whenever I can afford it. When the money is gone, I go back to work. Salvage work. Retirement comes when you are too old to enjoy it completely, so I take some of mine whenever I can. What good are beaches without beach bums? What would the little vacationing lady urchins do for their holiday pleasures were not some of us out there wastreling away? After the large money was all stowed and quite safe, I went digging into the big locker drawer under the bed in the guest stateroom. It is always packed with girl clothes. They get left aboard. They are purchased in the ports I can reach with my old houseboat, and they are left aboard for another time. No trouble to have them cleaned and put them away. And having the supply facilitates spur-of-the-moment decisions.

I found her some navy flairs and a pink sleeveless turtleneck shirt. And I found the kind of terry robe which fits anyone. It fit her and dragged on the floor behind her. She helped me make up the guest bed. She was yawning with every second breath. Her eyes were glazed with fatigue. When I went in not more than three minutes later to ask her if she'd like some hot chocolate or a drink, she interrupted the question with a long, gentle, purring snore.

I stood for a few minutes leaning against the doorframe, looking at her in the semidarkness, remembering her. I remembered the pre-Ben Carrie Dee, a pretty girl who worked at Peerless Marine and was seen now and again at some of the parties in and around Bahia Mar. We are never the best judges of what is meaningful and what is trivial in our lives, I guess. The accidents of time and place change the script, and later we say it happened on purpose.

Carrie didn't happen to me on purpose. Or I to her. There was a TV crew at Bahia Mar making a commercial. The Alabama Tiger had them at his permanent floating house party every night of the week they were there. The boss fellow was squat and hairy and very loud. Mod clothes and a glossy wig and a conviction that his profession and personality made him irresistible. I went topside at midnight on the *'Bama Gal* to get some air and see if there were any stars to look at. Boss Fellow had a girl down on the deck by the overturned dinghy and was mauling her around, riding her clothes up over her hips as she kicked and bleated and yelped, her protests lost in the Tiger's two hundred amps of speakers.

I plucked him off her and, while he flailed and cursed, I carried him to a place along the rail where I could get a clear drop into the boat basin. He made a mighty splash after the twelve-foot drop. When I was sure he could swim, I let him fend for himself. It was Carrie, and she was not in great shape. She was ripped and scuffed and close to hysterics. She was certainly in no shape to rejoin the party, so I walked her back to *The Busted Flush* and found some clothes that would fit her. She spent a half hour alone in the head, getting herself back together.

It had shaken her badly. He had come all too close to taking her. She looked spooked and sallow. By all the accepted rules of human behavior, she should have been so turned off by the near rape she would have felt neuter for quite a while. And I should have been reluctant to give her any new reason for alarm. But in some strange way the episode became a stimulant. We sat and talked, moved closer and talked, moved closer yet and kissed, and I took her to bed. It was a very gentle time, and very sweet in a strange way. In body language she was saying, *This* is the way it should be. And I was saying, Replace that memory with *this* one.

It was an isolated episode. Except perhaps by glance or by fleeting expression, we did not mention it again. Knowing her in that biblical sense changed my status with her to that of benign uncle. She sought me out to ask my advice about how she should live her life. She was so determined, months later, that I should approve of Ben Milligan, I think she convinced herself that I had approved. She wanted a good life. It is not an unusual hope, but a very unusual attainment.

I pulled the door shut. I made myself the drink and dressed while I worked at it. After the drink it was time for juice and coffee. After coffee, it was time to go find her purse. False dawn let a little light into the stateroom. I moved silently on bare feet and found the purse at the pillow end, shoved between mattress and box springs. I eased it out and took it to the galley and opened it at the table in the breakfast booth, under the light.

And hello to you, Carolyn Milligan. Florida registration receipt on a two-year-old Datsun, tag number 24D-1313. I found the car keys and put them in my shirt pocket. The occupation, which used to be given on the driving license, no longer appears there. Assume she is still a secretarial type. I copied down the tag number of the car and the address as given: 1500 Seaway Boulevard, Apt. 38B, Bayside, Florida. Comb, lipstick, dental floss, matchbooks, payroll stub, airplane tickets, used. Misc. intimacies. So Mrs. Milligan worked for Superior Building Supplies in Junction Park in Bayside, Florida, and she made $171.54 per week after deducts. She had been in Jamaica, at a Montego Bay hotel, in April. She had six hundred and some dollars in the purse. And a Master Charge card. And three kinds of pills. Everybody has three kinds as a minimum allowance. It is the creature adjustment to a rapidly changing world.

By then real dawn had arrived, and I locked up the *Flush* and walked through the deceptive coolness and the varying shades of gray, looking in the lots for her car. I found it. Bright orange. Imitation leather. Thirty-one thousand miles on it. Nothing significant in the glove compartment. A case of twelve bottles of an industrial abrasive in the trunk. Tru-Kut, it was called. I opened one, wet my fingers, rubbed and snuffed. Industrial abrasive. A milky white solution that smelled like men's rooms, overly sanitized, and contained a gritty cutting agent. So secretary makes deliveries for the boss fellow of Superior Building Supplies.

Nothing else of any moment. The tires were new, doubtless recently replaced. Windshield starred by a kicked-up pebble. Half a tank of gas. I relocked the car. Nobody seemed to be paying any attention to me. Over on charter-boat row they were getting ready to go rumbling out of the basin and roar out to the edge of the Stream. Early birds were beginning to arrive to get the shops ready to open. The early maid shift was reporting to the motel housekeeper. The early bird who gets the worm works for somebody who comes in late and owns the worm farm.

I sauntered back to the *Flush* by a different route. I unlocked it, slipped keys in purse, slipped purse under mattress while she still snored on and on into this new day. By morning light she did indeed look as if she had not weathered the years too well. New deep lines bracketed her mouth. Her eyes were pouched, her chin slightly doubled, her skin grainy. She frowned in her sleep. By my count, she was thirty. The body was younger, the face older than thirty. Some great-looking couple, those two. Ben and Carrie. Travel-poster people. Photograph them on red bikes in Bermuda, and you would sell tickets on the airplanes. Too much boyish petulance in Ben's face. Too much pseudo-masculine heartiness in his manner. His momma had loved him, all too well.

2

CARRIE slept through the morning and into the afternoon. At three I went in and put my hand on her shoulder and shook her gently. She made a blurred noise of complaint and then gave a great start and snapped her eyes open. She looked terrified. Then she knew me and the lids got heavy again and she put a fist in front of a creaking yawn.

"Whassamarra?" she said. "Whatimezit?"

"Three P.M. on Thursday, love. Keep sleeping. You seem to need it. I'm going to lock you in and go over to the beach for a while."

"Look. When you come back. Wake me up again? Okay?"

"Sure."

It had taken such a great effort of will and so much pain to get back in good shape, I had vowed never to let myself get sloppy again. And that meant hot sun and sweat and exercise every day, no tobacco ever again, and easy on the booze, heavy on the protein. Meyer was involved in writing a long and complicated dissertation on the lasting effect on international currencies of

18

the Arab oil production disputes, and he quit each day at three and joined me on the beach to get in his daily stint. Meyer never looks fat and he never never looks slender. He is merely broad and durable in a rubbery way, and hairy as an Adirondack black bear.

He believes in exercise in moderation. He says that he is not interested in celebrations of masochism, and so, aside from a part of the swimming, we do not see much of each other until the exercise hour is over.

He was already sitting on his towel at the hightide line when I finished sprinting the last hundred yards of my one-mile run. When I stopped puffing and panting and groaning, I took a final dip and then stretched out close by.

"You ought to run a little," I told him.

"Would that I could. When the beach people see you running, they know at a glance that it is exercise. There you are, all sinew and brown hide, and you wear that earnest, dumb, strained expression of the old jock keeping in shape. You have the style. Knees high, arms swinging just right, head up. But suppose I came running down this beach? They would look at me, and then look again. I look so little like a runner or a jock that the only possible guess as to what would make me run is terror. So they look way down the beach to see what is chasing me. They can't see anything, but to be on the safe side, they start walking swiftly in the same direction I'm running. First just a few, then a dozen, then a score. All going faster and faster. Looking back. Breaking into a run. And soon you would have two or three thousand people thundering along the beach, eyes popping out of the sockets, cords in their necks standing out. A huge stampede, stomping everything and everybody in their path into the sand. You wouldn't want me to cause a catastrophe like that, would you?"

"Oh, boy."

"It might not happen, but I can't take the chance."

"Meyer."

"Once it started, I could drop out and they would keep on going. The contagion of panic. Once you see it, you never forget it."

"Meyer, do you remember Carrie Milligan?"

"A thundering herd of . . . what? Who?"

"About six years ago. I loaned Carrie and Ben *The Busted Flush*. Not to take on a cruise. Just to live aboard, during a honeymoon."

"And told me to keep an eye on them. Very funny. I think I saw them come out into the daylight once. Let me see. She worked in the office over at Peerless Marine. Pretty little thing. I forget why you loaned them the *Flush*."

"I owed Dake Heath a favor and that's what he asked for. He was her half brother and he wanted things nice for her. Carrie and Ben were broke and so was Dake. So I broke a rule and said okay."

"To answer your question, yes. I remember her. Why?"

So I told all. I had promised Carrie not to tell anyone. But all rules are off when it comes to Meyer. Also, it was a form of protection. When somebody comes up and gives you that much money to tuck away for safekeeping, special precautions are in order. Checking the purse and the car, for example. And telling Meyer everything, including my checking the purse and the car. If the law moved in, I wanted to be able to give some plausible answers, with somebody to verify them if need be. Also, if somebody grabbed Carrie and bent her until she told them where to look for money, it would be nice to have Meyer know exactly why my luck had, at last, run out. And it will run out. Maybe not this time, or the next time. Sometime, though. And like everybody else, I will go down with that universal plea blazing in the back of my mind. "Not me! Not yet! Wait!"

Meyer was curious about the money, so I described the stacks to him, each neatly tied with white cotton string, each of mixed denominations, each totaling ten thousand. And, of course there were the loose bills, probably from a broken stack, which could mean that she had spent fifty-eight hundred. Each stack had an adding-machine tape stuffed under the string. Yes, all apparently from the same machine, but I hadn't examined them closely. It was used money, but reasonably clean and tidy. Under black light, it might fluoresce. Or somebody might have a list of serial numbers. Or it could all be funny, printed in a small room by night.

"You know her better than I do," Meyer said.

"I don't know her well."

"Have you formed any opinions about her and about the money?"

"Like what? Like did she steal it? I don't know. She's not a bum. She's a worker. Something happened that makes her feel she's got some sort of a right to the money. She arrived physically and emotionally exhausted. She didn't know if she was being followed. She thought she might be. Anyway, I'll hold it for her. If she comes and gets it, no fuss, it's a very easy ten, so easy I'll have an uneasy conscience."

A late-afternoon breeze riffled the water out beyond

the lazy breakers and hustled some candy wrappers down the wet brown beach. Two tall young ladies came sauntering by, brown, brawny, and bikinied, as confident and at home in their bodies as a pair of young lionesses, their hair sun-streaked and salt-tangled, their hips rolling and canting to the slow cadence of their long walk in the sunshine.

Meyer smiled his smile and sighed his audible sigh. It is both a pleasure and a sadness to watch the very young ones walk by. They know so very little, and so frighteningly much. They are on the edge of life, thinking they are in the midst of it. Pretty soon we got up and snapped the sand off the towels and went trudging back across the pedestrian bridge. We parted, and as I stepped aboard the *Flush* I had the sudden strong feeling that harm had come to Carrie, that harm had come aboard, a feral, crouching, bone-gnawing creature.

But all was well. Such hunches happen all the time, for every one of us. We forget them all—except when one turns out to be right. Then we say, I knew! I knew!

She waited to be awakened, waited there with brushed hair, touch of lipstick, new smudge of eye shadow. She faked a sweet awakening from her drowse to pull me down into the mint taste of my own toothpaste, murmuring, "Hello, hello."

It was supposed to be very easy. No need for talk, for claiming and disclaiming. All inevitable because she had made it so through contrivance and through the directness of invitation. Worm my way out of the swim pants and glide sweetly into the lady. Thank you, ma'am. The good-boatkeeping seal of approval. Only a total fink person would decline an offer so frankly made. But the problem of her motive got in my way.

Was this supposed to be in addition to the ten? Was it supposed to cloud my mind and make me less curious? Was she setting up some justification or rationalization of her own? The problem of playing somebody else's game is the problem of finding yourself stuck in a role you can't play. You can't say your lines.

So I disentangled her and sat up from the steamy kiss and smiled down at her and thumbed a strand of hair back from her round forehead. "You certainly needed a lot of sleep."

"I guess I did," she said, looking sullen.

"While you were sleeping, I was thinking."

"Goody!"

"Let's say it gets to be June fifteenth and Carrie doesn't come for her money. Don't you want me to try to find out why you couldn't make it? Or who kept you from making it?"

"It wouldn't matter a damn to me by then, would it?"

"That's what I'm asking."

"The answer is no. Just get the money to my sister. That's all."

"And she'll want to know where it came from."

"Tell her it's from me."

"Maybe she's so straight she might not take it. Then what?"

She bit her lip and looked thoughtful. "I could write her, I guess. Phone her. Something to clue her a little."

"Want to clue me too?"

"No. I don't want to talk about it and I don't want to think about it, okay? It's my personal problem."

"You're paying me enough so you can ask for help."

"I better not try asking for anything else, huh? A girl

shouldn't make it too obvious. Not and get turned down."

"I just get suspicious of free gifts."

"Some gift. From a fire sale. We had us one night, a long time ago. Remember? I was okay for you then, but not now. Not the way I am now. It was a dumb idea. Sorry, fellow."

I took her hand and then despised myself for checking to find those little fingertip calluses acquired from operating office equipment. McGee checks everything, as do all paranoids.

I kissed her slack, cool, unresponsive mouth, and as I straightened up she said, "No charity, thanks. The impulse has come and gone."

"Suit yourself."

"Am I doing something to spoil your day?"

"You don't leave me any options. Any move I make is wrong."

"That's the way it goes. Check with an expert."

"At least I can tell you that you are still very attractive to me, Carrie."

"Sure, sure, sure."

"I mean it."

"Six years ago you meant it, but that was a different girl, six years ago."

"You confuse two things. Okay, I didn't react the way I was supposed to. My guard is up. What do you expect? After six years you show up with a bundle of money and want me to keep it for you. You claim you've shed Ben. I stay alive by keeping my inputs open. Is it gambling money? Is it street money? Is it ransom money? I know some people who are hungry enough to nail me, they'd unearth a girl from six years ago and use her to get to me, to set me up. Marked money. Counterfeit money. Nearly everybody can be manipulated. McGee is alive and well because he is very very careful about a lot of things. Carrie, if you had been Miss Universe stretched out here waving your eyelashes at me, the word would have been the same word. Whoa! Look out for free gifts. I check everything I can check. What I found in your purse about working in an office matches the fingertip calluses on your hands. The industrial goop in the trunk of your car tastes and smells like legitimate industrial abrasive solution."

She spun quickly and stuffed her hand under the mattress, looking for the purse.

"It's there," I said. "I put it back."

She sat up, hauling the sheet up under her chin. She stared at me. "Jesus! You *are* jumpy."

"And alive. Be glad you are leaving your money at the right place, if you still want to leave it here."

"I still want to leave it. It could have been more."

"It's a tidy sum. You are overpaying me."

"I'll decide that. Look, don't worry about the money. Okay? It isn't marked or anything. It's sort of ... my share of some action. But somebody might grab it." Suddenly she grinned. "Hey! Thanks for giving me back my pride."

"Any time. Want some steak and eggs?"

She looked wistful but refused. She wanted to be on her way. She wore the borrowed clothes and carried her soiled ones in a brown paper bag. She waited for full dark before she left. She marched away under the dock lights, taking a roundabout route to her car. I expected her to look back, but she didn't.

There was a residual affection for her. The six years had aged her more than she could reasonably expect and had tested and toughened her. Her eyes were watchful, her merriment sardonic. There are too many of them in the world lately, the hopeful ladies who married grown-up boy children and soon lost all hope. They are the secretaries and nurses and switchboard people, the store clerks, schoolteachers, cab drivers, and Avon ladies. They lead the singles life. Lots of laughs and lots of barren mornings. Skilled sex, mod conversation, and all heartaches carefully concealed. They are not ardent libbers, yet at the same time they are not looking for some man to "take care." God knows they are expert in taking care of themselves. They just want a grown-up man to share their life with, each of them taking care. But there are one hell of a lot more grown-up ladies than grown-up men.

I wished her well. Lonely ladies can get into damned fool capers. I wished her very well indeed.

3

So two weeks went by. A pair of lovely weeks in May. A steady breeze off the Atlantic kept the bright tacky strip of Florida seacoast reasonably free of smodge, fugg, and schlutch. Old parties tottered out of their condominiums and baked themselves black in the white high glare of the beaches, pleased that their eyes didn't water and they could breathe without coughing.

On the tube the local advertising for condominiums always shows the nifty communal features, such as swimming pool, putting green, sandy beach, being enjoyed by jolly hearty folk in their very early thirties. These are the same folk you see dancing in the moonlight aboard ship in the tour ads. These are the people who keep saying that if you've got your health, you don't need anything else. But when the condominiums are finished and peopled, and the speculator has taken his maximum slice of the tax-related profits and moved on to crud up somebody else's skyline, the inhabitants all seem to be on the frangible side of seventy, sitting in the sunlight, blinking like lizards, and wondering if these are indeed the golden years or if it is all a big sell, an inflation game that you have to play, wondering which you are going to run out of first, your money or your life. The developers leave enough to go wrong in each condominium apartment that it becomes an odds-on bet the money runs out first. Nursing homes are a big industry in sunny Florida.

Anyway, it was Meyer who picked it up, a minor item on a back page, and brought it over to the *Flush* on the thirtieth day of May. It was early afternoon and I was topside, wrestling with too many yards of white nylon canvas, and with a borrowed gadget which, when properly operated, puts brass grommets into the fabric. I was irritated at how slowly my self-imposed chore was going. I was dripping sweat onto the grommet machine and the clean white nylon and the vinyl imitation-teak decking.

"Now what?" I asked sourly.

"This is what," said Meyer, and handed me the clip he had torn out of the paper.

PEDESTRIAN FATALITY

The City of Bayside registered its fourth traffic fatality of the year when Mrs. Carolyn Milligan was struck and killed at 10:30 Wednesday night while walking on County Road 858 just inside the city limits. Roderick Webbel, driver of the farm truck which struck and killed the Milligan woman, claimed that he did not see her until the moment of impact when she apparently stepped from the shoulder of the road into the path of the vehicle. Mrs. Milligan, who lived alone at 1500 Seaway Boulevard, was employed by Superior Building Supplies, Junction Park, Bayside. Police are investigating the accident and no charges have been filed as yet.

A fat drop of sweat fell from the tip of my nose and made a dark pattern of a sloppy star on the newsprint, the same color as the sweat smudge from my fingers. Meyer followed me into the shade of the canopy over the topside controls.

I leaned my rear against the instrument panel and propped one bare foot on the pilot's chair. The breeze began to cool me off.

"Accident?" Meyer asked. When I stared at him he said hastily, "Rhetorical question, of course."

"Of course. And who the hell knows? Damn it, anyway!"

I am cursed by an imagination which turns vivid when I wish it would turn itself off. She had been sturdy bone and sinew, sweet flesh and quick blood. She had been scents and secrets. Then a great bewildering bash, a tiny light in the back of the brain flickering out, as spoiled flesh, crushed bone, ripped connective tissue went slamming off into the roadside brush, spraying blood as it spun.

"Meyer, she gave me the orders. Just get the money to my sister, she said. That's all, she said. She said that if she couldn't come back and get the money, she wouldn't give much of a damn who kept her from it."

"And," Meyer said, "she paid you to do just what she said."

"I know."

"But?"

"I look at it this way. Two thousand would have been more than fair. It would have paid my way to Nutley and back, with a nice hunk left over. So she's got eight thousand worth of service coming."

"Posthumous service?"

"Which she didn't want." I doubled my right fist and gave myself a heavy thump on the top of the thigh. Painful. "It is the merry month of May, Meyer, and the lady is going to be dead for a very long time. I would be doing what she wanted. Giving the money to the sister. And making certain there are no strings attached, nobody following the scent, nobody mashing the sister too."

"I admire your talent for instant rationalization."

"This is not romanticism, dammit."

"Did I say it was?"

"By the expression on your face. Patronizing, amused, superior."

"You are reading it wrong. The face is just some skin and fat and muscle stretched over bone. I was actually looking apprehensive."

"About what?"

"About what you might be getting me into."

"You can stay right here and work on your treatise."

"I'm at a stopping point, waiting for translations of some Swedish journals to arrive. I could struggle through them myself, but . . ." He shrugged and went over and picked up some of the canvas, inspected a grommet. "Is this crooked?"

"Very."

"Then it won't look very good, will it?"

"No. It won't."

"Travis, do we know anybody at all in Bayside?"

"I keep thinking there was somebody."

So we went below, and while I checked out the book in the desk, Meyer opened a pair of cold Tuborgs. No friends in Bayside. None. Meyer blew across the top of the Tuborg bottle, a foghorn note far away. "So why are we up there fussing around?" he asked.

"A question which will be asked."

"Insurance?"

"Possibly, but it doesn't feel right."

"Good old united Beneficent Casualty and Life. Those are such beautiful blank policies. I can type in all the—"

"I know. I know. But it could be a dead end. Accidental death, fellows. And these days you get checked out too often. It just doesn't feel right. I think that when she was here two weeks ago I borrowed some money from her. Maybe I gave her a promissory note. I'm in shape to pay it back, but I'd just as soon not pay it back to her heirs and assigns, not if I can get my hands on the note I signed."

"And you take some cash along. For credibility."

"Right! Maybe we both borrowed it and both signed. We're a pair of real-estate gunslingers trying to cheat the little dead lady's estate. We'll pay up if we have to. But we'd rather not."

Meyer closed his eyes and thought long and hard, taking a deep draft on the Tuborg as he did so. He nodded. "I like it."

"We'll take all the cash along," I said.

He looked startled. "All?"

"We'll operate from this gallant watercraft. In comfort. Even in certain vulgar luxury. Go pack your toothbrush, my friend."

After he left I checked my Waterway Guide and picked out what looked like the best of Bayside's several marinas. It was called Westway Harbor, operated by Cal and Cindy Birdsong. I phoned and got a young man in the office named Oliver. Yes, he had a nice slot for *The Busted Flush,* one that would take up to a sixty-footer, one with water, electric, and phone hook-up and about a hundred feet from the facilities. I said we'd check in on Friday, probably around noon. The fee sounded a little bit on the high side. Oliver wanted to know how long we would be with them, and I said it was hard to say, very hard to say. He told me to look, for a high round water tower north of the center of town, and when I was opposite it, I was to look for their private channel markers and they would lead me right in, and he would be there to direct me to the slip. "You can't miss it," he said.

By the time I'd notified the office we were taking off, exchanged a few lies with Irv Diebert, picked up the laundry, arranged with Johnny Dow to take the mail out of the box and hold it, unplugged the shoreside connections, topped the tanks, and tied the *Muñequita* well off in the slip, tarped and snug, it was after four o'clock. We chugged out to the channel and turned north.

At drinking time I left Meyer at the wheel and went below and broke out the very last bottle of the Plymouth gin which had been bottled in the United Kingdom. All the others were bottled in the U.S. Gin People, it isn't the same. It's still a pretty good gin but it is not a superb, stingingly dry, and lovely gin. The sailor on the label no longer looks staunch and forthright, but merely hokey. There is something self-destructive about Western technology and distribution. Whenever any consumer object is so excellent that it attracts a devoted following, some of the slide rule and computer types come in on their twinkle toes and take over the store, and in a trice they figure out just how far they can cut quality and still increase the market penetration. Their reasoning is that it is idiotic to make and sell a hundred thousand units of something and make a profit of thirty cents a unit, when you can increase the advertising, sell five million units, and make a nickel profit a unit. Thus the very good things of the world go down the drain, from honest turkey to honest eggs to honest tomatoes. And gin.

I put cracked ice in two sturdy glass mugs, dumped in some sherry and dumped it out again, filled with Plymouth gin, rubbed peel around the rims of mugs, squeezed oil onto surface of gin, threw peel away, and carried mugs up to the topside controls, where Meyer was using his best twelve-syllable words on a yuk who had pounded by us, lifting a nine-foot wash behind him. I saw it coming and had time to prepare. I did some twinkle toes myself: three to port, three to starboard, never spilling a drop.

We clinked glasses, took the testing sip, then the deep single swallow. Delicious. The birds were circling, the sun needles were dancing off the water, and the *Flush* was lumbering along, slowed imperceptibly by a fouled bottom. It is unseemly to feel festive about checking out the death of a dead friend. But there is something heartening about having a sense of mission. A clean purpose. A noble intent, no matter how foolish. Behind us, a couple of slow hours back of us, the 17,000 resident boats and the thirteen big marinas of Lauderdale, where 150,000 people grow ever more furious in the traffic tangles. Ahead, some murky mystery locked in the broken skull of a dead lady. The knight errant, earning his own self-esteem, holding the palms cupped to make a dragon trap. Peer inside. S'right, by God, a dragon! But what color, fella?

Before nightfall I found the anchorage I had used before, a sheltered slot between two small mangrove islands. Fortunately nobody had yet built a causeway to either island, or erected thereon one of those glassy monuments to the herd instinct. I nestled the houseboat into the slot and went over the side and made four lines fast to the tough twisted trunks of mangroves, at ten, two, four, and eight o'clock. The night air was full of bugs homing on my earlobes, screaming their hunger, so we buttoned the *Flush* up, testing night breezes and screens until it was comfortable in the lounge.

While Meyer was broiling a very large number of very small lamb chops, a skiff went churning across the flats, heading out toward the channel. The people aboard were yelping like maniacs, making wolf yelps, panther screams, rebel yells. I heard the crazed laughter of a woman. And then there was a sharp authoritative barking. Thrice. *Bam, bam, bam.* Tinkle of glass inside the lounge. Sharp knock against paneling. The skiff picked up speed. The woman laughed in that same crazy way. I stopped rolling and got up onto one knee, then raced topside and yanked the shark rifle out of its greasy nest. No point in firing at one small light far away, the sound fading.

"Why?" Meyer said, beside me.

I didn't answer until we were below again, out of the bugs' hungry clasp. "For kicks. For nothing. For self-expression. Good ol' Charlie shows those rich bastards they don't own the whole goddamn world. It was a handgun and it was a long way off, and having one hit us was pure luck."

"It could have been between the eyes. Pure luck."

"Stoned and smashed. Beer and booze and too much sun. Uppers and downers, hash and smack, all spaced out. Take any guess."

Meyer went quietly back to his broiling. He seemed moody during the meal, working things out his own way inside that gentle, thoughtful skull. The misshapen slug had dented the paneling but had penetrated so shallowly I had been able to pry it loose with a thumbnail. It was on the table beside my cup, a small metallic turd dropped by a dwarf robot. I had stuck Saran Wrap across the starred hole in the glass port.

"Let me give it a try," he said.

"You think you can explain why? Come *on!*"

"When I was twelve years old I received on my birthday a single-shot twenty-two rifle chambered for shorts. It was a magical adventure to have a gun. It made a thin and wicked cracking sound, and an exotic smell of burned powder and oil. A tin can would leap into the air at some distance when I had merely moved my index finger a fraction of an inch."

"Meyer, the killer."

He smiled. "You anticipate me. There were good birds and bad birds. One of the bad birds was a grackle. Of the family *Icteridae,* genus *Quiscalus.* I do not recall why it was in such bad repute. Possibly it eats the eggs of other birds. At any rate, it seemed to be acceptable to shoot one, whereas shooting a robin would have been unthinkable. I had watched grackles through my mother's binoculars. A fantastic color scheme, an iridescence over black, as if there were a thin sheen of oil atop a pool of india ink. I had shown enough reliability with the rifle to be allowed to take it into the woodlands behind our place, provided I followed all the rules. There was no rule about grackles. I went out one Saturday afternoon after a rain. A grackle took a busy splashing bath in a puddle and flew up to a limb. I aimed and fired, and it fell right back down into the same puddle and did some frantic thrashing and then was still. I went and looked at it. Its beak was opening and closing, just under the surface of the water. I picked it up with some vague idea of keeping it from drowning. It made a terminal tremorous spasm in my hand and then it was still. Unforgettably, unbearably still. As still as a stone, as a dead branch, as a fence post. I want to say all of this very carefully, Travis. See this scar on the edge of my thumb? I was using a jack-knife to make a hole in a shingle boat for a mast, and the blade of the knife closed. This bled a good deal, and because it sliced into the thumbnail, it hurt. It hurt as much as anything had ever hurt me up until that time. And that had happened about two months before I murdered the grackle. The grackle lay in my hand, and all that fabulous iridescence was gone. It had a dirty look, the feathers all scruffed and wet. I put it down hastily on the damp grass. I could not have endured dropping it. I put it down gently, and there was blood left on my hand. Bird blood. As red as mine. And the pain had been like mine, I knew. Bright and hot and savage."

He was silent so long I said, "You mean that . . ."

"I'm looking for the right way to express the relationships. Travis, the gun was an abstraction, the bullet an abstraction. Death was an abstraction. A tiny movement of a finger. A cracking sound. A smell. I could not comprehend a gun, a bullet, and a death until the bird died. It became all too specific and too concrete. I had engineered this death, and it was dirty. I had given pain. I had blood on my hand. I did not know what to do with myself. I did not know how to escape from myself, to go back to what I had been before I had slain the bird. I wanted to get outside the new experience of being me. I was, in all truth, in all solemnity, filled with horror at the nature of reality. I have never killed another bird, nor will I ever, unless I should come upon one in some kind of hopeless agony. Now here is the meat of my analogy. Those young people in that boat have never killed their grackle. They have not been bloodied by reality. They have shed the make-believe blood of a West that never existed. They have gawped at the gore of the Godfather. They have seen the slow terminal dance of Bonnie and Clyde. They have seen the stain on the front of the shirt of the man who has fallen gracefully into the dust of Marshal Dillon's main street. It is as if . . . I had walked into those woods and seen a picture of a dead grackle. They do not yet know the nature of reality. They do not yet know, and may never learn, what a death is like. What an ugly thing it is. The sphincters let go and there is a rich sickening stink of fecal matter and urine. There is that ugly stillness, black blood caking and clotting and stinking. To them, that gun somebody took out of his fish box is an abstraction. They find no relationship between the movement of the index finger and the first stinking step into eternity. It is emotional poverty, with cause and effect in a state of disassociation. And they . . ."

He had become hesitant, the words coming more slowly, with less certainty. He smiled with strange shyness and shrugged and said, "But that doesn't work, does it?"

"I think it works pretty well."

"No. Because then they could only kill once. But some of them go on and on. Pointlessly."

"Some of them. Weird ones. Whippy ones."

"Theorizing is my disease, Travis. A friend of mine, Albert Eide Parr, has written, 'Whether you get an idea from looking into a sunset or into a beehive has nothing to do with its merits and possibilities.' I seem to get too many of my ideas by looking into my childhood."

"They didn't nail either of us between the eyes this time."

"Ever the realist."

We cleaned up and sacked out early. I lay wakeful in the big bed, resentful of Meyer nearby in the guest stateroom, placidly asleep. When he had been involved in a government study in India, he had learned how to take his mind out of gear and go immediately to sleep. I had known how, without thinking about it, when I had been in the army, but in time I had lost the knack.

Meyer had explained very carefully how he did it. "You imagine a black circle about two inches behind your eyes, and big enough to fill your skull from ear to ear, from crown to jaw hinges. You know that each intrusion of thought is going to make a pattern on that perfect blackness. So you merely concentrate on keeping the blackness perfect, unmarked, and mathematically round. As you do that, you breathe slowly and steadily, and with each exhalation, you feel yourself sinking a tiny bit further into the mattress. And in moments you are asleep."

He was, but I wasn't. Once I had explained Meyer's

system to a very jumpy restless lady, telling her it wouldn't work for me and it wouldn't work for her. I said, "Go ahead. Try it. It's just a lot of nonsense, Judy. Right, Judy? Hey! Judy? Judy!"

Tonight I was too aware of all the world around me. I was a dot on the Waterway chart between the small islands. Above me starlight hit the deck after traveling for years and for trillions of miles. Under the hull, in the ooze and sand and grass of the bottom, small creatures were gagging and strangling on the excreta of civilization. The farthest stars had moved so much since the starlight left them that the long path of light was curved. After the planet was cindered, totally barren of life, that cold starlight would still be taking the long curved path down to bound off black frozen stone. Ripples slapped the hull. I heard a big cruiser go barreling down the Waterway, piloted by some idiot racing to keep his inevitable appointment with floating palm bole or oil drum. Long minutes after the sound had faded, his wash tipped the *Flush,* creaked the lines, clinked something or other in the galley. It disturbed a night bird, which rose from one of the islands, making a single horrid strangled croak. Far off on the north-south highways there was the insect sound of the fast-moving trucks, whining toward warehouses, laden with emergency rush orders of plastic animals, roach tablets, eye shadow, ashtrays, toilet brushes, pottery crocodiles, and all the other items essential to a constantly increasing GNP.

My heart made a slow, solemn ka-thudding sound, and the busy blood raced around, nourishing, repairing, slaying invaders, and carrying secretions. My unruly memory went stumbling and tumbling down the black corridors, through the doors I try to keep closed. A tickle of sweat ran along my throat, and I pushed the single sheet off.

Where had Carrie Milligan gotten the money?

Had she told anyone I had it?

What had the money to do with being in the same clothes too long?

Kidnap?

Smuggling?

Casino?

Robbery?

Let's take it to Nutley and give it all to the little sister and then go fishing, preferably down off Isla de las Mujeres.

But first, friend, let us try to get the hell to sleep. Please? Please? Keep the black circle absolutely round. Sink deeper with each exhalation. Absolutely round.

4

A good marina—and rare they are indeed—is a comfort and a joy. The private channel to Westway Harbor was about six hundred yards long. It was a seminatural basin, dredged to depth, with the entrance narrowed for protection from wash, storm waves, and chop. The gas dock was inside the entrance, tucked over to the south side. Small-boat dockage was on the southern perimeter of the basin. There were an estimated eighty berths for bigger craft dead ahead and to my right as I came through their entrance.

A brown young man in khaki shorts came out of the dockmaster's office, gave me a follow-me wave of his arm, and hopped onto an electric service cart. I eased to starboard and followed him to the indicated slip, then swung out and backed in between the finger piers as Meyer went forward and put loops over the pilings as we eased past. When the young man sliced the edge of his hand across his throat, Meyer made both bow lines fast to the bow cleat, and I killed my little diesels. The young man was polite. He helped with the lines. He asked permission to come aboard. He handed me a neatly printed sheet of rules, rates, and regulations, services available, and hours of availability. I asked him if he was Oliver, and he said Oliver had gone to lunch. He was Jason. Jason had a jock body, a Jesus head, and gold-wire Franklin glasses.

The instructions were clear and precise. I helped him plug me into the dockside electricity. He took a meter reading. I said we'd like phone service, and he said he'd go bring an instrument. I tasted the hose water and told Meyer to top off the water tank while I went to the dockmaster's office to make arrangements.

As I walked, I admired the construction of the docks. Concrete piers and big timbers and oversized galvanized bolts holding them together. The trash cans were in big fiberglass bins. There were safety stations, with life rings and fire extinguishers. The water lines and power lines were slung under the docks, out of sight. They had about thirty empty berths. The fifty boats in sight looked substantial and well kept, especially a row of a half dozen big motor sailers. A calico cat sitting on the bow of a big Chriss stopped washing to stare at me as I walked by.

There was a big tall lady behind the counter in the office. She had very short black hair and strong features. She was barelegged and barefooted and wore yellow shorts and a white T-shirt and a gold wedding ring. She stood about six feet high, and though the face was strong enough to look just a little bit masculine, there was nothing masculine about the legs or the way she filled the T-shirt. And she was almost as tan as I am. It made her cool blue eyes look very vivid, and it made her teeth look very very white.

"Mr. McGee?"

"Yes. You've got a fine-looking marina here."

"Thank you. I'm Mrs. Birdsong. We've been open exactly two years today."

"Congratulations."

"Thank you." Her smile was small and formal. This was an arm's-length girl. With a long arm. Twenty-eight? Hard to guess her age because her face had that Indian shape which doesn't show much erosion from eighteen to forty.

We made the arrangements. I paid cash for three days in advance, saying we might stay longer. I asked about a rental car, and she walked me over to a side window and pointed to a Texaco sign visible above the roof of the next-door motel and said I could get a car there.

Just as we turned away from the window there was a roar, a yelp of rubber, and a heavy thud as someone drove a dusty blue sedan into the side of the building.

A big man struggled out from behind the wheel and walked unsteadily to the doorway and paused there, staring at her and then at me.

"Where have you been? Where—have—you—been?" she asked. Her eyes looked sick.

He was six and a half feet tall, and almost as broad as the doorway. He had a thick tangle of gray-blond hair, a mottled and puffy red face. He wore soiled khakies, with what looked like dried vomit on the front of the shirt. There was a bruise on his forehead and his knuckles were swollen. He wafted a stink of the unwashed into the small office.

He gave her a stupid glaring look and mumbled,

"Peddle your ass anybody comes along, eh, Cindy? Bangin' dock boys, bangin' customers. I know what you are, you cheap hooker."

"Cal! You don't know what you're saying."

He turned ponderously toward me. "Show you not to fool around with somebody's wife, you bas'ard, you rotten suhva bish."

She came trotting toward him from the side, reaching for him, saying, "No, Cal. No, honey. Please."

He swung a backhand blow at her face, a full swing of his left arm. She saw it coming and tried to duck under it, but it caught her high on the head, over the ear. It felled her. She hit and rolled loose, with a thudding of joints and bones and skull against the vinyl tile floor, ending up a-sprawl, face down.

Cal didn't look at her. He came shuffling toward me, big fists waving gently, shoulder hiked up to shield the jaw. If he'd left enough room for me to slide past him and bolt out the doorway, I would have. Dog drunk as he was, he was immense and seemed to know how to move. I did not want to be in the middle of any family quarrel. Or any wife-killing. She was totally out, unmoving.

One thing I was not going to do, and that was stand up and play fisticuffs. Not with this one. I was getting a good flow of adrenaline. I felt edgy and fast and tricky. I put my hands out, palms toward him, as though pleading with him not to hit me. He looked very happy, in a bleary way, and launched a big right fist at the middle of my face. I snapped my open palms onto that thick right wrist and turned it violently clockwise, yanking downward at the same time. The leverage spun him around, and his wrist and fist went up between his shoulder blades. I got him started and, with increasing momentum, ran him into the cement block wall. He smacked it, dropped to his knees, and then spilled sideways and sat up, blood running down into his eye and down his cheek from a new split in his forehead. He smiled in a thoughtful way and struggled up and came hunching toward me again. This time I moved inside a pawing left hand and hit him as fast and as hard as I could, left-right, left-right, to throat and belly. I knew it damaged him, but as I tried to slide past him, once more thinking of the doorway, he hit me squarely in the forehead. It creaked my neck, turned the bright day to a cloudy vagueness, and put me into slow motion. As I was going down, my head cleared. I hooked my left foot around the back of his right ankle and kicked his kneecap with my right foot. He grunted and tried to stomp me as I rolled away.

As I came to my feet I saw he was having trouble making his right leg hold him up. And the blood obscured his vision. And he was gagging and wheezing. But he was coming on, and I wanted no part of him. I had lost the edge of my reflexes. I was halfway aware of the whirling blue lights of the cop car outside, and of men moving smartly through the doorway.

"Cal!" some man yelled. "Cal, damn you!"

Then they walloped the back of his head with a hickory stick. They rang the hard wood off the skull bone. He tottered and turned and pawed at them, and they moved aside and hit him again. He puddled down, slowly, still smiling, with the unbloodied eye turning upward until only the white showed.

One of the officers rolled the limp hulk face down, brought the hands around behind, and pressed the cuffs onto the wrists. He said, "Hoo-wee, Ralph. He do have a stink onto him. We want him riding in with us?"

"Not after the last time we don't."

Jason, who had helped us dock, was kneeling on the floor. He had lifted Mrs. Birdsong into a sitting position. Her head was a little loose on her neck, and her eyes were vacant. He was gentle with her, murmuring comfort to her.

"She okay, Jason?" an officer asked.

"I . . . I guess I'm all right," she said.

"How about you?" he asked me.

I worked my arms, massaged the back of my neck. My head was clearing the rest of the way, taking me out of slow motion. I felt of my forehead. It was beginning to puff. "He hit me one good lick."

"Why?"

"I haven't the faintest idea. I was checking in."

"He brought his boat in a little while ago," Jason said. He helped Cindy Birdsong to her feet. She pulled free of him and walked over to a canvas chair and sat down, looking gray-green under her heavy tan.

"Want to prefer charges?" the officer asked.

I looked at Cindy. She lifted her head and gave a little negative shake.

"I guess not."

The cop named Ralph sighed. He was young and heavy, with a Csonka mustache. "Arthur and me figured he might head back here. We've been trying to catch up with him for two hours, Cindy. We got all the charges we need. He run two cars off the road. He busted up Dewey's Pizza Shack and broke Dewey's arm for him."

"Oh, God."

"Earlier he was out to the Gateway Bar on Route Seven eighty-seven, and he pure beat the living hell out of three truck drivers. They're in the hospital. I'm sorry, Cindy. It's since he got on the sauce so bad. And being on probation from the last time . . . look, he's going to have to spend some time in the county jail. I'm sorry, but that's the way it is."

She closed her eyes. She shuddered. Suddenly Cal Birdsong began to snore. There was a little puddle of blood under his face. The ambulance arrived. The cuffs were removed. The attendants handled him with less difficulty than I expected. Cindy got a sweater and her purse and rode along with the snoring gigantic drunk, after asking Jason to take care of things.

Jason leaned on the counter and said, "He was okay. You know? A nice guy up to about a year ago. I've worked here since they opened. He drank, but like anybody else. Then he started drinking more and more. Now it makes him crazy. She's really a very great person. It's really breaking her heart, you know?"

"Booze sneaks up on people."

"It's made him crazy. The things he yells at her."

"I heard some of them."

The part of his face not covered by the Jesus beard turned redder. "She's not like that at all. I don't know what it is with him."

"Where do they live?"

"Oh, right over there, in this end unit in the motel. They built the motel the same time as the marina, and leased it out, and in the lease they get to use the unit at this end, a little bigger than the others. Cal inherited

some money and they bought this piece of waterfront
and put up the marina and the motel. But they could
lose it if it keeps up this way."

He went and got a mop and a pail and swabbed up
the blood. While he was at it he mopped the rest of the
floor. A good man.

I stepped around the wet parts and went back to the
Flush. Meyer was annoyed. Where had I been? What
had happened to my forehead? What were we going to
do about lunch?

I told him how I'd happened to meet the Birdsongs.
Lovely couple.

When we went to get a car and get lunch, I saw a
different fellow in the office. This one was beardless
and smaller and rounder, but just as muscular.

"Jason here?"

"He went to lunch. Can I help you?"

"I'm McGee. We're in Slip Sixty."

"Oh, sure. We talked on the phone. I'm Oliver Tar-
beck. I understand you and Cal went around and
around."

"Sort of. If I can get a rental car, where should I
park it?"

"In that row over there where it says Marina Only.
If it's full, come here to the office and we'll work
something out."

"Place to eat?"

"A block to the left, on this side. Gil's Kitchen. It's
okay for lunch."

We had lunch first. The place wasn't okay for lunch.
Gil had a dirty kitchen. A fried egg sandwich was
probably safe. We went from there to Texaco, which

had some sort of budget rental deal, and I tested to see if I could get my knees under the wheel of the yellow Gremlin before giving him the Diner's Card. Nobody will take a cash deposit on a car any more. It forces everybody into cards. As the world gets bigger, it gets a lot duller.

I asked him if he could tell me how to find Junction Park. He gave me a city map and marked the route.

The Gremlin did not have air, but it had some big vents. Meyer read the map and called the turns. It was easy to see the shape and history of Bayside, Florida. There had been a little town on the bay shore, a few hundred people, a sleepy downtown with live oaks and Spanish moss. Then International Amalgamated Development had moved in, bought a couple of thousand acres, and put in shopping centers, town houses, condominiums, and rental apartments, just south of town. Next had arrived Consolidated Construction Enterprises and done the same thing north of town. Smaller operators had done the same things on a smaller scale west of town. When downtown decayed, the town fathers widened the streets and cut down the shade trees in an attempt to look just like a shopping center. It didn't work. It never does. This was instant Florida, tacky and stifling and full of ugly and spurious energies. They had every chain food-service outfit known to man, interspersed with used-car lots and furniture stores.

Junction Park was inland and not far from a turnpike interchange. It had been laid out with some thought to system and symmetry. Big steel buildings were placed in herringbone pattern, with big truck docks and parking areas. The tall sign at the entrance said that Superior Building Supplies was the fourth building on the right.

I parked and told Meyer to see what he could pick up at the neighbor establishments, a heating and air-conditioning outfit, a ladder plant, and a boatbuilder.

I went into the front office of Superior Building Supplies. A slender and pretty girl in a dress made of ticking was taking file folders out of a metal file and putting them into a cardboard storage file. She straightened and looked at me and said in a nasal little voice, "It isn't until Monday."

"What isn't?"

"The special sale of everything. They're taking inventory over the weekend. And right now."

"Going out of business?"

She went over to her desk and picked up a can of Coke and drank several swallows. She gave me a long look of appraisal.

"We sure the hell are," she said finally. She shook her gingery hair back and wiped her pretty mouth with the back of her hand, then belched like any boy in the fifth grade.

A man came through the open door that led back to the warehouse portion. He had a clipboard in his hand. He was sweaty and he had a smudge of grease on his forehead. Lots of red-brown hair, carefully sprayed into position. Early thirties. Outdoor look. Western shirt with a lot of snaps and zippers. Whipcord pants. Boots. A nervous harried look and manner.

"We're not open for business, friend. Sorry. Joanna, find me the invoices on that redwood fencing, precut, huh?"

"Cheez, I keep telling you and telling you, it was Carrie knew where all that—"

"Carrie isn't here to help us, goddammit. So shake your ass and start looking."

"Listen, Harry, I don't even know if I'm going to get paid for this time I'm putting in, right?"

"Joanna, honey, of course you'll get your pay. Come on, dear. *Please* find the invoices for me?"

She gave him a long dark stare, underlip protruding. "Buster, you've been talking just a little too much poremouth. Just a little too much. And you've been getting evil with me too often, hear? I think you better go doodle in your hat. I'm going to go get my hair done. I might come back and I might retire. Who knows?"

She slung her big leather purse over her shoulder. He tried to block her way to the door. He was begging, pleading, insisting. She paid no attention to him. There was no expression on her face. When he took hold of her arm she wrenched away and left, and the glass door swung shut.

Harry went over to a big desk and sat in the large red leather chair. He closed his eyes and pinched the bridge of his nose. He sighed and looked at me and frowned. "Friend, we are still not open for business. We are even less open than we were. Let me give you some sound advice. Never hump the help. They get up-pity. They take advantage."

"I came by to ask about Carrie Milligan."

"She used to work here. She's dead. What's your interest?"

"I heard she was killed. I'm a friend of hers from Fort Lauderdale."

"Didn't she used to live there?"

A bare-chested young man in jeans came out of the warehouse area and held up two big bolts. "Mr. Hascomb, you want I should count every damn one of these things? There's thousands!"

"Hundreds. Count how many in five pounds and then weigh all we got. That'll be close enough."

The boy left, and Harry Hascomb shook his head and said, "It's hard to believe she's dead. She worked day before yesterday. That's her desk over there. It happened so sudden. She really held this place together. She was a good worker, Carrie was. What did you say you want?"

"She came to see me two weeks ago. In Fort Lauderdale."

He was so still I wondered if he was holding his breath. He licked his lips and swallowed and said, "Two weeks ago?"

"Does that mean anything?"

"Why should it mean anything?"

I did not know where to go from there. The loan of money seemed all at once frail and implausible. I needed to find a better direction. "She came to see me because she was in trouble."

"Trouble? What kind of trouble?"

"She wanted to leave something with me for safekeeping. It happened it wasn't the best time for me to try to take care of anything for anybody. There are times you can, and times you shouldn't. I hated to say I couldn't. I was very fond of Carrie Milligan."

"Everybody was. What did she want you to keep?"

"Some money."

"How much?"

"She didn't say. She said it was a lot. When I heard about her being killed in that accident, I began to wonder if she'd found anybody to hold the money. Would you know anything about anything like that?"

Once again Harry went into his motionless trance, looking over my shoulder and into the faraway distance. It took him a long time. I wondered what he was sorting, weighing, appraising.

At last he shook his head slowly. "My God, I wouldn't have believed it. She must have been in on it."

"In on what?"

He undid a snap and a zipper and fingered a cigarette out of his Western pocket, popped it against a thumbnail, lit it and blew out a long plume of smoke. "Oh, shit, it's an old story. It happens all the time. You never expect it to happen to you."

"What happened?"

"What's your name again?"

"McGee. Travis McGee."

"Don't ever go partners with anybody, McGee. That's my second piece of advice for you today. Jack and I had a good thing going here. My good old partner, Jack Omaha. It wasn't exactly a fantastic gold mine, but we lived very well for quite a few years. And then the ass fell right off the construction business. We had to cut way back. Way way back. Trying to hold out until conditions improve. I think we might have made it. Things are looking a little bit better. I've always been the sales guy and Jack was the office guy. Anyway, he took off two weeks ago last Tuesday. On May fourteenth. Know what he was doing before he took off? Selling off warehouse stock at less than cost. Letting the bills pile up. Turning every damned thing into money. The auditors are trying to come up with the total figure. I'm a bankrupt. Good old Jack. Come to think of it, I guess he had to have Carrie's help to clean the place out. She only worked two days that week. Monday and Friday. Went out sick Monday afternoon. Came back in Friday. That was the day I finally decided Jack hadn't just gone fishing, that maybe he was gone for good. When did you see Carrie?"

"Thursday."

"It figures. I never figured her for anything like that. Even though she and Jack did have something going. No great big thing. It was going on for maybe three years, like ever since she started working for us. Just a little something on the side now and then. An overnighter. What we used to do, we'd send the girls, Carrie and Joanna, on another flight up to Atlanta, and then Jack and me would go up to catch the Falcons and stay in the HJ's next to the stadium. Just some laughs."

"And you think that was the money Carrie wanted me to keep for her?"

"Where else would she get it? Maybe Jack wanted her to run away with him. He was more hooked than she was, you know. Think of it this way. She helps him and gets a nice piece of change, and everybody thinks Jack took it all. When the dust settles, she can get the money and who'd know the difference?"

"Except she's dead."

"Yes, there's that. I want to make one thing clear, McGee. If you come across that money it belongs right here in this business. It was stolen from this business. It was stolen from me, and if you find it, it belongs right here."

"I'll keep that in mind."

He squashed his cigarette out. "None of this had to happen," he said softly. "I wake up in the night and think about it. If I'd had the sense when the money was rolling in, I would have put it in a safe place. Instead I farted it away on boats and cars and houses. If I'd kept it, I could have bought Jack out when things got slow. I could have squeaked through. In the night I think about it and I get sweaty and I feel like my gut was full of sharp rocks."

"What will happen?"

"I have to sell off what we've got left and throw it in the pot. It gets divided up among the creditors. I guess I'll lose the house too, maybe the cars. Then I'll start hitting my friends for a job. That son of a bitch said he was going fishing Tuesday and he'd be in Wednesday, and he said he had some money lined up to tide us over. I wanted to believe him. By Friday I got worried. I got some phone calls about bills I thought were paid. I called Chris. Jack's wife. She didn't know where the hell he was. She thought he was off in the boat somewhere. I phoned the marina and the boat was tied up there, nobody aboard. You know what? I just remembered. I had Carrie check out the bank accounts. She acted like she hated to tell me he had cleaned them out. He'd left ten bucks in each of them. He's a wanted man. I brought charges. I signed papers. It was on the news. I hope they find the son of a bitch, and I hope he has a lot of money left when they find him."

"You never thought Carrie was involved?"

"Not until you told me about her being in Lauderdale when I thought she was sick in bed. Not until you told me she wanted you to hold a lot of money for her. I swear. I mean I thought Jack was smarter than let

some girl in on a thing like that. I wouldn't ever give
Joanna any kind of leverage. I guess it was just that she
kept a close enough eye on the books, he couldn't work
it without her help. And, knowing that, she cut herself
in pretty good. Maybe she was afraid Jack might come
back to her for the money."

"Did you case her as a thief?"

"Her! I thought I was surrounded by friends. I guess
they decided that since the business was going to fold
no matter what anybody did, the thing to do was grab
the goodies and run. Like maybe running into a burning motel and grabbing a wallet. Shit, maybe I would
have cleaned the place out first if I'd thought of it before Jack did. And if I knew how. I wonder where Jack
is now. Brazil?"

For once Meyer followed my standing instructions.
He came in and folded his arms and leaned against the
wall beside the door. He didn't say a word.

"We're closed," Harry told him.

I said, "He's with me."

Harry stared at him. Meyer stared back, letting his
underlip and his eyelids sag. With all that hair and with
that inch of simian forehead he looked so baleful as to
be almost subhuman. Of course the effect is ruined if
he opens his professorial mouth.

Harry swallowed and said, "Oh. Uh . . . what kind
of work are you in, Mr. McGee?"

He rolled a yellow pencil under his palm, the flat
sides clicking against the top of the desk. I let him roll
it four times before I said, "Oh, I guess you could call
it investments."

He smiled too brightly. "Want to buy a nice build-
ing-supply business?"

I gave it a slow four count while the smile faded.
"No."

The kid came out of the warehouse again. "For Chrissake, there's supposed to be almost two dozen wheelbarras and I can't find a good goddamn one out there."

"Wait a second," Harry said. He took a sheet of letterhead, turned it over, and with a marking pen printed C L O S E D on it, and put pieces of Scotch tape on the corners. He stood up and said to me, "Nice to have met you, Mr. McGee."

"I'll stay in touch," I said. It didn't seem to make him happy.

After we left I looked back and saw him tape the sign to the inside of the glass door.

Meyer said, "What kind of fantasy were you selling him in there?"

"I was making it up as I went along. I was throwing in stuff to keep him talking. I dropped the loan idea."

As I drove slowly back toward town, I briefed Meyer on what I had learned. Then it was his turn. He gave it such a long dramatic pause, I knew he had done well. Why shouldn't he do well? I have busted my gut to learn how to make people open up. Meyer was born with it. A loving empathy shines out of those little bright-blue eyes. Strangers tell him things they have never told their husband or their priest.

He said that the secretary to the president of the Bayside Ladder Company, Inc., was one Betty Joller and, being Carrie Milligan's best friend, Betty was all racked up over the accident. Once upon a time Betty and Carrie and girls named Flossie Speck and Joanna Freeler had shared a little old frame house on the waterfront, at 28 Mangrove Lane. When Carrie moved out, they had gotten another girl to share rent and expenses. Meyer couldn't recall the new girl's name.

Anyway, Carrie Milligan was at the Rucker Funeral Home on Florida Boulevard, and there was to be a memorial service for her tomorrow, Saturday morning, at eleven o'clock. The sister, Susan Dobrovsky, was down from Nutley. She had arrived late last night. Betty Joller had picked her up at the airport and taken her to the Holiday Inn.

"You did well!" I told him. "Very very well."

It made him beam with pleasure.

I found 1500 Seaway Boulevard. I reminded him that Carrie had lived in 38B. I dropped him off and told him to see what he could get from the neighbors, and then work his own way back to Westway Harbor, and wait for me there if I wasn't back yet.

5

The Omaha house was in a fairly new subdivision called Carolridge. The developer had bulldozed it clean in his attempt to turn it from flatlands to slightly rolling contours. The new trees were all growing as fast as they could. In twenty years, when the block houses were moldering away, the shade would be pleasant and inviting. But in the mid-afternoon heat, all the houses sat baking white in the sun, and the spray heads made rainbows against immature gardenia bushes.

There were two cars in the carport at the Omaha place, and a fairly new cream-colored Oldsmobile in the driveway. A little wrought-iron sign was stuck into the parched grass, spelling out THE OMAHAS.

They give the development houses names. This was probably called The Executive or The Diplomat. It looked like eighty to ninety thousand, the top of the line for the neighborhood. Purchase would guarantee membership in the Carolridge Golf and Country Club. You could read the house from the outside. Three bedrooms, three and a half baths, colonial kitchen, game room, cathedral ceilings, patio pool, fiberglass screening.

I pushed the button and heard the distant chimes inside. Bugs keened in the heat. Some little girls went creaking and grinding past on their Sears ten-speeds, giggling. Somebody was running some kind of lawn machinery three houses away. A cardinal was sitting on a wire, saying *T-bird, T-bird, T-bird—cool, cool, cool.* I pushed the button again. And finally again. Just as I was about to give up, a woman opened the door. She had a broad, coarse, pretty face. She wore fresh lipstick, a sculptured blond wig, tie-dye jeans, and a white sunback blouse with no sleeves.

"Mrs. Omaha?"

"Yes. We were out in the back. I hope you haven't been ringing the doorbell long?"

"Not very long."

"I didn't know you'd come so soon. What happens is I keep getting a dial tone all the time, even when I'm trying to talk to somebody." She had a thin little-girl voice. She had the dazed glazed manner of someone awakened from deep sleep. Her mouth was puffy, her eyes heavy. The fresh lipstick missed its mark at one corner of her mouth. The sculptured wig was slightly off center. There was a red suck mark on the side of her throat, slowly disappearing as I looked at it.

"I'm not from the phone company," I said.

Her gaze sharpened. "Oh, boy, you better not try telling me you're selling something. You just better not try that."

"My name is McGee. Travis McGee from Fort Lauderdale. A friend of Carrie Milligan."

She was puzzled. "So what? What do you want here?"

"Did I come at a bad time?"

"Brother!"

"Suppose I come back later?"

"What for? Carrie is dead, right? Jack took off. Let's say they were very very good friends and I couldn't care less."

"I was talking to Harry over at Junction Park. He says Jack cleaned out the partnership accounts on May fourteenth. Carrie came down to Lauderdale to see me on the sixteenth. She was jumpy. She thought she was being followed. She gave me some money to keep for her."

"How much?"

"Maybe some other time would be . . ."

"Come on in, Mr. Gee. It's real hot this afternoon, isn't it?"

I followed her through the foyer to the long living room. She filled the rear of the stretch jeans abundantly. As she walked she reached up and patted the wig. The draperies were pulled shut. The subdued daylight came from the outdoor terrace area where, through the mesh of the drapery fabric, I could see a screened swimming pool as motionless as lime Jell-O in the white glare.

A tall and slender man stood in front of a mirror, combing his dark hair down with spread fingers. He wore a pair of quiet plaid slacks and a white shirt. His necktie hung untied. Over the back of a nearby chair I saw a dark blazer with silver buttons.

He said, "Honey, I'll get in touch again about the . . ."

He spotted me in the mirror. He whirled and said, "Who the hell are you?"

"This is Mr. Gee, Freddy."

"McGee," I said. "Travis McGee."

"This here is Fred Van Harn, my lawyer," Chris explained.

I put my hand out. He hesitated and then shook hands and gave me a very pleasant smile. "How do you do?"

"Honey, I asked him in because he says he's got some of the money. Maybe he's got all of it. Tell him he has to give it to me, dear. Mr. McGee, it's my money."

I looked at her in astonishment. "I haven't got any money!"

"You said Carrie gave it to you to keep for her!"

"She did, but I gave it right back. I couldn't accept the responsibility."

"How much was it?" Chris Omaha demanded.

"I'm sure I wouldn't have the slightest idea. She said it was a lot. She didn't say how much. What is a lot to one person is not a lot to another person."

Chris said, "Oh, God damn everything." She plumped herself down on a fat hassock which hissed as she sat on it.

Freddy said, "Do you know who did agree to keep the money for her?"

"She didn't say who she was going to try next."

"Where did this happen? And when?"

"On Thursday, May sixteenth, at about three or four in the morning aboard my houseboat moored at Bahia Mar in Fort Lauderdale."

"Why would she come to you?"

"Perhaps because she trusted me. We were old and good friends. I loaned her my houseboat for her honeymoon."

Freddy had long lashes, rather delicate features, olive skin. His eyes were a gentle brown, his manner ingratiating.

"Why did you come here, Mr. McGee?"

"I had a long talk with Mr. Hascomb. I just thought Mrs. Omaha would like to know about Mrs. Milligan coming to me. I thought it might answer some questions about her husband."

"You wouldn't listen to me, would you?" the woman said to Freddy in a whiny and irritating voice. "I told you that Milligan slut had to be in on it somehow, but you wouldn't listen to me. I happen to know as a fact that Jack was screwing her for years, even though he didn't know I knew, and—"

"Be quiet, Chris."

"You can't tell me to be quiet! You know what I think? He cleaned out the business and mortgaged everything in sight, this house and even the boat, and she was going to run off with him, but she probably had some boy friend and they decided it was safer and easier to chunk my husband on the head and throw him into—"

He moved close to her. "Shut *up*, Chris!"

"I can put two and two together even if you can't, Freddy, and let me tell you one thing—"

She didn't tell him one thing. He was one very fast fellow. He had a sinewy hand and a long whippy arm and a very nice clean pivot. He slapped her so fast and so hard I thought for one crazy moment he had shot her with a small-caliber handgun. It knocked her completely off the hassock. She landed on her hip and rolled over onto her shoulder and ended up face down on the carpeting. He got to her quickly, turned her, and pulled her up to a sitting position. Her eyes were crossed. The impact area was white as milk. I knew it would turn pink, then red, and finally purple. She was going to be lopsided for quite a few days. A little trickle of blood ran from the corner of her mouth down her chin.

He sat on his heels, holding her hand, and said, "Darling, when your attorney tells you to be quiet, there might be a very good reason for it. So you have to learn to be still when he tells you to."

"Freddy," she said in a broken voice.

He pulled her up to her feet and turned her toward a doorway and gave her a little push. "Go in and lie down, darling. I'll come in and say good-bye in a few minutes. Close the door, please."

She did as ordered. He turned mildly toward me and said, "Now let's understand where you fit, Mr. McGee. You just wanted to get involved?"

"Doing my duty as a citizen."

"I'm familiar with your type. The smell of money brings people like you out of the woodwork. I can't think of a way you can work any kind of a con in this situation. So give up and go home."

"I'm familiar with your type too. I saw the way you tied that tie. Very quick and neat. Ready Freddy, servicing another client. I bet you're in and out of those clothes as often as a fashion model."

I saw the little flare behind his eyes and hoped he would try me. I tried to look smaller and slower than I am. Finally he smiled and looked at a microthin gold watch gold-clamped to a lean and hairy wrist.

"With a deposition at four o'clock, there's no time for schoolyard games, my friend."

"Nor will there ever be, eh?"

A sudden flush made him look healthier, and then pallor turned him gray-green. "I think you'd better leave, McGee. Now!"

So I left that enchanting place. Pale shag, silk lampshades, velvet wing chairs, brocade, imitation Tiffany stained glass, Japanese lacquer, gilt mirror frames. Somehow like a matinee in a department store. Van Harn looked about thirty, or a shade under. The lady looked well over. They were consenting adults, consenting to afternoon games in the tangly bed under the long exhalation of the air conditioning.

As I backed out a phone truck pulled up. I smiled and waved at him and wondered what kind of reception he'd get. Good luck, fella. Must be an interesting line of work.

It was quarter to four. The yellow Gremlin was hot enough to bake glaze on pottery. The steering wheel was almost, not quite, too hot to touch. I stopped wondering what to do next and ran around for a mile or two trying to get cool in a hot wind.

I found a shopping center and discovered that they had left some giant oaks in the parking lot. This runs counter to the sworn oath of all shopping center developers. One must never deprive thy project of even one parking slot. And, wonder of wonders, there was an empty slot under one tree, in the shade. As I got out of the Gremlin, a cruising granny glowered at me from the air-conditioned, tinted-blue depths of her white Continental.

I found pay phones in a big Eckerd Drug, the phone stations half hidden by huge piles of pitchman's merchandise.

At the Holiday Inn they had a Miss Dobrovsky registered in Room 30, but she did not answer the phone. I looked up Webbel, who had driven the truck. There were about fifteen of them, but no Roderick. I wondered why Susan Dobrovsky would stay in the Holiday Inn instead of in Carrie's apartment. Squeamish, maybe. But sooner or later she would have to decide what to do with Carrie's personal belongings. That made me think of personal arrangements, and so I looked up the number for the Rucker Funeral Home and asked for Miss Susan Dobrovsky. After a long wait the man came back on the line and said that Miss Dobrovsky was busy with Mr. Rucker, Senior. I told him to tell her to wait there for me. Wait for McGee. Right there.

Rucker's Funeral Home was from the orange plaster and glass brick era. It had arches and some fake Moorish curlicues along the edge of the flat roof. A small black man was listlessly rubbing a black hearse parked at the side entrance. There was a large cemented area at the side and in back where doubtless they shaped up the corteges. I saw Carrie's bright orange Datsun in the parking lot on the other side of the building. On one side of the home there was a savings and loan branch, and on the other side a defunct car wash. I stuck my yellow Gremlin beside the orange Datsun, wondering if the industrial abrasive was still in the trunk. The bright colors screamed at each other.

She was sitting on a marble bench in the hallway just inside the front door. She looked enough like Carrie so that I was able to recognize her at once. She was a taller, younger, softer version of Carrie. She had on a dark gray tailored suit, a small round hat. She carried a purse and white gloves. Her eyes were swollen and red. She looked dejected and exhausted. But she was a marvelously handsome lady.

"I'm pleased to meet you, Mr. McGee."

"Did Carrie write you about me?"

"No. It was just . . . she phoned me long distance over a week ago, one night about ten. I was getting ready for bed. She talked a whole hour. It must have cost a fortune. She was funny. She kept laughing and saying silly things. Maybe she was drinking. Anyway, she made me get a pencil and paper and write down how to get in touch with you. She said that if anything happened to her, it was important I should get in touch with you. She said I could trust you. She said you're a nice person."

"She was in a loyal minority, Miss Susan."

"I . . . I don't know what to do about this," she said. She took a sheet of letterhead paper, folded once, out of her dark plastic purse and handed it to me. It was a heavy, creamy bond, and the statement of account had been typed with a carbon ribbon electric, flawlessly. It added up to $1677.90. It contained all manner of processing charges and service charges and mortuary overhead charges. It contained a coffin for $416 including tax, and it included an embalming fee, crematorium fee, death certification fee.

"She wanted to be cremated. It's in her will even. I can't pay all that. He has some kind of installment note he wants me to sign. He seems very nice . . . but . . ."

By being very firm with a chubby sallow fellow I gained an audience with Mr. Rucker, Senior. If you shaved Abe Lincoln and gave him a thick white Caesar hairpiece, and left the eyebrows black, you would have a reasonable duplicate of Rucker, sitting there in perpetual twilight behind his big walnut desk.

His voice was hushed, gentle, personal.

"I should be pleased to go over the billing with you, sir, item by item. Let me say I am glad the little lady has someone to help her in this time of need."

"Shall we discuss the coffin first?"

"Why not, if you wish? It is very inexpensive, as you can see."

"The decedent is to be, or has been, cremated."

"Cremation will take place this evening, I think. I can determine for sure."

"So there's no need for a coffin."

He smiled sweetly and sadly. "Ah, so many people have that misconception. It is a regulation, sir."

"Whose regulation?"

"The State of Florida, sir."

"Then you will be willing to show me the statutes which pertain?"

"Believe me, sir, it is standard practice and . . ."

"The statutes?"

"It may not be specifically spelled out in the law, but . . ."

I reached and took the pen from his desk set and drew a thick black line through the coffin and said, "Now we're down to twelve sixty-one ninety. I see you've charged for embalming."

"Of course. And a great deal of cosmetic attention was required. There were severe facial lacerations which—"

"It wasn't ordered and is not required by law prior to cremation."

He gave me a saintly smile. "I am afraid I cannot accept your judgments on these matters, sir. I must refer them to the sister of the deceased. We must bring her in on this. I must caution you that this is a very difficult situation for her, all this petty squabbling about the account as rendered."

"It's easier on her to just go ahead and pay it?"

"This is a very sad occasion for her."

"Wait right here," I said.

I went and found Susan on the bench in the hallway. I sat beside her and said, "We can cut that bill by a thousand dollars, but he thinks it will be such a rough experience for you to haggle over price, we should go ahead and pay it. What do you think?"

For a moment she was blank. Then I saw the tender jaw clamp into firmness and saw her eyes narrow. "I know what Carrie would say."

Mr. Rucker Senior stood up behind his desk when I walked in with Susan Dobrovsky. "Do sit down, my dear. We'll try to make this as painless as we possibly—"

"What's this crap about you overcharging me a thousand dollars?" she said in a high, strident, demanding voice.

He was taken aback but he recovered quickly. "You don't quite understand. For example, it may not be absolutely legally necessary for you to purchase a casket, my dear, but I think it would be a gross disrespect to your poor sister to have her . . . tumbled into the burning chamber like some kind of . . . debris."

She braced her fists on his desk and leaned closer to him. "That is not my sister! That is a body! That is debris! My sister is not in there any more and there is no reason for you to . . . to try to get me to worship the empty body, damn you, you greedy old man!"

He moved around the side of the desk, his face quiet as any death mask, and said, "Excuse me. I'll have this account recomputed. It will take just a few minutes."

He went out a side door. When it was open I could hear an electric typewriter rattling away. When he closed it behind him, she turned blindly into my arms. She rolled her head against my shoulder and gave three big gulping sobs and then pulled herself together, pushed away from me, honked into a Kleenex, and tried to smile.

"Was I okay?" she asked.

"You were beautiful."

"I was pretending I was Carrie and it was me who was dead. She'd never let him take advantage. I was just so confused when he gave me the bill before."

"Is the memorial service to be here?"

"Oh, no. Betty Joller sort of arranged it. It's going to be on the beach there at Mangrove Lane where she used to live."

Rucker Senior came back into the room and tried to hand her the new billing. I reached across her and took it. It was far more specific. It came to $686.50. I noticed he had included a sixty-dollar urn, sixty-two forty with tax. I was tempted to strike it but decided it was best to let him have a minor victory.

"Here are the rings from the deceased," he said, holding out a small manila envelope. She hesitated, and I took that also and slipped it into my shirt pocket.

"Satisfactory arrangements for payment will have to be made," the man said.

I took out my money clip, slipped the currency out of it, and counted out seven one-hundred-dollar bills on the front edge of his desk. "We'll need thirteen fifty in change and your certification on this bill, Mr. Rucker."

He expressed his opinion by looking most carefully at each bill, back and front. He made change from his own pocket and receipted the bill. *Paid in Full. B. J. Rucker, Sr.*

"You may pick up the urn here between one and two tomorrow afternoon," he said.

I nodded. There were no good-byes. We walked out.

Out in the afternoon sunshine of the parking lot, she swayed against me, leaned heavily on my arm as we walked. She shook her head and straightened up and lengthened her stride.

"He had me go back in there and see her," she said. "I thought there was some mistake. Her face wasn't the right shape even. She looked like she was made of wax. He showed me how the inside of the casket is all quilted, the kind he was selling me. Would he have really had it burned up, or would he have saved it for the next person?"

"I think B.J. would have had it burned up."

The lower angle of the sun had stretched casuarina

shadows across our two bright little cars. Before she unlocked the Datsun she turned to face me and said, "About that money in there, I'll be able to . . ."

"It was your money."

"What do you mean?"

"I owed it to Carrie."

"Is that true? Is that really true?"

"Really true."

"How much did you owe her?"

"It's a long story."

"Well, I'd like to know."

"She told you to trust me."

"Yes . . .?"

"Trust me not to tell you now, and trust me to have good reasons not to tell you. Okay?"

She looked at me for a long moment and then slowly nodded. "Okay, Mr. McGee." Her hair was long, and a couple of shades darker than Carrie's cropped silvery mop. The face was as round as Carrie's, the cheekbones high and heavy, but her eyes had more of a Slavic tilt, and their color was a seagreen-gray.

I made her try calling me Trav, and after three times it came easier and she smiled.

"How long are you going to stay?"

"Well, I guess until the lawyer says it's okay to go back to New Jersey. I've got to sort out all her stuff in that apartment. It's in a terrible mess. Somebody broke in and tore up the furniture and rugs and emptied everything out on the floor."

"When did this happen?"

"So much is happening, I'm getting confused on the dates. She was killed Wednesday night. Betty Joller was in bed and heard it on the eleven o'clock news. Betty, being her best friend, got dressed and drove to the apartment figuring my phone number would be in Carrie's phone index someplace, and I should be told. Betty has a key to the apartment that Carrie gave her. Betty got to the apartment about midnight and found it all in such a mess it took her a half hour to find my phone number. She was crying so hard I couldn't understand what she was trying to tell me. And when she did . . . wow, it was like the sky falling down. Carrie was seven years older, and I saw her just once in the last six years, when she came back to Nutley five years ago for our mother's funeral. I had no idea it would hit me so hard. I guess it's because she was the only close family I had left. There's some cousins I've never seen since I was a baby."

"Did Betty Joller report it to the police?"

"I don't really know. I guess she would have. I mean it would be a normal thing to tell the police about it. I told the lawyer about it, and he asked me if there was any specific thing we could report as being taken in the robbery, and I said maybe Betty could figure out what was missing, that I wouldn't know."

"Who's your lawyer?"

"He's a good friend of a girl that lives at 28 Mangrove Lane. I keep forgetting his name. But I've got his card here. Here. Frederick Van Harn. He just has to straighten out about the will and the car and all that. I guess it will be okay because he is the one who drew up the will for her. After she broke up with Ben she wanted to be sure he didn't get a dime that was hers if anything happened to her. Ben was at the funeral too, five years ago, but I can't remember him at all." She looked at her watch. "Hey, I've got to get going. Betty is com-

ing over to the Inn, and we're going to work it all out
about tomorrow. You're coming, aren't you?"

"Of course."

She drove away and I drove back to Westway Harbor.

6

I parked my rental in one of the reserved slots. As I walked past the office toward the docks, Cindy Birdsong came to the door and said, "Can I speak to you a moment, Mr. McGee?"

"Of course."

She had changed to a white sunback dress, and she wore heels, which put her over the six-foot line. A big brown lady with great shoulders and other solid and healthy accessories. And a mighty cool blue eye, and a lot of composure and pride.

"I want to apologize to you for the trouble my husband gave you this noon. I am very sorry it happened."

"It's perfectly all right, Mrs. Birdsong."

"It's not all right. It was a very ugly scene. If they release him on bail, I am sure he will want to apologize personally. I'm going to visit him this evening in the hospital, and I know he will be very ashamed of himself."

"He had a few over the limit."

"A few! He was pig drunk. He never used to get like ... well, I shouldn't burden you with our personal his-

tory. Thank you for giving me the time. If there is anything you need we are . . . always anxious to serve our
customers. Oh, and I meant to thank you for not signing a complaint." Her smile was inverted and bitter.
"There are enough of those to go around as it is."

"If there's any way I can help . . ."

She blinked rapidly. "Thank you very much. Very
much."

Meyer was aboard *The Busted Flush,* dressing after
having just gotten back from taking a shoreside shower.
I broke open a pair of cold beers and took him one and
sat on the guest stateroom bed and watched him put on
a fresh white guayabera.

"Fifteen Hundred Seaway's one of those bachelor
boys and girls places," Meyer said. "Everybody seems
to laugh a lot. It's very depressing. Eighty small apartments. There's a kind of . . . watchful anxiety about
those people. It's as if they're all in spring training, trying out for the team, all trying to hit the long ball, trying to be a star. And in a sense, they're all in training.
They're pretty trim and brown. Very mod in the
clothes and hair departments. They're all delighted that
there's a long waiting list for Fifteen Hundred. Pools
and saunas and a gym. Four-channel sound systems.
Health fads. Copper bracelets. *The Joy of Sex* on each
and every coffee table, I would guess. Water beds, biofeedback machines. There doesn't seem to be any kind
of murky kinky flavor about them. No group perver-
sion scenes. Just a terrible urgency about finding and
maintaining an orgasm batting average acceptable to
the peer group. Their environment is making terrible

demands upon them. I bet their consumption of vitamins and health foods is extraordinary."

We went up onto the sun deck and sat in the shade of the big canopy over the topside controls. "It doesn't sound like the kind of place where Carrie would want to live."

"No. It doesn't. It isn't. I didn't say why I was asking about her. I imagine they assumed I'm some kind of relative of hers. There was a coolness toward her. They thought she was standoffish, too much of a private person. She didn't get into the swing of things. I guess the pun is intentional."

"An outcast in Swingleville, eh?"

"Not exactly. More like a special friend of the management. The management is Walter J. Demos. He owns it and manages it and is sort of a den mother to all. He lives there, in the biggest apartment. He personally approves or disapproves of every applicant. He won't accept tenants who are too young or too old. He settles quarrels and disputes. He collects the rents, repairs plumbing, plants flowers, and he laughs a lot."

"How old a man?"

"I wouldn't want to guess. He looks like a broader, browner version of Kojak. He has a deep voice and a huge laugh. He is a very charming and likable man. He is very popular with his tenants. He is Uncle Walter. I think Uncle Walter is a smart businessman. The rents start at three hundred and seventy-five a month, and his occupancy rate is one hundred percent. By the way, he told me about Carrie's apartment being burglarized the same night she—"

"I heard about it. Was the door forced?"

"No. The layout is arranged for maximum privacy. If you go from your apartment to visit somebody, there's very little chance of your being seen. And it seems to be local custom to have a batch of keys made and hand them out to your friends."

"How long had she lived there?"

"Four months only. I picked up the rumor that Uncle Walter had moved her to the top of the list. They all seemed miffed about it. Jealous, almost. They don't want Uncle Walter to have a special girl."

"Did you get the feeling from him that she was special to him?"

"He seemed very upset about it, about her being killed. He said all the usual things. She had the best years of her life ahead of her. A pointless tragedy. And so forth."

"Seems like high rent for Carrie to pay."

"That's something that kept cropping up in conversation. Those tenants seem to feel they have to give a continual sales talk about the joys of living in Fifteen Hundred. They claim that because they don't have any urge to go out at night or away for vacations, it really saves money to live there. The little shopping center is so close you can walk over and wheel the stuff home. The ones who work close, some of them at least, have given up cars and use bikes. It's fascinating, in a way. A village culture. Maybe it's part of the shape of the world to come, Travis."

"Let us hope not."

"You seem a bit sour."

I stretched and sighed. "Carrie is in an upholstered box at Rucker's, her face reassembled with wax and invisible stitching. Tonight they will tote her off to the electric furnace and turn her into a very small pile of dry gray powder. So I am depressed."

"I don't think I can add anything of interest. Carrie didn't make any close friends there."

"Pun intended?"

"Not that time. Maybe you're not as sour as you act?"

"I'll tell you my adventures," I said. And did.

When I had finished he said, "I suppose we'll learn that young Mr. Van Harn is the attorney for Superior Building Supplies, which would account for his doing Carrie's will and being recommended to the sister, and being with Mrs. Omaha."

"I had the same feeling."

"What next?"

"We have a drink with a little more authority, and then we find a place to eat."

"Please don't give Gil's Kitchen another chance."

"And you call yourself fair?"

"You wouldn't!"

"You are right. I wouldn't. But between the drinking and the eating, let's go see where Carrie was killed."

By seven o'clock we had found the approximate place where it had happened. County Road 858 was called Avenida de Flores. It was an old concrete road, the slabs cracked and canted. Weeds stood tall on the shoulders. The shoulders slanted down into overgrown drainage ditches. There were a few old frame houses, spaced far apart, on the west side of the road. On the east side was a grove, with high rusty hurricane fencing installed on the other side of the drainage ditch. I went on out past the city limits sign and turned around in the parking area of a large new shopping plaza and came back, driving slowly.

I pulled off into the weeds of the shoulder, car at a big list to starboard, and stopped.

"For what?" Meyer asked.

I nodded toward the house two hundred feet ahead. An old man was riding a little blue power mower back and forth across the big expanse of front yard. "We just get out and start looking up and down the shoulder, and he'll come over and tell us all."

That is one of the few bonuses when looking into a fatal accident. People do love to talk about it.

In a few minutes I heard the mower cough, sputter, and die. Cars whooshed by, whipping the weeds around, blasting the hot wind against us. I looked up and saw the old man fifteen feet away, walking smartly, his face aglow with the terrible delight of someone loaded down with ghastly details.

"Hey, you wouldn't be looking for the spot where that there Mulligan woman got killed Wednesday night, would you?"

I straightened up and said, "Milligan. The name was Milligan. Carolyn Dobrovsky Milligan, Fifteen Hundred Seaway Boulevard, Bayside, tag number Twenty-four D, thirteen thirteen. Her name was not Mulligan, it was Milligan."

I used the voice and manner of the small-bore bureaucrat, petulant, precise, and patronizing. I needed no further identification as far as he was concerned. I was one of Them.

"Milligan, Mulligan, Malligan. Shoot, you're looking on the wrong side of the road is what you're doing."

"I doubt that," I said. "I doubt that very much."

He peered up at me. "Well, by Jesus H. Sufferin' Christ, you are something, you are! You may know her name right, but you don't know the first goddamn thing about the rest of it."

"I think he might be able to give us a little help," Meyer said, right on cue.

"Your partner here has got a little bit of sense," the old man said. "My name is Sherman Howe, and I've lived in that house there twelve years now, and you wouldn't believe the number of idiots get smashed up and killed on this straight piece of road in the night-time. One drunk son of a bitch about six months ago—see over there where that fence by the grove is fixed up new?—he come off the road and went through that fence, and he went weaving amongst the trees until he zigged instead of zagged and hit one dead center and mushed his skull on the windshield, dead as a fried mule. I keep my clothes on a chair by my bed and I keep a big flashlight handy, and when I hear that crunching in the night, I dress fast and come see what help I can give because that's the Christian thing to do. If it's bad, I blink the light back at the house here, and Mabel is watching for it, and she phones for the ambulance, and that's exactly what happened Wednesday night, and I was down here before that poor boy had even found the body, so don't tell me what side of the road it was on, mister. I know what side. Come with me. Watch out, now, you don't get yourself killed. Nobody slows down. Nobody gives a shit anymore what happens to anybody else in the world. Let me see now. . . . Sure. Here's where her car was. She was heading north, out of town, when she ran out of gas and pulled over onto the shoulder right here. See where she drove in? See the tracks? And the grass is still matted where the wheels set. It happened at twelve minutes after ten by my digital clock on my bed stand, and I'd just turned out the light to go to sleep. Mabel was in the living room watching the teevee. She still likes it, but it's got to the point where all that slop looks alike to me. I think the dead woman was . . . wait, follow me and I'll show you where the body was. I'm the one found it. That Webbel kid didn't have a flashlight at all. It was right about here I seen her arm kind of laying up against the side of the ditch in the grass, and the grass sort of hid the rest of her. She was right here, down in this dry ditch, her head aimed that way and her feet this way, neat as you please. Would have played hell finding her if that arm hadn't been up like it was and bare, so it caught the light from my flashlight. Sixty-five feet from the point of impact. I paced it off. Lordy, she was a mess. That whole left side of her face and head. . . . Anyway, I put the light on her and that boy fainted dead away. He fell like his spine had give way on him. I put my fingers on that girl's neck and thought I felt something, but I couldn't be sure. I ran and flashed my light three times at the window where Mabel was waiting, and she phoned it in. Then there was a terrible screeching and nearly another accident on account of that Webbel kid had parked half on the road and half off, being so shocked by hitting her the way he did. His motor was still running, so I run the truck off all the way onto the shoulder and turned it off. He was sitting up by then, moaning to himself. Pretty soon I heard the sirens coming from way off. The cops got here first. Those blue lights tamed traffic down. They took flash pictures of the two cars and the body, and they measured the skid marks, which didn't start until he was right at or a little past the point where he hit her. Any fool could see it wasn't the kid's fault."

"Would you care to explain your . . . theory, Mister Howe?"

"Theory! Goddammit, it's fact! Now you look and see that she was parked real close, too close, to the pavement. Maybe it was as far as she could get, running out of gas like that. The car lights were off. That's supposed to be what you ought to do if you are over on the grass at night, because, you leave taillights on, some dumb stupid drunken son of a bitch is going to aim right for those taillights thinking he's following you. Now the Webbel boy was driving one of those big Dodge pickups that's built like a van in the front, where the driver sits high, right over the wheels. You can see that this road is two lane and pretty narrow lanes at that. They talk about widening it, but all they do is talk. I heard them question the boy. There was a car coming the other way. He couldn't swing out around that girl's car. No room. He had to cut it pretty close. Now she must have slid across and got out the passenger side so as not to open her car door into traffic. Then she walked around the front of the car and stepped right in front of that farm truck. It sort of dented in the front right corner of that truck. Busted the right headlight, dented the metal, and so on. You could see where the post hit her head. She didn't realize a car would be so close. He said he saw her out of the corner of his eyes just as he hit her. He said there wasn't anything he could have done about it, and that kid is absolutely right. He was on his way home, and my guess is she was on her way to that gas station up across from the plaza, that stays open way late. When the ambulance came the medical fellow said she was dead. Massive skull fractures, he said. But he said it would be declared a DOA and the certificate would be made out at the hospital. Let me see. They took her away, no need for sirens. They'd got her ID from her purse in the car. The keys were in the ignition. It wouldn't start. When the wrecker came, the fellow looked at the gas gauge on the woman's car, and he had a can of gas on the back of the wrecker. He put some in and it started right up. I forget who drove it away. They took it down to the City Police Station. By that time the television truck was here, but there was nothing to take pictures of. So they just got the facts and used their radio to call them in. There was no cause to hold the Webbel boy. He was too shook to drive, but by then his father and his brother had arrived, and the brother drove the truck on back home. Their place is in the northwest part of the county. I guess that's all of it. You got any other . . . theory, mister?"

"When all the facts are in, all the *pertinent* facts, Mister Howe, I'll be able to summarize."

He turned toward Meyer. "Summarize, winterize, I feel sorry for you, friend, having to work with this sorry son of a bitch." He marched away without a backward glance. When I heard the mower start up again, I looked and saw him riding solemnly back and forth in the fading light of day.

Meyer said, "You couldn't have gotten any more under hypnotherapy. What are you looking at?"

I was down on one knee in the weeds, between the

matted places where the rear wheels had rested. I pointed to the place where the weeds and grass were withered and blackened. It began at a point midway between the wheels and slightly behind them. There was an area six inches in diameter and a random line half that width leading down the slope into the dry ditch, getting narrower and less evident as it approached the ditch.

"Gasoline spill will do this," I said. I dug down into the dirt with thumb and finger and pinched some of it up and sniffed it. It had a faint odor of gasoline. "I think her car fills on the left corner, aft of the wheel. But if it fills there or in the rear center, no matter how clumsy the man was who dumped gas into it, he could hardly manage to spill this much way under here without getting a lot right under where he was pouring."

"It soaked in before it got to the ditch," Meyer said.

"There had to be a lot of spill for it to run down the slope at all. It's been dry lately."

Meyer nodded. "And so she didn't stop because she ran out of gas. But it had to look as if she had a good reason for stopping. Is there some kind of drain under there, on the underside of the gas tank?"

"We'll be able to check that out. For now let's say yes."

"Am I following your scenario, Travis? X is in the car with Carrie. X is driving, let's say. He pulls off the road and stops. He picks a place a long way from any house. No street lights. He strikes her on the head with the traditional blunt object. He leans across her and opens the door. He pushes her out. The weeds are tall enough so that she would not be picked up in the lights of any passing car. He wiggles under the car with a wrench and a flashlight and opens the drain valve. When all the gas has run out, he closes the valve. He pulls her around to the front of the car, waits until he gets the right traffic situation and the right kind of oncoming vehicle, then boosts her up and walks her into the front corner of it. Then he takes off. Isn't that a little bit too much to get out of some weeds and grasses killed by gasoline? Isn't that too much of a dreadful risk?"

"Maybe it's too much. If X wears dark clothing, that would diminish the risk. He could stretch out flat beside her just ahead of the front bumper. He could look under the car for oncoming traffic heading the same way."

We went to where the front of the Datsun had been and looked at the weeds. It is too easy to let your imagination interpret the patterns.

"If so," Meyer said, "he didn't have much time to get out of sight. Too risky to go across the highway. Over the fence?"

I studied the fence line. "Under it. Where it's washed out. I think this was one very cool cat who checked his escape route first."

"Would your scenario include some telltale dark threads caught on the wire at the bottom?"

"There could have been, until you mentioned it."

I slid under the fence, on my back. Meyer stayed outside. There were inches to spare. I searched a quarter-acre area and came up with the startling conclusion that it was a very well-maintained grove. Nothing more. He could heave her into the front of the Webbel truck and spin and hit the hole before the truck could stop. Then, in dark clothing, he could melt back into the black shadows of the night and walk parallel to the fence line until it was safe to go over or under the fence.

Or, I thought as I went back under the fence, another vehicle had stopped there. Maybe a wife got nervous about a can of gas in the trunk of the family car. Dump it out this minute, dearest. Or maybe a can started leaking and somebody abandoned it there, and later somebody picked up the can, thinking it usable. Many false structures have been built from the flawed assumption of the simultaneity of seemingly related events.

As we got into the rental car, Meyer said, "We have no way of knowing that the gasoline was spilled—"

"At the same time. I just went through that."

"There are certain concepts which offend emotional logic. You have stopped beside a two-lane road at night. Traffic is light but fast. You walk to the front of your car, after sliding out on the passenger side. What are you going to do? Cross the road? Hitchhike? Open the door on the driver's side? Assume there is a good reason, do you step out, or do you look first?"

"If you are smashed, maybe you step out."

"If you are drunk, you would have opened the door on the driver's side, wouldn't you?"

"I don't know. But what the hell was she trying to do? Walk to one of those houses and phone? If so, Meyer, would she leave her purse and car keys?"

"Nice point. Now what?"

The wrecker stood beside the large gas station across from the entrance to the shopping center. It was a very muscular beast. It was painted bright red. It had warning lights, emergency lights, floodlights, and blinkers affixed to all available surfaces. The big tires stood chest high. The array of winches and cables and reels on the back end of it looked capable of hoisting a small tank up the side of an office building.

"Something I can do for you?" the bald sunburned man said.

"I didn't know they were making them so big."

"Mister, when you get a tractor trailer rig totaled across three lanes of an Interstate, you need something big to get it out of the way fast."

"Did that go out Wednesday night when that woman got killed just down the road there?"

His face twisted in pain. He spat and sighed. "Oh, Jesus, yes, it went out. Ray took it out. I had two guys out with flu. That goddamn Ray. You know what the payments run on this brute son of a bitch?" He kicked a high tire.

"No idea."

"Four hundred a month. A *month*. And Ray, the dummy, has to diagnose. Is he some kind of mechanic already? Hey, he says, no gas. So he puts some in. So what does that cost me? Thirty bucks' tow charge. Jesus!"

"Is he around?"

"Look, what's your interest in this thing, mister?"

"It's a case study project for the Traffic Advisory Council for the State Department of Transportation."

"Oh. Well, that's him at the far island there, checking the oil on the green Cadillac. Just don't hold him up on working the island, okay? It's money out of my pocket."

Ray was a stumpy nineteen with blue eyes empty of guile and with a face ravaged by acne.

"Gassy smell? Well, yeah. The way it was, see, I leaned inside to check the gear it was in and the brake. I was glad to see the keys there because it was in park, you know, and I was moving it to N when on account of the gassy smell inside it I looked at the gauge and seen it was empty. I turned the lights on. It's best at night, a short tow, keep the lights on, all the lights you got. I put gas in, figuring if it would run what's the sense towing it. I didn't know the boss would get his ass in such a big uproar about it, see. And I didn't even think who is going to pay for the couple gallons I put in, or the service call. That made it worse. Jesus, he's been all over me all the time since Wednesday. I'm about ready to tell him to shove his job."

I went to the boss and thanked him and said, "I have to interview the dead woman's sister. I can give her the bill for the gas and service, if you want."

He brightened up. We went into the office. He made out the bill. I looked at it and shook my head and handed it back. "Not like that, friend. Two gallons, not five. Five dollars' charge, not ten."

"So what are you, her brother? Look, the dead lady is in no shape to care what the bills are."

"Do you want to take a dead loss or fix the bill?"

"Everybody is all of a sudden getting weird," he muttered, and made out a new bill.

At ten o'clock we were back aboard the *Flush,* up on the sun deck under hazy stars, in two unfolded deck chairs like old tourists on a cruise ship. The events of the long day had been more abrasive than I had realized while they were happening. I felt a leaden weariness of bone and spirit.

I whapped a mosquito which tasted the side of my neck and rolled him into a tiny moist gobbet of meat and dropped him out of his life onto the deck. In many ways the Hindu is right. All life in all forms is so terribly transient there is an innocence about all acts and functions of life. Death, icy and irrevocable, is the genuine definition of reality. In my unthinking reflex I was doubtless improving the mosquito breed. If, over a millennium, man whapped every side-of-the-neck biter, maybe the mosquito race would bite only neck napes.

"Mr. McGee?" the polite voice said from the dock. I got up and walked aft to look down. There was Jason with the Jesus face and wire glasses standing under the dock light in a T-shirt with the short sleeves torn off, ragged blue-jean shorts, and a pair of boat shoes so exquisitely and totally worn out it looked as though he had wrapped his feet neatly in rags.

"Hi, Jason."

"Permission to come aboard?"

"Come on."

He came up the side ladderway like a big swift cat. He accepted a can of beer from the cooler. He had something to say, but he seemed to be puzzling out how to say it. He sat on his heels, on those brown legs bulging with big muscles.

I finally had to give him some help. "Something bothering you?"

"Sort of. I mean maybe it isn't any of my business.

What I wouldn't want is her having a worse time than she's having already. Okay?"

"Her being Mrs. Birdsong."

"She's really a great person. If I could have got to the office quicker, maybe the two of us, you and me, we could have grabbed onto Cal and quieted him down. I know how he could get. Did you hit him with anything? Did you pick up anything and hit him on the head?"

"I sort of hurried him into the wall once. Ralph or Arthur rapped him on the head with a hickory stick, a couple of good licks."

"Hey! That's *right*. I forgot that part. Then maybe it was from them. Look, can you tell—not you but medical doctors—can they tell which knock on the head did the most damage?"

Meyer answered. "I don't think so. Provided, of course, there's no depressed fracture or anything like that. The brain is a jelly suspended in a lot of protection, and oftentimes the greatest damage happens in the area directly opposite the point of impact. This could be in the form of a subdural hematoma, a bleeding which gradually creates enough pressure inside the brain to suppress the vital functions."

"Well, she visited him and then went out and got something to eat and went back and found a half dozen people working on him, but he was dead. There's going to be an autopsy. She came back in terrible shape. They gave her some pills. She's asleep now. A girl friend of Oliver's is sitting with her. Bet you it was a heart attack, or maybe a stroke that didn't have anything to do with getting hit on the head."

My neck was still sprained from being popped on the forehead. I hadn't enjoyed meeting the fellow, but had not wished him dead.

"Thanks for letting me know," I said.

"It's okay. I've been here the whole two years, you know. He was a pretty great person until he got to boozing real bad. And until just a little while ago, even though he got too drunk when he got drunk, he wouldn't drink when there was something he had to do that was best done sober. Like when Jack Omaha would hire him to captain."

"Jack Omaha!"

He turned toward me. He was slowly and carefully folding his empty beer can the way somebody might fold a Dixie cup, turning it into a smaller and smaller wad. "You knew Jack?" he said.

"No. But I heard he took off with a lot of money."

"That's what they say."

"You don't believe he did it?"

"No. But that's because somebody told me he didn't."

"Who would that be?"

"Somebody that knew him better than I did."

"Carrie?" I said.

I heard the air whoosh out of him. He stood up. "Who the hell *are* you?"

"Carrie's friend. When she married Ben Milligan she honeymooned aboard this old barge."

"Hey! I remember something about that. Sure. Have you got a great big shower stall aboard, and a big tub? And . . . uh . . ."

"A big bed? All three."

He leaned his rear against the rail and stood with ankles crossed and arms folded.

"Cheez. That Ben came by a year ago. She was still living at the cottage then. She and Betty Joller and Joanna Freeler and some bird name of Flossie. How come she ever married him, I wouldn't know."

"Nor anybody else. It happens."

"Mister America. Mister Biceps. He was in some kind of movie deal they were making up in Jax, probably an X movie. He came down to con some money off of Carrie. He'd done it before. She didn't have any. He said he would hang around until she got some. Betty came over and got me. It was a Sunday afternoon. Mangrove Lane is right down the shoreline to the south of us. I got there and he was sprawled out in the living room. I told him it was time for him to get on his Yamaha and into his helmet and head north. So we went out into the side yard and he began jumping back and forth and yelling 'Hah! Hah!' and making chopping motions. He came toward me and I kept moving back. I picked up the rhythm of the way he was hopping, and when he was up in the air, or starting up, I stepped into him and hit him in the mouth so hard it pushed this middle knuckle back in, and the first thing that hit the sod was the nape of his neck. He jumped up with both hands on his mouth, yelling, 'Not in the mouth. My God, not my mouth. Oh, God, my career!' So the girls babied him a little and I stood around until he got on his bike and roared away. I haven't seen him since. I don't think Carrie saw him either before she got killed. Are you coming to the service tomorrow morning?"

"At eleven? Yes. The sister asked me."

"She seems nice, that Susan. Carrie was too old for me. Maybe she wasn't, but she thought she was, which is the same thing. We had some laughs. She was making it with Jack Omaha. I told her that was dead end, and she said, What the hell, everything is. And there's not much answer to that, I guess."

"Where did Omaha keep his boat?"

"Right here. There it is, tied up to that shoreline dock at the end there, past the office, over beyond the lights."

I stood up. It was hard to see. "Bertram?"

"Right. Forty-six-foot with all the high-speed diesel you can use. All the extras. One hell of a lot of boat."

"I can believe it. It's one hell of a lot of price too."

"You can get that one at a pretty good price right now. The bank wants off the hook on it. I understand they'll take ninety-five cash."

"They ought to get that with no trouble if it's been maintained."

"Two years old and clean."

"Do you mean Omaha couldn't run it himself?"

"No. He could run it. But you can't fish and run it at the same time. When he got an urge to go billfishing, he'd get Cal lined up. He liked the edge of the Stream up beyond Grand Bahama. That's a good run, so they'd take off way before daylight and come back in by midnight or later. It makes a long day. Sometimes Carrie would go along."

"When was the last time?" Meyer asked. "Do you remember?"

"Only on account of the cops being here asking us. It was on a Tuesday, the fourteenth of . . . this month? Is it still May? Yes, the thirty-first. May is one of the months I always think should have thirty days. Yes, Jack Omaha took off with Cal about three in the morning, and they didn't come back in until after midnight. They questioned Cal about it. Just the two of them alone? Where had they fished? How had Jack acted? What time did they get back? How was Jack dressed? What was he driving? And so on and so on."

He stood up, shrugged, moved toward the ladderway.

"What time is it?" he asked. "I've got to go help Oliver lock the place. Anything you want, just ask either one of us."

After he was gone I strolled over and looked at the Bertram. It was called *Christina III*. It looked very fit and very husky. When I went back, Meyer was in the lounge. He was tilted back in a chair, hands laced behind his thick neck, staring at the overhead and frowning.

"Now what?" I asked.

"Do you know how they locate invisible planets?"

"No. How do they do that, Professor?"

"Because the visible ones act in erratic and inexplicable fashion. Their orbits are . . . warped. So you apply gravitational theory and a little geometry of moving spheres and you say, Aha, if there is a planetary body right *there* of such and such a mass and such and such an orbit, then all the random movements of the other planets become logical, even imperative."

I sat on the yellow couch. "So what kind of mass and orbit are we looking for?"

"Something large, important, illegal, and profitable."

"Involving a fast cruiser?"

"Possibly."

"Okay. Sunken treasure or Jamaican grass, routed via the Bahamas."

"Isn't there a lot of cannabis coming into Florida?"

"All the way from Jax around to Fort Walton Beach. Yes. Based on what they've intercepted and what they think they've probably missed, it would be at least ten tons a week. From Colombia, Mexico, Jamaica, and maybe some other BIWI islands."

"Big money?"

"Not as big as you read in the papers. Street value doesn't mean a hell of a lot. It passes through a lot of hands. The biggest bite is in getting it into the country and into the hands of a distributor. That's where you double your money, or a little better. Five thousand worth of good-quality, nicely cured Jamaican marijuana will go here for possibly twelve thousand. But if it is intercepted, they'll call it a quarter-million street value. It has to go from distributor to big dealer to little dealer to pusher-user to user. Everybody bites."

"How do you know all this?"

"What I don't know, I make up."

"Seriously, Travis."

"Boo Brodey wanted me to come in with him on a run last year. He laid it all out, including the comparison with Prohibition and so on. I said, Thanks but no thanks."

"Didn't he get picked up?"

"He's out again."

"Did you disapprove?"

"Can't you read me on that?"

Meyer chuckled. "I guess I can. You don't like partnership ventures and middleman status. You don't like large investments. You don't like coming to the notice and attention of the law. You wouldn't want anybody to have the kind of hold over you that Boo would have had. It's not your idea of high adventure. It's what the British would call a hole-and-corner affair. Tawdry. A gesture of defiance for the very young."

"So why ask questions you can answer?"

"I guess I meant, Do you disapprove of a person using the weed?"

"Me? I think people should do whatever they want to do, provided they go to the trouble of informing themselves first of any possible problems. Once they know, then they can solve their own risk-reward ratios. Suppose somebody proved it does some kind of permanent damage. Okay. So the user has to figure it out if there is any point in his remaining in optimum condition for a minimum kind of existence. For me, it was relaxing, in a way, the couple of times I've had enough to feel it. But it gave me the giggles, warped my time sense, and made things too bright and hard-edged. Also it bent dimensions somehow. Buildings leaned just a little bit the wrong way. Rooms were not perfectly oblong any more. It's a kind of sensual relaxation, but it gave me the uneasy feeling somebody could come up behind me and kill me and I would die distantly amused instead of scared witless."

"I am trying to imagine you giggling."

"I can still hear it."

"What about it being sunken treasure, Travis?"

"I am thinking back to the money. How it was packaged. Hundreds on the bottom, then fifties, twenties, tens. Some had fives on top. Tied with white cotton string, in both directions. With an adding-machine tape tucked under the string. Bricks of ten thousand.

Somebody very neat. It smacks of retail business, my friend. Think of it this way. Suppose you are taking in a lot of cash from various sources, and you use that cash to buy from several other sources, after removing your own share. Assume you do not want to change little ones into big ones at your friendly bank. Okay, if you put all the hundreds together, you have some thin little bricks to buy with. But at the other end you've got some great big stacks of little bills to add up to the same kind of round number. So you mix them up, and you have fairly manageable sizes."

"Sounds less and less like doubloons," Meyer said.

"Yes, it does."

"When I get this pain right between my eyes it means I've done enough thinking for now—on a conscious level. Now the subconscious can go to work. Do you have the gut feeling Jack Omaha is dead?"

"Yes."

"Then that makes the *Christina III* a very unlucky vessel."

"Jack Omaha, Carrie Milligan, and Cal Birdsong."

"And," he said, "the invisible planetary body which warped the other orbits. Good night."

After I had puttered around aimlessly and had at last gone to bed, I found myself reliving the memory of Boo Brodey when he tried to recruit me. He's big and red and abraded by life—by hard work and hard living, by small mercenary wars and thin predatory women. Yet there is something childlike about him.

He paced up and down in front of me, his face knotted with anxiety and appeal, chunking his fist into his palm, saying, "Jesus, Trav, you know how I am. Somebody tells me what to do and when, it gets done. I work something out myself and it's a disaster. Trav, we're talking about the money tree. Honest to Christ, you wouldn't believe it, the kind of money. Kids, weird little kids, are bringing in bags of grass right and left. Anything that'll fly, that's the way to do it. You can lease an airplane to fly up to Atlanta and back. Okay, you put it down on the deck and go to Jamaica and buy ten thousand worth and come back, and you got thirty thousand before the day is over. It's coming in on boats and ships and everything, Trav. Come *on!* The narcs aren't all that hard-nose about grass. They know they can't keep it out, and a lot of them, they don't know for sure it hurts anybody anyway, right? Come on in with me and help set it up. You know, the contacts and all. Help me out, dammit!"

When I told him I didn't want in, he wanted me to set it all up for him. I could stay outside and get a piece of it in exchange for management skills. I said no, I didn't want to go down that particular road. If you make it with grass, you find out that hash and coke are more portable and profitable. You kid yourself into the next step, and by the time they pick you up, your picture in the paper looks like some kind of degenerate, fangs and all. And all you can say is, Gee, the other guys were doing it too.

If I were really going to do it, I would refit the *Muñequita* for long-range work. Tune her for lowest gas consumption and put in bigger tanks. She's already braced to bang through seas most runabouts can't handle. Then I would . . .

Whoa, McGee. There is larceny in every heart, and you have more than your share. So forget how far it is across the Yucatan Straits, leaving from Key West.

7

I T was an overcast morning with almost no wind at all. The wide bay was glassy calm, the outlying headlands misted, looking farther away than they were.

There was a narrow, scrabbly, oyster-shell beach beside the cottage at 28 Mangrove Lane where Carrie Milligan had once lived. A narrow wooden dock extended twenty feet into the bay. It was still solid, just beginning to lean. It was good, I guessed, for another couple of years. Two old skiffs were high on the beach, overturned, nosing into the sea grapes.

Jason sat on the end of one of the skiffs. He wore a white shirt and white trousers. He had a big plantation straw hat shadowing his face. He was playing chords quite softly on a big guitar with a lot of ornate fretwork against the dark wood. The chords were related but did not become any recognizable song. They were in slow cadence, major and minor.

Meyer and I joined the group, standing a bit north of most of them, in the shade of a small gnarled water oak. I saw Harry Hascomb and the young man who had been counting stock in the warehouse. I saw Mrs.

Jack Omaha, Gil from Gil's Kitchen, Susan Dobrovsky, Frederick Van Harn, Oliver from the marina, Joanna from Superior Building Supplies, and a man it took me a few moments to place. He was Arthur, the younger of the two cops who had subdued Cal Birdsong.

There were seven young ladies in long pastel dresses. The dresses were not in any sense a matched set. They were all of different cut and style, but all long and all pastel. Susan wore a long white dress which was just enough too big so that I suspected it was borrowed. Susan and the other girls all had armfuls of the lush Florida flowers of late springtime.

A young man stepped out of the group and turned and faced us. He had red hair to his shoulders and a curly red beard. He wore a sports jacket and plaid slacks.

In a resonant and penetrating voice he said, "We are here today to say good-bye to our sister, Carrie." The guitar music softened but continued. "She lived among us for a time. She touched our lives. She was an open person. She was not afraid of life or of herself. She was at home being Carrie, our sister. And we were at home with her, in love and trust and understanding. In her memory, each one of us here now most solemnly vows to be more sensitive to the needs of those who share our lives, to be more compassionate, to give that kind of understanding which does not concern itself with blame and guilt and retribution. In token of this pledge, and in symbol of our loss, we consign these flowers to the sea."

He moved to the side. The guitar became louder. One by one the pastel girls walked out to the end of the dock and flung the armloads of blooms onto the gray and glassy bay. There were tear marks on their cheeks. The flowers spread and began, very slowly, to move outward and in a southerly direction with the current. It was a very simple and moving thing. I had the feeling of a greater loss for having so undervalued Carrie. I excused myself by saying I had really not known her very well. But that was what Red-beard had said, that we should be more sensitive to the needs of others— and more sensitive, I added, to their identities as well. If she had meant this much to these people, then I had slighted her value as a person.

The music trailed off and stopped. Jason stood up and bobbed his head to indicate that was all. The murmur of voices began. Susan went a little way down the beach and stood, watching the floating flowers.

I looked at the twenty or so people I did not know, and I realized anew that there is a new subculture in the world. These were mostly young working people. Their work was their concession to the necessities. Their off-work identities were contra-establishment. Perhaps this was the only effective answer to all the malaise and the restlessness and the disbelief in institutionalized life, to conform for the sake of earning the bread and then to step from the job into almost as much personal freedom as the commune person.

I realized Meyer was no longer at my elbow. I looked around and did not see him. Jason nodded to me and said, "Was it okay?"

"It was beautiful."

"I figured if I just noodled around it would be better. If you play something, people start making the lyrics in their heads and they miss the other words. Robby did fine, I thought. He's an architect. Cindy wanted to make it to the service here, but she's still too shook."

"She shouldn't have even thought about it."

"Well, she thought a lot of Carrie. When Cindy was sick last year, Carrie came over and straightened out the books. It took her a whole weekend to do it, the way Cal had screwed things up. Look, I think I ought to talk to Susan. You think it would be okay?"

"I think it would be fine."

He moved off down the beach. Meyer came up to me and said, "There's a hex nut on the bottom of the gas tank. The undercoat is off it on one of the surfaces, and the metal is shiny where the undercoat flaked off."

I stared at him in disbelief. "With all these people around, you were damn fool enough to—"

"I was flipping my lucky silver dollar and catching it, like this. I dropped it and it hit the toe of my shoe and rolled under the Datsun. I didn't get a good look or a long look."

"Don't try to be cute about these things."

"Don't try to be McGee, you mean?"

"Don't get huffy. If you want to travel with the team, learn the ground rules. I've told you before. Don't *ever* take a risk you don't have to take, just to save time or inflate your ego."

"Now wait a minute—"

"There are a lot of things you can tell me that I would never know or guess unless you told me. You have a lot of special information in your head. So have I in mine. My information can make you live longer. And better."

"Better than what?" a girl asked. I turned. Joanna.

Miss Freeler, recently of Superior Building Supplies. Dear friend of Harry Hascomb. Ex-friend. Slender girl with a delicate and lovely face, long fall of ginger-colored hair. Green eyes, slightly protruding and very challenging. The girl challenge, old as time.

"Live better than Harry is going to live for a while."

"That wouldn't be hard," she said. "Bet your ass. Harry is going to have to give up a lot of goodies. I know you from the office yesterday, when I quit. I remember you because you've got weird eyes. And for other reasons too, I might add. I bet you hear that from all the girls. You know, you got eyes the color of gin. What's your name?"

"McGee. And this is Meyer. Joanna Freeler."

"Hello, Meyer," she said. "Hello, McGee. What are you two dudes doing here at the memorial?"

"Friends of the deceased," I said. "From Lauderdale."

"Sure. That's where she married that muscle bum. Why didn't she marry you? Weren't you available, McGee?"

"Weren't. Aren't. Won't be."

"Now you're singing my song," she said.

She was wearing a long orange dress. The color was not good with her coloring. She had thrown her flowers farther and spread them wider than any of the others.

"You seem to be in good spirits," I said.

She clenched her jaw and glared up at me. "That's a shitty thing to say, friend. I miss her like hell. And in one way or another, I'll always miss her. Okay?"

"I didn't mean anything by what I said."

"Then apologize for letting your mouth run with your head turned off, McGee."

"I do so hereby apologize."

She hugged my arm and smiled and said to Meyer, "You run along, dearie. I have to ask this man something."

Meyer said, "I'll walk back to the boat."

"You've got a boat here? At Westway? Hmm. A fast boat?"

"If you really really press her, she'll do seven or eight knots."

"You a pilot? Like in an airplane?"

"No."

"Come along. I just don't like to say some kinds of things in front of two people. All right?"

She led me well away from the others, over to the far edge of the lot. One water oak had sent out a huge limb, parallel to the ground, the top of it almost as high as my shirt pocket. Joanna gave a little bounce and put her palms on the limb and floated up, turning in air to sit lightly. She patted the limb beside her. "Come into my tree, friend."

I sat beside her. She took my hand and inspected it carefully, back and front.

"Hmm. You've had an active past."

"You could have said that in front of Meyer."

"It's hard to say what I want to say in front of just one person. I mean it's so easy for you to get the wrong idea. I'll miss Carrie. But she *is* dead, right? And the world goes on. One thing I know from all this, maybe the same thing Carrie figured out, there's got to be

more to living than sitting on your butt forty hours a
week in an office and getting laid once in a while by the
joker who signs your paycheck. I could retire, maybe.
If I play it right. But what I want is more interesting
work. Like what Carrie was doing."

"What was she doing?"

"Don't try to get cute, McGee. Listen, I *knew* that
girl. There's four of us in the cottage now. Me and
Betty Joller and Nat Weiss and Flossie Speck. So before she moved out and since, Carrie was supplying the
cottage with free grass for her friends, like a paper bag
this big half full. We must have two pounds left. Do I
have to spell it out? What I wasn't told, I can guess. So
it all fell apart for you people. She went to Lauderdale.
Now you are here to put it back together again, right?
So this is a job application. I'm very smart and I know
how to keep my mouth shut."

"I wouldn't say you know how to keep your mouth
shut."

"This one time I have to take the chance, or where
am I? Outside, as usual."

"Who do you think I represent?"

"You are sitting in my tree playing stupid. You look
smart and rough. You're in distribution after the crazy
people bring it in. I want to be a crazy people because
I need something weird to do, and the money is nice. I
told Carrie she shouldn't be involved, and here am I
asking to get involved. What did happen to Jack?"

"Didn't Carrie tell you that?"

"She said he got scared and probably grabbed his
share and ran. But that doesn't . . ."

"Doesn't what?"

"Never mind. Skip it."

"Did Harry know what was going on?"

"Cowboy Harry? He's a jerk. How could he know what was going on? It takes him both hands to find his ass. Why did you come to see him anyway?"

"To talk to him about Carrie."

"Why would you want to talk to him about Carrie?"

"You can keep your mouth shut?"

"You know it!"

"Just trying to get a line on who pushed Carrie in front of that truck."

The color drained out of her face. She wiped her mouth and shuddered. "Come on, now!"

"She was killed. I guess you could call it an occupational hazard, right? If you want to accept that kind of risk, maybe we can find something for you."

"But who . . . who . . ."

"The competition, probably."

She looked down and plucked the orange dress away from her body. "I'm getting all hot and sticky. I better change. Don't go away, huh? I want to think this over, okay?"

Joanna dropped lightly from the limb and went to the cottage, striding long, and disappeared inside. A lot of the people had left. Some had gone into the cottage. Others were talking, by twos and threes. I saw Susan walking toward the Datsun, so I dropped down and got to the car just as she did. Her eyes were red, but she managed a smile.

"I think Carrie would have liked it," she said.

"I'm sure she would. Yesterday I walked off with her rings. I forgot to give them to you. And I left them on the boat. We could go get them now."

She frowned and shook her head. "There's no hurry.

I have to be here a few days anyway, Fred . . . Mr. Van Harn says."

"Do you want me to go and pick up that package from Mr. Rucker?"

"Oh, no, thanks. I already talked to Betty about it, and she's coming with me now and we'll go over there before two o'clock. It's perfectly all right, really. But thank you."

A sturdy girl in a yellow dress came hurrying to the car, saying, "Sorry, Sue. I got to talking to somebody."

"Betty, this is Travis McGee. Betty Joller."

She had one of those plump pretty faces which go with wooden shoes and beer festivals. Her eyes were Dutch blue, and her smile was totally friendly and not the least bit provocative. "When I saw you standing with Meyer, I figured it had to be you," she said. "Carrie told me once that the only really happy time she could remember was when you loaned her and Ben your houseboat for their honeymoon. We're all going to miss her so much around here."

They got in, and Susan hitched her white dress up above her knees and then backed smartly around and they left. At my elbow Joanna said, "Now that Susan is some kind of great package."

"And Jason has his eyes on it."

"I noticed that. She's too young for you, chief."

"So are you."

She laughed so hard it bent her over. The laugh was silver bright under the shade trees, unfitting for the occasion. "Me? Me?" she gasped. "I'm the oldest person around anywhere." She wore little salmon shorts and a soft gray top. She had wound her ginger hair into a pile atop her head and pinned it in place casually. Ends were escaping. It made her throat look very slender and vulnerable.

She looked around. "Where did you leave your wheels?"

"We walked over from the marina."

"So I'll walk back with you, okay?"

"Okay, Joanna."

"We haven't made our deal yet."

"Deal?"

She carried a small white canvas beach bag. She twirled it by its draw cord. "Keep playing dumb and I'll brain you, honey."

So we went out to the sidewalk and walked through sun and shade, past little frame houses and new little stores, to the marina. Jason was back at work. He was in his khaki shorts standing on the bow deck of a big Chris, hosing it down, washing off the salt, and the new arrivals, a pair of small round white-haired people in bright boat clothes, stood sourly watching his every move. "Get that cleat too," the man yelled. "The cleat!"

"Yessir," said Jason the musician. "Yessir, sir."

Joanna was loudly enthusiastic about the below-decks spaces of *The Busted Flush*. While she was trotting around, oh-ing and ah-ing, Meyer told me he had some errands. I gave him the car keys. I did not know if he had errands or a sudden attack of discretion.

I caught up with her in the head, standing in front of the big mirror, touching her hair, turning and looking back at herself over her shoulder. She saw me in the mirror and said, "This is really some kind of floating playpen. It's funny. I keep feeling left out. I keep thinking that it isn't right that all this has been going on without me. After all, I'm the best in the world. You didn't know?"

"You hadn't mentioned it before."

"Don't tell me you designed all this?"

"No. It was as is when I won this barge in a poker game."

"Ah. Hence the name."

"There was a Brazilian lady that went with it, but I wouldn't let him bet her."

"Are Brazilians so great?"

"I wouldn't know. Anyway, I kept the decor."

She was smiling. Then suddenly she slumped her shoulders, shook her head, her face somber. "It's so great to kid around, isn't it? I guess the real reason I'm quitting the job is because it wouldn't be the same there without Carrie. Can I have a beer?"

"Of course."

We sat in the galley booth, facing each other across the Formica top. She was pensive, silent, unreadable.

Finally she said, "So it isn't any game. So I don't want in, thanks just the same. Sorry I bothered you."

So I told her the truth about my relationship to Carrie. And why I was here with Meyer. She turned beet red and had to get up and pace around to control her restless embarrassment. It took me about five minutes to get the record straight. I left out the part about the money.

"You must have thought I'd lost my mind!"

"I decided you weren't too tightly wrapped, kid."

"You encouraged me, damn you!"

Finally she calmed down and sat down, sipped her beer, and said, "Okay, I can see why you think she was killed. The purse and the gas and so on. But why? She wasn't into anything *that* rough. Everybody and his brother is hustling grass into Florida. There's absolute tons of it coming in all the time. It's about as risky as running a stop sign."

"Did she tell you how it worked?"

"Not in so many words. It was no secret they used Jack's cruiser. There is no way this coast can be policed. Too many small boats and little airplanes and all."

"Didn't anybody at the cottage ask Carrie where she got it?"

"Betty always did, and Carrie would say something different every time. Like she'd say they had a special on it at Quik-Chek. It was top quality, cured right. Jason says it's the best he's ever run into. It was fun, the four of us, Betty and me, Carrie and Floss. Betty got a little machine and made cigarettes. And we had the cookbook, too, and made those hash puppies. Like on an evening, there'd be eight or ten of us sitting around, and maybe Jason making music, and we'd get onto a real nice level. And there'd be good relaxed talk that made sense, not like when everybody is drinking and people get ugly or silly. They say now it can mess up having babies, and it can lower your resistance to colds and flu and infection and so on. So? Automobiles can kill you, and people don't stop driving."

"The imperatives aren't the same."

"The what aren't what?"

"Excuse me. Let's not get into a hard sell."

"Are you opposed?"

"Joanna, I don't know. A fellow who was pretty

handy with a boat once said that anything you feel good after is moral. But that implies that the deed is unchanging and the doer is unchanging. What you feel good after one time, you feel rotten after the next. And it is difficult to know in advance. And morality shouldn't be experimental, I don't think. I find that the world is full of things which are unavoidable and which cloud my mind. When my mind is clouded, I am experiencing less. I may think it is more, if the mind is warped, but it is less, really. The mind looks inward, not outward. So I just . . . try to make sure there's always somebody in the control room, somebody standing watch."

"Somehow it sounds dull."

"It isn't."

She wrapped her fingers around my wrist. "Okay, smart-ass. Do you think you'd feel good after me?"

"If the reasons are right, sure."

"Is there more than one reason, friend?"

"The biggest and most important reason in the world is to be together with someone in a way that makes life a little less bleak and solitary and lonesome. To exchange the I for the We. In the biggest sense of the word, it's cold outside. And kindness and affection and gentleness build a nice warm fire inside. That's okay. But if you want to set some new international screwing record, or if you want to show off the busiest fastest hips in town, forget it."

The fingers slackened their hold on my wrist and she pulled her hand back. Tears stood in her eyes. She smiled and shook her head and said, "No way, McGee. Whatever it is you're selling, I can't afford it. I went that route once, and it stung. It stung a lot. If that's the kind of dressing you want on the salad, eat elsewhere. I am a very good lay for the Harry Hascombs of the world, and I always feel good afterward, thanks."

"Always?"

"Go to hell!" she said and got up. "All I am is your garden-variety man-eater. I like it. Go to hell!"

"To each his dagnab blue-eyed own."

She smiled. "And I'll always miss Walt Kelly too." She held her hand out to me. "Friends? I didn't exactly come here to set up a friendship. But it'll have to do. God! I am starving. What have you got here?" She had opened the refrigerator. "Is this corned beef? Cheese. Where's the bread? I have this terrible food engine inside me. I eat enough for three truck drivers and I'm always hungry and I never gain one little ounce. I could give you bone bruises, dear."

I sat and watched her make sandwiches. She was very deft, and she made a lot of them. She ate about twice as much as I ate. She ate with such enthusiasm it made her sweaty, even in the air conditioning. She ate with such a lusty, bright-eyed joy that I had the wistful wish to have played her game and bundled her into the sack five minutes after Meyer stepped off the boat. She was intensely alive, as vital and immediate as anyone I had met in a long time.

"How often did she bring the samples?"

"What? Oh, when we were about to run out. Her moving to that Fifteen Hundred place had something to do with the deal. She told me she was getting a free ride on the apartment. But she missed us."

The phone rang. It startled both of us. I went into

the lounge and answered it. It was Meyer. "About the autopsy on Birdsong, it was heart. Some kind of aneurysm. Thought you'd like to know. I hope I . . . haven't disturbed you by phoning."

"You can come back aboard any time."

"Oh."

"What's this with the Oh?"

"Just Oh. Nothing complicated. Oh."

She sauntered into the lounge and stretched out on the yellow couch, placing her second mug of milk on the coffee table. "This is truly some great boat."

"What is Chris Omaha like?"

"Nobody can ever figure out how come Jack stayed with her so long. She's dumb, loud, and greedy. Rotten to him and rotten to the kids. Ever since the kids got old enough to be sent off to school, they've been away. She likes to be alone in the house in case something wearing pants comes by to make a delivery or fix something. Jack caught her a couple of times. But leave her? No. Carrie thought for quite a while maybe he would leave Chris and marry her. I don't know what the hold is. It was a kid marriage for them. Seventeen and eighteen they were. It finally got to be an arrangement, I guess. He could have Carrie, and she could have anybody who happened to come along."

"Like Ready Freddy Van Harn?"

"Ready Freddy? Wow, you read him right. I'll have to tell Floss what you called him. No, Fred is the lawyer for the business, and he's Jack and Harry's personal lawyer, and he'll be handling the estate, what's left, but he wouldn't boff around with old Chris, not when he can tag the best there is."

I recounted my reasons for contradicting her. She looked astonished. "What *about* that! What do you know? I guess old Chris snuck up on his blind side or something."

"He was Carrie's lawyer?"

"From being the lawyer for the business. When she wanted to make out a will so that Ben couldn't get her savings or her car or anything like that, she asked Fred one day when he was in to see Harry about something, and he made some notes and drew up a will and had her come into the office and sign it. I guess he made himself the executor. That would be okay by Carrie. And Betty told me she'd warned Susan about Fred. Susan seems like such a nice kid. Fred even got to Betty one time. I guess it was sort of a challenge to him. Betty is sort of sexless, you know? She has all the equipment and she's pretty, but something's left out. Fred got her a little bit bombed on wine and then he took her. It wasn't exactly rape, but it was as close as it could get and still not be. She hates him. He really hurt her, because she's built small, and that Fred has . . . well, all I can say is that you'd never know, looking at him, so kind of slender and girlish almost. And pretty. But he's a bull. He's huge. He's so huge he's sort of scary. And . . . he likes to hurt. I don't like kinky things. I like it, you know, for fun. It doesn't seem to be fun for him. Oh, he knows a lot of tricks and so forth. But it's more like he read up on it in engineering school. Once was enough for me. He's with you but he isn't. He's . . . I don't know how to say it."

"Remote?"

"Ri-i-ght! I think Fred is trying to score every girl in

Bayside and surrounding area. He's real hell on wives. Maybe that's why he put Chris on his list. Men have tried to beat up on him for messing around, but he is just as quick and just as mean as a snake. He's a good lawyer, but he's not a very nice person. I don't know how marriage is going to work out for him. He's going to get married. It was in the paper. Jane Schermer. Very social and very very rich. It's grove money from way back. He has some ranchland out near all her groves, lots of it, but nowhere near as big. The Van Harn family used to have money, but about the time Fred was in Stetson Law, his daddy shot himself and it turned out he was almost totally busted. It was something to do with letter stock. I don't even know what that is. But that's what they say. Something about pledging letter stock for bank loans, and him being the lawyer for the bank. Fred works hard. I think he's maybe made back a lot of money. Everybody says he does a good job. But I think that way down deep he's a creepy person."

"Bayside seems like a busy place."

"It's okay, I guess. I really don't know whether I'll stay around. I left once before and came back. Maybe I'll come to Lauderdale and live on this boat with you for a while. Okay?"

"We'll keep your name on file, Miss Freeler."

"You are so nice to me."

My alarm bell bonged as Meyer stepped aboard, onto the mat on the stern deck. He knocked and came in and smiled at pretty Joanna on the yellow couch. "I like to see healthy young girls drinking milk," he said. She had set aside a couple of sandwiches for him, neatly packaged in Saran. She stirred herself and got up, yawning, and said she was going back to the cottage for a nap. I took her by the shoulders and turned her around and gave her a little push toward the state-rooms. She trudged off, scuffing her heels, and when I looked in on her she was snoring, a large snare-drum sound for such a small lady.

I sat with Meyer while he ate at the booth in the galley.

"I tracked it down," he said. "The place Carrie had her car serviced. It's a big Shell station right across from the entrance to Junction Park. It was handy for her because she could leave her car there while she was working. It was in last Tuesday. They looked up the ticket. They changed the oil and the filter and put on new wiper blades—and filled the tank."

"And if it was filled Tuesday, and she didn't go on any trips . . ."

"She worked all day Tuesday and Wednesday."

"Very nice work, Meyer."

"Thank you."

"About that planet theory of yours, how they find the invisible one by seeing what it does to the orbits of the others, I have a candidate for planet. One attorney by the name of Frederick Van Harn. He impinges on the lives of too many of the people we're interested in."

"Including Mrs. Birdsong."

"Huh?"

"He was coming out of her motel unit when I drove in."

"Oh, that's just great. Anyway, he's top priority. All we can find out. Right?"

"Yessir, sir."

And despite my protestations that it wasn't all that urgent, he headed on out again after reborrowing the car keys.

8

JOANNA woke up at four and said a sleepy farewell and went tottering off. I wrote a note to Meyer and left it where he would see it. I locked the *Flush* and walked all the way to 1500 Seaway Boulevard, estimating it at a little less than two miles south of the marina. At first it was very hot, but then a quick thunderstorm came slamming in. I stepped over a hedge and took refuge under a tremendous old banyan. A small white dog yapped at me from a screened porch, some of his yapping drowned by thunder. A pale woman came out onto the porch to see why he was making such a fuss. Over the rain sound I yelled, "I'm trespassing!"

"You can trespass on the porch here if you want."

"I'm terrified of the savage dog. Thanks anyway."

She smiled and went back into the house. When the rain stopped, mist rose from the pavement.The air was washed clean and was much cooler. I stepped along faster than before.

Fifteen Hundred was a jumble of villas and town houses, of joined and separate structures interconnected by arcades and roofed walkways. The layout estab-

119

lished small courtyards of various sizes. It did allow for a maximum privacy of approach and departure, but at the expense of security. In a world where violence is ever less comprehensible and avoidable, people—especially the middleaged and the old—settle more comfortably behind barred gates, locked lobbies, roving guard dogs. They seek to die in bed, of something gentle and merciful.

I roamed, looking for Walter J. Demos. His was number 60, the ground floor of a town house near the back of the property, looking out at the pool area. A pretty lady in jeans and work shirt and tousled hairdo opened the door and said, liltingly, "No vacancies, none at all; so sorry." She started to close the door.

"I want to talk to Mr. Demos."

"He isn't even adding any names to the list, it's so long now." She had sweat beads of exertion on her forehead and upper lip. Behind her I could see a mop pail with a wringer fastened to it.

"I don't want to live here."

"Then you must be out of your tree. If it's about something else, well, let me think. Mary Ferris was after him to do something about her disposer. I think he'll be there by now. That's Twenty-one. Go past the pool and through that arch at the right and it will be . . . the second? No, the third doorway to your right. Go up the stairs and come back toward the front of the building."

Walter J. Demos wore gray coveralls and an engineer cap. The coveralls were wet-dark around his middle in a wide irregular band. He did indeed look something like a shorter broader Kojak, his face and jaw massive, almost acromegalic.

He showed me what he had in his hand. It looked like a tangled ball of dirty string.

"Do you know what this is? Can you guess?" he asked.

The woman giggled. She was plump and coy and underdressed.

"I wouldn't know."

"Miss Mary here had a lovely artichoke yesterday, and she put all the inedible parts of it into her disposer. Artichoke leaves, my friend, are made of string. And in a little while the string wound itself into a tangled mess and stopped the machinery."

Mary giggled again and switched back and forth, chewing a knuckle, scuffing her sandaled foot.

She thanked him and he gave her the string to dispose of in a less damaging manner. He picked up his tin toolbox, and we left to walk slowly back toward his apartment.

"I could tell them all to call the repair people. I could spend all my time in the pool. But it would drive me quite mad, I think. I have to keep busy. That's the way I am, Mr. McGee. And it saves my people money, which is increasingly important these days. Everyone chips in and helps whenever and wherever they can. We're a family here, helping and protecting each other."

"Meyer told me he got that impression."

"Oh, then *you* must be the friend he mentioned. I chatted with him for just a few minutes, but he struck me as charming and highly intelligent. I like intelligent people. That's the way I am."

"Have you found out who trashed Carrie's apartment?"

"What? Oh, no, we haven't. And I doubt we ever will. No one resident here would ever do a thing like that."

"Even though she was resented by the other . . . members of the family?"

He stopped and peered at me. "What would give you that idea?"

I was tempted to remind him of Meyer's intelligence, but I thought I could make a little more mileage by using the dead lady, so I said, "Mrs. Milligan was quite aware of it."

He grunted and we walked on, right to his door. The lady had stopped sweating. He took her hand in both of his. "Thank you so *very* much, Lillian. You know how much I appreciate it."

She went smiling off, purse in hand. He closed the door and looked around. "Nice job," he said to himself. "Very nice." He turned to me and made a wry grimace. "I have to be so very careful. If one of them cleans up for me too often, the others get jealous. Please sit down. You were telling me that Carrie had some fantasy about resentment."

"Purely a paranoid fantasy. She thought that because you put her at the head of the list and gave her the first empty apartment, the others resented her. She thought that because she was getting a rent-free ride, they resented her. She thought that because she didn't care to mingle, they resented her. She would rather have stayed with her friends in the cottage at Mangrove Lane. Maybe you should have told the whole family that Carrie wasn't a very special and dear friend, but just part of the pot distribution system. Jack Omaha, Cal Birdsong, Carrie Milligan, and you."

He was good. He stared at me. At first he chuckled and then he laughed and then he roared. He slapped his thighs and rocked back and forth and lost his breath. Finally he held his wrists out and, still choking, said, "Okay, officer. I'll go quietly. You've got me."

"Why the special treatment she got from you? Tell me so we can all laugh."

He lost all traces of mirth. "You're beginning to annoy me. It's no business of yours, but I'll tell you anyway. A friend of mine asked me to make the apartment available to Mrs. Milligan. Jack Omaha asked me. My books show the rent paid every month. She may have had a free ride, but it wasn't from me. Probably Jack felt that it would be more pleasant to have . . . more privacy and more access to the lady."

I lifted eyebrows and looked at him politely. "I'm beginning to annoy you, Mr. Demos?"

"Frankly, yes."

There are a lot of choices in every instance. And it is easy to make a bad choice. A man will react badly to the promise of some unthinkable punishment. The musician will buckle at the thought of smashed hands. The choice cannot be made with the thought of taking any pleasure in the choice. It has to be businesslike, or it will not be convincing. This man was the benign daddy, the solid meaty big-skulled patriarch, full of such amiable wisdom and helpfulness that he would appeal to the little girl in any woman who might be still searching for poppa. A gregarious man. A sensualist. A skilled,

successful, and unlikely womanizer who had built himself a profitable world teeming with prey. He was
pleased with himself, and evidently still greedy.

"I'm thinking of alternate ways of annoying you, Mr.
Demos."

"What do you mean?"

"We have a specialist we could import. His nick-
name is Sixteen Weeks. He's very bright about guessing
just how much punishment a given person can endure
and still recover. He can guarantee you sixteen weeks
in the hospital, Walter. At your age you might not ever
get about as well as you do now."

His attempt at a smile was abortive. "That's grotesque."

"Or, if we decide to head in another direction, I'd
turn the problem of dispositon over to Meyer. He
works things out so there isn't any fuss. As you noted,
he's highly intelligent. We gave him the problems of
Mr. Omaha, Mr. Birdsong, and Mrs. Milligan. He'd
find something plausible for you. They could find you
on the bottom of the pool some morning."

I think he tried to smile again. It gave his mouth an
odd look. "Are you quite mad? Why are you saying
such terrible things? What do you *want* from me?"

Rhetoric, all by itself, is too abstract. It needs punc-
tuation. Show and tell. I stood up, smiling. I moved
slowly. He watched me with some agitation. I walked
slowly around to the back of his chair. He leaned forward and craned his neck around to watch me. I knew
he was wondering whether or not to get up out of the
chair.

It takes a reasonable amount of precision. In the

clavicle area, where the muscle webs of the trapezius and deltoid are thinned out, the descending brachial plexus, which includes the big ulnar and radial nerves to the arm, is close to the bone. I chopped down, a short swift smashing blow, and hit him just as he started to move, hit him on target, mashing the nerves against bone with the bone ridge of my knuckles.

Walter J. Demos screamed in a very aspirated hissy way and came floundering up out of the chair. His right arm hung dead. He clasped his right shoulder in his big left hand. He stared at me with bulging eyes and roared with pain. Tears ran down his face.

There was a flurried rapping at the door. "Walter?" a woman cried. "Are you all right? Walter?"

"Tell her to call the cops," I suggested. "We can all sit around and talk about how much pot you moved out of this place."

"Walter?" she yelled.

"Everything is fine, Edith," he called. "Go away!" He sat down again and said, "You broke my shoulder!"

"It isn't broken. It will be okay again in a week."

"But I can't move my arm. It's numb."

"The feeling will come back, Wally."

"Nobody ever calls me Wally."

"Except me. I can call you Wally, can't I?"

"What do you want of me? Were they really killed? Really?"

"What we want is an established outlet in Bayside. Your previous source has dried up, Wally. Now tell me how you got into it and how you've been operating."

He found a hanky with his left hand and patted his

eyes and blew his nose. He rubbed his numb arm. He talked and talked and talked.

He had always purchased supplies for apartment repairs and redecorating from Superior. He became friendly with Jack Omaha and they would have coffee together at a diner near the industrial park, within walking distance. One day he told Omaha that a lot of his tenants had become ill from smoking grass adulterated with some unknown compound. Jack said that his personal supplier, his milkman, had recently been busted, and he was buying it at a gas station and paying too much. Omaha had taken a lot of his vacation time in Jamaica. Half joking, he had told Demos he was tempted to go get his own, but it wasn't worth the risk unless he arranged to have a lot of it brought in, and he couldn't see himself peddling it. Demos told Omaha that quite a bit could be absorbed at 1500 Seaway Boulevard, and some of his tenants could probably get rid of a lot more at the offices where they worked.

It wasn't long before they had talked themselves into it. Omaha came back from Jamaica with guarantees, having talked to local hustlers named Little Bamboo, Popeye, Hitler, John Wayne, and so on.

At that point it was decided that Walter would be better off if he did not know any of the details of the smuggling operation, and if Omaha did not know a thing about his wholesale operation. The first shipments were small. As they got bigger, Demos brought in his most trusted tenants and it became a cottage industry, taking the bulk and weighing, measuring, and bagging it for the smaller wholesalers and the retail trade.

"We thought we'd be able to avoid getting mixed up with any—excuse the expression—hoodlums. We didn't see that there was anything terribly sinister about it. We were filling a demand at a fair price. We tried to cut our risks. Bringing Carrie here to live was part of the risk-cutting. She'd tip me in advance as to when a shipment would be coming in. I'd get my people ready. On those nights she'd be driving one of the little panel trucks from Superior instead of her own car. When it was unloaded, checked, and weighed, I'd give her the money. We'd work all night. I wanted it all out of here by the following morning. Except personal supplies, of course."

"When was the last shipment?"

He looked dispirited. He nursed his shoulder. He sighed. I could feel a certain satisfaction in having diagnosed him so precisely. But with satisfaction there was also regret. Demos had been full of himself, full of a big-bellied confidence, sure of his place in his world. But in had come the pale-eyed stranger who had said terrifying things and who had sickened him with pain. His world had become fragile all of a sudden. His heart was heavy. He was not a bad man, everything considered. He had been a jolly sly man, a manipulator, a greedy chap, overconfident. He had changed.

"Do you want me to annoy you some more, Wally?"

"No! No, I was trying to remember exactly. A Tuesday night. That would make it May fourteenth. Yes. I can't remember the exact time, but it was before midnight."

"How much was there?"

"An average shipment. Ten sacks, I think. Forty

kilos each. Over eight hundred and fifty pounds. I think I gave her about ninety thousand dollars."

He described, by request, the way the money was wrapped. It fit the way it had been packaged when Carrie gave it to me. The adding-machine tape was from his office machine. He handled the money, figuring the commissions to his peddlers.

I pressed him to find out how well he had done. He was evasive. In the beginning he had plowed everything back into increasing the shipments. He guessed Jack Omaha was doing the same. They were on a cash-and-carry basis with each other. When they got to maximum weight coming in, he had started to skim, and he guessed that Omaha had started too. He said he was having a problem legitimizing the cash, trying to work it out in such a way that he could apply it to the outstanding mortgages on Fifteen Hundred. He guessed that probably Jack Omaha was having the same problem, but he hadn't discussed it with him. He started to ask me about Jack Omaha and changed his mind. He didn't want to know anything about Omaha. Or Carrie.

I asked to see Carrie's apartment. He said that a Miss Joller and a Miss Dobrovsky, Carrie's sister, had gone through everything and packed up some things for shipment to New Jersey, and had called Goodwill to come pick up the rest. It had been cleaned and the new tenant was moving in tomorrow morning. So there was nothing to see.

He said he had a headache and would like to lie down. I told him we had some more ground to cover first. I asked him what Carrie did with the money.

He said he had the impression she took it down to

Superior and put it in the safe. It seemed logical that she would have some safe place to put it.

"What do you want from me?" he asked again.

"You have a nice operation, Wally. It's cleaner than some loft or old warehouse or a trailer parked in the woods. And you have those nice clean little clerks and bank people doing the pushing and being very careful because they don't want to mess up this great life-style you created for them. I don't have to put you out of business because you're already retired. You've got no supply, right? Do you know what I'm going to recommend? I'm going to say you should be our exclusive distributor in Bayside. How *about* that?"

I couldn't detect any genuine enthusiasm in his response.

"What does . . . it entail?"

"We'll guarantee top quality. We'll guarantee no hassling by the law. We'll expect you to absorb, say, a ton a month, cash on the line, half again what you were paying Omaha. In time we'll have you broaden the line. Coke and hash."

"Oh, I just couldn't handle that, Mr. McGee. I really couldn't. That quantity and price. . . . This has been just a small operation. An amateur thing. You know. I just couldn't. . . ."

I stood up, smiling at him. "It's all settled."

"Don't I have any choice?"

"Choice? Of course! You stay right here and hang onto that cash, because when we make a delivery, you have to be able to pay. You have to accept what we send you. Don't try to look for another supply source. You just wait. If you want to fuss and bob and weave and make trouble, that's your choice. If so we'll kill you and make our deal with whoever takes over this place. It might be a couple of months before we set you up as a distributor, Wally. Hang in there."

He didn't move. I let myself out. I was a little depressed by my own childishness. It was a fair assumption it could work exactly as I had outlined it to Demos. The contact would probably be a lot less melodramatic than I had made it. Actually the setup would probably not appeal. It was too unusual. Hoodlums are the true conservatives. When you are winning, never change the dice. Distribution would be limited to the candy-store, horse-room, bartender, cocktail-waitress, coin-machine, call-girl circuits. Demos's arrangement was too fancy and made too much sense.

I took a small detour to go around by the pool. The after-work residents crowded the pool area. They made a youngish, attractive throng in their brown hides and resort colors. The scene looked like a commercial for swimming pools.

They made gay little cries of glee and fun. A game of water tag was in progress.

Wally's Paradise. There was one thing wrong with it, and that was what probably created the slightly frantic gaiety. They all loved it here. They were all going to stay. They were going to obey all the rules, and pay the rent, and stay and stay and stay.

It was a life-style designed for the young. Twenty years from now it was going to look a lot less graceful and productive. Unless all leases were canceled at age thirty-five, and your family throws you out. It was a pretty problem for Wally, and a dreadful one for his tenants.

I skirted the jolly crowd and walked back to the marina. I needed the long walk in order to sort out everything I had learned from Walter Demos and fit it into the facts and inferences I had acquired before chatting with him.

9

*T*HE day was darkening prematurely by the time I got back to the marina. As I passed the office there was a bright blue click of lightning, a white dazzle, and an enormous crash of thunder. I ran through the first heavy drops and boarded the *Flush*. . . .

It was still locked, the security system still operative. Meyer was not back yet. My note to him was still where I had left it. He arrived, soaking wet, ten minutes later.

After he had changed, we sat in the lounge and exchanged information.

"Frederick Van Harn is a very impressive young man," Meyer told me. "In a very short time he has built up a very wide-ranging and profitable practice of law. He has been pulling together the shattered remnants of the Democratic Party in this county. He will very probably run for the state legislature and very probably make it, after he marries Jane Schermer. Her Uncle Jake is the power and money behind the party. Van Harn can speak very persuasively in public. A lot of people don't care for him personally, but they have a

132

grudging respect for the way he came back and started building a career right on the top of the ruin his father made of his life. About two years ago Van Harn bought the Carpenter ranch twelve miles west of town. The Schermers live out that way. Jane has extensive grove land out there."

"From what Joanna said, I'd think his reputation as a womanizer would get in the way of his electioneering."

"The general feeling around the area seems to be that he has a way with the ladies, but he'll settle down after he marries Jane. It isn't doing him any harm that I could see. And I spent my time drinking beer in a place across from the courthouse. Bail bondsmen. An investigator for the state's attorney. Bartender. A lady from the tax office. There was just one questionable area that turned up."

"Such as."

"Gossip. About money. It just seems to the spectators that Freddy has bought too much too fast. They wonder if maybe Freddy's father killed himself because he couldn't avoid being caught, but left a stash of cash around somewhere. They say the ranch he bought is twelve hundred acres, high and dry. It had to be at least a million one, even without the ranch house and the man-made lake and the airstrip and hangar. So even if he made out well in the law, how could he pay his taxes and still have enough left over for his lifestyle? He's about thirty years old, and he's been at it here just six years, but he started slow and small."

"Did you get any information on how well his father lived?"

"Oh, very well, apparently. Cars, boats, hunting lodges. women."

"You've come back with a lot."

Meyer smiled. "It's a cozy bar. The conversation was general. Everybody joined in. Freddy has charisma. He's one of the people that other people like to talk about. So it was easy. Besides, due to constant pressure from you, I'm getting better at being a sneak."

"That isn't a word I would have chosen."

"Once you face up to reality, everything is easier."

From time to time the rain came down with such a roar we couldn't hear each other. Wind buffeted the *Flush,* thudding her against the fenders I had put out and made fast to the pilings. Then the rain steadied down into a hard, continuing downpour. I opened two cans of chili, and Meyer doctored the brew with some chopped hot pickled peppers and some pepper seeds. He does not approve of chili unless the tears are running down his cheeks while he eats. His specialty, Meyer's Superior Cocktail Dip, is made with dry Chinese mustard moistened to the proper consistency with Tabasco sauce. The unsuspecting have been known to leap four feet straight up into the air after scooping up a tiny portion on a potato chip. Strong men have come down running and gone right through the wall when they missed the open doorway.

It was a good night to stay aboard. It was a good night to conjecture, to try various possible patterns of human behavior and see how well they fit, much like kids in the attic trying on old uniforms, wearing old medals.

I got out charts of the Caribbean and worked out alternate routes from Bayside to Kingston and to Montego Bay. It was easier to route back in pre-Castro days. (Maybe everything was easier.) I made it 650, if you were a straight crow. But avoiding Fidel's air space with enough of a margin of comfort made it 1,000 miles. No great problem for the huskier variety of private aircraft, provided fuel was available at the Jamaica end.

So add in the Bertram. From predawn to after dark would give you, say, sixteen hours. Allowing for variations in wind and weather and the size of the seas, call it an outside distance of 120 or 130 out and the same back. That would also allow some time at the far end, for rendezvous.

As I had to start somewhere, I picked 220 mph for the aircraft cruising speed. Give it an hour at the far end for gassing and loading. Ten hours would do it. Leave in daylight, return by daylight. Okay, so why push the boat so hard? Probably two reasons. First, because the seas close to Florida are so full of small craft, you have to go a long way to get out of the traffic. Second, once you are in open empty water, you are too hard to find from the air. So you have to head for some distinctive land mass that the aircraft can find without too much trouble.

I drew a 130-mile half circle on the chart, with the point of the compass at Bayside. Of the areas included, I was willing to vote for the north side of Grand Bahama, over away from the folks and the casinos, where the water is tricky. Big stuff goes way north to come around into the Tongue of the Ocean. Little stuff stays inside, south of Grand Bahama. If they picked a tiny island off the north shore, a pilot could orient himself by the configuration of Grand Bahama, head for the tiny island, and the rendezvous point could be, for example, a mile north of that crumb of land.

If they had a source in the Bahamas for the Jamaican weed, then I was wrong. But that was not likely. Too much risk and too low a margin.

And our Freddy Van Harn had an airstrip and a hangar. And he was Jack Omaha's lawyer. Chris Omaha's lawyer. Lawyer for Superior. Lawyer for Carrie, and Susan, and the marina.

"The invisible mass," Meyer said, "distorting the orbits."

"Distorting the orbits, or removing the planets?"

"But why?" Meyer asked.

"You know, that's really a rotten question."

"It has to be answered. Otherwise there's nothing."

"Let's find out first if he has an airplane."

"How?"

"The direct approach. Let's go look. Very very early tomorrow."

Somebody came hurrying out of the rain and boarded the *Flush*. We both heard the warning bell. I snapped on the aft floods, and through the rain curtain we saw Joanna scuttle close to the door for shelter. She was holding a package.

I let her in. She was one very damp lady.

"Hey!" she said. "This is such a rotten Saturday night, all things considered, I decided we ought to have some kind of celebration. Okay?" She turned and put her package on the table, her back to me. "And it just so happens—"

There was a huge white ringing crash, blinding light, deafening sound, and I was spun and dropped into darkness, hands out to break the fall that never ended. . . .

I opened my eyes and looked up at a white ceiling. There was an annoying whining ringing sound going on which made it difficult to think clearly. I looked back up over my head and saw the familiar white tubular headboard of your average hospital bed and thought, Oh, Christ, not again! A quarter millimeter at a time I rolled my head to the left and saw a narrow solitary window with the venetian blinds almost but not quite closed. A white floor lamp beside the window was turned on. The chair in front of the window was empty. My head made a funny sound against the pillow as I rolled it back into place. I brought up from beneath the covers a slow brown enormous hand and willed it to feel of my head. It felt bandage and then moved dumbly back to lie inert against my chest. So. The other arm worked. Both legs worked. I wished somebody would turn off the ringing. I rolled my head to the right and saw a closed door. A long sigh ended in sleep.

I woke up. The ringing was not quite as loud. There was night instead of sunshine between the slats of the blind. I thought nothing had changed until I found I couldn't move my right arm. I turned my head and studied the arm. It was strapped to a board. There was a needle in the vein inside my elbow. The needle was taped in place. I saw a rubber tube that went up to a bottle hanging over me. It seemed to be about half empty. The stuff in it was gray-white and semitransparent. I reached around in my head for the nurse word: I.V. Meaning . . . intravenous. Meaning I was having dinner.

After considerable fumbling around I found a push button safety-pinned where I was least likely to be able to reach it with my left hand. But I managed, and I thumbed it down.

After a few minutes the door was slung open and a dainty little white-haired nurse about fifty years old came trotting in. "Oh, hey!" she said. "Oh, good!" Then she said something I couldn't hear because of the ringing.

"What? Somebody turn off the damn bell."

She leaned close. She laughed. "Bell? It's in your ears, sweetie. From the bomb."

"Bomb?"

She checked the I.V. and said, "You're doing okay here. They're not going to have to go into your skull, sweetie. Now be patient. I'm supposed to get Dr. Owings to check you."

"Where am I?"

"Ask your doctor, sweetie." And she was gone, the door hissing slowly shut behind her.

Dr. Owings really took his time. I found out later that he was out of the hospital. And I found out that one Harry Max Scorf wanted to be present when I came out of it, if I came out of it.

After an hour, Dr. Hubert Owings came in, wearing that familiar look of the distracted, overworked professional. If you ordered a doctor type from central casting, they wouldn't have sent Hubert. He looked like a cowhand in a cigarette ad, even to the lock of hair falling forward across the hero forehead. The man who followed him in was small and spare and old. He wore a thick ugly gray suit, a frayed and soiled shirt in a faded candy stripe. It was buttoned at the throat, but he wore no tie. He wore a gleaming white ranch hat, the Harry Truman model, and, as I found out later, gleaming black boots. His face was small, withered, and colorless.

"Mr. McGee," said my doctor irritably, "Captain Scorf may want to read you your rights."

"Now, Hube," Scorf said in a plaintive voice, "it's nothing like that. Son, I'm Harry Max Scorf, and I just want to know if you'll freely and willingly answer any questions I might have about the death of Miss Freeler."

I stared at him. "Miss Freeler?"

"Captain, if you would just sit over there and let me handle the usual questions?"

"Sure, Hube. Sure thing."

Hube shone a sharp little light into my eyes, first one and then the other. "Your name?"

I gave it at once. He straightened up and stared down at me in perplexity. I didn't know what was wrong, and then like an echo, I heard my voice giving my name, rank, and serial number.

"I don't know why I did that," I said.

"What do you remember doing last?"

"While waiting for you, doctor, I've been trying to remember. The last thing I know is that I was standing in a very heavy rain under a banyan tree, and a little white dog on a screened porch was barking at me. I was on my way to see . . . someone at Fifteen Hundred Seaway Boulevard, and I don't know if I ever got there. I don't know how I got here, or why. This *is* Bayside?"

"It is. You were brought in unconscious with a severe concussion and a deep laceration on the back of your head, triangular, with a flap of scalp dangling."

"What about Meyer?"

"At the time you were brought in—"

"What about Meyer!"

"He's jes' fine," Harry Max Scorf said.

"Thanks, Captain."

Looking annoyed, Hube said, "If you'd remained unconscious any longer we were going to have to—"

"What day is this?"

"Thursday evening. Nine thirty on Thursday evening, Mr. McGee. The sixth day of June."

"For the love of—"

"Hold still, please. I'm trying to check you."

I became aware for the first time of the catheter. He sent Scorf out of the room for no good reason while he uncoupled me from the input and output tubes. He asked me if I thought I could stand up, as if I felt like trying to stand up. I did, in the ridiculous hospital long bib, and walked carefully and shakily around the bed and got back in, sweating with the effort it had taken.

He left me with Scorf, saying, "If you feel you are getting too tired, just say so, and the captain will leave."

After the door closed, Scorf said, "Now just why did you and your friend come up here from Lauderdale, McGee?"

"No answers at all, Captain. Not until the blanks are filled in. What happened? I remember now that Joanna's last name was Freeling."

"Freeler. Now what I know about the bomb comes from the two experts we had come in and check it all over. You and Meyer were on your houseboat Saturday night. It was raining hard. That girl came aboard with a package. She put it on the table and bent over it to unwrap it. It went off. You and your friend were lucky because you were both standing behind her and not too far apart, so her body took the major force of the explosion. It blew the girl practically into two halves. She never knew what happened. It knocked both of you down, you and Meyer. You hit your head and he didn't. He's lost the hearing in one ear, but they think it's coming back."

"What did it do to the boat?"

"Blew out all the glass. Blew a small hole in the deck, and blew a great big hole in the overhead, like ten feet by ten feet. Then it rained into the hole all night long. It's a mess. They're working on it now."

"They?"

"At that Westway Harbor Marina. Jason and Oliver and a friend of theirs. With Meyer helping."

"Where's Meyer?"

"Waiting for me to get out of here. He got called the first thing. Anyway, it was what they call a primitive-type bomb."

"Primitive?"

"No timing device or anything like that. They explained it to me after they found enough to know how it probably worked. The package was about so big, tied with string. There were four sticks of dynamite in there, taped together and taped into place. There was a battery and a cap and a little switch, a contact switch. What the fella who made it did, he stuck a thick piece of cardboard between the switch terminals. Then he tied string to the cardboard and led the string out a hole in the side of the box and fastened it to the string he tied around the box. So anybody unties it and pulls the string off, they pull that cardboard out and contact is made and it all goes *bam*. It went off about eight inches from the middle of that girl. Bombs are so damned ugly and messy. I can't get inside the head of a fella who'd use a bomb."

"Who are you, anyway?"

"Harry Max Scorf."

"I mean your official capacity."

"Oh, I should have said. I'm with the City and County of Bayside. Used to be just with the County. What I am, I'm kind of a special investigator. Odds and ends of this and that. I work when I please and how I please."

"Must be nice."

"It's worse than having hours. A man works longer. Then again, there isn't anything I'd rather be doing. No family. No hobbies. Tuesday I drove on down to Fort Lauderdale and I walked around that Bahia Mar Marina and asked questions about you and Meyer. You don't seem to have much visible means of support, McGee."

"Salvage work. Here and there. It's spotty."

"I combed every dang inch of what's left of your houseboat."

"What's left of it!"

"Steady there. It floats. I came to a conclusion."

"Which is?"

"I don't really think you came up here to straighten out the distribution of pot in Bayside County."

"Thanks, Scorf."

"Somebody will come along soon. No place along

the coast can stay amateur. They'll take in the ones who'll play along and kill those that won't, and turn it from nickels and dimes into big money, like it is other places. I thought they were already here. Maybe they are. But it's not you and Meyer."

"Why not?"

"Because the job calls for running the hard stuff, and running women, and selling to everybody, grannies and little kids. It calls for buying the law and buying the courts, and you and Meyer are quick enough in your own way and hard enough in your own way, but you got stopping places that are way short of what it takes. If you got a stubborn bartender and you bust both his arms and change his face, the replacement bartender is willing to do business with you. Bars are a nice distribution point for off-premises use."

"Are you working on a book?"

"Don't get snotty with an old man. I could write one."

"Why *are* we here?"

"Well, Harry Hascomb has one story, and that Miss Dobrovsky, she's got another, and Jack Omaha's wife has another. They add up to Carolyn Milligan having been a friend of yours. But if you thought that girl was killed, and you came here to find out who did it and why, and you didn't check in with us and show credentials—which you haven't got—then you're in trouble, aren't you?"

"I know she was killed and so do you. I just wonder if it was entirely an accidental death. That's all."

"And you wanted to attend the service?"

"Right!"

"Now you lunged at that like a bass, boy."

"Remember, I hit my head when somebody killed Joanna."

"We can set here and josh each other from now till the end of time. And you can duck and bob and weave all you want. The thing I've got the most of is time. If somebody did kill Carolyn on purpose, who is your guess?"

"Shouldn't this be some kind of a trade?"

"It is. You've been busy. You've been lying to people. Maybe you've been obstructing justice, or concealing the evidence of a crime, or impersonating an officer. Things like that. I won't act on any of that, at least right now. That's the trade."

"Take me in, officer. Read me my rights."

He sighed and shoved his white hat farther back on his head. "Well, let's see now. What have I got to trade? How about this? So far we've kept a lid on that autopsy on Cal Birdsong. It was heart, all right. But Doc Stanyard didn't like the way it looked, that big soft clot in the pleural cavity and no real sign of any aneurysm. He checked it slow and small and found that something went into there on Cal's left side, between the ribs, smaller than a knitting needle or an ice pick. It could have been a piece of stiff piano wire, sharpened to a needle point. A person could roll it between thumb and forefinger like one of those Chinese needles, to make it go in easy. The heart really hops around in there when it beats. Run that needle in there back and forth a couple of times, and you'd probably pick an artery open or puncture the sac around the heart or mess up a valve somehow. Doc found the entrance track and laid it open and took slides. I saw them this morning, all developed. The track shows up nice."

"And what was Birdsong doing?"

"Seems he was dog tired. They tried to keep him awake on account of his being hit on the head. They don't like people sleeping with head injuries. But he was pooped and he slept hard. And forever. It wouldn't probably wake him, just that little prickle when it went through the skin."

"Does his wife know this?"

"She was one of the ones with him. We're keeping the lid on while we watch how people act."

"One of the ones with him?"

"That's all the trading material you get for now. Your turn."

"You probably know everything I could tell you."

"Try me."

"Well. . . . Adding two and two, the *Christina* came in on May fourteenth, on Tuesday night, with over eight hundred pounds of marijuana aboard. Just two people went out before dawn Tuesday: Jack Omaha and Cal Birdsong. Sometimes Carrie Milligan went, but she didn't go that day because she was sick and said she would be in when she felt well enough. I would guess that Carrie went to Westway Harbor that night in a panel delivery truck owned by Superior Building Supplies. The boat is docked in a good area for privacy. It's beyond the range of the dock lights, but you can drive up close to it. The grass was loaded onto the truck, and Carrie took it to Fifteen Hundred Seaway Boulevard. After it was off-loaded, Mr. Walter Demos took over, and he paid Carrie in cash for the delivery at the rate of a hundred dollars a pound. My guess is that she drove down to Superior and parked the truck where she had picked it up. She had left her own car there. Standard procedure was for her to put the money from Demos into the office safe. She and Jack Omaha had the combination. End of trade. Anything new?"

"Here and there," he said comfortably. "Here and there. Of course you spoiled any chance of us finding anything at all by scragging Demos in his big love nest. There won't be a scrap anywhere."

"He's anxious to . . . wait a second. It fades in and out, like a bad projection bulb. Sorry. My memory quits when it comes to Demos. Your turn," I added.

"Let me see. Oh, here's something you wouldn't know. In that rain Saturday night somebody had left off a package on the porch of the cottage, well back under the overhang, for Joanna Freeler. Betty Joller told me that when Joanna came home she knew what was in the package. She said it was some wine and cheese and like that, for a snack, a present from some-body who couldn't keep a date that night. Now there was just going to be the three of them in the cottage that night. Joanna and Betty Joller and Natalie Weiss. I think it was intended for the package to be opened with the three of them there. Instead, on an impulse, that girl came running through the rain with it. She was a girl who'd rather be with men than girls any time. Your turn, McGee."

I thought it over and then I decided, What the hell, why not? I went through the whole Carrie Milligan death item by item, stressing the illogic of her supposed behavior, the gassing of her car the previous day, and the signs of fresh tampering with the gas tank drain cock.

He glared down at a freckled fist and said, "Even after years, you miss the damnedest things. You know,

I decided that what she was going to do was cross the road and walk to a lighted house and ask to use the phone. With her purse setting there on the front seat in an unlocked car? Nonsense! It was right there and I missed it cold." He thought it over, and finally said, "That would do for now."

"You owe me one."

"I don't have any more to trade." He was distracted by the conjectures swarming in his head. He wanted to be up and off and away. I had put him onto the possibility of a new pattern.

He stood up. I said, "When do you lock me up?"

He focused on me completely and silently. Harry Max Scorf was no figure of fun. He was one hard and determined little man.

"I'll do whatever needs to be done," he said, and turned and left, tugging his hat to the correct angle as he went through the doorway. Before the door had wheezed entirely shut, Meyer came bursting in, grinning.

10

"WELCOME back!" said Meyer.

"Thanks. What about the *Flush?*"

"It floats."

"Really, how is it?"

"There's nothing that about ten thousand dollars can't fix. Don't worry about it."

"Good God, what's left of it?"

"Don't *worry* about it. You do a lot of talking about the way possessions hold us all in thrall. Pretty things are chains and shackles."

It made me gloomy. I could see a listing hulk with huge holes, with wisps of smoke rising from the interior debris. And it worried me that I should care that much. The important loss was the death of that lively girl. Blown in half. Into two girl parts. Such a great and bitter waste.

I realized that if the *Flush* were entirely gone, if it had burned to the waterline and sunk, I would be able to adjust more easily than to the uncertainty. Baubles and toys should disappear, not become broken litter.

Meyer sat beside the bed. He looked like an apprehensive owl as he said, "I kept wondering what the hell to do if you didn't wake up. People stay in a coma for years. They seem to have families to look after them."

"And you could see yourself stuck?"

"I could see myself tottering down to the drugstore saying, Yep, he's still asleep. Been nineteen year now. Gimme some more of that goo for bedsores."

"Look, I blank out during my walk that Saturday afternoon. Tell me about Joanna."

He told me. I could not make it seem real. It was easier to make the service seem real. They did the same thing for her as they did for Carrie. One less girl in a long dress to throw flowers. Good-bye, my sister Joanna. Her widower father attended, full of indignation and stiffness at such an informal heathen ceremony. But, Meyer said, it melted him quickly and he wept with the rest. It loosened the adhesions in his heart, freeing him from other rituals.

"We're losing too many girls," I told Meyer.

"You've added a new one."

"Hmm. The spry nurse lady?"

"No. Cindy Birdsong. She's spent a lot of time here, so someone would be with you when you woke up. She was sure you would. Then she missed by a few minutes. She left a little while before you came out of it, apparently. She's out there now, waiting her turn."

"Why the devotion?"

"I don't know. It's some kind of penance, maybe. Or maybe she is the kind of person who has to have somebody to fret about. Cal is gone. You were at her marina when we got blown up."

"What did it do to you?"

"Gave my back a little wrench and gave me a sore shoulder and one deaf ear."

"So this is Thursday, everybody keeps telling me, June sixth, they keep saying, and it is five days gone out of my life, and what useful thing have you done with those days? I don't like it any more around here, Meyer. I want to go home. Every time I get blown up by a bomb I get that same feeling. Let's go home."

"That wrapped head makes you look strange. It's like a turban. Lawrence of Arabia, or some damned mercenary. You're dark enough for an Arab, but the pale eyes make you look very savage somehow."

"Meyer, what did you find out?"

"Oh. While you were unconscious? Let me think. Oh, yes. That's quite a nice hangar out there at the ranch. Quonset-type construction. That's where ranch equipment gets repaired and maintained too. There's a slow charger for batteries, and a battery cart to boost the aircraft batteries when starting the aircraft up cold. There's a fifteen-hundred-gallon gas tank and a pump to service the aircraft and the ranch vehicles. There's about six employees out there, which means a pretty good payroll, wouldn't you say?"

"Meyer!"

"Are you supposed to sit up like that? There, that's better. Okay. Travis, he has . . ." Meyer paused and took out his little pocket notebook and flipped through the pages, grunting from time to time.

"Meyer!"

"He has a Beechcraft Baron, designation B fifty-five. It has two two-hundred-and-sixty-horsepower Continental engines, designation Ten four-seventy L.

The fuselage is twenty-nine feet long, and the wing-span is thirty-seven feet ten inches. At ten thousand five hundred feet, at a long-range cruising speed of two hundred and twenty miles per hour, with optional fuel capacity of a hundred and thirty-six gallons, he can carry two people and over eight hundred pounds of cargo for sixteen hundred miles, less ten percent safety factor, which gives us fourteen hundred and forty miles. It has an automatic pilot and a lot of other things which I didn't write down here. He bought it used a year ago for sixty-five thousand. He financed it. It can carry four people. It is white with a blue stripe."

I stared at him. "And you went out there and went in the hangar!"

He stared back. "I wish I could say yes."

"What did you do?"

"You reminded me to be cautious when I looked under that Datsun."

"What did you do?"

"I did what all economists do. I went to the library. And after a two-hour search I found an article about him and his place in a magazine called *Florida Ranchorama.* It had a picture of the hangar, with airplane inside. Then I went to the airport, over to the private airplane area, and talked with some mechanics there about airplanes. I asked some questions and then I did a lot of listening. I found out more about airplanes than I care to know."

"You did very well, old friend."

"Shall I blush and simper?"

"If you don't keep it up for long. I hate blushing and simpering in a grown man when it goes on and on."

"You seem to be doing a lot of yawning."

"I am dead tired for some unknown reason, and I am starving. I've never been so empty."

We got hold of the sprightly little old nurse, who said the kitchen was closed and who then went off and checked with Dr. Owings to see if it was all right for Meyer to bring food in. He said fine, and he would approve it because I had a private room.

When Meyer left on his errand it was after eleven, and I did not expect Mrs. Birdsong to be waiting that late. But she was. She came in, and her face went from somber to beautiful in the glow of her smile. She came around and sat on the chair and then stood up again. Awkward moment.

"Please sit down," I said.

"I am so used to sitting right here without . . ."

"You don't need any invitation, really. Meyer told me how faithful you've been."

She had seated herself again, on the edge of the chair. She wore khaki slacks, fitted and faded almost white. She wore a tan shirt with silver buttons. She clutched a brown leather purse with both hands. She wore a trace of lipstick, nothing more. When she looked down the dark glossy hair would have swung forward, would have softened her face, had she not worn it cropped so desperately short. In manner and looks it was almost as if she were trying to deny her femininity, or perhaps she was so shrewdly aware of herself, she knew that any attempt to deny it merely emphasized it.

"Faithful," she said, giving the word a bitter emphasis. "Sure, I guess so. I . . . didn't want you to wake up and not have anyone close by to tell you what happened. But I missed out on that . . . too."

"I appreciate it. Maybe it was good to have someone nearby. I think that people are never totally completely one hundred percent unconscious. I think that they are always aware to some degree of what is going on around them. I think I knew you were here."

"How could you know it was me?"

"Maybe just that someone was here who cared."

"Cared. Yes, that word is okay, Mister McGee. Cared if you lived or died. I'll buy that word."

"I'll give it to you free."

She smiled and again that transformation, but the smile did not last long enough. She flushed visibly and said, "I didn't think about it being hard to talk to you when you woke up."

"Is it hard?"

"Well, I don't know what to say. We buried my husband Monday. I've hired another person. With Jason, Oliver, and the new man, Ritchie, everything can go on . . . as before. After the insurance people told Meyer that you're not covered, he said it was okay if I told the boys to work on your houseboat whenever they have the time."

I sat up. "I'm covered!"

"For lots of things, yes. If your tanks had blown up, yes. Or sinkings or collisions or fire or running aground. But not for people bringing a bomb on board, you're not covered. Should you be sitting up like that?"

I settled down again. She reached and gave a quick shy pat on my arm.

"It's sort of in their spare time, so I'm only billing you for supplies."

"It wasn't your fault."

"I don't know. Sometimes things happen that maybe a person could have stopped."

"And people can take too much onto themselves. If I had done this . . . or that . . . or the other, then maybe this or that or the other would never have happened. The world-mother syndrome."

She thought it over. "I guess I am sort of that way."

She looked down and away, lost to me, wandering in the backwoods of her mind. It was a strong clear face, clean and dark and timeless, like the face of a young monk seen in an old drawing. It was somber and passionate, withdrawn yet intensely involved. The curve of the lips, shape of the throat, set of the eyes, all spoke of fire and of need carefully suppressed, held down in merciless discipline.

Meyer came back. She stirred to leave, but he had brought food for her too. He said it had not been easy at that time of night. Quarter-pounders with cheese, in square cartons, still hot. He had brought six of them, and a container of milk and two containers of coffee. Meyer sat on the foot of my bed. I was certain I could eat three of them. I was famished. Yet it was all I could do to finish the first one. I drank the milk. I sagged back. I thought I would close my eyes for just a moment. I heard them talking, and their voices sounded strange to me, as if I were a child again, half asleep in the back seat while the parents talked together in the front seat. When the little white-haired nurse woke me up to find out if I wanted a sleeping pill, Meyer and Cindy were gone and the room was darkened. I heard a siren far away. I turned back into my sleep, wormed my way back to dreaming.

On Friday at eleven thirty Dr. Hubert Owings changed the dressing on my head, making it much smaller, getting away from the turban effect. He checked me over and approved me for release. I phoned the marina and got hold of Jason, who got hold of Meyer. Meyer said he would be along to pick me up in a half hour. I told him to bring money. And clothes. The clothes I had been wearing when I arrived were too badly dappled with the blood of Joanna to ever consider wearing again.

I borrowed a shower cap and took a shower. Meyer arrived and said he had stopped at the cashier's office and bought me out, and given the release ticket to the nurse at the floor station. I got up too quickly and felt dizzy. I had to sit down for a minute before I could get dressed. Meyer was worried about me.

"Hube said I'm fine. A heavy concussion. No fracture. I came out of it okay, he says. If I start to have fainting spells, come back in for observation. They are short of beds or they'd keep me longer."

The world looked strange. There were little halos around the edges of every tree and building. I did very deep breathing. It is strange to sleep for five days and five nights and have the world go rolling along without you. Just like it will keep on after you're dead. The wide busy world of tire balancing, diaper changing, window washing, barn dancing, bike racing, nose picking, and bug swatting will go merrily merrily along. If they were never aware of your presence, they won't be overwhelmed by your absence.

On the way back Meyer told me that Cindy Birdsong had made arrangements for me to have a unit at the motel, next to hers. I could not get any rest aboard the *Flush* because of all the sawing and hammering. I was supposed to get a lot of rest. The prescription would make me drowsy. I said it was a lot of nonsense.

But when I got out of the car I gave up all hope of walking out to look at my boat. I saved everything I had left for the immense feat of tottering over to the motel and collapsing onto the bed which Cindy and Meyer guided me to.

I slept through lunch and woke up at five, o'clock. I put my shoes on and latched my belt and went on the long walk out to the *Flush*. The sun was still high and hot. I heard the power saw long before I recognized who was running it. Jason was brown and sweaty, and he was cutting some heavy-duty marine plywood to size. He let go of the trigger on the saw and put it on the uncut sheet and stuck his hand out. "You don't look so bad, Mr. McGee."

"Neither does my vessel."

"Not so bad on the outside until you notice it blew all the ports out of the lounge. It isn't so great in there."

"Do you know how to do . . . what you're doing?"

"Does it make you nervous? I can cut plywood to fit, for God's sake. The thing is to get it sealed before it rains again. We're into the rainy season now. I fixed the two broken cross members, those beam things. They were splintered. I cut out the bad parts and bolted in new pieces. It's okay now. Stronger than before."

"In case I get another gift bomb?"

"Nobody around here makes any jokes about that."

"I'm sorry."

"Joanna was an okay person. Not like Carrie, but

okay. I mean there was no need for anybody to blow her into pieces."

I climbed aboard and up the side ladderway. There was one hole left, a neat rectangle about two feet by five feet. There was new plywood over an area at least sixteen by thirty feet, the major portion of the sun deck. Jason came up with the last piece and laid it in place. It fit so snugly he had to stomp it into place with his bare heels. He knelt on it and took the nails from his canvas apron and smartly whacked the nails home. He threw one to me. It had a twist like a screw, and it was heavy-duty galvanized.

"These won't let go," he said.

"You're doing a good job."

"Ollie and I both think we are. He did part of this. What I plan on doing is caulk all these seams with a resin compound before I lay the new vinyl decking. It doesn't exactly match this stuff but it's close. Here's a sample. Close enough?"

"Nobody will ever notice. What about the ports?"

"That's another story. I got a guy coming to make an estimate tomorrow morning. At ten, if you want to be in on it."

I left him to his hammering and went below and went down into the forward bilge area. It took thirty seconds to make certain nobody had located my hiding place between the fake double hull, not even the impressive Harry Max Scorf himself. I checked out three weapons. If he found them, he had had the sense to leave them where they were, entirely legal.

The lounge was a sorry mess. It was damp as a swamp and already sour with mildew, a gray-green scum spreading across the carpeting. The yellow couch lay with its feet in the air, a dead mammoth from earlier times. Shards and splinters of coffee table and chairs lay here and there in profusion. A large splinter protruded from the precise center of a stereo speaker. Another had pierced a painting I was fond of, right between the Syd and the Solomon of the painter's lower-right-corner signature. There were thick brown stains of dried blood. There was a chemical smell, like cap pistols and ammonia.

Meyer came hurrying in. "Hello! Should you be roaming around like this?"

"I'm roaming around crying."

"I know. I know."

"Is the wiring messed up? Would the air conditioning work?"

"It kept blowing circuits at first, and I found out that it was the lamp that used to be on this bracket over here. It smashed the inside of it. But now things work."

"Then instead of letting the place rot, let's get some sheet Pliofilm and staple it over the ports and get the air conditioning going to start to dry it out in here. And let's pull up this carpeting and get it trucked away."

"All right. But spare me the 'us' part of it. Go back and rest."

"Is there any ice?"

There was. I assembled a flagon of Plymouth and carried it topside and sat at the controls and sipped and watched the sun sliding down the sky on the other side of Florida. That drink really slugged me. I had to pay special attention to every shift of weight and balance as I walked back to the motel. Every footfall was an engineering problem. My ears had started ringing again.

Cindy heard me and opened the interconnecting

door and stood staring at me. I realized that I was visibly smashed, and I realized she'd had all too much of that in her marriage.

She shook her head. "Travis, good God. Sit down before you fall down."

"Thank you very much indeed."

"Are you going to be sick?"

"I don't think so. Thank you very much indeed."

"Here. Let's swing your legs up. Let me get your shoes."

"Thank you very much indeed."

11

I opened my eyes. It was night. There was a small lamp with an opaque shade on a table in a corner. Cindy Birdsong slept in the wing chair beside the table, long legs extended, ankles crossed, head tilted way over to rest on her shoulder, mouth slightly agape. I spied upon the privacy of her sleep. She rifled the closets and drawers of memory while her body lay a-sprawl, clad in gray cardigan, pink blouse, dark blue slacks.

I looked at my watch. I pressed the button. No display. The batteries had died. I had such an evil taste in my mouth I knew I had been asleep a long time. I felt as if I could eat a bison. Raw. With a dull fork.

I tiptoed to the small bathroom and eased the door shut before I turned the light on. I looked at a gaunt, weathered, and most unfamiliar face. I brushed my teeth with foaming energy and drank four glasses of water. My tan looked yellowed, as if I had jaundice. The white scar tissue in the left eyebrow seemed more visible than usual, the nose more askew. The eyes looked shifty and uncertain. Some kind of hero. Some kind of chronic girl-loser. Some kind of person on the edge of life, unwilling and/or unable to wedge himself into the heartlands.

When I turned the light off and opened the door, Cindy was sitting bolt upright on the edge of the chair, knees together. She hugged herself, rubbing her left shoulder, and said, "I must have dozed off. I'm sorry."

"Why be sorry? What time is it?"

She gave a little start as she looked at her watch. "Good grief, it's a quarter to four! I . . . I really haven't been sleeping well lately. Until now. I guess you were so deep in sleep it was contagious. How do you feel?"

"I'm starving. You asked. I have to tell you I'm going to faint from hunger. I'll fall heavily."

At her invitation I followed her into the larger unit she had shared with Cal. There was a kitchenette arrangement behind folding doors, scrubbed to a high shine. We inventoried the possibilities, and I opted for Polish sausage and lots of eggs. She went into the bathroom and came out with minty breath and brushed hair.

She made an ample quantity and served herself a substantial helping. It was not a meal where conversation was encouraged. It was a meal which required more eggs, and she hopped up and scrambled more. She served good coffee in big mugs.

At last I felt comfortable. I felt cozy. I leaned back. She caught my eye and flushed slightly and said, "I haven't been eating hardly anything. Until now. I've lost about six pounds in the past week or so. I want to keep it off."

"You seemed about the right size and shape when I checked into your marina, lady."

"I get hippy. That's where it all goes."

The silence between us was comfortable—and then uncomfortable. The awareness grew, tangible as that ringing in the ears. She looked down, flushing again. When she got up I reached for her and caught her wrist, then tugged her gently around the corner of the table toward me. She came with an unwillingness, looking away, murmuring "Please." I pulled her to stand by me, against my thigh, and slid my hand to her waist, slid it under the edge of the pink blouse to clasp the smooth warm flesh where the waist was slimmest.

"No," she said in a soft dragging voice, far away.

"I have been losing girls," I said. "It has to stop."

"I'm not a girl. Not any more, I'm not."

I stood up and put my hands on her shoulders, felt a gentle shuddering that was awareness, not revulsion.

"Cindy, I could say an awful lot of dumb things. What it would boil down to is, I'm alive, glad to be alive, and I want you."

"I . . . I just can't quite . . ."

And I steered her slowly and gently to the relative darkness of my connecting unit, through the door ahead of me, arm around her waist, blundering together to the bed.

At the bed, after she sat and I began to undo the buttons of her blouse, she pushed me away and said, "I have to say something first. Before anything happens. Listen to me. Wait. Please. When I heard he was dead there was . . . some kind of dirty joy in me. I cried and carried on because people expected me to."

"It's like that sometimes."

"I don't want it to be like that for me." Her voice was uneven. "I know what they think: It was all just dandy great until he got on the booze. Well, it wasn't all that great. It wasn't even half good between us. He wanted it to be great. I couldn't really love him. I tried to imitate loving him, but he knew it had all gone away for me. He knew I felt empty. That's why he started drinking like that. People got it all backward. And I feel so . . . so rotten. So sick. So really terrible about . . . what I did to him."

It was all the confession she could handle. Guilt broke the dam inside her. I held her and she rocked herself back and forth in her inner agony. Guilt is the most merciless disease of man. It stains all the other areas of living. It darkens all skies.

I held her and eased her and soothed her. When she was nearly quiet, except for the occasional hiccup sob, I wondered if she was too spent for love. I peeled her gently and quietly out of her clothes. When we were naked and enclasped, facing each other on the motel bed, there seemed to be a great deal of her, long and firm and rich, with a body heat degrees above mine.

We were the wounded, she from all the trauma of her tears, me from the concussion and the five lost days. So it was not a physical, sexual greed that motored us.

It was an affirmation, a way to be less alone. In fact for quite a long time it seemed as if it would be love-making without climax, with only slowness, tenderness, and affection.

With the first of morning light she found a slow and lasting release and faded from that crest into the downslope of sleep. I eased out of the bed to close the slats of the blinds and shut out the increasing brightness. As I went back to bed I carried an uneasy afterimage of something, some shadow or substance, flickering swiftly away from the space under the window, out of sight.

On Saturday afternoon I left Meyer and Oliver to finish stapling the Pliofilm over the ports and over the smashed doorway, and went back to the motel, feeling pleasantly tired, and curious as to how she would accommodate herself to this new fact of her life.

She wore a brief yellow sun dress. She came toward me and looked cautiously beyond me to see if we were observed. Then she kissed me quickly on the lips and pulled me inside her quarters for a more emphatic kiss after the door was shut.

She was smiling. She said, "I don't know what I ought to say. But what I want to say is, Thanks for a lovely evening, for a lovely late date."

"You are most very certainly absolutely welcome, ma'am."

"Can you eat beef stew?"

"Indefinitely."

"I want you to keep your strength up."

"That's the best invitation I've had today. You're blushing."

"The stew is canned, dammit. I had to spell Ritchie at the office and didn't have time to fix anything special. But I added a couple of things to make it taste better."

It was excellent stew. We sat across the table from each other, by the window. We could see most of the marina from the window.

I said, "Cindy, my darling, I want to ask you some things. You might wonder why I have to ask them. But it would be a very long story, and I will tell you that long story some day but not right now. Okay?"

"Questions about what?"

"About a lot of things. First question: When Cal went off before dawn on those boat trips with Jack Omaha, where were they going?"

She tilted her head, frowning. "Off Grand Bahama Island after billfish, dear. Sometimes little Carrie Milligan went too. Jack's secretary and . . . well, playmate. I think it was a chance for them to play while Cal ran the boat. The other times they were after tuna and marlin and so on."

"Was Cal getting any extra money from anywhere, in large amounts?"

"Cal? God, no! He was good at spending it, not making it."

"Did you think those trips were strange in any way?"

"Listen, darling. I didn't much care if they were strange or not. I didn't think very much about what Cal did or didn't do. There was very limited communication between us. Before I met him I had been going with someone and I was in love with him, very deeply in love. We had the most horrible fight ever, and he went off and got married. So I went off and got married. He showed me and I showed him. I married Cal, and it was a lousy reason to get married. It was sort of okay in a limited way. The physical part was okay at first, and then it didn't hold up very well, especially not when he was drinking. About his trips, if I thought about them at all, it was to wish they'd happen oftener and last longer. And there was no extra money from anywhere. I guess I ought to tell you that these are almost the same questions our lawyer asked me."

"Fred Van Harn?"

"Yes. He was very solemn and insistent. He said that he wanted to make certain I wasn't mixed up in anything that Cal might have been doing that was against the law. I told him exactly what I've been telling you. He said that he couldn't protect me unless I was frank and open with him. He said that anything I told him was privileged information. I had to say I just didn't know anything, and that it had been a long time since Cal and I had talked much about anything. It wasn't exactly the friendliest conversation in the world."

"What do you mean by that?"

"Oh, it's just that Fred is . . . well, constantly horny. About a year ago he made a pretty startling pass at me. It was in his office. He came up behind me and hugged himself up against me and had both hands roaming all over me. I'm a very strong person."

"I noticed."

"Hush. I picked his hand up and set my teeth in his thumb. He screamed. He had to have a tetanus shot. He got over his problem very quickly. So we haven't been very chummy with each other."

"I wouldn't think so."

"Men like that have an instinct about wives, when they might be vulnerable. Something must show, somehow. For one little instant when he was doing what he was doing, I thought, Well, why not, what the hell? But then I realized that if I was going to say what the hell with somebody, it wouldn't be with Freddy. He's too conscious of those long black eyelashes of his. So I bit him to the bone."

"That pleases me."

"What *was* Cal doing on those trips?"

"Smuggling narcotics."

She stared at me. "You've got to be kidding! You really have got to be kidding!"

"Jamaican marijuana."

"Oh. Just grass. Well . . . "

"What's the matter?"

"That's where he got that stuff. He insisted I try it. A sloppy cigarette, twisted at the ends. A toke, he called it. A joint. He showed me how you're supposed to do it. Then we made love after he knew I was feeling it a lot. Love was strange and dreamy. I could hear the sound his hand made on my skin, a little brushing sound. Things went on forever, and I knew every part of it while it was going on. And I started crying and couldn't stop. It was so sweet and sad I couldn't stop crying. That made him angry and he went storming out. That was the last time we ever made love together, and that was . . . months ago. I guess that was part of what he was smuggling, he and Jack?"

"Probably."

"I liked it and I didn't like it. I would like to try it with somebody I really love sometime, but not until I'd tried everything else first with that person."

She got up and took the dishes to the sink.

I watched her, appreciating the way the brief yellow dress made her legs look uncommonly tan and uncommonly long.

Yet I had the curious feeling that I had not really made love to her. We could make small bawdy jokes together. We could kiss in excellent imitation of new-found lovers. I could look upon her in happy memory of the last time and steamy anticipation of the next time, but at the same time feel as if we were theater people, trained to give a convincing imitation of desire. We were close. We knew all the motions. Yet in a way I could not define we were insulated from each other, not quite touching in some deep and important way.

As a test I went up behind her and put my arms around her and pulled her close. She tilted her head back and said, "You risk a tetanus shot, sir."

"Worth it, ma'am."

"Listen. Where did the money go? If he was taking risks like that, where is the money?"

"I don't know. Maybe he hid it in some safe place, or somebody was holding it for him."

As I turned her around she said, "He used to worry so much about the money we owe on the marina. He used to fret and fume. Hey! What are we doing now?"

"It's siesta time. This is called getting you ready for your three o'clock nap."

"Don't you think you better move back onto your houseboat?"

"Right now?"

"Well . . . not exactly right now, okay?"

By Sunday afternoon the air conditioning was making good headway against the dampness aboard the *Flush*. A milky light and blurred outlines of nearby boats shone through the Pliofilm. The carpeting had been jettisoned, and Meyer had samples to study, before rendering advice.

The ninth day of June. I hadn't adjusted to the five-day gap in my memory. I was being hustled along too fast into the time stream. Ears ringing. A sweet and greedy lady to be with.

"Make some sense of things," I asked Meyer.

He stopped playing solitaire with his carpet samples. "I cannot come up with an overview," he said. "I can sense no paradigm that later events will prove out. I can construct no model from what we have."

"Thanks."

"Believe me, it's nothing."

"I know. I know."

"How about this blue? Indoor-outdoor. Won't fade."

"It's truly lovely, Meyer."

"Come on. Don't you care how it's going to look?"

"Intensely."

"All things considered, you should be jollier, Travis."

"Than whom?"

"Than whom has not such a handsome lady tending his convalescence."

"I feel disoriented. I have a dull ache in the back of my head, and I live in a motel."

Further discussion of my melancholy was terminated by the arrival of Jason-Jesus with Susan Dobrovsky. She looked sallow and subdued, with smudges under her eyes and a listless manner. Jason was being very firm and forthright. The protector. No social strokes. No discussion of the weather. He planted his feet and got right into it.

"Susan and I have been developing a useful dialogue about her situation here. We've decided that it is more important for her to get away, to get back to Nutley, than it is to hang around while Van Harn takes care of the last little legal details regarding Carrie's death."

She sat on the edge of the yellow couch which was going to have to be re-covered. "I want to leave," she said, in a very small voice. "Everything here has been so rotten."

"Mr. McGee, Susan told me that you told her that you owed Carrie some money. You paid off the funeral home in cash. Is there more money Susan should have?"

"Yes."

"How much?"

"What's your special interest in this, Jason?"

"Somebody has to care about situations like this. People have to take care of people."

"Granted. Let me talk to Susan alone. Meyer, why don't you go topside with Jason?"

When they had left and the Pliofilm curtain had fallen back into place, I went over and sat beside her on the couch. She became very still, quite rigid. It seemed a curious reaction. I touched her arm and she made a huge flinching motion, ending up two feet farther away from me.

"Hey," I said. "Whoa. Settle down."

"I'm sorry. I'm sorry. It's just that I'm not reacting to things . . . normally. To being touched by anybody. I can't help it."

"What happened to you?"

She gave me a wide, bright, terrible smile. "Happened? Oh, I was a guest at the V-H Ranch yesterday and the day before. That's all. Mr. Van Harn raises Black Angus and breeds horses. He has twelve hundred acres out there, and the old Carpenter ranch house was built out of hard pine in nineteen twenty-one and it's still as solid as a rock. I . . . nothing . . . can't. . . ."

She bent abruptly forward, face in her hands, hands resting on her knees. I reached to touch her and pulled my hand back in time.

"Were you forced?"

Her voice was muffled. "Yes. No. I don't know. I don't know what to say. He kept after me and after me and after me. It went on and on. I got so tired. So I thought . . . I don't know what I thought. Just that if I let him that would be the end of it."

"Susan, I have to know something. Did he ask you anything about Carrie?"

"There wasn't much talking."

"Did he ask you anything at all about Carrie?"

"Well, he wanted to know the last time I'd talked to her, and so I told him about the long phone call, the one I told you about too. He made me remember everything she said. One part that I told him was about you. You know. Carrie said to me that if a person named Travis McGee got in touch with me I was to trust him all the way."

"Did he seem interested in that?"

"Not any more than in any of the rest of it. He just kept me going over it and over it until he saw there wasn't any part of it I hadn't told him. That was the only talking there was, mostly."

"When did this conversation take place?"

"Yesterday, I think. Yes, yesterday. Early in the morning, I think. I remember the sounds the birds were making. Early sounds."

"How did you get back?"

"He drove me in and let me off at the Inn. He had a meeting. Maybe it was three o'clock yesterday afternoon. Jason came over this morning. I . . . told him about it. I wanted to tell somebody about how damned dumb I was."

"How did Jason react?"

"He wants to go kill him. What good would that do anybody? I shouldn't have gone out there with him. Joanna told me enough about him so I should have been careful, more careful. Mr. McGee, is there any more money? And you still have Carrie's rings. I remember Mr. Rucker giving them to you. He tried to give them to me and I couldn't take them then. I can now. Is there any money?"

"A lot of money."

"A lot?"

"Ninety-four thousand dollars in cash."

Her face went quite blank as she stared at me. She rubbed the palms of her hands on her forearms, one and then the other. "What?"

"Ninety-four thousand two hundred, less six hundred and eighty-six fifty that I paid Rucker. Ninety-three thousand something."

She rubbed the palms of her hands together. She narrowed those tilted gray-green eyes. She swung her hair back with a toss of her head. "Where would . . . Carrie get that?"

"From something she was involved in."

"From smuggling marijuana?"

"Did someone suggest that to you?"

"Betty Joller. It had something to do with why she left the cottage and went to live at that Fifteen Hundred place, Betty said. Would she make that much all for herself?"

"It's possible."

"She always wanted to have a lot of money."

"On the other hand, maybe the money is Van Harn's."

Her sallow round face looked stricken. "Would she be mixed up with him in anything? I wonder if he ever . . . made love to my sister. Jesus! That word doesn't fit. Love!"

"I wouldn't know."

She looked thoughtful. "She was always a stronger type person than me. I mean she could probably handle that kind of a man better than I could. Being older and married and so on. I never knew about men like that. He just kept confusing me. I guess I want that money now. Where is it?"

"In a very safe place."

"Can you get it for me?"

"Do you want to travel with that much in cash?"

"Oh. No, I guess not."

"I can get it to you later. What are you going to do with it when you get it?"

"I don't know. Put it in a deposit box, I guess. I don't know about taxes and so on. And her estate. On the phone something she said made me think she gave you some money too."

"She did. I hope it's going to be enough to get my houseboat fixed up. It was a fee for services. I am trying to find out who killed her."

"Who killed her! You're confusing me."

"Fly out of here. Fly home. I'll bring the money."

"When?"

"When I find out what went on here."

"And you'll tell me? Did somebody actually kill Carrie?"

"It's a possibility."

"Because of what she was doing? Because of the smuggling?"

"I would think so. In the meanwhile, Susan, not one word to anybody. Not even Jason."

"But I am very—"

"Not even Jason. Damn it, she told you to trust me. So trust me. Don't stand around dragging your feet."

"Well, then. Not even Jason."

As I went out onto the side deck with her, I saw Oliver trotting toward the *Flush*. He looked solemn. "Judge Schermer wants to talk to you, Mr. McGee."

"Send him along then."

"Oh, no. He wants you at his car. He's up there by the office."

12

IT was a spanking new Cadillac limousine, black as a crow's wing. It had tinted glass. I saw the black chauffeur walking offstage toward a shady bench.

A young woman stood beside the car. She put her hand out. "I'm Jane Schermer, Mr. McGee. Sorry to disturb you like this, but my uncle is anxious to talk to you."

She was a young woman with a sunburned flavor of ranchlands, cattle, and horses. She had a prematurely middle-aged face, doughy and slightly heavy in the jowls. She was oddly built, tall and broad, with vestigial breasts and very little indentation at the waist. The accent was expensive finishing school, possibly in Pennsylvania.

Jane opened the rear door and said, "Mr. McGee, Uncle Jake."

"How do you do, Judge Schermer," I said politely.

"Jane, you go take a little walk for yourself. This is man talk. Give us fifteen minutes. McGee, come on in here, but don't sit beside me. You can't talk to a man

175

sitting beside you, damn it. Open up that jump seat and sit facing me. That's fine. Please don't smoke."

"I had no intention of so doing."

He chuckled. "No intention of so doing. You ever read for the law? Can't get the stink out of the upholstery."

He looked ludicrously like Harry Max Scorf. He looked as if somebody had taken Harry Max and inflated him until his skin was shiny-tight and then had spray-painted him pink. His round stomach rested on his round thighs. He wore khakis and a straw ranch hat. The motor purred almost soundlessly. The compressor for the air conditioning clicked on and off.

"You're one sizable son of a bitch, aren't you?" he said. "That's some goddamn pair of wrists on you. You go about two twenty-five?"

"Few people guess it that close."

"I guess a lot of things close. It's been a help over the years."

"Do you want to get to some kind of point?"

"Saving us both time, eh? I have a protégé."

"Named Freddy Van Harn, who is engaged to be married to your niece, Jane Schermer. People think he has a political future. Then there could be those who don't think he has any future at all."

"You are a quick one, all right. You surely are. Frederick and I discuss his future and his current problems from time to time. You came up as one of his current problems."

"Me?"

"Pure bug-eyed astonishment, eh? Frederick is a lively young man. It's entirely possible for a fellow like him to become involved in something foolish out of a sense of risk and adventure. At his age—he's only twenty-nine—a single man can do some foolish things, never quite realizing that he might be destroying his whole future and destroying the dreams of the people depending on him. A man can have his sense of values warped by expediency sometimes, McGee. In Frederick's case, he's wanted to make money fast and make it big to wipe out the local memories of his father, a man who made a terrible mistake and took his life. Frederick became overextended, and he took a foolish risk in an effort to make some quick money. I've been very severe with him about that."

"What kind of risk?"

"We don't have to go into that here."

"Then let's say he was flying in grass, dropping it to a friend in a power boat. That would be profitable and foolish enough, don't you think?"

"Out of the goodness of my heart, I would advise you not to get too smart-mouth and high-ass around me. It makes me irritable, and when I get irritable, I'm harder to deal with."

"I'm not after a deal."

"You might be sooner than you know."

"Whatever that might mean."

"Frederick Van Harn is a very talented attorney, and he has that special kind of charisma which means he can go far in public service. It's past time that me and my little group had somebody in Tallahassee speaking up for this county and our special problems here. We've all he'ped him along ever' way we could, ever since he got out of Stetson and set up practice here. Once he's married to Janie he won't have any more money problems to fret about and do foolish things trying to solve them. You get what I mean. Janie inherited ten thousand acres of the most profitable grove lands in this whole state."

"How nice for her."

"McGee, we're talking about image here. We're building an image people are going to trust. You ought to hear that boy give a speech. Make you tingle all over. What I wouldn't want to happen, I wouldn't want anybody to come here, some stranger, and try to make a big fuss based entirely on the word of some dead thieving slut."

"You wouldn't?"

"Especially when it would be bad timing for Frederick in his career. A man shouldn't lose his whole future on account of one foolish act. It wouldn't be fair, would it?"

"To whom?"

"To those of us working hard to see dreams come true."

I shook my head. "Judge, you picked the wrong protégé. You picked a bad one."

"What are you talking about?"

"This Ready Freddy is kinky, Judge. He's all twisted in the sex areas."

"By God, there's nothing twisted about a man liking his pussy and going after it any danged place he can find it. When I was that boy's age I was ranging three counties on the moonlight nights."

"He likes it to hurt them, Judge. He likes to force them. He likes to scare them. He likes to humiliate them. He leaves them with bad memories and a bad case of the shakes."

"I'd say you've been listening to some foolish woman

with too many inhibitions to be any damn good in bed. I'd stake my life that boy is normal. And when he's got a wife and career he'll be too busy to go tomcatting."

"That sexy wife ought to keep him at home, all right."

"Watch yourself! You got a lot more mouth than you need."

"Judge, we have arrived at the end of our discussion. Weird as it may seem to you, I think your protégé is a murderous, spooky fellow. I think he has been going around killing people. I think he killed two friends of mine. Tell him that."

I reached behind me for the door handle. "Wait!" he said sharply. "What are you trying to pull? You can't believe that shit!"

"But I do!"

We locked stares for ten long seconds. And then he looked down and away, lips pursed. "We couldn't be that far wrong," he said softly, wonderingly. He shook himself and glowered at me. "You want to raise the ante. All right. Here is your deal. Twenty-five thousand dollars cash to get out of this county and stay out."

"Not for ten times the offer, Judge."

"You are dead wrong about Frederick. Believe me."

"I'll have to prove that to myself in my own way."

"Stop reaching back of you for that door handle. Set a minute. Everybody wants something bad. What is it you want?"

"It isn't nice to go around killing people."

"Frederick wouldn't kill anybody. Have you got some romantical notion about getting even for Carrie Milligan? My God, McGee, these people that get into drugs, they've got the life expectancy of a mayfly. That girl probably didn't know where she was or what she was doing. She walked into traffic."

"Like Joanna."

"A bomb? Frederick Van Harn fooling around with bombs? That's ridiculous. What do you want? What are you after?"

"Nothing you'd understand, Judge."

"I understand a lot of things. I understand the world is too full of people and half a billion of 'em are starving this year. I understand there's a few million tons of phosphate under the ranchlands down in the southeast corner of this county, and the ecology freaks have kept National Minerals Industries from strip-mining it, and there's a group of us thinks if we put Fred in the State Senate, that might get changed around and a lot of people might make out pretty good. I understand that we're not going to stand for anybody coming in here and messing up our plans. People are starving because of the shortage of fertilizer. Phosphate is high priority, McGee. Now who's going to do the most good in the world, Van Harn or you?"

"It's nice to know why you're so interested in me."

"You know what I'm going to do for you? I'm going to set up a little session between you and Frederick, and I'll let him tell you just what his involvement was."

"Are you sure you want to do that?"

"What's the matter? Afraid he'll shoot your theories full of holes?"

"I met him once. He didn't impress me, Judge."

"You caught him at a bad time. He told me about it."

"Why should he tell you?"

"I asked him if he'd ever met you."

"I'll talk to him, sure. Send this car back with him in it, and I'll talk to him right here. Like this. Alone. If he's willing."

"He's willing to do what we want him to do."

"Let's make it tomorrow. There isn't enough of today left. I seem to get tired easily."

"Tomorrow morning."

I got out. Jane Schermer was strolling slowly toward the limousine. When she saw me holding the door for her, she quickened her step. The Judge kicked the jump seat back into its niche. I handed her in and closed the door. The driver climbed in and chunked his door shut, and the car moved off through the late heat of the day, with barely audible hum of gears and engine.

Cindy was in the office. A man from Virginia was settling up, preparatory to leaving in the early morning on Monday. He was signing travelers' checks. He wore red-white-and-blue shorts and a yellow shirt, funny shoes, and a funny hat. He had narrow little shoulders and a yard of rump. He was telling Cindy how great it had been, except when the bomb went off. She said she was sorry about that bomb. He said he didn't know what people were thinking of these days. Like in Ireland.

He went out with his receipt and with Cindy's wishes for a good cruise back to Virginia. The door swung shut and she said, "You look practically gray. What is it, dear?"

"The Judge wore me down. I'm going to go lie down."

"Before you fall down."

"I'm going to swim in that motel pool first."

"Should you?"

"If I don't get the dressing wet."

"Somebody ought to be with you."

The new fellow came in. Ritchie. A little older than Ollie and Jason, a lot less hairy. He said Jason was out on the docks and sure, he'd take the desk.

I went to the *Flush* and got swim trunks. Meyer wasn't aboard. I changed in the motel, and by the time I got to the pool Cindy was there, taking long sweeping strokes, a fast crawl from end to end, using kick turns. The dusk light was turning orange, making the world look odd, as though awaiting thunder. I sat on the edge of the pool and admired the smooth flexing of the muscles of her back and hips and thighs as she made those turns. Then I lowered myself into the pool and paddled lethargically around, keeping my head high. She wore a white suit, white swim cap.

When I clambered out, refreshed and relaxed, she was still swimming hard, but she was beginning to labor, beginning that side to side roll of exhaustion. At last she came to the edge and clung, panting audibly. I went and took her wrists and hoisted her out. She stumbled against me and recoiled, turning away from me.

"What was that all about?"

"What was what all about?" She walked over to her towel and mopped her face, tugged the cap off, shook her dark hair out, and sat on an aluminum chaise and closed her eyes.

I sat on the concrete beside the chaise and took hold of her hand. It was brown and boneless, without response. "What was the compulsive swimming all about?"

"Exercise. That's all."

"All?"

"Well. I guess I was fighting us. Working off anger."

"Why?"

"It just seems too pat. Just too damned easy, that's all. Nothing comes for free. Everything costs. I walk around all day wanting to be in bed with you. Knowing I will be. But maybe I won't be."

"Why not?"

"Weren't you listening? I said it was too easy for us."

"And that makes it bad? That makes it ugly?"

"I didn't *say* that."

"Meyer is the one with the erudition. Meyer is the one with all the smarts. I can give you something secondhand from Meyer which might help. It comes from a smart tough old Greek by the name of Homer. I'll tell you what he said . . . if you'll use it."

"I'll try."

"He said, 'Dear to us ever is the banquet and the harp and the dance and changes of raiment and the warm bath and love and sleep.' "

She kept her eyes closed and her face told me nothing. Finally she said, "Dear to us ever. Yes." She turned her head toward me and opened her eyes and linked her fingers in mine. "Maybe that old Greek meant that a thing in and of itself is okay, without deadlines or promissory notes or anything. Just in and of itself alone."

"In and of itself together."

"Well, sure."

And so we went into the motel where there was a last pink tinge of sunlight dimly reflected on a far wall. Out of the wet suits our bodies were enclasped clammy cool, but swiftly heating. There was no constraint in her, only a merging and changing energy, quite swift and certain of itself, strong and searching.

When I awoke she was gone. There was a rusty old projector in the back of my mind, showing underexposed film on a mildewed screen. The projection bulb kept burning out and the film kept jamming in the gate, but by watching closely I could make most of it out. Memory was healing itself, taking me from banyan shelter in the rain to Fifteen Hundred to my talk with the bald man. It was all of a piece, but with murky places which I hoped would become more clear to me as time went on.

It was four in the morning. I was on the edge of sleep, beginning to hallucinate back into my dreams, when the creak of the interconnecting door brought me awake. I smelled her perfume. Her groping hand touched my shoulder. She whispered my name.

I turned the sheet back for her and she came shivering in beside me, chattering her teeth. She wore something gauzy and hip-length.

"What's the matter?"

"I dreamed you were d-d-dead too, darling."

"I'm not."

"I just had to come in and hold you. That's all I want."

"Everything is all right. It's all right."

"I'll be okay in a little wh-while."

I held her, close and safe. She felt restless for quite a

long time, and then gradually her breathing slowed and deepened. I tried to visualize her face but could not, and at the edge of sleep I had the nightmare vision of face without features, of a rounded, tanned expanse of flesh, anonymous as the back of her shoulder.

When I awoke at dawn she was still with me. I thought I was aboard the *Flush,* and for a time I did not know who she was. Her leg jumped twice and she made a whining sound before turning back into heavy sleep.

As once again she became restless, I tried to find the answer to my feeling that I could not seem to get truly close to her. I did not know enough about her. Had she fallen out of apple trees, ridden a red bike, built castles in a sandbox, scabbed her knees, worshiped her daddy, sung in a choir, written poetry, walked in the rain? She did not tell me enough. I wanted to know all of the complex of experience which had finally brought her to this place and time, to this moment with her dark hair fragrant and pressed against the edge of my chin. A widow, now indulging herself in the delights of the flesh, so long denied by the hulking drunken husband, and feeling guilt for such indulgence. I was being used, and wanted a deeper and truer contact. I wondered if I wanted her to be in love with me, as a sop to my ego, perhaps.

There was a change in the feel of her, in the textures of her, that told me she was now awake. Gently, gently, she disengaged herself as I feigned sleep. She sat on the edge of the bed and groped for the short nightgown, then stood and put it on. Through slitted eyes I saw her put a fist in front of a wide yawn, a yawn so huge it made her shudder. She moved silently across the room and slipped through the interconnecting door. I heard the soft click of the latch and the second metallic sound that meant she had locked the door behind her. A gesture for the motel maid? A disavowal? Or the end of the episode?

13

FREDERICK Van Harn sat in the same rear corner
of the limousine as had the Judge. The black chauffeur
sat upon a different bench because the shade patterns
were different at ten o'clock on that Monday morning.
The engine ran as quietly as before, the compressor
clicking on and off.

I sat on the same jump seat, turned to face him. I
wore boat pants, sandals, a faded old shirt from Gua-
temala. He wore a beige business suit, white shirt, tie of
dark green silk, dark brown loafers polished to satin
gloss. As he looked directly at me I saw that his side-
burns were precisely even. The sideburn hair was long,
brushed back to cover the ears. Neat little ears, I imag-
ined. Maybe a bit pointed on the top. Olive skin, delicate features, long dark eyelashes, brown liquid eyes.

I had been an annoyance to him when we had met at
Jack Omaha's house. He studied me quietly, very much
at ease, not the least bit uncomfortable. His hands were
long and sinewy, and he clasped his fingers around a
slightly upraised knee.

"Mr. McGee, you got under my skin pretty good when we met at Chris's place."

"You went into a massive tizzy."

He smiled. "Are you trying to do it again?"

"I don't know. What are *you* trying to do?"

It was an engaging smile. Very direct. "I'm trying to get you off my back. Uncle Jake thinks you could hurt me."

"Don't you?"

The smile faded. He looked earnest. "I really don't see how. Oh, if you were politically inclined you could give me some static by bringing up the dumb-ass bit about flying marijuana in, but you'd have no proof of that, and I think I could deny it convincingly. Besides, I don't think people are as dead set against it as they used to be. The use of it is too prevalent. I hear that a long time ago the rumrunners were folk heroes along this coast. It's getting to be much the same with grass. I'm not sure you could hurt me."

"What if somebody got notarized statements from Betty Joller and Susan Dobrovsky? Do you think your kinky love life could hurt you any if it came out?"

He colored but recovered quickly. "People must find it remarkably easy to talk to you, McGee. I don't think there's anything kinky about enjoying the hard sell. Reluctance stimulates me. Maybe in retrospect they see it differently than it was. But in both those cases there were plenty of squeals of girlish joy."

"Joanna thought you were tiresome."

"Please stop trying to bait me. Let's try to get along at least a little bit. Try to understand each other."

"What do you want me to understand?"

He shrugged. "How I was such a damned fool. I'd

flown to most of the islands. I'm a good pilot. I've got a good airplane and I keep it in first-class condition. As lawyer for Superior Building Supplies, I knew Jack and Harry were in bad shape and things were getting worse. I think it was Jack who brought it up, like a joke. I had said something about falling behind on the ranch payments and trying to get an extension on the loan. He said we ought to work out a way to bring grass in. He said he could find a nice outlet for us. We met again and planned how we could do it, still treating it as a joke. Finally I went down and lined up a source in Jamaica and then we . . . went ahead. We couldn't afford much the first time. But it all worked out okay."

"Tell me about it."

He shrugged again. "We'd rendezvous off the north shore of Grand Bahama. The coast was always clear because it's difficult water. I'd circle and drop the stuff. We would have put the big bags inside plastic bags from Omaha's stock and tied the neck so they'd float and the seawater couldn't get to the grass. They'd gather them in with a boat hook. Very simple."

"How about the last trip?"

"What about it?"

"Who was involved?"

"Just the four of us. Carrie went with me. Jack and Cal were aboard the boat. I had headwinds and I was a little late coming to the rendezvous point. At about five fifteen Carrie started horsing those sacks out the door. She was a strong person. They picked them up. Nine, I believe there were. So I put my ship right down on the deck and crossed the coast north of here and came down to the ranch and landed. She got in the little truck and went to the marina late that night, and they loaded the stuff into the truck. She drove it to the outlet and got paid off and took the money down and put it in the safe at Superior."

"What happened to Jack Omaha?"

"I have a theory."

"Such as?"

"I think some professionals were moving in on us. It was too easy to score. I think they got to Jack and scared him badly. I think that he stayed with Carrie and they went down and emptied the safe and went their separate ways. A lot of that money was supposed to be mine. It would have helped me a lot to have it. As it was I had to arrange to . . . borrow it."

"From Uncle Jake Schermer?"

His smile was ironic. "And a lot of advice went along with the money. He was upset about the whole thing. I couldn't make him understand that it wasn't as important as he was making out. It was . . . a caper. It was fun, damn it. Everybody in the group got along all right. Low risk and good money. We were planning on making one or two more trips and then splitting the money and calling it a day. I wanted to come out of it with two hundred thousand clear. And that's what Jack Omaha felt he needed to save the business."

"Harry Hascomb wasn't in on it?"

"Harry talks to make himself important. He talks in bars. And bedrooms. Harry is a jerk. I'm talking to you now, McGee, but there is no part of this you can prove. There is no basis for indictment by anybody."

"And the Judge and his group are going to make certain you have a nice clean record because you are going to make them all rich and happy."

After a flash of anger he spoke slowly and judiciously. "I don't know how much good I'm going to do them. I really don't. The timing is right. I can get elected. The campaign will be well financed. The incumbent is senile. I've built a good base here. I plan to announce right after the wedding. I love this part of Florida. I'm not at all certain I'd be in favor of a new deepwater port and a lot of phosphate mining and processing. It's a dirty industry. The port will bring in other industries. Maybe a refinery. But those are low-employment prospects. They won't keep young people from leaving the Bayside area. And they will pollute the water and the air. On a risk-reward basis I can't make it add up. I have the feeling I want to work in the best interests of the people who will vote me into office, not the few men who have been grooming me for office."

He was impressively convincing. He emanated a total sincerity. Right at that moment he had my vote. I could see what it was about him that made the Judge label him charismatic. He talked to me as if I were the most interesting person he would meet this year.

"What do you think I ought to do?" he asked me.

"Do what you think is right."

"That sounds so easy. Right and wrong. Black and white. Up and down. It divides the substances of life unrealistically. The world is often gray and sideways. According to the game plan, if I go to Tallahassee I ought to be able to move the situation along in five to six years. If there is world famine by then, it will be the thing I should do."

He sighed and shrugged.

"Well, it's my problem and I will have to make the decision. I know I'm going to run for the office. I'll just have to take one step at a time. McGee, I want to thank you for listening to me. I haven't killed anybody. I don't know where the money went. I got into a foolish situation because I didn't weigh all the consequences. And I'm glad now that it's over. I know that the chemistry between us is not good. I can't help that. I don't expect everybody to like me. I'll depend on your sense of fair play."

I found myself shaking hands with him. I got out of the car hastily, and after it drove away I wiped my hand on the side of my trousers. I felt dazed. He had focused a compelling personality upon me the way somebody might focus a big spotlight. He had that indefinable thing called presence, and he had it in large measure. I tried to superimpose the new image upon the fellow I had met in Jack Omaha's house, listlessly tying his tie after a session in Jack Omaha's bed. That fellow's anger had been pettish, slightly shrill. I could overlap my two images of the man. I wondered if my previous image had somehow been warped by the great blow on the back of the head when the explosion had hurled me off my feet.

This man had been engaging, plausible, completely at ease. He made me feel as if it were very nice indeed to be taken into his confidence. There were dozens of things I wanted to ask him, but the chance was gone. The chance had driven away in a gleaming limousine, cool in the heat of the morning.

Yes, if he could project all that to a group, he could be elected. No sweat.

Yet where were you, Van Harn, when big Cal Birdsong was dying in the hospital, with a thin wire sticking him in the heart? Were you beside the bed, charismatic and relaxed? When your men clear new ranchland, do they blow the pine stumps with dynamite? Did those lean sinewy hands hoist Carrie into the front corner of the Dodge truck? Exactly how did you make Susan look so sick at heart, so defeated and sad?

I had been trying to make it all a single interrelated series of acts of violence. But his convincing presence was making it all come unstuck, turning it all into unrelated episodes.

Harry Max Scorf said, "Have a nice chat?"

Usually I can sense people who move up close behind me. Something gives me warning. Not this time. I leapt into the air.

"Jesus!"

"Nope. Only me. Harry Max Scorf."

"Of the City and County of Bayside. I know. I know."

"Your nerves aren't real good, son."

"Yes, I had a nice chat. What else is new?"

"Let's set," he said, leading the way to a shady bench.

I sat beside him, leaning back, squinting from the shady place out at the white dazzle of boats at the marina. I could see a brown lady in lavender bikini prone on the foredeck of a Chris, her head near the gray bulk of a big Danforth. Nearby was the silent gleaming bulk of Jack Omaha's muscular Bertram. Was it beginning to look slightly dingy? The unused boat so quickly acquires that abandoned, unloved, uncherished look. Chrome gets foggy. Bronze turns green. Aluminum pits and flakes. The lines get whiskery and the fenders get dirty. By looking to my right I could see into the office to where Cindy Birdsong stood working on a ledger, elbow on the counter, fingers clenched in her hair, tongue sticking out of the corner of her mouth. Looking beyond the Bertram, beyond the bikini, I could see Meyer and Jason working, sweat-shiny on the sun deck of the *Flush,* setting and cementing the vinyl sheets. Behind me was the traffic roar of the busy Monday streets and highways. Florida no longer slows down for June. A pity.

Harry Max Scorf produced a blue bandanna and flicked a shadow of dust off the toes of his gleaming boots. He took off his white Truman hat with care, wiped the sweatband, and placed it between us on the weathered wood of the bench. He seemed to doff force and authority along with the hat. His head was oddly pointy.

"What is new," he said, "is that the special task force hit Fifteen Hundred Seaway Boulevard at first light this morning. And some sight it was. Nine cars. Twenty-five men. Feds and state people. I was local liaison, sort of observing. They tested me out long ago and know I can keep my mouth shut. I went along with the four who hit Walter J. Demos's apartment. He'd been entertaining a little schoolteacher person in his bed. They found about thirty pounds of cannabis in a plastic bag hanging on a hook about three feet up inside his fireplace. I can tell you it was sorry shit, my friend. Weak and dusty, a lot of big lower leaves cured bad, powdery as senna leaves. Well, those two had got some clothes on and they stood in the living room, both of them crying. The little schoolteacher was crying because she was ashamed and scared for her job, which she will lose. And that ball-headed Demos was crying because he was so goddamn mad at himself he couldn't hardly stand it. All the other men were going through the other apartments. There was one crazy scramble of folks trying to get back to their own beds. I think I've got the figure right. They made fifteen 'arrests for possession, not counting Demos and the teacher. Of course with Demos with that quantity, it will be for dealing, and that is heavier. You want to put it together for me?"

"You already have."

"I know. I know. But you tickle me. You've got cop sense."

"I can't remember a word of my little talk with him."

"What do you think you might have said?"

"Oh, something to open him up. Come on very very heavy, like somebody from the Office taking over the operation. An amateur like Demos would buy an act that wasn't exactly plausible. Then I suppose I would have told him to hold onto his money and wait for a delivery and not get impatient."

"You just suppose you might have said all that?"

"And left him a posture he couldn't maintain. He is big jolly old Uncle Walter, head of the family. He is supposed to take care of everything and provide everything to make life juicy for his tenants. So when somebody showed up with some product, Uncle Wally bought it, and then they turned him in. I'd say that he was put out of business by the real professionals, easily, quietly, no fuss. He was buying enough for Fifteen Hundred, to maintain the life-style there. The squire of swingleville. The professionals wouldn't bother to work him over. The professionals use the law to weed out the amateurs."

"Did they weed out that girl, that Carolyn Milligan?"

I didn't have to think long. "You don't like that any better than I do, Captain. Makes no sense. I could never believe that."

He sighed and said, "Neither can I. I tried to figure they'd wipe out the supply group: Omaha, Birdsong, Milligan. Then go after distribution. The trouble is, they wouldn't get into that much trouble for the sake of one channel of supply in Bayside County. There's three or four other groups. It isn't all that big. It's all businesslike. Nobody kills anybody unless there is absolutely no other way at all. This whole thing won't hang together because I don't know some things I ought to know. That's always the way it is. When you know enough, all of a sudden you know it all."

"What about Carrie? Did you look into that?"

"I got with Doc Stanyard on that. We went over his autopsy notes. Her left arm was badly abraded on the outside of the forearm and upper arm, with some paint fragments driven into the skin. See what that means?"

"No."

"Use your thick head, McGee."

It took about twenty seconds before light dawned. "Okay, if she was sober enough to pull her car off the road, then she was alert enough to have the normal instinct of lifting her arm to ward off the truck bearing down on her. She would step out and try to ward it off and dodge back. Her arm was hanging at her side when she was hit, so the assumption is that she was unconscious."

"Or suiciding. Waiting for the right vehicle. Left her purse in the car. Shut her eyes and stepped out. *Bam.*"

"Which do you think?"

"I think that unless I learn more, I won't ever know which it was. Why did you have a conference with the Judge yesterday and a talk with Freddy this morning?"

"We were talking about his appeal to the electorate."

"His daddy was pleasant. Weak and pleasant and crooked. Funny thing. They say Freddy won't ever have his hand in the till because of what happened to his daddy. It did him good instead of bad. They like the way he's come up so fast."

"Too fast, Captain?"

"They changed the retirement rules when it got to be City and County of Bayside. I've got thirteen months to go. If somewhere down the road, before thirteen months are up, I get thrown off, I ride an old bicycle and eat dog food. If I last it out, I'm better off than I would have been under the old rule. If Judge Jacob Schermer and his buddies are playing poker some night and somebody at the table says they've got tired of my face, I'm through the next day."

"Scare you?"

He turned and looked at me. Those old eyes had seen everything, twice. They had looked into a lot of people. An echo of a smile touched the corners of his mouth. "Scared shitless," he murmured.

"Then I better not tell you Freddy was flying the grass from Jamaica and air-dropping it to Omaha's boat off Grand Bahama."

"No, you shouldn't tell me because it would fit too close with the arithmetic I've worked up about Freddy. He dresses fancy, drinks fancy, drives fancy. He's got the ranch and the airplane and forty pair of boots. But then you got to remember that Miss Janie has ten thousand acres of grove, and under management it must turn her sixty dollar an acre a year net, on which she can afford Fred Van Harn as a play toy, but if I were Jake I wouldn't be hoping my niece would marry up with a fellow with some kind of wrong twist in his head. Two years ago something got hushed up. They got delay after delay so by the time it was ready to go to court that girl had grown some inches taller. It's said he claims he never had any idea she was only fourteen. Anyway, she got taller and older and smarter, and settled for the money. They've been grooming him for politics, first the State Senate, then maybe Governor. They really don't give a damn what kind of a man he is. What they care about is that, he goes on local television on a public issue, you never seen such mail as comes in. Begging him to run for office. That's all they care about. In fact the other stuff kind of helps them out because it makes it easier to control him. Oh, they'll have him married to Miss Janie, and she'll be a good hostess, and she'll bear him some healthy kids, and there you are. He can turn that charm on. He can charm a five-thousand-dollar fee out of a five-hundred-dollar case and make the sucker come back for more advice. What did he tell you?"

"He told me he didn't kill anybody."

"My hunch is he probably didn't. But he sure got into the pants of just about ever' woman involved in it. You got a list?"

"Carrie Milligan. Joanna Freeler. Betty Joller. Chris Omaha. He made a try at Miz Birdsong, but she bit him."

"Good for her."

"And Susan Dobrovsky."

He stared at me, registering shock. "That girl too? Son of a *bitch!*"

"He took her out to the ranch. She was supposed to leave for home this morning. Jason was going to see her off."

"Ever since that boy was fourteen damn years old, he's been lifting every skirt he sees. There's stories about him. He goes after ever' one as if there was never going to be any more. And there's something about him, they say. The ones you'd never expect, their eyes cross and they lay back and put their heels in the air for him. There's no law against it, at least no law anybody enforces. And he doesn't seem to ever get tired of looking for it. And he finds it places you wouldn't even think of."

I had to admit to myself there were, indeed, a lot of places I would never think of. And a fair portion of every day when I did not think of it at all, at all.

"Vote for Van Harn," I said.

"They'll do that. Senator Van Harn. They need a man up there riding point on what they want around here. Deepwater port for the phosphate down in the south county. Refinery. And all the goodies that go along with it that only a few fellows get a piece of."

"The Judge offered me twenty-five big ones to go away and forget all about Freddy."

Harry Max Scorf looked mildly startled. "What do they think you know?"

"No more than I've told you. That he's a kink. He rapes people and kills people and spends too much money and flies grass in."

He stood up and carefully fitted his white hat back

over the pointy skull, tugging it to the right angle. He gave me a sharklike smile. "What the hell do they want for a front-runner? Some kind of nance fellow? See you around, son."

When I went into the office, Cindy looked up with her customer face, cool and polite. Then the great warm smile came. "Hello," she said. It was just one word, but it was about fifteen words long.

"And hello to you. Books balance?"

"They do now. What I did, I wrote a hundred and sixteen dollars when it was supposed to be a hundred and sixty-one. I saw you out there. Captain Scorf has been around forever, and they say he's always looked exactly the same. Was he being rough with you?"

"No. He says I've got cop sense."

"Is that a good thing to have?"

"They have finished the noisy parts of repairing the *Flush*. I think I better pay my motel bill and move my toothbrush back to the boat."

She showed quick sharp dismay and disappointment before she caught herself. "Anything you wish, dear."

"If you want to bring a small portable fire extinguisher, I'll talk Meyer into cooking some of his renowned chili tonight."

"That would be nice," she said, forcing it.

"Anything wrong?"

"Nothing at all, thank you."

"Are you sure?"

"Certainly I'm sure!"

There is no going past that point. All the roads are

barricaded and all the bridges are blown. The fields are mined and the artillery has every sector zeroed in.

So I went and moved my toothbrush and accessories out of the unit, went to the front, and paid a fat lady my accumulated charges. She asked me if I was feeling better, and I said I was feeling just great. She said, "It's so nice that Mrs. Birdsong has a friend nearby in her time of need. Have you known her long?"

"A very long time."

"He drank, you know."

"Yes. Cal drank."

"In a way, it's a blessing."

"There are a lot of ways of looking at everything, I guess."

"Oh, yes, that's so true."

A small fire fight, with no decision. Both sides retreated.

When I got to the boat, the glass people had arrived. There were four of them, in white coveralls, with the pieces all cut to size, tempered glass for marine use. The foreman said they would be through by four at the latest. Jason and Meyer were celebrating the completion of the vinyl job on the sun deck by having a cold beer in the shade of the canopy over the topside control panel. I inspected the job and gave my approval.

I am skeptical of all of the so-termed marvelous advances of science. And I am suspicious of anything which tries to look like something it isn't. Thus it would seem that a coal-tar derivative patterned to look like bleached teak would turn me totally off. But it is so damned practical. If you should ever have an artery which can't be repaired, it can be replaced with woven Dacron. And, wearing that in your gut, it would be unseemly to go about muttering about the plastic world full of plastic people.

So I stand on my plastic deck and mutter whatever I please. When did I make any claim about being consistent? Or even reasonable?

I went below and checked out my stereo set. I put on the new record, Ruby Braff and George Barnes. It is nice to have one that is just out and know that it is destined to become one of the great jazz classics. I knew I had lost one speaker. I suspected I had lost more. Delicate microcircuitry cannot take that kind of explosive compression. When the noise came out, sounding like someone gargling a throatful of crickets, I snapped it off in haste.

Back to the shop. No new components. Get the Marantz stuff fixed. I did not think I could placidly endure another gleaming salesman tell me that I had to have quadraphony sound, coming at me from all directions. I have never felt any urge to stand in the middle of a group of musicians. They belong over there, damn it, and I belong over here, listening to what they are doing over there. Music that enfolds you, coming from some undetectable set of sources, is gimmicky, unreal, and eminently forgettable.

Jason went back to work his turn in the office. Meyer and I made some sardine sandwiches. He was glad to learn I was back aboard for good. We sat at the booth in the galley and ate. And compared notes and reports.

"We are absolutely nowhere," Meyer said.

"A perfect summary."

"Are you sure you feel okay?"

"Don't I look okay?"

"Glassy. You stare at me in a . . . goggly way."

"Come to think of it, I feel goggly and glassy."

"Just this minute. Or . . ."

"Most of the time. The light seems too bright."

"When the windows are done—"

"The ports."

"When the windows are done, we could go."

"Home?"

"And forget this whole mess, Travis."

"Tempting. Who are we supposed to be, going around finding out who did what and why?"

"That's why they have police."

"Right!"

We beamed at each other, but we both knew we were talking nonsense. The habit of involvement is not easily broken. It is even more pervasive than the habit of noninvolvement, the habit of walking away when the action starts.

I told him we couldn't leave because we had a guest coming for dinner. I told him he was cooking chili.

14

WE three had sat with tears running down our cheeks and told each other in choked voices that the chili was truly delicious. She and Meyer had cleaned up, telling me that I was still on semi-invalid status.

By the time they were through, there was a large dark night outside, wide as a country, high as the stars, and hot with the night winds of June.

We killed the lights and went topside to a shadowed part of the sun deck, out of the reach of dock lights. The sky was pink orange over Bayside, all its outdoor advertising glowing against a mist made of hydrocarbon fartings of trucks and other vehicles. We aligned deck chairs on the newly repaired decking so as to look out at the stars over the Atlantic. We were into the rainy season now. The night of June tenth. Bulbous black lay low to the southeast, sullenly flickering an unseen artillery of lightning.

She on my left, Meyer on my right, the night air stirring across us and then fluttering back to stillness. Her hand had crept over to my thigh, stealthily, nudged a welcome, and was enclosed by my hand, unseen by

Meyer, as if we were children in church. With my thumb I rubbed the thick warm pads at the base of her fingers. I wondered if she had been told or had guessed that her husband had not died of natural causes. They would have to tell her, sooner or later, no matter how pessimistic the law felt about catching whoever had done it. Harry Max Scorf had indicated quite plainly that she was on his list of suspects. Though I knew her very well in certain limited ways, I knew her not at all in many aspects. But I could not imagine her killing in that stealthy way, jabbing a wire into the great chest while the king slept.

Harry Max Scorf, in a dogged and plodding pattern, would have long since established the identity of every person who could have gotten close to Cal Birdsong long enough to do him in.

"It always seems such a waste when it rains way out there," she said. "Sort of badly managed, to rain into the sea."

"It's moving this way," Meyer said. "But your average thunderstorm has a total life span of fifty-five minutes."

She sat up and looked across me at Meyer. "You've got to be kidding."

"Believe him," I said.

"When the conditions are right a pod will be forming in the area as the older pod is dissipating its energies. Thus we get the impression of one single storm lasting for hours. Not so."

She settled back and made a small sound of mirth and wryness. "The rest of my life," she said, "I'll see a thunderstorm and say to myself they only last fifty-five minutes."

Her hand still rested on mine, her hand warm and dry. I thought of lies and polygraphs and biofeedback. One type of biofeedback machine requires strapping a pair of electrodes to the palm of your hand. When you are tense and nervous, your palm is moist and cool and the conductivity of your skin is increased. The machine has a dial and a little electronic tone, thin and insectile. As you make yourself more calm your hand becomes more dry, the dial needle swings slowly downward, and the electronic note moves down the scale. By giving you the visible and audible results of different mental and emotional postures, in time you learn, without the machine, how to impose a great calm upon yourself, an alpha state, if you will.

Soon she would be told her husband had been murdered. The required Grand Jury hearing could not be delayed indefinitely. I rubbed my thumb back and forth across the pads on the palm of her hand, and tried to think of how to word my trick remark, and felt disgusted with myself. A rotten game to play with this woman.

Suddenly, without a word being said, I felt her palm go cold and wet. She tugged her hand away and got up and moved over to the rail and turned to lean against it, her arms folded, her shoulders hunched forward.

"What's wrong, Cindy?"

"I guess somebody walked over my grave."

She was silhouetted against the intermittent glow of distant lightning. "Did you think of something that upset you?"

"I think I'll go home now," she said.

"I'll walk you."

"I'm okay."

"No trouble."

I tried to make conversation as we walked to the motel, but she gave one-word responses. She unlocked the door and pushed it open and turned to me. I took her in my arms. Her lips were cool and firm. There was no response in lips or body, and then there was a lot. A hungry lot.

We went in and the door clicked shut. "No lights," she said. "Don't let me think about anything. Don't give me time to think about anything. Please."

The bed was by big windows. The draperies were open. The storm moved closer. The lightning flashes were vivid. Each one made a still picture of her in black and white. Black eyes and lips and hair and nipples and groin. White, white, white all the rest of her. The lightning arrested movement. It caught her in a fluid turning, mouth agape with harsh breath and effort. It froze a leg, lifting. It stopped her, astride, arms braced, halting the elliptical swing of hips, turning her into a pen and ink drawing of greatest clarity. I kept her for a long time within the prison of her own tensions, though she escaped to partial release from time to time. Each lightning stroke seemed to be brighter, each stroke bringing the thunder closer and sharper. At last the lightning made a ticking sound, filled the room with a strange hard blue light, and the great following bang of thunder made her gasp and leap. The ensuing crashing downpour of the rain was like a signal to us.

We lay damp and slack in a close and sweaty embrace, content, heavy-breathing, detumescent. The storm air moved across us, cooling our bodies. The intensity of the downpour began to slacken, but it was still a heavy tropic rain.

"Ruthie took those pills," she said.

"What?"

"You didn't know her. It was a long time ago. Bud—he was her husband—ran off a curve and hit a big tree. They gave her pills to make it easier. God, she took so many pills you couldn't talk to her, hardly. Huh? She'd say. Huh? Wha'? And sleep? She'd sleep twenty hours a day. Toby—you didn't know him either —his wife went back to see her sick mother and the airplane fell out of the sky. For Toby it was booze. After a year they had to put him away and dry him out. People use things, don't they? I'm using sex. I want it to be more and more, every time with you. It was more this time than ever. When it's so much, I can't think about anything else. The thing about me is, I'm not like this. Not really. I told you Cal hadn't touched me in ever so long. But it didn't make me feel . . . deprived. I mean it was okay. I guess I'm the way I am now, with you, because I try so hard to get my mind turned off. I try so hard, I get way way into the sex thing, like I couldn't before. I always felt a little odd about it. Ashamed, almost. I mean being so big and strong and healthy and looking . . . as if I would like it."

"You need never feel odd again."

"I won't. I won't."

"And you've got a talking jag."

"I know. And you have to listen, don't you? We don't really know each other. It's strange. I guess the way men think about these things, without me sounding like an egomaniac, what you did was luck out. You came along at the time when any presentable and sympathetic guy would be right where you are right now, doing what you were doing."

"Flattery will get you everywhere."

"Trav, please don't make flip little remarks. What our relationship is, it's backassward. It started at the end, and I want to find our beginnings. I want to know you as a person, not just want you terrible for the way you can turn my head off. It's a genuine compulsion, really."

"Okay. No flip remarks. No bedroom comedy. I saw the vulnerability and I took advantage. So that makes it seem unreal to me too. But it's more than pure physical hunger."

"What else is it?"

"Liking you. Wanting things to be right for you. Wanting the world to be a special place for you. Also, there's guilt."

"About what?"

"About knowing that Cal was murdered. Harry Max Scorf told me. I don't know if he knew I'd tell you."

She sat up, with sharp hissing exhalation. "How?" she whispered.

I told her. She made a sick sound and closed her fingers around my arm with impressive force.

"Jason," she whispered.

"Are you sure?"

"I can't prove anything. Once . . . after things had been very bad—Cal was drunk and he beat me—Jason came to me and said that there were ways Cal could be killed that nobody would ever know. I made him be still. I knew he was going to say he'd do it for me. And he would have. He's a strange boy. He can't stand any kind of cruelty. He was a battered child. He nearly died of it. And he has been . . . a little bit in love with me, I think."

"It showed, after Cal knocked you out."

She settled slowly back down again, cheek against my chest, arm heavy across me. "I thought I saw him at the hospital the evening Cal died. I was going out to eat. I thought I saw Jason riding his bike toward the hospital at the far end of the parking lot. I didn't think any more about it until now. When I came back from eating, all those people were working on Cal so frantically. What it probably was was a piece of stiff leader wire. Cal was in one of those security rooms, single rooms, but he wasn't guarded. But I don't really *know*. So I don't have to go and tell anyone, do I?"

"Are you angry at Jason?"

"I don't *know*. Cal was killing himself in any case. They'd told him his liver was going bad and he shouldn't drink at all. I can understand why Jason did it. If he did it. Trav, help me."

"Captain Scorf will ask questions of you, sooner or later. It would look better if you went to him. Ask him if your husband died of natural causes. If he levels with you, register shock and then tell your suspicions. It will have to be your choice as to whether you tell Jason you're going to see Scorf and, if Jason runs, how much lead time you give him."

"Okay. I'll do it that way. But I wish you hadn't told me anything, dear."

"Why did you get upset tonight when we were looking at the stars and the storm?"

"Upset? Oh, I just remembered a nightmare Cal had, about a week before he died. He woke up roaring. I couldn't seem to make him wake up. I looked up at the dark sky and remembered. He had a nightmare about something falling toward him out of the sky that was going to kill him, that was going to land on him and kill him, and he couldn't get out from underneath it. He was so really terrified that I guess it left a mark on me. Half nightmare and half delirium, I guess it was. His mind had gone all warped and nasty from the drinking. Then he didn't want me to tell anybody about his nightmare! As if anybody in the world would give a damn! Tonight I remembered, and it made me feel weird and crawly."

The rain stopped. Another pod formed and came grumbling toward us through the night. She talked in a slumbrous, murmurous voice, and then the voice ended and her breathing changed, slow, deep, and warm against my throat. I watched the flashes against the window and against the ceiling. The new storm moved closer, and at last the thunder became loud enough to awaken her. She started, then settled back. "I was dreaming," she said.

"Pleasant dreams?"

"Not really. I was in front of a judge's bench. It was very high, so high I couldn't see him at all. They wouldn't let me move back to where I could see him, and it made me angry. I knew he would never believe me unless I could see him and he could see me. I was accused of something about Jason, doing something wrong."

"Such as?"

"I don't *know*. I guess I was guilty of something, all right. I mean when somebody is attracted to you, you know about it. And it feels good to be admired that way. So you . . . respond to it. Do you know what I mean? It changes the way you look at the other person, and the way you walk when you walk away from them, and it changes the pitch of your voice when you laugh. So I guess . . . those little things would add up, and maybe that's why he did what he did. *If* he did it."

"Don't go around looking for guilt."

"I miss Cal. I miss him every single day of my life. It had gotten to be a rotten marriage, and I miss him terribly."

"Involvement doesn't have to be good or bad. It just is. It exists. And when it stops, it leaves emptiness."

"Something happens, and I think how I'll have to tell Cal about that. Then I know I can't. Oh, hell."

She began to weep, without particular emphasis. Gentle tears for a rainy night. When they subsided she began an imitation of need, a faking of desire. But the textures of her mouth were unconvincing. The storm time had worn us both out. I was glad she did not persist, as male pride would have made the responsive effort obligatory. The second storm was upon us, the wet wind blowing across weary bodies. I covered us with the sheet. The lightning once again took still pictures of the room, of her head on the pillow beside me. After the crashing downpour turned to a diminishing rain, she slept. When the rain stopped I slipped out of the bed, closed the draperies, groped my way into my clothes, and left without awakening her, testing the door to be sure it had locked behind me.

The storm had knocked the power out. There were stars in half the sky. My eyes were accustomed to darkness. I found the path without difficulty and walked between the black shapes of shrubbery, down the slope past the office, and out onto the dock.

Meyer had locked the *Flush* and gone to bed. I found the right key by touch. In the darkness of the lounge I gave my left shin a nasty rap against the new coffee table. I limped to the head and, by darkness, took a long hot sudsy shower. The great bed swallowed me up like a toad flicking a fly into the black belly.

15

B Y the time I came out to fix my breakfast, Meyer was having his second cup of coffee.

"You are running for office?" he asked.

"I thought you knew I owned a white shirt and a tie."

"I guess I'd forgotten."

"I want to look safe and plausible."

"To whom?"

I poured my orange juice and selected a handful of eggs.

"Five eggs?" he asked.

"These are the super supreme extra large eggs, which means they are just a little bit bigger than robin eggs. Stop all this idle criticism and take a look at the back of my head, please. I took the dressing off."

I sat on my heels. He came from the booth and stood behind me and turned my head toward the light. "Mmm. Looks sort of like the stitching on a baseball. Nice and clean, though. No redness that I can see."

He went back to his coffee. I broke the eggs into the

small skillet, sliced some sharp cheddar and dropped it in, chopped some mild onion and dropped it in, folded that stuff in with a fork, took a couple of stirs, and in a couple of minutes it was done.

When I sat down to my breakfast Meyer said, "You were saying?"

"I'm saying something new now. We've been playing with a short deck. With a card missing, the tricks won't work. Maybe it is a variation of your invisible planet theory. I'll describe the missing card to you. The Van Harn airplane comes winging through the blue, and in the late afternoon it spots the Bertram off the north shore of Grand Bahama, as before. There are eight or nine bags of gage, plastic-wrapped to keep the water out. They are about a hundred pounds each. Van Harn makes a big circle at an altitude of a couple of hundred feet. The circle is big so that each time he comes around, Carrie has time to pull and tug and wrestle one of the bags to the passenger door and shove it out on his signal. That would be the way to do it, right? Nine passes. They hope to drop them close enough so they can be picked up quickly with a little maneuvering and a boat hook. Cal Birdsong and Jack Omaha are busily and happily hooking the bags aboard. Probably Birdsong is running the boat and Omaha is doing the stevedore job. Van Harn and Carrie are having a dandy time too. A little bit of adventure, a nice piece of money, and all the bugs have been worked out of the system. The payoff is big. Have you got the picture?"

"It seems plausible. What are you getting at?"

"Cindy told me that a week before he died Cal had a nightmare about something falling out of the sky and killing him."

I saw Meyer's face change. I saw the comprehension, the nod, the pursing of lips.

"One drop was too good," he said.

"And Jack Omaha was careless. He wasn't watching. He was maybe leaning to get the boat hook into a floating bag. There would be a hell of a lot of impact. A good guess would be that it hit him in the back of the head and snapped his neck. And all of a sudden it wasn't a party any more. It wasn't fun any more."

Nodding, Meyer spoke in an introspective monotone. "So Birdsong wired weights to the body and dropped it into the deeps, after dark. Van Harn flew back to the ranch with Carrie. When Birdsong was due in, she was waiting here at the marina with one of the little panel trucks. Birdsong loaded the sacks into the truck. They got their stories straight. She drove to Fifteen Hundred where the truck was unloaded and Walter J. Demos paid her off. She drove the truck down to Superior Building Supplies. She had probably left her car there. She put the money into the safe and took her share, because she knew the game was over. And she brought her share to you to hold. Travis, how do you read Van Harn's reaction?"

"Sudden total terror. I don't think the money mattered one damn to him any more. Marrying Jane Schermer would take care of the money problem forevermore. He knew he had been taking a stupid chance, perhaps rebelling against a career of fronting for Uncle Jake and his good old boys. He would know that if it all came out, it would finish him. It wasn't a prank. He was involved in the death of a prominent local man while committing a felony. Good old Jack Omaha of

Rotary, Kiwanis, and the Junior Chamber. He wouldn't even keep his ticket to practice law. So I think that all of a sudden he was very anxious to please Uncle Jake."

"The eyewitnesses were Carrie Milligan and Cal Birdsong."

"Exactly, Meyer. A hustling lady and a drunk. I just thought of something else: Freddy's matinee with Chris Omaha. There probably isn't a better way of finding out how much the lady knows about anything. He wanted to know how much Jack had told her about the smuggling, or if he had told her anything at all. He evidently hadn't."

"And the burgled apartment?" Meyer said.

"Same reason. Find and remove any written evidence."

"What about Joanna and the bomb?"

"That won't make any sense until we know more."

"If you can ever make sense out of a bomb. The Irish tried it. Except for the people getting killed, it's turned into a farce to amuse the world. The Irish have forgotten why they set off bombs, if indeed they ever knew. It's probably because there's so damned little else to do in that dreary land."

"You won't be popular in Ireland."

"I've never had any urge to go back, thank you."

"Joanna came aboard bearing goodies. A little feast left off at the cottage for her. Meyer, we were both moving toward her as she started to open the box. If she had been a string-saver, a careful untier of knots, we'd both be dead. But she was the rip and tear type. God, I can still smell the stink of explosion in here."

"I know. It's a little less every day."

After I finished off the eggs, I answered his first question. "I am going to visit the brilliant young attorney at his place of business. And I may have to see Judge Schermer. And I may have to see the Judge's niece."

"With what objective?"

"Application of pressure."

"What do you want me to do?"

"Be right here where I can get you if and when I need you."

Cindy Birdsong was alone in the office when I walked up there from the docks. She got up from the desk and came around the end of the counter quickly, then glanced guiltily out of each of the windows before tiptoeing to be kissed. A brief kiss, but very personal and emphatic. "You sneaked away," she said.

"Like a thief in the night."

"I slept like dead. I woke up and didn't know where I was or who I was, darling."

"I'll try to keep track."

She became more brisk and businesslike as she backed away from me. "Something strange, Travis. Jason was supposed to tend the office this morning. Ollie says he isn't around. And Ritchie has got some kind of a bug."

"Where does Jason stay?"

"He and Ollie have been living aboard the *Wanderer*. Over there at the end. It's ours . . . mine, I mean. But she needs new engines and an awful lot of other things."

I could see that the *Wanderer* was an old Egg Harbor fly bridge sedan, white hull and a rather unhappy shade of green topsides, something under forty feet in length.

Ollie came into the office, round, brown, and sweat-shiny, and gave me a good morning and gave Cindy a dock slip and said, "I put that Jacksonville Hatteras in Thirty-three instead of Twenty-six. It's new and he can't handle it worth a damn. It's easier to get in and out of Thirty-three. Okay?"

"Of course."

"They'll sign in personally when they get it hosed down. They're very fat people, both of them. Not real old. Just fat."

"Oliver," I said, "do you think Jason took off for good?"

He stared at me. "Why would he do that?"

"I don't know. He's missing. That's one possibility, isn't it?"

"I didn't think of him exactly as being missing, Mr. McGee."

"Did you notice if his personal gear was gone?"

"I didn't even think to look."

"Could we take a look right now?"

He looked at Cindy and when she nodded he said, "Why not?"

We both stepped aboard the *Wanderer* at the same moment, making it rub and creak against the fenders. As we went below Oliver said, "We slept here in the main cabin, Jason in the port bunk and me over here. If anybody was entertaining anybody, the other person slept up in the bow. There's two bunks up there. You can see that he slept in his bunk at least for a while and

. . . you know something? I don't see his guitar any-place."

We checked the locker and stowage area. His personal gear was gone.

"What kind of car does he have?"

"No car. A bicycle. Ten speed. Schwinn Sports Tourer. Blue. He keeps it chained to a post behind the office under the overhang. His duffel bags are the kind that hang off the back rack on a bike. Panniers, they call them. The guitar has a long strap so that he can sling it around his shoulder so it hangs down his back. He loves that bike. He does the whole bit. Toe straps. Racing saddle. Hundred miles a day. That's how come those fantastic leg muscles."

I sat on Jason's bunk and said, "I don't even know his last name."

"Breen. Jason Breen," he said, sitting facing me.

"Okay to work with?"

"Sure. Why?" He looked defiant.

"How much do you really know about him?"

"What business is it of yours?"

"The boss lady has had enough trouble, don't you think?"

He looked uncertain. "I know. But what has that—?"

"Jason could have done something very bad and very stupid, because he thought he was helping Mrs. Birdsong. I want to get a reading from you about his capacities. You strike me as being very bright and observant, Ollie."

He blushed. "Well, not as bright as Jason. He reads very heavy things and he has very heavy thoughts."

"About what?"

"Free will, destiny, reincarnation. Stuff like that."

"What kind of person is he?"

Oliver pondered, his forehead wrinkling. "Well, he's a mixture. He likes to be with people. People like him. When there's a group, people end up doing what he wants to do without him having to push. When he's having a good time, everybody is having a good time, and when he isn't, nobody is. At the same time he's a loner. You never really know what he's thinking. He does nice things for people without making a big fuss about it. The ladies really like him a lot. You saw how he sort of stepped in and took care of Carrie's sister, Susan. Got her on the plane and everything. About doing anything wrong, I don't think he'd do anything he thought was wrong. But there would be no way in God's world of stopping him from doing something if he thought it was right."

"Did he have a thing about Mrs. Birdsong?"

Oliver blushed more deeply. "No more than . . . anybody. I mean she's a very decent person. And she looks . . . so great. And Cal was such a son of a bitch to her. Really dirty mean. He's no loss to anybody."

"Except to her. She misses him."

"That's her, all right. She's the kind of a person who could even forgive that rotten bastard. Look, I know what's going on with you two. If you give her a hard time, I'm going to take my best shot."

"I think you really would."

"Believe it."

"What do you think is going on, anyway?"

"Jason told me. He's never wrong about things like that. He sleeps a couple of hours at a time. He prowls around a lot. He always knows what's going on over at the cottage and on the boats and in the motel and the whole neighborhood."

"How did he act about it when he told you? Just how did he tell you? Can you remember the words?"

"Close enough. I came in the other night and he was in the bunk reading and he looked over and said, 'McGee is screwing Cindy.' It was just a statement of fact. It stung me, you know. I said you were a bastard to be laying her so soon after Cal died, and he told me that was a sentimental and stupid attitude. I couldn't tell what he thought about it."

"Current girl friend?"

"He hasn't got any particular person at the moment that I know of. He goes over and sees Betty Joller. You know, she's alone in the cottage now. Unless she can get somebody to come in with her, a couple of girls, she can't swing the rent and upkeep."

"Wasn't there another girl there?"

"Two. Nat Weiss and Flossie Speck. After the bombing, Nat went back to Miami and Floss decided to try it out in California. She was bored with her job here anyway. She was working for the phone company."

"Didn't Jason have something going with Carrie and with Joanna?"

"Probably. Sure. It wouldn't be any great big deal in either direction. It would just have to be the right time and place is all, and it would just happen."

"Would Carrie have confided in him?"

"What about?"

"Anything that might have bugged her."

"I don't see why not. People talk to Jason about the goddamnedest things. He doesn't pass it along. You know you can tell him things. Funny, come to think of it, how he never tells things about himself to other people. I guess he's had a hard life. He was in foster homes. They took him away from his own folks because they nearly killed him beating him. He wasn't even two years old. That's the only thing he did ever tell me. He had about six broken bones. Maybe more. I forget."

"Did the storms wake you up last night?"

"Hell, yes!"

"Was Jason in this bunk?"

"Let me think. No, he wasn't. I could see in the flashes of lightning. I mean it wasn't anything unusual. He's always roaming around by himself. Or visiting people. He's a very restless person."

"But he's been here two years, ever since they opened."

"I don't mean restless like that. We've talked about moving on, but we never do. You get kind of hooked. Boats and water and working outside mostly."

"But now he's packed his gear and moved on."

"I can't believe he'd just go without a word. But maybe he would. Maybe he would. He'd have pay coming. I don't know why he'd leave without picking up his pay. Maybe he figures on sending for it. Or maybe he didn't leave. Maybe he moved into the cottage."

"Want to check that out for me?"

"For myself too. Sure."

As I walked slowly back to the office, alone, I could guess at what would convince Jason Breen it was time to pack and leave. If he had been under the open awning windows, crouched a couple of feet from the bed, he would have heard a conversation about Cal's murder. A little bonus for the restless voyeur of the marina. A little lead time on the blue bike. I wondered if he had sheathed his guitar in rain-proof plastic.

I briefed Cindy and we waited for Oliver. He came back panting for breath, overheated. "Not there," he said. "Betty hasn't . . . gone to work yet. She said . . . she hasn't . . . seen Jason."

After Oliver left Cindy said, "You don't suppose Jason . . . could have listened?"

"Could be. He'd know you were going to talk to Scorf."

"But does a person . . . flee on a bicycle?"

"A person flees on what they have at hand, if they are anxious to flee."

"It makes me feel . . . sort of rotten to think anybody could have been listening."

"Ollie says Jason did a lot of prowling."

"But he seemed so nice!"

"We like the people who like us."

"I suppose. Rats. Phone call? Sure. Here's the book."

I phoned the offices of Frederick Van Harn, Attorney-at-Law, in the Kaufman Building. A soft-voiced girl answered by speaking the number I had just dialed.

"May I speak to Mr. Van Harn, please?"

"Who is calling?"

"A certain Mr. McGee, my dear."

"Is it a business call or a personal call?"

"Let's say business."

"He won't be in the office today."

"Out of town?"

"No, sir. He won't be in today."

"Where can I get in touch with him?"

"You could phone here tomorrow, Mr. McGee."

"What if I said personal instead of business?"

"You already picked one, sir."

"Is he out at the ranch? What's the number there, please?"

"Sorry, sir. That is an unlisted number. You can reach him here tomorrow morning."

I thanked her and hung up. I wondered vaguely if Freddy was stupid enough to be making another run to Jamaica and decided he wasn't. I asked Cindy if she could aim me toward the Van Harn ranch. She was blank on that, but she knew the road to take to get to Jane Schermer country, out amongst the grapefruits, and Meyer had told me they were adjacent.

I threw jacket and tie into the back seat of the bright little oven, opened all windows, and headed a little bit south and then turned west on Central Avenue. At first it was a six-lane avenue fringed with motels, the Colonel's chicken, steak houses, gift shops, dress shops, savings and loans, and small office buildings. After a few blocks of this, I was in used-car country speckled with tired old shopping centers and convenience stores. After a mile or so of that, the road became divided and I went through a long expanse of decaying residential. The pseudo-Moorish and old frame houses had once been impressive—and expensive. They were cut up into apartments and rooming houses. The yards were rank and littered, and the palms in the medial strip looked sickly. The road became two lane, and I went through an area of huge new shopping centers and small dreary-looking developments where, on the flat-lands, the developers had peeled off every tree and had big bonfires before putting in the boxy little houses. As these dwindled I saw For Sale signs on raw acreage, and at about nine miles from where I had made my turn, I came to the first ranchlands, with some Brahman, some Black Angus, some Charolais. Windmills flapped near the water holes. Salt blocks were set out in little open sheds. Where there were trees, the cattle had eaten the bottoms of the boughs off in a straight line, so that at a distance it had something of the look of African landscape.

There was more contour to the land on the right of the road, and more of that was used for geometric groves, laid out with a painful precision. I saw some spray trucks working in the groves, tall booms hissing white into the trees, agitating the leaves and the young fruit.

Big trucks used the narrow road and used it fast. Their windy wake snapped at my little rental. The landscape was beginning to turn a rich and glorious green with the heavy rains. Kingfishers sat on high wires, looking optimistically down into the drainage ditches. Grease-fat bugs burst on my windshield.

The entrance was so inconspicuous I nearly missed it. The narrow driveway was marked with two gray posts. A varnished sign not much larger than a license tag was nailed to one post, saying V-H Ranch. The entrance drive was lumpy and muddy. Wire fencing was snugged close on each side of it. Ahead was a distant grove of pines. On either side was a hell of a lot of empty space, flat as a drafting table, with some faraway clots of cattle wavering in the heat shimmer. The fencing on both sides turned away from the road just before the grove. The grove was a huge stand of ancient lob-lolly, home for hawk and crow and mockingbird and some huge fox squirrels which menaced me with fang and gesture of profane chatter. Once through the grove I could see the house a couple of hundred yards away, spotted in the middle of giant live oaks hung with moss.

It was squarish, two stories, with two broad verandas which encircled it completely, one at each level. Steep tin roof, big overhang. Porch furniture. The house looked rough and comfortable. A pair of dogs came around the corner of the house at a full run, arfing to-ward me. They were part German shepherd, but broader across chest and brow. One put his feet up on the side of the yellow Gremlin and grinned at me, tongue lolling. He lifted his lips to show me more tooth and made a sound like a big generator running in a deep basement. My window was up before he could draw breath.

An old man came out onto the porch, shaded his eyes, and then put fingers in his mouth and blew a piercing blast which silenced birds and dogs and could possibly have stopped traffic on the distant highway. The dogs backed away and dwindled. They walked sideways, knees bent, tails tucked under. They swal-lowed, lapped their jowls, and looked apologetic.

"Git on out back!" he yelled, and they did git, in scuttling fashion. Then he stood on the porch, feet planted, arms crossed, and waited for me to approach, and waited for me to say the first word. He was a tall scrawny bald man with tufts of white over his ears. He was all strings, except for his watermelon belly, and he wore crisp khakis and new blue sneakers.

"It's nice to see animals pay attention," I said.

"They know I kicks their ass nine feet in the air ef'n they don't. State your business."

"I would like to see Mr. Van Harn."

"Sorry."

"He isn't here?"

"I didn't say that, did I?"

"Then he is here?"

"He could be."

"My name is Travis McGee. To whom am I speaking?"

"I'm Mr. Smith."

"Mr. Smith, your loyalty is commendable. I would like you to take a short message to Mr. Van Harn. I think he will want to talk to me."

"I don't know as I want to do that. He's in a real bad temper this morning. He had to shoot Sultan. Busted his fool leg. Fifteen-thousand-dollar horse. He don't want no help with it. He's got a backhoe down there, and a jeep with a blade, and he's burying that fool horse by himself. He sent Rowdy and the boys off to string fence. Wants to be alone with the fool dead horse. I don't want to mess into that, Mister McGee."

"The message is very important to him."

Smith studied me for long long seconds. This was a character reading. "You say you snuck by here after I told you to git?"

"I put my car back in the pines and snuck by. Where did I go to when I snuck by, Mr. Smith?"

"You followed the ruts there to the side of the house. Two hundred yards, you came to a plank bridge. Cross it and turn left past a stand of live oaks and you can see the stables and some storage sheds, and past that the hangar and the landing strip. He'll be on high ground right across from the stables. You'll see the backhoe and jeep before you can make him out."

"Mr. Smith?"

"Yes."

"What about those dogs?"

He took me around the house. The dogs crawled forward and I extended my hand. They both snuffed my hand. "Leave him alone, hear?" Smith roared. The dogs nodded. "They won't bother you none," he said.

Smith was right. I saw the vehicles first. The yellow jeep with a front-end blade was crawling slowly across the infield of a rough track, dragging the glossy red-brown body toward the slight rise and the cabbage palms at the far side, where the backhoe stood near a large mound of dirt.

Van Harn saw me walking toward him and stopped the jeep.

"What are you doing here, McGee? How'd you get past the house?"

"Smith told me to get lost. I parked in the pines and snuck around. Sorry about your horse."

He had wrapped chain around the hind legs and fastened it to the tow hook on the back of the jeep. The great head of the horse was at rest. I had seen it bobbling across the stubble. The visible eye bulged nastily from the socket. The shot had been perfectly centered, above and between the eyes, making a caked mess of the brown gloss. A swarm of bluebottle flies settled onto the horse when the jeep stopped. He was a grotesque parody of a horse at a full run, front legs reaching, back legs extended, head high.

"What do you want?"

"I tried the office first."

"What do you want?"

"Why don't you go ahead and bury the horse and then . . ."

"What do you want?"

He wanted the leverage right away, right in the blazing sun of midmorning, in the infield of his little track. He wore big oval sunglasses, aviator type, and a white canvas cap. He was stripped to the waist. He wore dirty khaki pants and old white boat shoes. I was surprised at how tanned his body was, and how slender and fit he looked. Thin tough musculature made ridges and knots under the tan hide at each slight move. He had a medallion of black hair in the middle of his chest, big as a saucer, turning into a thin line of black hair that disappeared behind his brass belt buckle.

Plausibility is the key. I said, "When we had our little talk in the limousine, there was an area we didn't get to."

"Such as?"

"Uncle Jake offered me twenty-five thousand to pack and leave. I wanted to talk to you about whether it is all the traffic will bear."

"It sounds like too much as it is. What can you do?"

"I can put things together. Carrie gave me enough to go on. It's a case of filling in the blanks."

"Blanks?"

"Such as who decided to fasten ballast to Jack Omaha and drop him in the sea after he got hit by the bag of grass when you and Carrie were air-dropping the stuff to Cal and Jack aboard the *Christina III*."

He opened his mouth and closed it, opened it again, and said, "You lost me on the first curve, McGee."

"I think you waited too long."

"Maybe I did. I've got to bury Sultan." He started the jeep up and once more the big head bounced along the ground, tongue protruding between the big square teeth. I followed along at walking speed. He went to the left of the big hole, as close as he could get to it, and cut to the right as soon as he was past it. When he stopped, the horse lay with his back at the edge of the hole. He backed to slack off on the chain, got out and unfastened it from the jeep and the horse's legs, and dropped it into the jeep. Next he bent and picked up the hind legs and pushed at them, rolling the horse onto its back. It slipped over the edge of the hole and fell four feet, turning the rest of the way over, gases bursting out of its body as it thudded against the bottom.

I backed out of the way when he got back into the jeep, after setting the blade to its low position, and began shoving dirt into the hole. It was pale dirt, a mix of sand, topsoil, and surface limestone which contained billions of small fossil shells.

A buzzard began a big lazy circle overhead. I squinted up at it against blue sky, wondering how it knew. The abrupt roaring of the jeep shocked me out of my stupid trance. The onrushing blade was a yard from my legs by the time I took a frantic sideways leap, like a man going into second base in a headlong slide. I sprawled and rolled and came up onto my feet with the jeep right behind me. I feinted one way and dived the other way, came to my feet, and ran around to the other side of the horse grave.

He idled down and stopped. Oval lenses looked at me from under the stubby bill of the white cap.

"You move good for the size of you," he said.

"Thanks. And what's one more dead person?"

"At this point in time, not very much."

"But you can't make it, not the way you've tried to make it, Freddy. You dropped the rock in the water, and you can't move around fast enough to flatten out all the ripples."

"I can give it a goddamn good try. I didn't know if you had a gun. I guess you don't."

"I should have. It was an oversight."

"Final mistake."

"What was Carrie's final mistake?"

He seemed puzzled. "Mistake? Walking in front of a truck?"

"Didn't you close her mouth for good?"

"Didn't have to. Carrie was bright. She was involved in Jack's death too, you know. And she had less leverage than I have."

It was convincing. I felt confused. I couldn't see him as the murderer of Cal Birdsong or the builder of the bomb which killed Joanna. So why was he so obviously intent on doing away with me?

"I think we ought to talk," I said.

"Make your move."

"What move? Run for it? How far would I get?"

He gunned the jeep toward the right. I lunged to the left, dipping to scoop up a handful of ancient oyster shells from the pile of dirt. They were thick, calcified and heavy, dating back to the time when the V-H Ranch had been on the bottom of a shallow sea. I wound up quickly, stuck my leg in the air, threw a shell with a followthrough that brought my knuckles to within an inch of the ground. I really whistled it, but it curved low and outside, missing his right shoulder narrowly. He backed away quickly and, out of range, stood up and pulled the windshield up and fastened the wing nuts before rolling back to position.

"That was very cute," he said.

"Freddy, I've talked to a lot of people about you."

"I'm sorry about that. But it doesn't change anything."

"Your odds are impossible already."

"You don't know how bad they really are, McGee. But they are the only odds I've got, and it's the only game there is."

I tossed the other shells away. They weren't going to help me. I could guess what he would do. He would start circling that big grave as fast as he could go. I could stay out in front but not for long, not in such heat. And as soon as I slowed, or headed for the trees or the stables, he'd have me. I didn't have much time to do any thinking.

In such a situation it is difficult to believe it is completely serious. A yellow jeep is a jolly vehicle. Pastureland is not menacing. The hour before noon is not a likely time for dying. It was some odd game of tag, and when it ended the eventual loser would congratulate the winner. Let's try it again someday, pal.

But it was real. A jeep with or without a blade is a lethal weapon. I could tell from the way it tracked that he had it in four-wheel drive. He was skilled, and the jeep was agile.

I thought of alternatives and discarded them as fast as they came up. I could head across the field and try to trap him into a circle out in the open. I could turn a smaller circle than he and maybe get near enough to the side of the jeep to jump him. No chance. He would read it, accelerate out of the circle, and swing around and come back at me. Or I could slow him enough, maybe, to go up over the blade and hood and drop in on him. But how do I slow him down that much?

Suddenly I thought of one slim chance. If I couldn't make it work, I was going to be no worse off. I was going to be dead. And if I didn't try it, I was going to be dead. A mockingbird flew over, singing on the wing, a melody so painfully sweet it pinched the heart. I do not want to leave the world of mockingbirds, boats, beaches, ladies, love, and peanut butter from Deaf Smith County. Especially do I not want to leave it at the hands of a fool, at the hands of this Van Harn who thought he could wipe out an event by killing anybody who knew anything about it. It has been tried. It never works. Any lawyer should know that.

I had to get him going counterclockwise around the horse grave. So I moved to my left and he gunned the motor and took the bait. He came on so fast he gave me a very bad moment. The big hole was a sloppy rectangle about ten feet by eight feet. Before I could get my feet untangled and get around the first corner, he nearly clipped me. He had shoved about three blade loads in on top of the dead horse, and so that side was filled to within about two feet of the original ground level, the whole front half of the horse still uncovered.

He pressed me. I had to lope around pretty good, with a constant fear I might slip and fall on the corners. He held it in an almost continuous controlled skid, the back wheels staying farther away from the hole than the front wheels. His reasoning was obvious. In such heat I could only make so many circuits. I had to make enough circuits to lull him. The sweat was running into my eyes. Each time I passed the decision point, I mentally rehearsed exactly how to do it. And I had to do it soon, before I was exhausted.

At last I felt ready. I rounded the corner, dropped down two feet onto the loose dirt, spun and leapt up beside the jeep, and dived for the top of the wheel. He tried to accelerate but I was able to stretch the necessary few inches. I snapped my right hand onto the top of the wheel and pulled it hard over, toward me. The jeep swerved into the horse grave, dropped, and piled into the straight side of the hole, over where it was deeper.

The left rear fender had popped me in the side of the thigh, throwing me into a deep corner of the hole, in considerable torment. I scrabbled and pulled myself up and saw Van Harn fold slowly sideways out of the jeep. The four wheels were still turning, settling it deeper, and then it stalled out.

His legs were still hung up in the jeep. One eye was half open, the other closed. He had a high white knot in the middle of his forehead, growing visibly. I hobbled to him and bent over him. He hit me in the mouth and knocked me back into the same corner of the hole. Before I could get up, he sprang out of the hole and went racing toward the backhoe. I came lumping along behind him, with no hope of closing the distance.

He went to the back of it and wrenched a spade out of some spring clips, a spade I wished I had seen earlier.

He darted to meet me and swung the spade, blade edgeways, at my middle. During my screeching halt I managed to suck my stomach back out of the way. He swung back the other way, from left to right, aiming at my head. I couldn't back away in time. I dropped under it, dropped to my hands and knees, felt it whip the hair at the crown of my head. That made everything real and deadly. A tenth of a second faster and he would have cleaved my skull.

From knuckles and knees I launched myself forward, getting one foot under me, coming up under him like a submarining guard, getting a shoulder tucked cozily into his gut, clapping an arm around his heels as he tried to bicycle backward. He smacked down hard and lost his spade. I crawled up him, straddled him. He was yipping, bucking, writhing. I didn't want to break my hands on the bones of his skull or face. I came down with a forearm across his throat, my other hand locked on my wrist for leverage. I tucked my face into the curve of my arm as protection from his flailings. After a frantic spasm he fluttered a little and went still. I kept the pressure on to be sure of him. Then I rolled off and got onto my knees and sat back on my heels, blowing hard. His white cap lay nearby. I picked it up and wiped the sweat off my face and out of my eyes.

His face was puffy and suffused with blood. His chest was moving. It seemed very quiet out there in that pastureland. I listened to the songs of the midday bugs and the liquid call of a distant meadowlark. Time to wrap him up and make delivery.

16

WHEN at last I felt partially restored and was not gagging with each breath, I got up onto my feet. My right thigh was cramping with the muscle bruise the jeep had given me. I managed a deep knee bend without screaming, and the second one did not hurt quite as much.

The jeep offered the best chance of something with which I could tie him up. I trudged toward the horse grave. If he could have come the whole distance across grass, he would have had me. He had to cross some of that dirt from the hole. The brittle limestone crackled under his running feet. I jumped sideways, ducked, and spun all in a single terrified bound. I heard the spade hiss past my head. His momentum carried him toward the hole. He tried to turn, tripped, stumbled, fell and rolled down the slope, and ended up beside the jeep.

I was after him quickly and got there as he lifted the spade over his head. I reached up and got hold of the handle. As soon as I had the handle he let go of it and hit me three very fast and very good shots. He had screwed his feet into the dirt. He had very good leverage, and he was too able to attempt the roundhouse blows of the beginner. He slammed them home, very close straight shots. They darkened the sky. The spade slid out of my hand. I stepped into him and hugged him like a big sick bear. I bore him down and suddenly he was in back of me instead of in front of me. I was on my hands and knees in the soft dirt and he had a wiry arm locked around my throat.

My air was shut off. Dazed as I was, I could not get the leverage to get out of that position or to throw him off. I tried to crawl to the jeep. He somehow held me back. I scraped with both hands like a dog digging a hole as I tried to plunge forward. The world swam. My lungs heaved against the obstruction. I began to feel a lazy floating pleasure. Oxygen starvation. Rapture of the deeps. I folded down and with darkening sight stared into the hole I had dug with my hands. I saw a piece of blue pipe, very pretty blue pipe. And just under it, as in some grotesque still life, I saw an unmistakable segment of suntanned wrist, dirt caught in the sun-bleached curling hair.

The dimming brain works slowly and with difficulty. Clean blue tubing. An azure blue. The size used for a bicycle frame. And why was that fellow under it, under the dry dirt that had come from a hole too deep for all the recent rain to reach? There was a stupid rhyme in the fading brain: Jason Breen and his Azure Machine.

The realization pierced the darkness that was closing in on me. What happened in my mind was not fright, not anger. It was an overwhelming dismay. A veritable crescendo of dismay, enough to galvanize my slackening body into a few moments of a terrible, terminal strength. I will never know how I was able to come to my feet with Van Harn plastered to my back. I took a single wobbly step and then fell toward the jeep, turning as I fell, so that I smashed him against the metal. I rebounded onto hands and knees, the stricture gone from my throat. I stretched out and breathed until the shadows lightened and the sun came out again. In sudden fright I pushed myself up and spun around. Freddy lay on his side.

I had the feeling he was going to bound to his feet and we were going to have to do it all over again, as if he were some mythological creature which could not be slain.

First I got the chain from the jeep. I rolled him onto his face, and chained his wrists together, tying a clumsy knot, and used the surplus to chain his ankles.

Then I knelt by the hole and carefully pulled the dirt away until I could see a hand, and most of a forearm, and more of the tubing of the blue bicycle.

From the angle, the rest of him was under the jeep, and under a foot of dirt. Somewhere under there could be found the stillness of the Jesus face, the wire glasses, the crushed guitar, the brown legs sturdy with the bicycle muscles. And somewhere in his head, lost forever in the death of the synapses, were the jellied memories of why he had come out here and what Van Harn had done to him. The idea had been splendid. Dig a big hole and bury the body under a horse. Who would ever look farther than the horse?

I dragged Van Harn up the slope toward the back of the jeep and left him in the shade of the rear overhang. I felt his throat. The pulse was strong and regular. Except for the knot on his forehead, there wasn't a mark on his face. The left side of my underlip felt like half a hot plum. When I opened my mouth to yawn width, experimentally, the hinges creaked. I had a dull headache behind my eyes. He could blow them in pretty good. His dark glasses were missing. I looked around and found them, stomped flat.

Just as I climbed out of the hole I heard the oncoming drumbeat of a galloping horse. It was one great big dark brown horse, and she looked good in her cowgirl hat, yellow shirt, and twill britches. But when she pulled it up short and slid off, she turned back into Jane Schermer, with pudding face, minimal neck, and neuter body.

"Smith said Frederick had to shoot . . ." She saw Freddy in the shade of the jeep. "What are you doing to him?"

"Nothing, at the moment. But he's kept me pretty busy."

"Get that chain off him at once!"

"First come take a look at this."

She hesitated, then dropped down into the hole. She had let the reins hang free. The big horse made munching and ripping sounds in the stubbly grass. I pointed to the hole, big around as a bushel basket and half as deep, with the arm and hand and the portion of blue bike in the bottom of it.

She stared and sprang back and turned quickly, making a shallow, gagging little coughing sound. "Who? What—"

"I'm pretty sure it's Jason Breen. He worked at Westway Harbor Marina."

"But did you . . ."

"Did I? For God's sake! Sure, I came out here and sort of borrowed that backhoe, which I don't know how to operate. Then I dug this big son of a bitch of a hole. Then I put Jason and all his gear in the bottom of said hole and covered him over good. Then I shot this horse and . . . look. Forget it."

"But Frederick couldn't have done it."

"Lady Jane, I don't think there's anything in this world that you or I could think of that Freddy wouldn't do, if he happened to feel like it."

She hustled over and knelt by Freddy. She felt his forehead with the back of her hand. She put her ear against his bare chest to hear his heart. She stood up and looked at the visible half of the horse. "Poor darling," she said softly. "Poor Sultan. Poor beast. My Graciela foaled him. He grew up on my place. I gave him to Frederick."

"That's nice."

She went to the front legs of the horse, lifted, and tested with strong hands. "Must be a hind leg," she said. "Take that stupid chain off of Frederick right away!"

"I don't think it's a hind leg either."

She stared at me. "What do you mean?"

"I think Freddy needed a dead horse."

"He has other horses here. Sultan was valuable."

"He needed a dead horse that was so valuable and he liked so much that it made sense for him to send his ranch hands off on other work while he took care of it himself."

"What makes you think a hind leg isn't broken?"

"I watched him slide it up to the edge of the hole and roll it in. By then he didn't care what I saw because he had already decided to put me in the hole next to Jason. Under the horse."

"You make him sound like a . . . Could you uncover those back legs? Please?"

I walked over and got the spade and went to work. Once I got into the rhythm of it, it didn't take long. Before I finished, her fool horse finally caught on to the fact there was a dead horse in the area. He came over and stared into the hole, then screamed and backed away, shaking his head, rolling his eyes, and clacking his teeth. Jane hustled and caught him and led him all the way to the trees and tied him to a branch and left him there, squealing and pawing at the ground.

She hunkered down and checked each back leg in turn, then stood up and dusted her hands and climbed up out of the hole. I followed her. She looked thoughtfully down at Freddy, and she didn't say anything about the chain.

"I raised Sultan," she said.

"I better go to the house and use the phone."

"Phone?"

"To report a body."

"Oh, of course. There's one in the tack room, an extension. Are you going to leave Frederick . . . like this?"

"I know. That chain looks as if I'm overreacting. But I feel a lot better with it wrapped right where it is."

She looked at me and through me. Her eyes were small and of no particular color. Dull hazel, perhaps. "The things people said about him. I knew they were all lies. They were jealous." She focused on me. "Is this all some kind of terrible trick? Did you shoot Sultan?"

"I am not terribly fond of horses, but I've never shot one."

"I have to believe somebody."

"It might as well be me. Freddy tried to kill me. He made some good tries. He tried with the jeep. He tried with the spade. He tried manual strangulation. He is a very tough animal. He is about twice as strong as he looks."

"Jane?" Freddy said weakly. "Jane, dear?"

"Yes?"

"Help me, please."

"You shot Sultan because he broke his leg?"

"No other choice, dear. Please help me. Unfasten the chain, please."

She moved closer, looking down at him. "I don't think I can help you, darling. I don't think anybody can help you. Just be patient. We're going to make a phone call. You won't have to stay there very long."

I was halfway to the stables and the tack room before I could no longer hear his voice calling her name. She cantered past me when I was almost there. I found the phone while she was shooing her horse into an empty box stall.

Captain Scorf was not available, so I asked for someone to whom I could report a dead body, a murdered body. Then I gave a very simple report and explicit directions.

Jane Schermer sat with her back against the box stall door, her knees hiked up. There was a broad overhang shading the walk which led by the stalls. I sat beside her.

After a long time she said, "They were telling the truth and he was telling the lies."

"What?"

"Nothing. I've been going over things that troubled me, that I asked him about. I've been such a fool."

"That is a very convincing fellow when he wants to sell you."

"I was too easy to sell. I wanted to get married."

"So you'll get married. But not to Freddy."

She turned and looked at me. "Men have never paid much attention to me. I know when it's the money. A person can tell. I wondered about him. I was never sure."

"Maybe it wasn't."

"You're trying so hard to be kind, aren't you? Why would he . . . spoil everything for himself?"

"In big ways, and little ways too, people do that all the time to themselves. We can't stand prosperity. We have to tinker with the machinery."

She looked out across the track at the distant scene, at the canted top half of the yellow jeep. She touched my arm suddenly. "Look!"

I looked out there and saw that Freddy had performed a feat I would have called impossible. With wrists chained behind him and ankles chained together, he had managed to worm his way out from under the back end of the jeep and get himself up out of the hole and onto his feet. He was on the far side of the hole, hopping up and down with terrible demonic energy, managing somehow to retain his balance, though without seeming to make any progress. He was springing high into the air. I thought I heard a distant shouting. Then we saw him fall, roll, and disappear back into the hole.

We both got up. Jane said, "Something's the matter with him."

"I could make you a list."

But she had started off at a flat-out run, too concerned to remember she could ride that big horse out to him. I loped along, feeling the lumpy pain in my thigh with each stride. When we got there she jumped down into the hole where he was flapping and churning around and yelled, "Fire ants! Fire ants! Help me with him."

I think he had five thousand ants on his face, arms, and torso, swarming and biting with that dedicated aggression peculiar to that innocent-looking little red-brown ant.

I jumped down and grabbed him and wrestled him up out of the hole and half carried, half dragged him about forty feet and put him down on the grass. All this while he was moaning, cawing, and whimpering, and Jane was slapping and brushing at the ants. About a hundred turned their eager attentions to me, so after I dropped him I hopped and slapped and brushed until the frequency dropped to a random nip from time to time. They are called fire ants because the bite feels like a very tiny red-hot coal on the surface of your skin.

She kept on getting rid of the ants while I quickly took the chain off ankles and wrists. He had stopped being a dangerous person. Though his gestures seemed weak and uncertain, he was of some help in removing the ants. The ones that were being brushed off were climbing back onto him, so I got him onto his feet and trundled him another fifty feet before he stumbled and fell.

When he was down I pulled his shoes and socks off, undid the brass buckle, and pulled his khaki trousers off. The ants were thick on his legs, way up to the upper thigh and the groin. I pulled his underwear shorts off and wadded them up and used them to brush away the ants. I noted that, dimensionally, he more than lived up to the billing Joanna had given him. I rolled him over and over, away from the area where the brushed-off ants could get back on him.

They are aggressive, these red ants, but they are certainly not the menace the farming fraternity and the petrochemical industry would have us believe. If you stand too near a nest, they will come out and climb up your shoes and sting your ankles. You know immediately, and you move away and knock them off. The bites make little white blisters which, if untended, are likely to fester. The easiest remedy is rubbing alcohol applied as soon as possible after being bitten. Vodka or gin will do.

Ninety-nine out of a hundred fire-ant horror stories are false. Freddy was the one in a hundred. I had never heard of anybody being so completely bitten. We had him free of the ants at last. He made sad weak sounds as he rolled his head from side to side. He was gray and sweaty. I wedged him back into his pants and clinched the big brass buckle.

I now knew why he had been so anxious to do me in. But it seemed idiotic to have killed Jason Breen.

I leaned close to him and said, "Hey! Why did Jason come out here?"

"Money," he said in a dull voice. "Called me at four in the morning on the private line. I chained the dogs. Waited in the grove. Twenty thousand."

"Why?"

"He'd snooped. Figured it all out. Saw the *Christina* come in without Jack. Told me he had killed Cal with a wire and he had to run, and unless I gave him money he'd claim I paid him to kill Cal. I said okay. He was very jumpy. Then he said he was going to beat up on me anyway, on account of what happened with the Dobrovsky girl. He hit me and I hit him. I caught him in the throat. It broke something. He grabbed his throat. Tried to breathe. Fell onto his knees. Made choking noises. Fell over dead in less than two minutes. By dawn light his face was black and his eyes bulged out. I dragged him down to the stables. Wheeled his bike down. Oh, Christ, everything is getting so . . . so far away."

He was looking worse by the moment, face bloating, tongue thickening. His lips were fat. He was close to blacking out.

"He told me once a bee sting can make him real sick," Jane said. "What's *keeping* . . . them."

A moment later we both heard the distant hooting as a cruiser blew its way through the highway traffic. When in another minute it hove into sight around the stand of trees, I stood up and waved my arms at it. It came bounding across the track and the infield, stopped near us, and two deputies piled out, very smart in pale blue shirts, dark blue pants, and trooper hats. They were big, young and ruddy, creaking with equipment.

"Hey, Miz Jane!" one of them said.

"Why, hello, Harvey!"

"Now just who is this here, Miz Jane?"

"You know him! This is Frederick Van Harn."

Harvey stared. "You've got to be kidding," he said in an awed voice. "What in hell *happened* to him?"

"He got into fire ants," I said, "and he's allergic. He's going into shock. Can you get a radio patch through to hospital emergency?"

"Yes, but—"

"You better get on it and tell them you're heading in there wide open. Tell them it's shock from insect bites. They'll know what to have ready. I think it's called anaphylactic shock."

"But—"

Jane stepped closer to him and said, "Maybe you *want* to explain to my Uncle Jake why you let Frederick die?"

That is one of the interesting things about power. Everybody who really has it seems to know exactly how to use it. The ones who pretend to have it make the wrong moves.

While he was on the radio, the other deputy and I lifted Freddy and put him in the back of the cruiser, on his back on the seat. The deputy said, "There's supposed to be a body here?"

"There is."

"Harv, I'll stay here and look into what the call was about. You come back or have them send somebody, okay?"

Jane had gotten in the back and she was kneeling on the floor, holding Freddy's hand. Harvey made a tight circle and went bucketing out of there. We heard him hooting his way down the highway toward the city.

The one left behind said, "Those far ants are mean."

I inspected the bites on the backs of my hands and between the fingers. "They're very convincing."

He took out his notebook. "Who was it phoned in?"

"Me. Travis McGee."

"My name is Simmons. Frank Simmons." He almost started to shake hands and apparently decided it wasn't professional.

"Have you been a deputy long?"

"Just over three weeks. Address, Mr. McGee?"

He wrote the ID information down, slowly and carefully. "Now where'd this dead body be?"

"Over there in that hole."

"Is it a real old dead body? I mean dead long?"

"Only since last night."

We walked to the hole. In a higher voice he said, "That there is a dead *horse!* You funnin' me? What's that jeep doing in there?"

"Frank, there's a small hole I want you to look in, there by the front of the jeep."

He went over and looked down into the smaller hole. There were some flies on the brown arm. He swayed slightly, then whirled and took two big steps and threw up. When he was finished he straightened up slowly and said, "That didn't give me a damn bit of warning. It just come on me all at once."

"It can happen that way."

"This is my first one on duty. Jesus! Look, don't tell Harv about my barfin', okay?"

"I'd have no reason to."

"He rides me. He thinks I won't make it. I'll make it. Now, who discovered the body? You or Miz Schermer or Mr. Van Harn?"

"I discovered it."

"Who put it there?"

"Mr. Van Harn."

"The *hell* you say!" He bent and slapped at his ankles. "Far ants all over the place. Let's get out of this here hole. You think there's a water tap around here anyplace?"

"Over there at the stables."

"Let's us walk over there. Now, you got any idea who the deceased is?"

"I think it is a fellow named Jason Breen."

"From Westway Harbor? With the beard?"

"Right."

"I'll be a son of a bitch," he said softly and stopped long enough to write the name in his notebook.

17

CAPTAIN Harry Max Scorf questioned me at the scene. By the time he was through they had Jason and his bike and his smashed guitar and his duffel bags out of the ground. I followed Scorf over and took a look at the body. The eyes glared up at the sky. The beard was chalked with limestone dust, giving me a hint of what he would have looked like as an old man, had the world given him a chance to live that long.

It had taken Mr. Smith a long time to notice that something was wrong. He came trotting across the field as they were loading Jason. "What are all these damn cars coming in and out? Is that fellow dead? He looks dead. Where is Mister Fred? Who's in charge here anyways?"

Scorf settled Smith down with an admirable economy of word and gesture. Then he suggested that I drive him to the hospital in my rental car, which would give him a chance to go over my story with me once more.

We turned the vent windows so the hot air blew in. I drove slowly. I went through the play-by-play description of our battle again. He chuckled and I told him

251

that it did not seem funny at the time, and it did not get any funnier with the passage of time. I told him that he could maybe think of a nice funny way to tell Uncle Jake that he was going to have to arrest Frederick Van Harn.

"While we're both being funny, McGee, you can tell me how you happened to know that Breen was buried under that dead horse."

"As I said, Captain, I was scrabbling in the dirt, trying to get a purchase, trying to crawl to the jeep so I could grab onto it and stand up. Which I finally did. But I uncovered part of Breen and the bike first."

"It's nothing you can prove, and I want to see just how Van Harn's story matches yours. I'll buy the story about how he killed Jason, because Jane Schermer heard that part of it too. And maybe the autopsy will verify. We know the autopsy verifies the way Birdsong died. But I would be a happier man if I could get a better way to tie Breen to that killing. He was on my list and looking better every day. But it isn't solid."

"I can make you happier. I think Cindy Birdsong will be willing to tell you without much urging that once upon a time after Cal beat her up, Breen went to her and said he could arrange to kill Birdsong very quietly for her. No one would suspect. She was horrified and told him to forget it. The same day I arrived, when Birdsong got ugly with me, he backhanded his wife in the office and knocked her cold. Jason Breen was the one who got to her and picked her off the floor."

He turned in the seat and I could feel him looking at me. "That means that I can't let you go back there alone. You could coach her. I want to come up on her cold with this."

"Captain, what difference does it make anyway? You don't have to build a case against Jason Breen. It doesn't have to stand up in court. It gets Birdsong off your books."

"I am a careful man, McGee. I like people, alive or dead, to get charged with what they did, not what somebody else did."

When we got to the hospital, we were told that Frederick Van Harn was in Intensive Care. I followed Scorf up to the fourth floor. A young doctor was sitting in the small waiting room outside the closed double doors, talking quietly to Jane Schermer. Tears were running down her prematurely middle-aged face. The doctor came and talked to us in the corridor. He said they had tried, but they just couldn't reverse the severe shock, not even with every radical treatment they could think of. He had responded slightly to massive injections of digitalis but had faded again until his heart had stopped and they had been unable to restart it. An intense allergic reaction, he said. Massive fluid imbalance. A pity, he said. Such a young man.

Harry Max Scorf looked indignant. One cannot ask questions of the dead. People were eluding him. He acted as if he thought it was unfair, a kind of trickery.

The murder and the poetic justice of the macabre death made the event a twenty-four-hour sensation. The wire services picked it up. It had the right words. Prominent attorney. Political hopeful. Possible blackmail. Involvement in drug smuggling suspected. Mur-

dered man believed intimate of ex-model recently slain
by bomb aboard houseboat.

But a news story is a fragile thing. It is like a hot air
balloon. It needs a constant additive of more hot air in
the form of new revelations, new actions, new suspicions. Without this the air cools, the big bag wrinkles,
sighs, settles to the ground, and disappears.

Judge Jacob Schermer put the clamp on any flow of
additives. He and his minions spread the word. They
apparently had leverage to use on the local radio stations and the Bayside television station and the mo-
nopoly newspaper. They also had the City and County
Police Department, the banks, the Chamber of Commerce, the service clubs, and every phase of local government.

No one knew a thing about anything. A blank stare
was better than no comment. The reporters who had
come in from Jacksonville, Miami, and Orlando went
hurrying right back out of town toward the next story.
People could barely remember what Van Harn looked
like or what he did. The usual eruption of sick, sad, violent events continued throughout the nation and the
world, like an unending, eternal string of those little
Chinese firecrackers called ladyfingers.

By Saturday morning, when Harry Max Scorf came
to see us aboard the *Flush,* the news story was so dead
it might as well have happened in some other year.

He sat in the cool lounge, took his spotless white hat
off and wiped the sweatband with a bandanna, and
placed it back on his head carefully, at exactly the right
angle.

"My feeling," he said to us, "is that I ought to waltz
you people to and fro and bounce you up and down

gentle-like until you let loose of something that makes sense out of where you fit in this picture. But it's one of those feelings I don't get to enjoy."

"Orders?" I asked.

"The official position is that there's no loose ends at all. Everything is solved and filed away. The Milligan woman was an accident. Jack Omaha lit out for places unknown. Jason kilt the Freeler girl with the bomb and kilt Birdsong with a wire. Then Freddy kilt Jason and the ants kilt him. And that's all she wrote, boys. You two fellas know, just like I know, that it adds up to a crock of shit."

"We really can't help you at all," Meyer said.

He sighed. "Anyway, one thing looks better. There's pretty fair grass coming in at a reasonable price. Somebody has knocked all them amateur wholesalers into a tight line. Some professional outfit has moved in like overnight and took over the whole county. Speaking purely as a cop, it's a relief. It's the amateurs screw everything up. With these pros, I know which way they'll jump, and what will make them jump and what won't. If they keep it tidy, we'll lay back and let it roll. When customs picks up forty-two tons at a time on the Mexican border, it's a signal that it is too big a business to hope to stop entire. If these pros start to get into any heavier action around here, then what we'll do is make their operation so expensive it'll take the cream off, and they'll back off to what they've got right now. It's the amateurs who drive you crazy. That Walter J. Demos would drive anybody crazy, the damned fool. Every time I try to talk to the son of a bitch, he starts crying. He sits down, wraps his arms around his bald head, and starts bellering. What I come by for is to say you can make everybody very happy by going back where you come from, as soon as you can untie your ropes and start your engine."

"This is a roust, Captain?" I asked.

"Not right at this minute, it isn't. It starts to be a roust when I tell somebody you won't move. Then that somebody goes to all the city and county departments that have got anything to do with boats and navigation. Then they come around here and they check you and your boat for every little paragraph in city, county, state, and federal law going back to when Lincoln got shot. Like any boat operating in county waters has got to carry two brass kerosene lanterns at least fourteen inches high as spare equipment, one with green glass and one with red glass, and if you can't show them to the inspector, it's a hundred dollars a day and costs for every day of violation, whether you're tied up or running. That's when it gets to be a roust. Want any more?"

"When you want us to move out, Captain," I said, "you just give the word and we'll move. You've convinced us."

He looked puzzled. "I thought I'd just given you the word."

Meyer cleared his throat and said, "I suppose you could change that official position you described if you could come up with something new?"

Scorf frowned. "It would have to be hard evidence. Very hard. I told you, people want this all forgot. Right now. If anything gets stirred up and it comes to nothing, I am retired with no pension."

"Sometimes you can't help thinking," I said.

"About what?"

Meyer said, "We did a lot of thinking and talking last night, Captain. We decided to check just a little bit further and then bring it to you. But you've rushed us. It's still all theory."

"Theory," he said, and seemed to be looking around for a place to spit.

I said, "Carrie Milligan's share of the ill-gotten gains was a little better than a hundred thousand dollars."

He snapped his head around and stared at me. "That sounds more like a fact than a theory, McGee."

"She gave it to me to hold for her, and to give to her sister if anything happened to her."

"We can come back to that," Scorf said. "Where does it lead you?"

"We had four people in business together. Carrie Milligan, Freddy Van Harn, Jack Omaha, and Cal Birdsong. Carrie had her own kind of twisted integrity. She'd take no more than what was hers. But she was afraid somebody might take her share away from her. With Freddy supplying the plane and Jack supplying the boat, and probably the two of them supplying the financing, would Carrie have been in for a full quarter of the pie? I'd say no. I would say a top of twenty percent. Jack was the banker. He was keeping it in the safe at the business. Carrie was the bookkeeper and courier. New buys were financed out of that money in the safe. When they eventually decided to call it quits, they would have divided it up according to the formula and gone their separate ways. If a hundred thousand equals twenty percent, then there was four hundred thousand left in the safe after she took hers."

"Four hundred thousand!" Scorf said slowly.

"Maybe more," Meyer said. "It is hard to read the

motives of a dead man you never met, but it struck us last night that Jack Omaha was setting himself up for total departure, deserting hearth and home, cashing in everything, even cleaning out the partnership. Maybe he left that money in the safe with the group funds, or maybe he hid it somewhere where he could get to it quickly."

"So maybe he did take off," Scorf said, "and took Van Harn's money and Cal Birdsong's money with him."

"Or, like I told you before, a bag of grass fell on his head and killed him, and that's why Freddy told me that Jason saw the *Christina* come in without Jack Omaha."

Scorf frowned. "So . . . Van Harn would want his money and he'd know where it was and who could give it to him."

I said, "There's a chance he would want to leave it right there for the time being. Jack and Carrie had the combination. Jack was dead and he could trust Carrie. It would be there when he needed it."

"You mean it could still be there?" Scorf asked, frowning in puzzlement.

"Suppose," Meyer said, "that Harry Hascomb walked in on Carrie when she was taking her share out of the pot that night of the day Jack Omaha died. He would know there was big money there, but no way to get to it. Harry was the outside man. Because Omaha and Carrie handled all the accounts and financial records, they would be the only ones who needed to know the combination of the safe. Insurance people like to ask that the number of people with access be kept to a minimum. Two is ideal. Because Harry saw her take the money, it would account for her being uneasy and leaving the money with Travis McGee in Lauderdale. Just in case."

Scorf displayed the quickness of the cop mind by saying, "And after he found out that Omaha was planning to clean him out, and maybe guessed from the Milligan woman's reactions that Omaha was already dead, the simplest way into the safe would be to have the Milligan woman die by accident so he could call the safe company and have them drill it open. It would be the reasonable thing for him to do."

I said, "We can assume Van Harn went there as soon as he heard of Carrie's accident. All Harry would have to do is act totally blank about there being any money in the safe. Van Harn wouldn't dare press it. Besides, Uncle Jake had already taken him out of his financial bind."

Scorf sighed. "All theory. Pretty theory."

"How about some fact?" Meyer asked him. "In the building supply and construction supply business, Hascomb either handled dynamite and caps and wire and batteries or knew how to get what he needed. He was the outside man, not the desk man, and apparently had some mechanical training or ability."

"And," I said, "Joanna Freeler told me she could retire, if she played it right."

"Are you trying to say she could have known that Hascomb killed Carrie, and she would blackm—"

"No! It really shook her when I told her I thought Carrie had been pushed in front of that truck. I think Carrie told Joanna there was a bundle of money in the office safe. They were the only two girls working in that office. And that would give her some leverage to use on Harry Hascomb. That could have been her retirement. If she played it right."

"She didn't play it right," Scorf said.

Meyer said, "We decided last night that if Harry had asked Joanna for a date she would have accepted. They'd had an intimate relationship for several years. Then, if he couldn't keep the date, he could have left off a consolation prize, a box of wine and cheese."

"Loud wine and cheese," Scorf said. He got up and roamed the lounge. He stopped and looked around. "This place was one damn mess when I checked it out. Sickened me. Dead girls get to me. A bomb is a cruel and ugly thing. Any kind of death is cruel and ugly, I guess. Except as a merciful end to pain. The worst are bombs and fire and knives. Look, I know about girls in offices. Jack Omaha and the Milligan woman were the two supposed to have the combination. Bet you a white hat Joanna Freeler knew it too, or knew where Miz Milligan had it wrote down. Know where every damn person in America writes down the combination to a safe? They write it on tape and stick it to the backside or underside of the top middle desk drawer. Half the safe jobs in the country are easy because everybody knows where to look for the combination."

"We don't want to start the voyage home just yet," I said.

"Whatever you've given me, I can handle," he said. "It's all theory. If Joanna let it be known to Hascomb that she accepted the date so they could have a little chat about how the Milligan woman died, she set herself up with wine and cheese."

"If we worked it out right," Meyer said, "it would be . . . gratifying if we could be present when you interview Mr. Hascomb."

Scorf looked bleakly at him. "Gratifying, eh?"

"So few things in life work out neatly, Captain Scorf, it would be reassuring to be in on one that does."

"And you think that this whole mess is neat?"

Meyer looked trouble. "Not in the usual sense of the word."

Scorf thought it over. "It's hardly one damn thing to go on. I don't want a committee, for God's sake. McGee, you can come along with me and watch me mess it up. Meyer, you better stay right here and get this thing ready to move on out into the channel. My orders are clear. I have to get you started on your way. And we'll be back soon."

I had expected Scorf to sit bolt upright behind the wheel of the dark blue unmarked Cougar and fumble it along at a stilted thirty-five. Instead, after he had belted himself in, he tipped his white hat forward to his eyebrows, lounged back into the corner of the driver's seat, put his fingertips on the wheel, and slid through heavy traffic like an oiled eel. He moved to where the holes were, moving the oncoming traffic over, and was able to avoid accelerations, decelerations, and the use of the brakes. He had looked too underprivileged to be an expert, but he was, indubitably. And I said so.

With mirthless smile he said, "I wasted a lot of time and money ramming stocks around the dirt circuits. I felt easy riding with you the other day. Except you're not good on picking lanes at the lights."

"Is there a secret I don't know?"

"Always haul in behind local plates on older cars with kids driving and crowd them a little so they'll pile on out of your way. Haul in behind local delivery trucks. On three lanes run the middle one, and swing to the curb lane when you're going to miss the light. A man turning is out of your way fast."

"Where are we going?"

"Pineview Lakes Estates. Twenty-one Loblolly Lane."

It was low land, five miles out. The developers had used the fill from the dug lakes to lift the ranch-type homes out of the swamp. It was eleven in the morning when we pulled into the river-pebble driveway of number 21, a long low cypress house with a shake roof out of some kind of fireproof imitation of cedar. It was stained pale silver and had faded blue blinds by the windows, the kind that are fixed in place and never cover the windows.

Two tanned skinny boys were working on a stripped VW with wide oversized tires. They gave us a sidelong glance and no further acknowledgment of our existence, even when we stood beside the VW.

"Either of you a Hascomb?" Scorf asked.

"Me," the skinnier one said.

"Your daddy around?"

"No."

"Miz Hascomb?"

"No."

"If it wouldn't strain your brain, sonny, maybe you could break down and tell me where I could find your daddy."

The boy straightened up and stared at him in bleak

silence. "What's this shit about brain strain, gramps?"

"I am Captain Harry Max Scorf, and I am tired of the hard-guy act from young trash. I get cooperation from you, and I get manners from you, and I get respect from you, sonny, or you go downtown for obstructing a police officer in his line of duty."

The bleak stare did not change. "Oh, goodness me," the boy said in a flat voice. "I did not for one moment realize. Tsk tsk. From what I overheard I believe you will find my dear father down at his place of business, Superior Building Supplies, at Junction Park. Actually it is no longer his place of business because the silly shit has lost it because he didn't know how to run it, and his partner screwed him and ran with the cash. But Cowboy Harry is just as bigmouth as ever. He is down there because some pigeon from Port Fierce wants to buy the junk that didn't get cleared out in the clearance sale. And now if you will give me your gracious permission to get back to work here."

Scorf smiled sadly and shook his head. "Thank you kindly, sonny. I am sure we will meet professionally one day."

"You can count on it," the boy said.

As we drove out Scorf said, "What makes so many of them so damned angry at everything lately?"

"It's a new preservative they put in the fried meat sold at drive-ins."

"As good an answer as any."

There was one car behind Superior Building Supplies, a recent-model Ford wagon with local plates, dinged and dusty, with a cracked window and a soft tire. One of the big sliding doors that opened onto the loading dock was ajar about three feet. We climbed onto the dock and went into the shadowy echoing areas of the empty warehouse. The air conditioning was off.

"Hascomb?" Scorf shouted.

"Yo! Who is it?"

Harry came out of the shadows, a pair of pliers in his hand. He peered and said, "Oh, hey, Harry Max! You were against the light." He looked at me. "What was your name, friend?"

"McGee."

Hascomb was stripped to the waist, the sweat rolling off his soft torso. His cowhand pants, cinched with a wide belt, were sweat-dark around the waistline. His abundant red-brown hair was carefully coiffed and sprayed into mod position, covering his ears. His boot heels clicked on the cement floor.

"You caught me, Harry Max," Hascomb said. "What I'm doing, I'm taking off the big junction box over there. I don't rightly know if it's mine or the owner's, so in case of doubt I'm taking it. The fellow from Port Fierce offered twenty bucks, and that is twenty bucks I wouldn't otherwise have. He took a lot of the small stuff and he's sending a bigger truck back for the desks, safe, chairs, and those two generators over there. And that cleans me out."

"Sorry to hear it," Scorf said.

Hascomb sighed and shrugged. "Hard times and a thief for a partner."

"What are you going to do?"

"I think we'll head out to Wyoming. Out to the mines. I can fix any damn thing that's got moving parts. New start. The equity in the house will give us a stake. Were you boys looking for me?"

I wondered how Scorf would approach it. Suspicion without proof is a dangerous thing and a clumsy thing.

Scorf said, "Harry, I hope you won't take this wrong, I surely do. In my line of work I have to do a lot of fool things I don't believe in, but I guess every line of work is the same. Anyways, I guess your prints are on file from army duty, but it would take a time to get them out of Washington or wherever the hell they keep them, and so they said to me, Captain, you go bring Harry Hascomb in voluntary and take his prints. You won't put up a fuss, will you?"

"Me? No. Hell, no. I won't put up a fuss, but what in the world is the point of it, Harry Max?"

"Maybe I shouldn't even tell you this, but we've known each other a long time. Maybe you know or don't know, a fragment of a print isn't worth a damn. This piece they got looks like it is one half of the pad of the third finger right hand."

"A print on what?"

Scorf scuffed at the cement floor. He shook his head. "Now you've got to understand how they think, Harry. It certainly wasn't exactly a big secret around the town that you and Joanna Freeler had a lot more than a business relationship. And lovers can have quarrels. Anyway—and don't get sore—the bomb experts, they recovered a piece of battery casing about so big, and they used some kind of chemical treatment to bring out the fragment of the print enough to photograph it. Once they compare yours, then you're off the list for keeps, Harry. It's something I plain have to do, and I'm sorry. I'm really sorry."

Harry Hascomb whacked the smaller man on the shoulder. "Chrissake, Harry Max. Don't feel sorry. I know when a man has a job to do, he has to do it. Right? You want me to go in right now? Let me get my shirt."

I noticed that Harry Max Scorf drifted along behind Hascomb as the man got his shirt, and I noticed that Scorf's heavy, drab suit coat was unbuttoned, and I could guess at the presence of the belly gun clipped to the waistband of his trousers.

Hascomb shouldered into his ranch shirt and tucked it in and buttoned it as we walked out. He slid the big door shut and snapped the heavy padlock on the hasp and smiled and said, "Have to finish stealing that box later." We were parked beside the Ford wagon, just to the right of it. Hascomb started to get into the Cougar and then he said, slapping his pocket, "Just a second, Harry Max. Let me get my other pack of cigarettes."

He leaned into the wagon and thumbed the button that dropped the door of the glove compartment. He was very good. Scorf was standing outside the open door of the two-door Cougar, holding the driver's seat tilted forward so that Hascomb could climb into the back. I was opposite the hood, walking toward the door on the passenger side.

Hascomb snatched an ancient weapon out of his glove compartment. Officers have smuggled them home from the last five wars. The Colt .45 automatic. I caught a glimpse of it as he turned and fired at Scorf at point-blank range.

Scorf got his left hand up to ward off the big slow slug. He was reaching for the belly gun with his right hand. The big slug went through the palm of his left hand and hit the shelf of brow over the left eye. The resistance of the thick ridge of bone snapped his head back and broke his neck. The white hat went sailing over the hood of the car. The relentless chunk of lead plowed through the brain tissues and took off a hunk of the back of the skull as big as an apple. It was all very immediate and messy. It spattered blood and tissue over the front half of the Cougar. I saw it all in slow motion. It was in the hard and vivid light of the hour before noon. It was a day of almost stagnant air. The wind had been moving steadily from north to south, bringing to Florida's east coast all the stained and corrosive crud of Birmingham and the rest of the industrial South. The horizons were whiskey-stained, and the sky above was a pallid saffron instead of blue. The bleared sun made harsh studio lighting on the parking lot scene. And Harry Hascomb saw Captain Scorf's horrid death under the dreadful lemon sky.

Scorf lay poised halfway across the dark blue hood. Meyer had been so right about the vivid reality of death. Harry Hascomb's face was absolutely slack, his eyes blank and dulled. He had expected to see the picture of the dead grackle. Here was the genuine article, smashed, leaking, stinking, and so sickeningly vivid that it immobilized him, froze him in an incredulous horror. I was caught on tiptoe for an instant, knowing that we were in a deserted parking lot in a deserted area, knowing that I could not expect any Saturday noon curiosity-seekers.

Scorf's coat was spread, showing the gun butt. With a swift and insane delicacy, with a mind-bulging awareness of my own madness, I leaned into the field of fire of the big automatic, snatched Scorf's weapon free, and fell to the cement on the far side of the Cougar from the immobilized Hascomb. He fired as I disappeared from his view, and like an afterecho of the hefty *bam,* I heard the slug chunk into the loading dock. An instant later Scorf slid off the hood onto his side, landing with a heavy clopping and thudding.

Doubtless Harry Hascomb had some sort of a script in mind. Maybe the automatic was due to end up in my dead hand, and Harry was due to end up in Peru.

I am not one for the shootout at the O.K. or any other corral.· I have no wish to stand in full view with steely nerves and draw a bead on the chap trying to blow my head in twain.

I hitched quickly into the prone position and steadied the short-barreled weapon by grasping my right wrist in my left hand and pushing outward. I aimed under the low road clearance of the Cougar, and I aimed at the front ankle creases in his Western boot and did not miss at that range. He yelled and started gimping around. I missed the other boot the first try and then got it on the second try. All of Harry Hascomb came tumbling down, making shrill sounds of total dismay. He thought to return the fire in the same manner, aiming under the car. I was after his hand or wrist, but I hit the automatic by accident. The slug spanged and went screeing off in ricochet, and the Colt killed the muffler on the Cougar before it went spinning away from him.

Without any conscious thought and without the awareness of any lapse of time, I found myself standing over Hascomb, picking a place right between his eyes.

Then I realized it would mean I would spend the best years of my life in Bayside, filling out forms and answering questions. He was not going anywhere, but to be safe I took both sets of car keys. I walked all the way to the phone booth beside the gas station, the one Carrie had patronized.

18

A wind had come up and blown all the smutch into somebody else's sky. Cindy and I sat on the deck chairs on the sun deck, side by side, and looked up at all the diamonds in the sky.

"You said they found it, Trav, but where was it?"

"In a box labeled Camp Stove. He was getting ready to go camping. And get lost in the woods. Forever."

"He said he killed Carrie?"

"Knocked her cold. Waited for the right kind of traffic and then took her by the crotch and the nape of the neck and slung her into the farm truck."

I sensed the way she shuddered.

She said, "I suppose, in a way, some of the money is mine."

"In a way. But your chances of getting it . . ."

"I know. I'll just have to make it anyway."

"Couldn't you sell out?"

"Sure. But then what?"

"What do you mean?"

"Trav, darling, I like to work. I like to run things.

And I like to have security. I've got a hundred thousand mortgage to pay off, and the place is worth ten times that. I am really going to have to pitch in."

"And I was going to ask you to pack a bag and come cruising."

"Well . . . someday, maybe."

"I gather that you are underwhelmed."

"Male pride talking. Can't you accept the fact that I'm tied to this place?"

"And you want to be tied to it."

"Please. I don't want to fight with you. Please, dear."

I stretched until my shoulders creaked. *"Okay, Cindy.* You are very realistic and diligent and all that. Maybe I have a grasshopper philosophy, but it strikes me there are a lot of dead people around here. Given advance warning, they could have done more living."

"We don't know each other."

"What does that mean?"

"I found out from you I'm a more physical person than I thought I was. Okay, so it makes me skeptical of myself and impatient about things. So, being a careful person, I need time. I just can't go mooning and dreaming around here and letting important things slide."

"Mooning and dreaming are very good stuff."

"Sure, sure, sure. We really don't know each other at all. And I am a drone. A worker. A builder. Maybe I can learn to play someday. But I have to have something solid, all built, before I'll dare. Please understand."

I gave up. I lifted her hand up and opened it and

kissed the palm. She shivered. I said, "Give me a call when you get all your ducks in a row. When you feel like getting acquainted."

"Could you call me?"

"I suppose so. Why?"

"It's very strange to feel so shy about somebody you've been to bed with. But I do."

"Cindy, I will call you. But when?"

She inhaled and exhaled deeply, a sign of relaxation and contentment and eventual anticipation.

"Just try me every once in a while, okay?"

And it was okay because it had to be. There wasn't any other choice. Sometimes it is a relief not to have a choice. I will have to get Meyer to explain this concept to me.

A MESSAGE THAT MAY SAVE
ALL OUR LIVES

"An eloquent and accurate assessment of the nuclear threat: the arms race which threatens our survival."

—Richard Barnet, Coordinator,
Institute for Policy Studies

"Helen Caldicott's message—delivered with sound facts, sincere compassion, and irresistible conviction—needs to be heard now!

—John W. Gofman, M.D., Ph.D., Chairman,
Committee for Nuclear Responsibility

"Required reading for all members of the human race, particularly for those of us blessed with the political freedom to make choices on our future direction."

—Dale Bridenbaugh,
Nuclear Engineer

"An excellent account for the lay public about the imminent dangers of the nuclear age. It should be read by all voting members of an informed democracy."

—Thomas Najarian, M.D.

"At last, a book that should awaken America to the dangers of the nuclear age, combining the authority of an expert, the passion of a mother, and the vision of a world citizen."

—Richard Falk, Ph.D.,
Professor of International Law,
Princeton University

ABOUT THE AUTHOR

Australian-born and educated, DR. HELEN CALDICOTT practices pediatrics at Boston's Children's Hospital Medical Center. An environmental activist since 1971, she virtually single-handedly educated and inspired the Australian public to protest—and bring a halt to—French atmospheric testing in the South Pacific. She later worked tirelessly to inform Australia's labor unions about the medical and military dangers associated with the mining and sale of Australian uranium on the international market. Married and the mother of three children, Dr. Caldicott is now a permanent resident of the United States—where she is rapidly becoming a leading critic of the nuclear power and armaments industries. In *Nuclear Madness,* and in her frequent lectures and T.V. and radio appearances, she urges us all to become better informed about the nuclear hazards we face—and challenges us to take action to assure human survival on planet Earth.

Nuclear Madness

What You Can Do!

With a new chapter on
Three Mile Island

Dr. Helen Caldicott

with the assistance of
Nancy Herrington & Nahum Stiskin

NUCLEAR MADNESS
*A Bantam Book | published by arrangement with
Autumn Press*

PRINTING HISTORY
Autumn Press edition published December 1978
2nd printing .... April 1979
3rd printing .... June 1979
4th printing .... December 1979
Excerpted in THE PROGRESSIVE, *December 1978; and* NEW AGE
Magazine, June 1978.

*A portion of this book appeared in "Accidents Will Happen:
The Case Against Nuclear Power" by Environmental Action
Foundation published by Harper & Row Publishers, Inc. 1979.*

Bantam edition | November 1980

**Bantam Books are published by Bantam Books, Inc. Its trade-
mark, consisting of the words "Bantam Books" and the por-
trayal of a bantam, is Registered in U.S. Patent and Trademark
Office and in other countries. Marca Registrada. Bantam
Books, Inc., 666 Fifth Avenue, New York, New York 10103.**

PRINTED IN THE UNITED STATES OF AMERICA

0 9 8 7 6 5 4 3 2

To Bill,
to my children Philip, Penny, and William,
and to all the children of the world.

Acknowledgments

I gratefully acknowledge the helpful criticism given by Tom Adams, Mary Baker, Richard Barnet, Rosalie Bertell, Dale Bridenbaugh, William Davidon, Lester del Ray, Richard Falk, Daniel Ford, Randall Forsberg, Ann Freedgood, John Gofman, Dolph Honicker, Charles Janeway, and Thomas Najarian.

Table of Contents

Nuclear Threats to Human Survival

NUCLEAR WEAPONS
(Design, Testing, Production,
Storage, Deployment)

↓   **UNDERGROUND EXPERIMENTS**

Ʊ   **UNIVERSITY REACTORS**

☒ · **MILITARY AND ERDA ('72) REACTORS
AND RESEARCH FACILITIES**
Accounting for 50% (appr.) of All Radioactive Waste

⌂ **NUCLEAR POWER PLANTS (Commercial)**
Accounting for 50% (appr.) of all Radioactive Waste

  ▲   **UNDER CONSTRUCTION**
  ■   **OPERABLE**
  ●   **PLANNED**

▙ NUCLEAR INDUSTRIES

▲ URANIUM MILL TAILINGS

▥ TRANSPORTATION/STORAGE OF RADIOACTIVE MATERIALS

▦ RADIOACTIVE WASTE BURIAL GROUNDS

Map prepared in 1972 by L. Franklin Ramirez, and designed by Mercedes Naveiro. Information from Another Mother for Peace. Commissioned by Women Strike for Peace.

1

Our Own Worst Enemy

I am a child of the Atomic Age. I was six years old when American atomic bombs were deployed against the Japanese, and I have grown up with the fear of imminent annihilation by nuclear holocaust. Over the years my fear has increased. Thousands of nuclear weapons are now being built each year. At this writing, 360 nuclear reactors are in operation in thirty countries around the world, 65 of them in the United States. Hundreds more are projected by the end of the century. The nuclear facilities stand to inherit the earth.

As a physician, I contend that nuclear technology threatens life on our planet with extinction. If present trends continue, the air we breathe, the food we eat, and the water we drink will soon be contaminated with enough radioactive pollutants to pose a potential health hazard far greater than any plague humanity has ever experienced. Unknowingly exposed to these radioactive poisons, some of us may be developing cancer right now. Others may be passing damaged genes, the basic chemical units which transmit hereditary characteristics, to future generations. And more of us will inevitably be affected unless we bring about a drastic reversal of our government's pronuclear policies.

I learned about the carcinogenic (cancer-causing) and mutagenic (gene-altering) effects of nuclear radiation during my first year of medical school, in 1956. At that time the United States and Russia were conducting atmospheric bomb tests. My genetics teacher did not connect his lectures on radiation to the fallout produced by these explosions, but the relationship became clear to me when newspapers reported that radioactive strontium-90, a by-product of atomic testing, had been carried around the world by high-level winds, deposited on the earth as nuclear fallout, and was being found in high concentrations in cow's milk and in the deciduous teeth and, presumably, the bones of children. At the same time, the long-term medical consequences of radiation were just beginning to appear, in the form of an increased rate of leukemia among Japanese A-bomb survivors.

Most Americans with whom I've spoken know very little about the medical hazards posed by nuclear radiation and seem to have forgotten (or suppressed) the atomic-bomb anxiety that was so prevalent in the 1950s. Back then, most Americans were aware of the devastation that nuclear war implies: Children were constantly diving under their desks and crouching in school corridors during simulated nuclear attacks, while the bomb shelter business boomed and the nation prepared a program of civil defense. Americans were justifiably scared. People recognized that nuclear disarmament could mean the difference between a secure future for them and their children, and no future at all.

But during the 1960s the American public became preoccupied with other matters: political assassination, the Civil Rights movement, the Vietnam war. The threat of nuclear holocaust was submerged by these more immediate problems. Only the Pentagon sustained its interest in nuclear development: in the effort to keep ahead of the Soviet Union, America's military strategists continued to stockpile more and more atomic weapons, while developing and refining delivery systems, satellites, and submarines.

Today, however, it is of the utmost urgency that we refocus our attention on the problems posed by nuclear technology, for we have entered and are rapidly passing through a new phase of the Atomic Age. Despite the fact that reactor technology is beset with hazardous

2

shortcomings that threaten the health and well-being of the nations that employ it, nuclear power plants are spreading throughout the world. Moreover, by making "peaceful" nuclear technology available to any nation wealthy enough to buy a nuclear reactor, we are inviting other countries to join the international "nuclear club" militarily, as well as economically. Following India's lead in 1974, many nations are bound to explode test devices in the coming years. Because of this proliferation of nuclear weapons, the likelihood of nuclear war, the most ominous threat to public health imaginable, becomes greater every day.

In view of the threat that nuclear technology poses to the ecosphere, we must acknowledge that Homo sapiens has reached an evolutionary turning point. Thousands of tons of radioactive materials, released by nuclear explosions and reactor spills, are now dispersing through the environment. Nonbiodegradable, and some potent virtually forever, these toxic nuclear materials will continue to accumulate, and eventually their effects on the biosphere and on human beings will be grave: many people will begin to develop and die of cancer; or their reproductive genes will mutate, resulting in an increased incidence of congenitally deformed and diseased offspring—not just in the next generation, but for the rest of time. An all-out nuclear war would kill millions of people and accelerate these biological hazards among the survivors: the earth would be poisoned and laid waste, rendered uninhabitable for aeons.

As a pediatrician, I have devoted most of my professional life to working with children born with cystic fibrosis, the most common inherited childhood disease. The abnormal gene that carries this fatal disorder is found in 1 in 20 Caucasians; the disease's incidence is 1 in 1,600 live births. Watching my patients die of respiratory failure, and seeing other children in the wards die of leukemia and cancer, has motivated me to speak publicly and write this book. Knowing that the incidence of congenital diseases and malignancies will increase in direct ratio to the radioactive contaminants polluting our planet, I cannot remain silent.

"But what can *I* do, as an individual?" is a refrain I hear whenever I draw people's attention to the problems threatening our survival. The international balance of terror, economic pressures, and the frustration of dealing with a biased government and unresponsive bureaucracy leave many Americans feeling helpless. Many seem to believe that it has simply become impossible for an individual to influence the course of national and world events.

I disagree. My experience in Australia from 1971 to 1976 taught me that democracy can still be made to work—that by exerting electoral pressure, an aroused citizenry can still move its government to the side of morality and common sense. In fact, the momentum for movement in this direction can only originate in the heart and mind of the individual citizen. Moreover, it takes only one person to initiate the process, and that person may be politically naive and inexperienced, just as I was when I first spoke out.

My personal commitment to human survival was sparked when I read Bertrand Russell's autobiography. In Russell I found the moving example of a man who faced up to the dangers of the Atomic Age and, despite all odds, dedicated himself to ridding the earth of nuclear weapons. By 1962 his "ban the bomb" movement had culminated in the International Atmospheric Test Ban Treaty signed by the United States, Great Britain, and the Soviet Union—and the world briefly waxed hopeful that the superpowers would begin to disarm. When, in 1971, I discovered that France had been conducting atmospheric tests over its small colony of Mururoa since 1966, contravening the treaty inspired by Russell's work, I became indignant. I knew that when an atomic bomb explodes near the earth's surface, the mushroom cloud

4

that billows into the sky carries particles of radio-active dust. Blown from west to east by stratospheric winds, these particles descend to the earth in rainfall and work their way through soil and water into the food chain, eventually posing a serious threat to human life.

At the time few Australians knew of the testing or were aware of its inherent dangers. I decided that it was my duty, as a physician, to protest France's disregard for the health of my fellow Australians, and I began by writing a letter to a local newspaper. That letter generated some supportive correspondence, and a TV news program asked me to comment on the medical hazards posed by fallout. France had tested another nuclear device, and planned to detonate four more in the next few months. Each time the French tested a bomb, I appeared on television again, explaining the dangers of radiation. As the public became better informed, a movement to stop the French tests coalesced around the medical facts.

The informal campaign that grew up around these televised talks gained greater momentum when I exposed a secret government report, passed on to me by a sympathizer employed by the State Government of South Australia, which confirmed that in 1971 a high level of radiation had been found in South Australian drinking water: In June 1972 government inspectors detected 1,860 picocuries of radiation per liter of rainwater, compared with a normal background radiation level of 50 picocuries and the "safe" maximum of 1,000 arbitrarily established by the International Commission of Radiological Protection. Shocked by the realization that their water supplies were now sufficiently contaminated to pose a genuine threat to them and their children, the citizens of Australia took action. Thousands joined marches held in Adelaide, Melbourne, Brisbane, and Sydney; a spate of editorials and statements by eminent scientists demanded an end to the testing; newspapers devoted full pages to angry letters from readers; dockworkers refused to load French ships; postal workers refused to deliver French mail; consumers boycotted French products. A Gallup poll showed that within a year 75 percent of the Australian public had grown opposed to the French tests. And on June 15, 1972, in response to enormous public pressure, the Australian government instructed its representatives to the U.N.'s Stockholm Conference on the Environment to vote in favor of a resolution calling for an end to all nuclear testing.

Although the Australian government was beginning to shift its position in response to public demand, the French remained unmoved, and it was decided by the committee coordinating the groups working together to stop the French tests that a delegation of concerned citizens should fly to Tahiti to lodge a formal protest with the governor of France's South Sea islands. The group was to include churchmen, union representatives, and Dr. Jim Cairns, deputy leader of the Australian Labor Party. I was invited to go along. Moments before we were to depart, however, we learned that French officials in Tahiti had announced that our group would be denied the right to disembark. We then decided to go to Paris with our protest. Twenty-four hours later, Jim, Ken Newcombe (leader of the Union of Australian Students), and I arrived in London, where we addressed a large crowd of Australians and New Zealanders in Hyde Park and delivered a letter of protest to the French embassy. Unfortunately, Britain's Parliamentarians were far more concerned with securing England's entry into the Common Market than with hearing about the radioactive fallout then contaminating Australia, and Prime Minister Harold Wilson declined to meet with us. We were not surprised when we met with an equally cold political reception in Paris the next day. The bureaucrats with whom we exchanged opinions were closed to our arguments; they insisted France needed its own *force de frappe* and that it would under no circumstances yield to public pressure. Stubbornly claiming that their nuclear tests were harmless, these professional bureaucrats nevertheless conceded that they would never consider conducting such tests in the Mediterranean: "Mon Dieu, there are too many people there!" We returned to Australia feeling that we had presented our case as forcefully as we could, but sorely disappointed by the arrogant disdain with which we were received.

In November, however, the momentum began to shift dramatically in our favor: A conference of Pacific nations convened by Australia and New Zealand spearheaded a U.N. vote to outlaw nuclear testing. The French countered with an announcement that 1973 would bring a new series of tests, including a 1-megaton hydrogen bomb blast over Mururoa Atoll. One month later, an enraged Australian public elected the Australian Labor Party, which opposed the action of the French, into office. Calling for an injunction to compel the French to desist from further atmospheric testing in the Pacific, the newly elected Australian government, and the government of New Zealand, took France before the International Court of Justice in the Hague. Although the Court's decision was disappointingly equivocal, France finally backed down in the face of world opinion and announced that it would restrict its testing to underground sites.

In our struggle to put an end to atmospheric nuclear testing, we had demonstrated that one voice was all it took to raise a warning call, and that once enough other voices joined in, that call would be heard around the world.

My experience in the struggle I have just described, and in others in Australia and the United States, has taught me many things: first and perhaps most important, that we can no longer afford to entrust our lives, and the lives and health of future generations, to politicians, bureaucrats, "experts," or scientific specialists, because all too often their objectivity is compromised. Most government officials are shockingly uninformed about the medical implications of nuclear

7

power and atomic warfare, and yet they daily make life-and-death decisions in regard to these issues. Some responsibility for this ignorance rests with my medical colleagues: too many of us are reluctant to look beyond our research laboratories or hospital corridors, and too many of us have remained silent about the medical hazards of nuclear technology and the radiation it produces, despite the fact that we acknowledge such radiation to be a certain cause of cancer and genetic disease.

My experience also taught me that the survival of our species depends on each individual. The growing controversy surrounding nuclear fission is the most important issue that American society and the world at large has ever faced. A national and international debate on this subject is long overdue, and the participation of each individual will determine its outcome. We must begin today by first of all learning as much as we can about the critical health hazards involved, because what we don't know about these dangers may kill us:

- The world's major military powers have built tens of thousands of atomic bombs powerful enough to kill the world's inhabitants several times over.
- Each 1,000-megawatt nuclear reactor contains as much radioactive material ("fallout") as would be produced by one thousand Hiroshima-sized bombs. A "meltdown" (in which fissioning nuclear fuel and the steel and concrete structures that encase it overheat and melt) could release a reactor's radioactive contents into the atmosphere, killing 50,000 people or more and contaminating thousands of square miles.
- Each reactor daily leaks carcinogenic and mutagenic effluent. These radioactive materials enhance the level of background radiation to which we are constantly exposed, increasing our risk of developing cancer and genetic disease.
- Each reactor annually produces tons of radioactive waste, some of which remains dangerous

8

for more than 500,000 years. No permanent, fail-safe method of disposal or storage has yet been found for them, despite millions of dollars spent during three decades of research. Despite recent proposals, there is good reason to suspect that we may never develop safe methods of disposal and long-term storage.

- Each commercial nuclear reactor produces approximately 400-500 pounds of plutonium yearly. Dangerous for at least 500,000 years, this toxic substance poses a threat to public health which cannot be overemphasized. Present in nature in only minute amounts, plutonium is one of the deadliest substances known. In addition, it is the basic raw material needed for the fabrication of atomic bombs, and each reactor yearly produces enough to make forty such weapons. Thus, "peaceful" nuclear power production is synonymous with nuclear weapons proliferation: American sales of reactor technology abroad guarantee that by the end of the century dozens of countries will possess enough nuclear material to manufacture bombs of their own. Moreover, the "plutonium economy" urged upon us by the nuclear industry and its supporters in government presents the disturbing probability that terrorist groups will construct atomic bombs from stolen nuclear materials, or that criminals will divert such materials for radioactive blackmail. Because of this terrorist threat we may find ourselves living in a police state designed to minimize unauthorized access to such nuclear materials.

Most early developers of nuclear energy explored its potential forty years ago to produce bombs that would inflict unprecedented damage. Seven years after the United States tested two such weapons on the populations of Hiroshima and Nagasaki, the collective guilt generated by the deaths of some 200,000 Japanese civilians prompted the American government to advocate a new policy: the "peaceful use of atomic energy" to produce "safe, clean" electricity, a form of power touted as being "too cheap to meter." Together, industry and government leaders decided that nuclear power would become the energy source of the future. Today, twenty-five years later, that prospect threatens the well-being of our nation and the world.

I believe it imperative that the American public understand that nuclear power generation is neither safe, nor clean, nor cheap; that new initiatives are urgently required if we are to avoid nuclear catastrophe in a world armed to the teeth with atomic weapons; and that these initiatives must begin with awareness, concern, and action on the part of the individual citizen.

One need not be a scientist or a nuclear engineer to take part in this emerging debate; in fact, an overspecialized approach tends to confuse the issue. The basic questions involved ultimately go beyond the technical problems related to reactor safety and radioactive waste management. Even if the present state of nuclear technology were to be judged fail-safe, for example, we must ask ourselves how much faith we would be willing to invest in the infallibility of the human beings who must administer that technology. Granted, we may someday be able to isolate nuclear waste from the environment: How confident can we be in our ability to control the actions of fanatics or criminals? How can we assure the longevity of the social institutions responsible for perpetuating that isolation? And what moral right have we to burden our progeny with this poisonous legacy? Finally, we must confront the philosophical issue at the heart of the crisis: Do we, as a species, possess the wisdom that the intelligent use of nuclear energy demands? If not, are we courting disaster by continuing to exploit it?

From a purely medical point of view, there really is no controversy: The commercial and military technologies we have developed to release the energy of the nucleus impose unacceptable risks to health and life. As a physician I consider it my responsibility to preserve and further life. Thus, as a doctor, as well as a mother and world citizen, I wish to practice the ultimate form of preventive medicine by ridding the earth of these technologies which propagate suffering, disease, and death.

2

Radiation

Radiation, the particles and waves emitted by unstable elements, has saved the lives of thousands of people when used to diagnose and treat disease. But little more than thirty years after its discovery in the late 1890s, scientists began to find that radiation had a schizophrenic nature: It could kill as well as cure. Working with primitive, high-dose X-ray machines, many early roentgenologists died of radiation burns and cancer. Well known for their pioneer work with radium, both Marie Curie and her daughter, Irene, died of leukemia. Studies conducted over the past forty years have shown that many people irradiated in infancy and childhood for such minor maladies as acne, enlarged thymus, bronchitis, ringworm, tonsillitis, and adenoids have developed cancers of the thyroid, salivary glands, brain, pharynx, and larynx up to thirty years later. Studies of uranium miners and people engaged in commercial activities, as well as of Japanese survivors of atomic explosions, have yielded enough evidence to demonstrate beyond doubt that cancer of the blood, lung, thyroid, breast, stomach, lymph glands, and bone occur in human beings as a result of exposure to radiation. Today, therefore, it is an accepted medical fact that radiation causes cancer.

To understand the dangers posed by nuclear power generation, nuclear weapons production, and nuclear warfare, we must acquire a basic knowledge of the nature of radiation and its biological impact on human body cells.

All matter is composed of elements, and the smallest particle of an element is an atom. Each atom has a central nucleus consisting for the most part of protons (particles with mass and positive electric charge) and neutrons (particles with mass and neutral charge). Around the nucleus revolve electrons, particles with very little mass, and negative charge. The number of protons in the nucleus gives us the element's "atomic number"; the sum total of both the protons and neutrons in the nucleus gives us the element's "atomic weight." All the atoms of a given element have the same atomic number, but because some atoms contain more neutrons than others, not all of an element's atoms have the same atomic weight. Atoms of the same element with different atomic weights are called "isotopes." Uranium for example, with an atomic number of 92, appears in nature in two forms: uranium-235 and uranium-238.

All elements with an atomic number of 83 or more are unstable or "radioactive," which means that their atoms can spontaneously eject—or "radiate"—particles and energy waves from their nuclei. This emission process, during which an element disintegrates into other nuclear forms, is referred to as "radioactive decay," and the rate at which it proceeds is calculated in terms of "half-life." The half-life of an element is the period of time it takes for the radioactivity of any amount of that element to be reduced by half. The half-life of strontium-90, for example, is twenty-eight years. Starting with 1 pound of strontium-90, in twenty-eight years there will be ½ pound of radioactive material; in twenty-eight more years there will be ¼ pound; in twenty-eight more years there will be ⅛ pound. After approximately 560 years, the radioactivity of a given sample of strontium-90 will be reduced to one-millionth of its original potency.

In the course of this decay, atoms give off three major forms of radiation: alpha, beta, and gamma, named after the first three letters of the Greek alphabet.

The equivalent of a helium nucleus, an alpha particle consists of two protons and two neutrons. Because of its relatively great size and weight, such a particle can be stopped by a sheet of paper, tends to lose momentum quickly, and can penetrate only short distances into matter. Nevertheless, it is very energetic, and if it is moving fast enough when it comes in contact with a living body cell, it can burst through the cell wall and do serious damage to the interior. In fact, for the same amount of total energy delivered, alpha radiation has greater biological effects than any other form of radiation.

Almost two thousand times smaller than an alpha particle, a beta particle, when negatively charged, is identical to an electron. Emitted by the nucleus, beta particles can penetrate matter much further than alphas: They can travel through a number of body cells before they lose energy and come to a stop.

Gamma radiation, electromagnetic energy waves emitted by the nucleus of a radioactive substance, has the greatest penetrating power and often accompanies alpha and beta emission. X-rays are similar to gamma rays.

Radiation is insidious, because it cannot be detected by the senses. We are not biologically equipped to feel its power, or see, hear, touch, or smell it. Yet gamma radiation can penetrate our bodies if we are exposed to radioactive substances. Beta particles can pass through the skin to damage living cells, although, like alpha particles, which are unable to penetrate this barrier, their most serious and irreparable damage is done when we ingest food or water—or inhale air—contaminated with particles of radioactive matter.

Radiation harms us by ionizing—that is, altering the electrical charge of—the atoms and molecules comprising our body cells. Whether the effects of this ionization are manifested within hours or over a period of years usually depends on the amount of exposure, measured in terms of *rem* (roentgen equivalent man) units. Nevertheless, even the smallest dose (measured in millirems) can affect us, for the effects of radiation are additive. If we receive separate small amounts of radiation over time, the long-run biological effects (cancer, leukemia, genetic injury) may be similar to receiving a large dose all at once.

A very high dose of ionizing radiation (say, of 3,000 rems or more) causes acute encephalopathic syndrome —an effect scientists sought when they designed a "neutron bomb" to be used against invading forces. The explosion of such a bomb will leave buildings intact (although they may remain radioactive for years); what is destroyed is the human brain and nervous tissue. Within forty-eight hours of exposure, the brain cells will swell and enlarge, producing increased pressure inside the skull. Confusion, delirium, stupor, psychosis, ataxia (the loss of neurological control of the muscles), and fever result; there follows a period of lucidity, then sudden death.

A dose of 600 rems or more produces acute radiation illness. Thousands of Japanese A-bomb victims died from this sickness within two weeks of the bomb explosions. Such exposure to radiation kills all actively dividing cells in the body: hair falls out, skin is sloughed off in big ulcers, vomiting and diarrhea occur, and then, as the white blood cells and platelets die, victims expire of infection and/or massive hemorrhage.

Lower doses of ionizing radiation can cause leukemia five years after exposure; cancer, twelve to forty years later; and genetic diseases and abnormalities in future generations.

Of all the creatures on Earth, human beings have been found to be one of the most susceptible to the

14

carcinogenic effects of radiation.* One of America's most dreaded killer diseases, cancer is like a parasitic organism, often causing slow and painful death. It is estimated that 1 in 3 Americans now living will contract the disease at some point. During the 1970s alone, 3.5 million people are expected to die of it.

The mechanism by which radiation causes cancer is not completely understood. It is currently believed, however, that it involves damage to the genes. Our bodies are made up of billions of cells. Inside each cell is a nucleus, and inside the nucleus are long, beadlike strings known as chromosomes. Arranged on these strings are genes consisting of DNA molecules. Genes control every aspect of the individual's hereditary characteristics: hair color, eye color, personality factors, brain development, and so forth. Half of one's genes are inherited from one's mother, half from one's father.

Genes also control cellular activities, and within every cell there is thought to be a regulatory gene which controls the cell's rate of division. If our bodies are gamma-irradiated from the exterior, or if we inhale a particle of radioactive matter into our lungs and one of its atoms emits an alpha or beta particle, this radiation can collide with a regulatory gene and chemically damage it, sometimes killing the cell, sometimes leaving it alive. The surviving cell continues to function normally, until one day, five to forty years later (i.e., after the "latent period" of carcinogenesis), instead of dividing to produce two new cells, it goes berserk and manufactures billions of identically damaged cells. This type of growth, which leads to the formation of a tumor, is called cancer.

Cancer cells often break from the main mass of a tumor, enter the blood or lymph vessels, and travel to other organs. Here again, they will divide uncontrollably to form new tumors. Because they are more aggressive

---

*Because their cells are growing and rapidly dividing, fetuses, infants, and young children are the most sensitive to radiation effects.

than normal body cells, cancer cells utilize the body's nutrients, causing normal tissues to waste away and die.

In addition to giving rise to cancer, radiation also causes genetic mutations, sudden changes in the inheritable characteristics of an organism. In 1927 Dr. H. J. Muller was awarded the Nobel Prize for his discovery that X-radiation causes an increase in the number of such mutations in fruit flies. Muller's findings have since been confirmed by many other researchers. The genes and chromosomes of the scores of animals tested have been found to be vulnerable to radiation. The reproductive organs of human beings are believed to be equally susceptible. Moreover, the number of mutations has been shown to be in direct ratio to the total amount of radiation exposure to the gonads, whether that exposure be a single large dose or many very small ones.

A mutation occurs whenever a gene is chemically or structurally changed. Some body cells die or become cancerous when they are mutated; others survive without noticeable changes. A genetically mutated sperm or egg cell may survive free of cancer but can seriously damage the offspring to which they give rise.

There are two kinds of genes: dominant and recessive. To clarify the difference, let us consider the example of eye color. Each characteristic is determined by a pair of genes (one member of the pair coming from the mother, one from the father). The gene for brown eyes is a strong, or dominant, gene. The gene for blue eyes is weak, or recessive. A child who inherits two brown-eyed genes will be born with brown eyes. The child with one brown-eyed gene and one blue-eyed gene will still have brown eyes, because the brown-eyed gene is dominant. The only way to get blue eyes is to inherit two blue-eyed genes.

A child formed from an egg or sperm cell mutated by radiation in a dominant way will show the results of that mutation. It may spontaneously abort or, if it sur-

16

vives pregnancy, it may turn out to be a sickly, deformed individual with a shortened lifespan. If this person then reproduces, statistically, half of his or her children will inherit the dominant gene and its deformities. Approximately five hundred such dominant genetic diseases have been identified. A typical example is achondroplastic dwarfism: individuals suffering from this disease are born with abnormal bones, resulting in short arms and legs and a relatively large head.

A radiation-induced recessive mutation might not make itself immediately apparent. A child might seem normal but carry the deleterious gene and pass it on to the next generation. Since the disease caused by a recessive gene will not manifest unless a child inherits the gene from both parents, it might not show up for generations. Diabetes, muscular dystrophy, hemophilia, certain forms of mental retardation, and cystic fibrosis are among the 1,500 recessive genetic diseases now known.

Radiation can also cause chromosomal breakage in a sperm or egg cell, leading to seriously deformed offspring. One disease associated with chromosomal damage is mongolism, or Down's syndrome.

Deformities can also occur even when the sperm and egg cell are genetically normal, if radiation kills specific cells in the developing embryo during the first three months of intrauterine life. If a cell destined to form the septum of the heart is killed, a baby may be born with a hole in its heart. Such intrauterine damage, known as teratogenesis, can produce deformities similar to those caused by the drug Thalidomide.

We are all constantly exposed to some radiation in the form of the natural, "background" radiation to which the earth has been subject for billions of years. When the ozone layer of the atmosphere was thinner, ultraviolet rays from the sun and cosmic rays from outer space, two natural forms of radiation, streamed in unhampered to cause genetic mutations in every species. As a result, the simple single-celled organisms found in

17

the ocean evolved into more complex creatures adapted to living in the sea, on land, and in the air. Eventually the human species, with its highly specialized brain, developed. Strong or beneficial mutations prevailed, while detrimental mutations died out. Almost all geneticists currently believe that humanity has reached an evolutionary peak in the number of beneficial mutations that the species can undergo. Most genetic mutations are therefore thought to be detrimental, causing disease and deformity.

Background radiation continues to affect us. The atmosphere is now protected by a thicker ozone layer, but ultraviolet and cosmic rays still filter in (inducing, for example, skin cancer in some people when they are exposed to excessive amounts of sunlight). Background radiation also comes from other natural sources, such as the radium, radon, potassium-40, and carbon-14 present in rocks, air, and our own body cells. In Kerala, India, an abnormally high level of radioactive thorium found in the local soil is believed to be responsible for a high incidence of mongolism and mental retardation. The average level of background radiation exposure for people living in both the Northern and Southern Hemispheres amounts to approximately 100 millirems per year (6 rems in 60 years). Although the exact percentage is unknown, this radiation is thought to be responsible for a portion of all the cancers and genetic disorders afflicting us today.

Equally hazardous to our health is the human-made radiation to which most of us are exposed. Human-made radiation, too, can initiate cancer and genetic mutation. How does it reach us?

Medical X-rays are the most prevalent source of radiation for the general public today. Since the effect of each dose is additive, each exposure carries with it a minimal carcinogenic and mutagenic risk. Thus, it is imperative that doctors, dentists, chiropractors, and patients alike take into account the potentially harmful effects of these rays, so that only those X-rays deemed absolutely necessary are performed. Dr. Karl Morgan, a health physicist formerly associated with the Atomic Energy Commission, estimates that 40-50 percent of all medical X-rays are unnecessary.

Nuclear power production and the process employed in the manufacture of nuclear weapons are the second most prevalent sources of public exposure. These processes result in the manufacture of hundreds of radioactive elements, which are starting to contaminate the food chain. The radioactive material finds its way into rivers, lakes, and oceans, where it is eaten by fish and incorporated into their biochemical systems, concentrating in their bodies thousands of times. Contaminated water is taken up by grass and other vegetation; again the radioactive elements are concentrated. Cows grazing on contaminated grass further concentrate the radiation and eventually pass the contamination on to us, in the form of milk or meat.

Prominent among the radioactive elements manufactured in the production of nuclear power are the beta emitters iodine-131, strontium-90, and cesium-137. Iodine-131 has a half-life of 8 days. Both this element and strontium-90 travel up the food chain, and, when ingested by humans, are absorbed through the bowel wall. Iodine-131 migrates in the blood to the thyroid gland and may cause cancer there twelve to fifty years later; strontium-90, which chemically resembles calcium, is incorporated in bone tissue, where it may lead to leukemia and osteogenic sarcoma (a malignant bone tumor). Cesium-137, with a half-life of 30 years, concentrates in animal muscle and fish; ingested by humans, it deposits in body muscle and irradiates nearby organs.

Whether natural or human-made, all radiation is dangerous. There is no "safe" amount of radioactive material or dose of radiation. Why? Because by virtue of the nature of the biological damage done by radiation, it takes only one radioactive atom, one cell, and

19

one gene to initiate the cancer or mutation cycle. Any exposure at all therefore constitutes a serious gamble with the mechanisms of life.

Today almost all geneticists agree that there is no dose of radiation so low that it produces no mutations at all. Thus, even small amounts of background radiation are believed to have genetic effects.

Similarly, there is no disagreement among scientists that large doses of ionizing radiation cause a variety of different forms of cancer. Starting fifteen years after the explosions, the incidence of cancers of the stomach, ovary, breast, bowel, lung, bone, and thyroid doubled among Japan's bomb survivors. Approximately five years after the nuclear attack on Hiroshima, an epidemic of leukemia occurred that within ten years reached a level of incidence thirty times higher among the survivors than among the nonexposed population.

The direct relation between cancer and even minute amounts of radiation has best been demonstrated by the British epidemiologist Dr. Alice Stewart, who found that only one diagnostic X-ray to the pregnant abdomen increases the risk of leukemia in the offspring by 40 percent.

Every medical textbook dealing with the effects of radiation warns that there is no safe level of exposure. Nevertheless, the nuclear industry and government regulatory agencies have established what they claim to be "safe" doses for workers and the general public, drawing support from scientists who believe that there is a threshold below which low doses of ionizing radiation may in fact be harmless. This claim is dangerously misleading and, I believe, incorrect. The International Commission on Radiological Protection (ICRP) originally proposed "allowable" levels of exposure for use by the industry, but not without conceding that these may not be truly safe. Rather, it admittedly accorded priority to the expedient promotion of nuclear power. As the ICRP noted in its 1966 Recommendations (Document #2), "This limitation necessarily involves a compromise between deleterious effects and social

20

benefits . . . It is felt that this level provides reasonable latitude for the expansion of atomic energy programs in the foreseeable future. It should be emphasized that the limit may not in fact represent the proper balance between possible harm and probable benefit."

The truth is that we are courting catastrophe. The permissive radiation policy supported by the American government in effect turns us into guinea pigs in an experiment to determine how much radioactive material can be released into the environment before major epidemics of cancer, leukemia, and genetic abnormalities take their toll. The "experts" stand ready to count victims *before* they take remedial action. Meanwhile, the burden remains on the public to prove that the nuclear industry is hazardous, rather than on the industry to prove that it is truly safe.

Today's safety standards have already been shown by several studies to be dangerously high. When investigations of low-dose ionizing radiation revealed that levels of radiation lower than those permitted were causing cancer, government agencies attempted to suppress the findings.

In February 1978 an illustrative case was vindicated at a hearing before the House Subcommittee on Health and the Environment. In 1964 the United States Energy Research and Development Administration (ERDA) had funded a study to be conducted by Dr. Thomas Mancuso, a physician and professor in the Public Health Department at the University of Pittsburgh. Its purpose was to determine whether low-level radiation induced any discernable biological effects in the nuclear workers at two of the oldest and largest atomic reactors in the United States, the facilities at Hanford, Washington, and Oak Ridge, Tennessee.

Dr. Mancuso's study was one of the broadest industrial epidemiological studies ever undertaken. Over a ten-year period, he pored through 1 million files and compiled data from the death certificates of 3,710 former atomic power workers. Because of the long latency period of carcinogenesis, his first results were

21

negative; that is, he did not find an incidence of cancer higher than the norms for the general public. In 1974 the Atomic Energy Commission began pressuring him to publish his findings. The AEC wanted to use Mancuso's report to refute an independent study conducted by Dr. Samuel Milham of the Washington State Health Department; after reviewing 300,000 case histories at Hanford, he had found that there was indeed a high rate of cancer among former employees there.

Dr. Mancuso refused, claiming that his statistics were incomplete and that he needed more time. In 1975 the AEC informed him that his funding would be terminated as of July 1977 and demanded that he surrender his data to the Oak Ridge laboratories at that time. Mancuso took advantage of the interim to call in epidemiologist Stewart and her associate, Dr. George Kneale, a biostatistician, and together the three scrupulously studied the material on the Hanford workers. They came up with results similar to Milham's: a 6 7 percent increase in radiation-related cancer deaths among Hanford workers, indicating that the disease is distinctly related to radiation exposure at today's "acceptable" levels.

In fact, Dr. Mancuso discovered that the radiation "doubling dose" (that is, the dose at which the incidence of a disease is doubled) is 3.6 rads* per lifetime for bone marrow cancer, and stands at 33-38 rads per lifetime for other forms of cancer. Previous estimates, based on atomic bomb survivor data and human X-ray research, had set these doses at 100 rads for leukemia and 300-400 rads for solid cancer induction. Today every civilian nuclear worker is allowed a radiation dose of 5 rads per year: that is, workers may be exposed to doubling doses for leukemia *each year,* for cancer every *7-7.5 years.* Dr. Thomas Najarian's study of Portsmouth, New Hampshire, nuclear submarine

---

*The *rad* (radiation absorbed dose) is a measure of radiation absorbed by a target expressed as the amount of energy (in ergs) per gram of absorbing material. The rem is a measure of the number of rads absorbed by a target multiplied by the relative biological effectiveness of the given type of radiation. In this case they are almost identical.

workers confirms Dr. Mancuso's estimates. Such figures suggest that the nuclear industry will have to start hiring workers who are over sixty years of age—so that they will not live long enough to develop malignancies!

The increasing radiation exposure of workers and the general public by the nuclear industries implies tragedy for many human beings. Increasing numbers of people will have to deal with cancer or, perhaps more painful still, deformed or diseased offspring. In 1969 Dr. John Gofman and Dr. Arthur Tamplin, scientists formerly with the AEC's Lawrence Livermore Radiation Laboratory, announced that if all Americans were annually exposed to the official allowable dose of 170 millirems of radiation (the equivalent of about six chest X-rays a year) over and above background levels, there would be an increase of 32,000-300,000 deaths from cancer each year. It is difficult to predict how many mutated children will be born in the world as a result of nuclear power and weapons production, or what the nature of their defects may be. But it is indisputable that the mutation rate will rise—perhaps far higher than we would care to contemplate. The massive quantities of radiation that would be released in a war fought with nuclear weapons might, over time, cause such great changes in the human gene pool that the following generations might not be recognizable as human beings.

It is important that we keep in mind the fact that the nuclear industries are relatively young. Nuclear power has been in commercial production in the United States for only twenty-five years; arms production for thirty-five. Since the latency period of cancer is twelve to forty years and genetic mutations do not often manifest for generations, we have barely begun to experience the effects radiation can have upon us. Nuclear power plants and military facilities will continue to release radioactive materials into the environment, until public pressure becomes great enough to bring such releases to a halt. Because the effects of these materials on us, our children, and our planet will be irreversible, we must take action now. What we have discovered so far should serve as ample warning that our future as a species is imperiled: We are entering a danger zone—an uncharted territory—from which we may never return.

3

The Cycle of Death

Australia possesses 20 to 30 percent of the free world's known supply of uranium, the raw material upon which virtually all forms of nuclear technology depend. Following the oil embargo in 1974, the Labor Government offered to sell that uranium on the world market. Ironically, only two years earlier that same government had brought France before the International Court of Justice at the Hague and forced that nation to test its nuclear weapons underground; moreover, it had already made it the nation's policy to forego nuclear power. Now Australia publicly announced its readiness to sell the raw material for nuclear power generation for national profit.

Appalled by what I considered to be an act of misguided—and ultimately self-destructive—opportunism, I went to see Dr. Jim Cairns. Three years earlier, I had accompanied him to Paris to protest to representatives of the French government about their atmospheric nuclear tests. Now Deputy Prime Minister, he was negotiating the sale of Australian uranium with the Shah of Iran.

Dr. Cairns is a politician in whom many people placed their trust. I could not understand why he would

24

disregard the medical dangers associated with the mining of uranium and the health hazards inherent in the nuclear fuel cycle. In discussing the matter with him, however, I realized that he was not even aware of the fact that the uranium-fission process produces plutonium, the material used to fuel atomic bombs, or that nuclear waste posed devastating health hazards.

This ignorance, unfortunately, is not unique. Over the past seven years, I have met many other politicians —in Australia, France, England, Ireland and the United States—who were equally uninformed. Nuclear power has been with us for more than three decades. Our public servants should have taken the initiative long ago to educate themselves on this life-and-death issue. Is it not their moral responsibility to do so?

The "front end" of the fuel cycle—the mining, milling and enrichment of uranium—is dangerous, because at every step, uranium decays into radioactive by-products which pose a threat both to workers in the nuclear industry and to the public at large.

MINING

In the United States, most uranium ore is mined in the Colorado Plateau and the Wyoming Basin. During the process, two highly carcinogenic radioactive substances are released: radium and radon. Radium, an alpha emitter with a half-life of 1,600 years, is a decay product of uranium which is found in uranium ore. If particles of the dust from uranium mines are swallowed, the radium is absorbed by the intestine and carried to the bone, where it can cause leukemia or bone cancer. Years ago, clockwork employees—predominantly women—painted the numbers on luminescent watch and clock faces using a radium-based paint. To make the figures more precise, many of them licked the tips of their paintbrushes, swallowing relatively large amounts of radium. A disproportionate percentage later died of bone cancer, leukemia, and acute radiation effects.

25

Radon, a gas, is a radioactive daughter isotope of thorium, which is a daughter-product of uranium. Inhaled, it can cause lung cancer. Changes in mining safety standards to protect against radon have now been implemented, but 20-50 percent of the American, German, and Canadian miners working under past conditions have already died—or will die—from cancer.

At certain levels of the Australian government, the hazards of uranium mining—and of radon—are recognized, and stringent regulations have been passed to protect miners' health. Thus, mines must be kept dust-free, and miners are required to wash their hands and faces thoroughly before they eat, in order to remove radium-contaminated dust. These hygienic measures, however, are inadequate. The miners I have spoken with said they had never been explicitly informed of the possible long-range cancer-causing and genetic effects of radiation; moreover, they reported safety regulations are not always enforced.

In 1976 I visited the only Australian uranium mine then in operation, the Mary Kathleen Mine located in hot, dry Queensland. I was given a tour and later spoke to the miners about the medical and military dangers of uranium and uranium mining. I asked the plant manager whether radon alpha emission near the men was being measured; he replied that it was not. The only radiation monitored was gamma radiation from the uranium ore at the mine face. The radon was safe, he told me, because the mine was open-cut, above-ground, and "the wind blows the dust and gas away." His rationalization was patently feeble. As we stood there, talking in the open in the heat of the day, the air was completely still; dust hung heavily around the mine and swirled about the trucks as they moved along the roads. One man was totally enveloped in dust as he sat in the open cabin of his truck while a load of freshly quarried ore was dumped into his vehicle's tray.

After I spoke to the workers at this mine, several told me that management had recorded high levels of radiation in their urine. Concerned, now that they had been informed about the dangers associated with radiation, they asked me what this condition might imply. I explained that by the time radiation is detected in the urine, it has probably already been deposited in various organs of the body—where it may have done irreparable damage.

MILLING

After uranium ore is mined, it is ground, crushed, and chemically treated. The end product is "yellowcake" (U_3O_8), a uranium compound. The waste ore, called tailings, is discarded outside the mill and left lying on the ground in huge mounds; over the last thirty years, about 100 million tons has been accumulating in the American Southwest. These tailings contain the radioactive materials thorium (half-life: 80,000 years) and radium.

Until recently, hundreds of acres of tailings thrown off from a once thriving uranium business lay on the ground in Grand Junction, Colorado. In the mid-1960s, city contractors hit upon the idea of using such tailings for cheap landfill and concrete mix. Construction firms used the waste ore to build a variety of structures, including schools, hospitals, private homes, roadways, an airport, and a shopping mall. In 1970, a local pediatrician noticed an increase of cleft palate, cleft lip, and other congenital defects among newborn babies in the area. Further investigation revealed that all these children had been born to parents living in homes built with tailings, and, when tested, many of these buildings demonstrated high radiation levels. Soon after this discovery, medical professionals at the University of Colorado's Medical Center obtained funding from the U.S. Environmental Protection Aegncy (EPA) to study the possible correlation between low-level radiation and a rise in birth defects. But a year later funds for the project were cut off: federal authorities claimed that the government had to cut back on many programs for

27

budgetary reasons. Clearly, it did not consider the Grand Junction study worth pursuing. It is our moral responsibility to these—and all—children, however, to undertake such follow-up studies. A similar instance of laxity has occurred in Australia.

The town of Port Pirie, South Australia, once hosted a government uranium mill, which, over the years, generated some 60 acres of tailings, which were dumped in a nearby tidal dam. After the mill closed, children began using the dam as a favorite spot to practice cricket, ride bikes, and play. During the late 1960s, a company specializing in rare earth materials bought the plant, refined pure thorium from imported rare earth sands, and exported it to Japan for use in color television sets. Soon after operations began, a shipload of the material was rejected at its Japanese port of entry when it was discovered that many barrels had ruptured during the rough voyage and were leaking the thorium onto the ship's deck. Sensitive to the hazards posed by radiation, and upset by the shipper's negligence, the Japanese refused the cargo and sent it back to Port Pirie —where it was immediately dumped into the tidal dam. The dam is periodically submerged by sea water, and radiation was undoubtedly absorbed by algae, mollusks, fish, and other marine life. At low tide, children would play in the dam, crawling through the empty thorium barrels, or fish in a nearby creek.

Radiation levels were monitored at the site in 1976, when the mill was again put up for sale, and in many locations, they were found to exceed World Health Organization standards. These disturbing data were eventually leaked to the press, initiating a public outcry: parents feared their children might contract leukemia or other forms of cancer. Government officials claimed that the children were in no danger and that there was no need even to have them checked regularly for possible ill effects. The parents apparently accepted the officials' word, and no program for medical follow-up was instituted.

Out of each ton of uranium ore extracted from the earth, 4 pounds is pure uranium. Of this amount, 99.3% is the unfissionable isotope uranium-238. Only somewhat less than half an ounce is the fissionable uranium-235. Since a specific minimal concentration of the latter isotope is needed for the fission process in most commercial reactors, but only 0.7 percent of the uranium found in its natural state is of this variety, uranium ore must be "enriched" so that its uranium-235 content comes to comprise approximately 3 percent of its bulk.

The enrichment process is extremely expensive, consumes vast amounts of energy (the Oak Ridge, Tennessee, enrichment plant consumes the electricity provided by two 1,000-megawatt nuclear reactors), and leaves radioactive tailings containing presently-unusable uranium-238. Enrichment is so costly that in the United States the federal government has to underwrite the process and operate America's three enrichment plants, located at Oak Ridge; Paducah, Kentucky; and Portsmouth, Ohio. Such subsidy has enabled this country to become the world's chief supplier of enriched uranium. It is a powerful position to hold, for it literally gives America almost complete control over—and responsibility for—the growth of nuclear power production throughout the free world at this time.

The United States may soon lose its nuclear clout, however. Not only are its uranium reserves declining, but both South Africa and France have already built small enrichment plants of their own. These foreign installations should be recognized as a legitimate cause for concern: They may well make access to nuclear fuel and the subsequent manufacture of atomic weapons uncontrollable. Approximately two tons of weapons-grade enriched uranium and plutonium have already disappeared from nuclear facilities in the United States: Some of it may have been stolen, possibly—as suggested by one CIA report—by Israel. Unfortunately, there is every indication that such acts—whether perpetrated by nations, or terrorist groups, or even criminal elements—will become a standard feature of a nuclear-powered world.

FUEL FABRICATION

After undergoing the process of enrichment, the uranium—in the form of uranium oxide (UO_2)—is converted into small pellets. These cylindrical pellets are then placed into 12-14 foot-long metal fuel rods less than 1 inch in diameter. A typical 1,000-megawatt reactor contains about 50,000 fuel rods comprising more than 100 tons of uranium in a cylindrical space about twenty feet in diameter and fourteen feet high. During the fabrication of these pellets, workers are exposed to the dangers of low-level gamma radiation emitted from the enriched fuel.

NUCLEAR REACTORS

When the fuel rods are packed into the center (or "core") of a "nuclear reactor" and covered with water, the enriched uranium is ready to undergo fission. In undergoing this process, the nucleus of a uranium-235 atom breaks apart into fragments (or fission products—the nuclei of lighter elements such as strontium or cesium), plus heat, and one or more free neutrons. The neutrons released by the splintering of each nucleus in turn break up the nuclei of other atoms. When each free neutron absorbed by a uranium nucleus is replaced by a free neutron released by another fissioning atom, the reactor "goes critical" and the chain reaction becomes self-sustaining. Control rods, which absorb the fast-moving neutrons, regulate the speed of the process.

Fission releases a tremendous amount of heat, which is used by the reactor to boil water. The boiling water produces steam, which turns a turbine—and generates electricity. Nuclear fission is thus a very sophisticated and expensive method of boiling water—analogous to cutting butter with an electric saw.

In addition to generating electricity, uranium fission throws off hundreds of radioactive isotopes—all carcinogenic and mutagenic, with half-lives ranging from several seconds to 24,400 years—or longer.

The operation of nuclear power plants presents many hazards which have been disregarded because, as frequently happens, short-term profit has outweighed the responsibility of industry and government to protect the public.

On February 2, 1976, three men with fifty-six years of combined work experience at all levels of the nuclear industry resigned from secure (and well-paying) positions as nuclear engineers at General Electric. Dale Bridenbaugh, Richard Hubbard, and Gregory Minor explained their reasons for leaving to the Joint Committee on Atomic Energy:

> When we first joined the General Electric Nuclear Energy Division, we were very excited about the idea of this new technology—atomic power— and the promise of a virtually limitless source of safe, clean and economic energy for this and future generations. But now . . . the promise is still unfulfilled. The nuclear industry has developed to become an industry of narrow specialists, each promoting and refining a fragment of the technology, with little comprehension of the total impact on our world system . . . We [resigned] because we could no longer justify devoting our life energies to the continued development and expansion of nuclear fission power—a system we believe to be so dangerous that it now threatens the very existence of life on this planet.
>
> We could no longer rationalize the fact that our

31

daily labor would result in a radioactive legacy for our children and grandchildren for hundreds of thousands of years. We could no longer resolve our continued participation in an industry which will depend upon the production of vast amounts of plutonium, a material known to cause cancer and produce genetic effects, and which facilitates the continued proliferation of atomic weapons throughout the world.

During their long testimony, these men claimed, among other things, that the defects and deficiencies in just the design of nuclear reactors alone created severe safety hazards, and that the combined deficiencies "in the design, construction and operation of nuclear power plants makes a nuclear power plant accident, in our opinion, a certain event. The only question is when, and where."

What makes an accident in a nuclear power station uniquely dangerous is the potential release into the environment of highly poisonous radioactive elements which can contaminate large areas of land and make them uninhabitable for thousands of years. What makes an accident seem inevitable is the human factor. The most advanced plant is still at the mercy of the fallible human beings who design, build, and operate it. Millions of parts are needed to construct a nuclear reactor, and each must be made, assembled, and operated with little room for error.

The design of a nuclear power plant is extremely complex; its construction very difficult. As the resigning engineers noted, these aspects of plant management are in the hands of specialists who do not necessarily understand the work of—or even communicate with—other specialty groups. In fact, today no one individual or group coordinates the complete process of building and operating such a reactor. The Nuclear Regulatory Commission (NRC)—formerly the Atomic Energy Commission (AEC), with no appreciable change of staff in between—is in charge of licensing and inspecting each plant. Its inspection, however, is generally confined to spot checks a few days each year. Daily responsibility for plant inspection and radiation monitoring rests with the licensees. Such an arrangement is similar to allowing restaurant owners to inspect the cleanliness of their own kitchens.

Nuclear power plants operate under many untested theoretical principles. Certain safety systems are built on the shaky test results of computer models. Many components are made of metals susceptible to failure from contact with the nuclear environment. As a result, corrosion causes cracks and subsequent leaks that are often difficult to remedy in certain sections of the plant, because localized intense radioactivity prevents entrance. The nuclear industry has avoided making certain necessary repairs by conducting computer studies which prove that a particular pipe or component part was unnecessary in the first place. In engineering language, this practice is termed a "fix."

In a nuclear plant, the repair of a mere pipe, a simple task under ordinary conditions, often requires that the plant be shut down; many workers must be called in. Some years ago, a pipe failed at the Indian Point I plant, located on the Hudson River 24 miles north of New York City. As a result, the plant was rendered inoperable for six months and 1700 certified welders— almost every certified union welder in the Consolidated Edison Company—were needed to repair the damage. It was necessary to hire that many because within a few minutes each worker would receive the dose of radiation deemed allowable for a three-to-six-month period.

Like the workers at the Mary Kathleen Uranium Mine, workers at nuclear power plants in America are told in only general terms that radiation can be dangerous; they are not informed specifically of its carcinogenic and mutagenic properties. While each person must wear a badge which monitors the level of radiation to which he or she is exposed, this device registers only gamma radiation, not the alpha or beta emissions that

33

can be swallowed or inhaled. Furthermore, workers are permitted to receive thirty to a hundred times as much radiation per year as the limit set for the general public.

At present the nuclear industry is required to keep employee medical records current for no more than five years while workers are on the job. They can be destroyed when employees leave. Radiation records must be kept, but if cancer shows up later in any of these workers, it is difficult to assess the relationship of the disease to the radiation. Medical follow-ups are rarely conducted to determine whether former employees have contracted malignancies, or to check whether their children have been genetically affected by preconception irradiation to their father's or mother's gonads. (In the event of such disability, no compensation is paid.)

At many plants the hiring of unskilled itinerant or migrant labor is a common practice. These employees work briefly for high wages, often in areas of intense radiation. After receiving their legal maximum dose at one facility (sometimes in only one day or less), they may be hired on at another plant without ever being questioned concerning their previous radiation exposure. Plants hire these transients in order to preserve the "body banks" of their full-time employees. At a reprocessing plant in West Valley, New York, which is now inoperable, "fresh bodies" were often recruited from local colleges and bars to do the industry's dirty work. From a medical standpoint, this practice is unsafe; it should be declared illegal.

The nuclear plant accident which poses the greatest threat to public safety is termed a "meltdown" or the "melt-through-to-China syndrome." Such an event could be initiated by a pipe breakage or safety failure—whether accidental or the result of sabotage—that would permit the coolant water at a reactor's core to drop below the level of the fuel rods. The rods would become so hot that they would melt; then the whole mass of molten uranium would burn through the "container" (the concrete base of the plant) and into the earth, possibly triggering a steam explosion that would blow the containment vessel apart, releasing its deadly radioactive contents into the atmosphere. Soon after a meltdown with release of radioactivity, thousands would die from immediate radiation exposure; more would perish two to three weeks later of acute radiation illness. Food, water, and air would be so grossly contaminated that in five years there would be an epidemic of leukemia, followed fifteen to forty years later by an upsurge in solid cancers. The genetic deformities that might appear in future generations are hard to predict, but they surely will occur.

Such a meltdown could have staggering consequences. The Union of Concerned Scientists recently conducted a two-year study of a hypothetical "expanded nuclear economy" and concluded that before the year 2000 A.D., close to fifteen thousand people in the United States may die of minor reactor accidents. Moreover, they estimated that in the same time period there is a one percent chance that a major nuclear accident will occur, killing nearly 100,000 people; most will die of radiation-induced cancers.

The United States has already come frighteningly close to experiencing a catastrophic meltdown. In 1975, the Brown's Ferry atomic power station near Athens, Alabama, witnessed the worst accident in the history of the U.S. nuclear industry. Two electricians, using candles to check for air leaks, accidentally set fire to some highly combustible polyurethane foam used as a sealant. The fire quickly spread to the plastic coverings around the cables controlling the operation of the reactor and the emergency core cooling system, or ECCS (a device designed to prevent a meltdown by piping in more water if the coolant water in the reactor core begins to fall uncontrollably below safe levels). The blaze raged in the bowels of the plant for seven and a half hours. In the process it severed thousands of cables, knocking out most of the reactor's control systems and the ECCS. Operators watched helplessly as the water level in the reactor core dropped sharply.

Then, after workers resorted to equipment not intended for emergency cooling services, the water began to rise. A major disaster was thereby averted, but by accident, not design.

A wide array of regulatory violations and inadequate safeguards were disclosed in the wake of this accident. First, it was revealed that the NRC had no fire hazard inspection program; only if a plant were insured for fire damage could an insurance company monitor fire-related problems. Since Brown's Ferry was not thus insured, it had never been subjected to fire-safety inspections of any kind. Second, it was eventually found that the cables were located too closely together, such that a single mishap would affect both the operational cables controlling the reactor's standard operations and the ECCS cables. Third, although the emergency menaced many lives, local citizens were never alerted—and evacuation plans were not put into effect—because no one informed the local authorities.

Another inherent deficency that was revealed concerned the design of backup safety systems. Such systems may be redundant (that is, built of multiple but identical components) or diverse (each designed to function differently). Brown's Ferry had a redundant cabling system and five diverse emergency core cooling systems. All were disabled by the single event. At the time of the accident, Greg Minor, one of the engineers who later resigned from GE, was in charge of control design for many of the systems at Brown's Ferry. Before the fire, he considered the redundancy–diversity setup extremely reliable. The near calamity convinced him that no reactor is safe in human hands. As he and the other two engineers stressed in their testimony, "Safety features are constantly being worked on, but the tremendous cost, schedule and political pressures experienced [by the industry] make unbiased decisions, with true evaluations of the consequences, impossible to achieve. The primary focus ... has been to 'prove' the plants are safe enough for continued operations—not to openly assess their true safety."

The fact that many plants are built and operate according to the same design has been a major drawback in the development of the nuclear industry. If a safety feature in one is found to be at fault, all other plants sharing that feature should also be shut down for inspection and repair. Since the industry's inception, plants have generally spent half their time idle because of breakdowns and failures, usually involving safety-related equipment. At present the inconvenience caused by delayed service is minor, because the nuclear industry contributes only 3 percent of the United States' total energy consumption, but if nuclear power becomes the nation's major source of energy, serious problems could arise when large sections of the nation are left without electricity for months at a time. Continual brownouts and blackouts might so try the public's patience that safety concerns may be sacrificed.

The world's first nonmilitary reactor began operating in Canada in 1947 and was soon plagued with breakdowns and accidents. By the late sixties, nuclear plants in Britain, the U.S., the U.S.S.R., and Switzerland had all experienced major accidents as well, which resulted in death or injury to personnel and were potentially dangerous to the general public.

In 1957, an accident at Britain's Windscale reactor on the Irish sea released a cloud of radioactivity across neighboring fields and villages. Soon afterward, the government supervised the disposal of thousands of gallons of contaminated milk into the sea nearby. This action may have spared the public temporarily, but not for long. The polluted ocean water contaminated marine life and fish-eating mammals, and the radioactivity eventually worked its way up the food chain. Later studies revealed high levels of iodine-131 in the thyroid glands of local residents.

Following the Windscale accident, the British government compensated local farmers for the contamination and loss of their milk. If a similar major accident or meltdown occurred in the United States, however, few people would be adequately reimbursed for radiation-induced illness, or loss of life or property, because the liability of the U.S. nuclear industry is limited. In the 1950s, private insurance companies recognized that nuclear power generation was an enterprise fraught with risk: They predicted that a nuclear accident of substantial proportions could financially destroy them, and they were therefore reluctant to provide insurance. Because Congress was eager to promote nuclear power, however, it passed the *Price-Anderson Act* which absolved America's power companies of major financial responsibility in the event of a nuclear disaster. This Act recognizes that the nuclear industry could never have developed if private insurance had to cover all contingent liabilities. In fact, former Pennsylvania insurance commissioner Herbert Deneberg has calculated that if insurance companies were willing to cover the risk, the premium required to insure a nuclear plant would be about $23.5 million per year—a figure roughly equivalent to the entire current costs of plant operation and maintenance.

The *Price-Anderson Act* limits U.S. government and private corporate liability to $560 million for each nuclear generator. Claims in excess of $560 million would require legislative action. But a major nuclear accident would cause billions of dollars in property damage alone, not to speak of massive loss of life. What dollar-value can we attach to each life lost?

In the event of a nuclear mishap, individual citizens have no recourse to their own insurance firms. Most homeowner's policies include a "nuclear exclusion" clause which denies an individual compensation for a "nuclear catastrophe"—whether caused by nuclear war or nuclear power generation.

While a major nuclear accident might result from internal plant safety failures, nuclear reactors are also vulnerable to terrorist takeovers and internal sabotage by dissatisfied or simply unstable employees. A recent U.S. government study concluded—in all seriousness—that, in order to ensure adequate protection, every plant should: 1) employ a full-time guard armed with a bazooka, to shoot down any threatening helicopters and aircraft; 2) obtain the services of a psychiatrist, to assess the behavior of employees; and 3) discourage gambling among workers lest it attract loan sharks and mobsters.

In fact, when a country is dotted with nuclear power plants, enemies and terrorist organizations need no nuclear weapons to wage nuclear war; they need only drop a conventional bomb on a nuclear reactor to release all the radiation it contains, killing thousands of people. Analysts have calculated that if Europe had been powered by nuclear generators during World War II, it would still be uninhabitable due to widespread radioactive contamination of air, food, and water.

The dangers intrinsic to the nuclear industry are unique. Not only is nuclear technology unsafe, the industry has virtually ignored the fact that a reactor's highly radioactive waste products are indestructible. Were all the dangers I have enumerated thus far miraculously overcome, the sole problem of waste disposal —and its impact on future generations—should be sufficient to give pause. For, once created, some of these nuclear by-products will remain in our biosphere for thousands of years—wreaking irreversible damage on plant, animal, and human life. What moral right have we to leave such a legacy to our descendants?

4

Nuclear Sewage

The only commercial nuclear-fuel reprocessing facility ever to operate in the United States was located at West Valley, New York, about 30 miles south of

Buffalo. From 1966 (the year that it opened its doors) through 1972, the plant repeatedly violated radiation-safety standards. In October 1976, Nuclear Fuel Services, Inc., the private firm that owned and operated the facility, closed the plant permanently—bequeathing tons of radioactive waste to the citizens of New York State.

In 1977, the U.S. Congress's Committee on Government Operations spent $1 million to determine what might be done with West Valley's 600,000 gallons of high-level neutralized liquid waste and 2 million cubic feet of low-level solid waste. It concluded that the problem was "gargantuan" and might cost as much as $600–$700 million to remedy.

While in Washington, D.C., to address the 1977 Convention of the Association for the Advancement of Science, I was invited to the office of the Congressman who represented the West Valley district. To my surprise, he proceeded to ask me what I thought could be done. I replied that I did not know, for as a physician, I have no answers for the problems posed by the "back end" of the nuclear fuel cycle: the disposal of the lethal radioactive wastes produced each year by America's commercial and military nuclear programs. Nor, unfortunately, does anyone else—including the nation's nuclear engineers.

The term "nuclear waste" ("radwaste") refers to all the unusable, radioactively contaminated by-products of the nuclear fuel cycle and the weapons program. Intensely radioactive, "high-level" waste consists of fission products of uranium in the form of either intensely radioactive spent fuel or as a concentrated liquid or solid. Both forms contain substantial quantities of deadly plutonium. "Low-level" wastes include contaminated articles of clothing, decommissioned plant components, and fission by-products given off by nuclear reactors in dilute aqueous and gaseous solution; the toxicity of "low-level" wastes is said to be reduced even further by dilution into the environment.

40

Hundreds of radioactive elements are produced as uranium is consumed by the fission process, and these isotopes gradually build up in a reactor's fuel rods and begin to hinder its efficiency. In addition, some uranium-235 remains unfissioned; it, together with plutonium, can be retrieved and reprocessed for use at the front end of the fuel cycle. Each year, therefore, reactors are shut down so that technicians can replace one-quarter to one-third of the fuel rods.

The disposal of these "spent" rods must be carried out with extreme care, for they are intensely radioactive: a few seconds of unshielded exposure would deliver a lethal dose.

The rods are also extremely hot and must be stored temporarily in a pool of water usually located near the reactor. The water cools the rods, preventing them from spontaneously melting and releasing their poisonous contents into the atmosphere, and permits their radioactivity to decline in isolation. The swimming pool-like structures are designed to hold the spent fuel for three to six months. The rods are then sent to a reprocessing plant in order to extract the residual uranium-235 and plutonium-239.

In 1977, President Jimmy Carter declared a moratorium on the operation of commercial reprocessing plants in the United States, in the hope that other countries would follow this nation's example and refrain from reprocessing their spent fuel to build atomic bombs. Because there are no commercial reprocessing plants in operation in the United States today, individual nuclear plants are required to store their spent fuel rods in the holding pools indefinitely, and the accumulation of such rods is causing the pools to become dangerously full. The Nuclear Regulatory Commission has granted several nuclear plants an interim license to pack their fuel rods even closer together, although a study on the safety of this procedure has yet to be completed. Such "compaction" however, may result in the production of a critical mass—causing a meltdown in the storage pool—and subsequent nuclear disaster. By the end of 1976, 3,000 metric tons of spent fuel lay in nuclear pools across the United States. By 1983, an estimated 13,000 tons will be dangerously straining the capacity of present storage pool facilities.

The U.S. military continues to reprocess the fuel in its nuclear reactors by first dissolving the spent rods in nitric acid. The solution that results is highly corrosive. Today, there are more than 74 million gallons of this high-level liquid waste in storage tanks in the United States; many of these wastes are so hot that they boil spontaneously and continuously. Most can be found at the Hanford Military Reservation in Washington and at the Savannah River facility in South Carolina. The major portion of these wastes lie in huge carbon-steel tanks which cannot withstand the waste's corrosive properties for more than twenty-five years; newer stainless steel tanks can last for fifty. But what is half a century compared to the thousands of years that this radioactive material must be kept isolated from the environment?

Moreover, many of these tanks have already sprung deadly leaks. From 1958 to 1975, twenty of Hanford's older, single-walled carbon steel tanks developed cracks through which 430,000 gallons of high-level waste leaked into the soil. In 1973 alone, an oversight on the part of a tank operator caused the escape of 115,000 gallons. These accidents may have disastrous consequences. The Hanford Reservation is located several hundred feet above the Columbia River. With no means to halt its descent, the escaped waste is migrating through the soil toward the water table and the Columbia River system, which supplies drinking water to cities in the Northwest.

Eight double-wall tanks at the Savannah River facility have shown stress corrosion cracks. In one tank, 175 cracks were detected: 100 gallons of high-level waste have leaked into the soil adjacent to the Savannah River. Local rainfall—4 inches per month—may hasten migration of the isotopes into the river.

Between 1946 and 1970, the U.S. military encased 47,500 55-gallon drums of low-level waste in concrete-lined steel drums and dumped them into the Pacific Ocean about thirty miles outside San Francisco Bay. One third of these drums are now leaking radioactivity into the Bay Area's major fishing grounds. Giant sponges, many of them over 3 feet high and believed by some to be mutants, have attached themselves to the drums.

In an attempt to minimize the corrosive properties of West Valley's high-level waste, scientists have used sodium hydroxide to neutralize the acid solution in which spent fuel rods were dissolved. Unfortunately, this procedure results in greater problems than it solves, for it doubles the waste volume and, over a period of time, precipitates a radioactive sludge consisting of strontium-90, cesium-137, other fission products, and some plutonium to the bottom of the tanks. Because of the probable high concentration of plutonium in this sludge, some experts fear that it may go "critical," initiating a reaction similar to a melt-down and releasing tons of deadly radioactive materials into the biosphere. If the 600,000 gallons of high-level waste stored at West Valley were to be dispersed in this way, the resulting radiation could devastate Buffalo and surrounding towns.

The consequences of such a disaster were foreshadowed by an accident that occurred in 1958 in Russia, at a vast nuclear complex in Kyshtym, a small town in the Ural Mountains. According to the Soviet scientist Dr. Zhores Medvedev, an "enormous explosion, like a volcano of radioactive waste" dispersed clouds of radioactivity "over hundreds of miles." He reports: "Tens of thousands of people were affected, hundreds dying, though the real figures have never been made public." The area around Kyshtym is now a wasteland, devoid of life. It will remain uninhabitable for years.

This Soviet disaster, apparently at a waste-repository site, was revealed in CIA reports which were released in 1977 under the Freedom of Information Act. It is not unfair to ask why the U.S. government covered up the occurrence of this accident for almost twenty years.

Many low-level wastes accumulate during the daily operation of nuclear reactors. Solid wastes in this category (contaminated plant equipment and clothing) are buried close to the earth's surface for easy recovery, since such burial is considered by technicians to be only temporary until safe, long-term storage facilities are arranged. Some 13 million cubic feet of solid military and research waste, containing 2,200 pounds of plutonium, are presently buried in five principal shallow-land sites in the United States, and it is estimated that by the year 2000 there will be 7 million additional cubic feet of commercial waste needing disposal. The radioactive elements emanating from these wastes are often leached into the soil by rainfall. In addition, these materials are readily susceptible to disinterment: Several years ago it was discovered that contaminated gloves, wheelbarrows, and shovels were missing from an unguarded, unmarked burial site in Nevada; it was later revealed that local citizens, totally unaware of the dangers involved, had dug up and used the equipment.

Animals that we do not use for food also act as carriers of radioactive particles. A study at the Hanford Reservation showed, for example, that jackrabbits had spread radioactivity over a wide area. They picked up the material by burrowing near trenches where radioactive waste was buried. They obviously ate or ingested some of this material, since traces of the radioactive isotopes were found in their feces. Such traces were also found in the feces of coyotes and the bones of dead hawks—animals which had apparently eaten the radioactive jackrabbits.

Government regulatory policies permit a certain amount of low-level liquid waste to be returned to

44

the environment. Nuclear advocates and government regulatory agencies claim that this liquid effluent leaks into the environment in "safe concentrations" and that "routine emissions" of this type containing long-lived isotopes are even further diluted by the ecosphere. However, even if these isotopes are very dilute, they will inevitably become re-concentrated in the aquatic food chain.

Government agencies similarly permit a certain amount of radiation to be "routinely" emitted from a reactor stack, arguing that the gaseous radioactive effluent consists primarily of krypton and xenon, two elements that will not be incorporated into biological systems to any appreciable degree for "many years." Nevertheless, scientists are uncertain about the long-range effect of krypton emission on the environment; a gamma-emitter, krypton has been found to concentrate in the fat layers of the lower abdomen and upper thighs, near the gonads. To claim that the radioactivity in these discharges is diluted to safe levels is fallacious: it in fact adds to the existing levels of background radiation, increasing the risk of disease.

In addition to "routine emissions," "abnormal releases" of low-level radiation often occur as a result of plant accidents. Frequently reported in the press, these releases are usually accompanied by a statement from the NRC claiming that the amount of radiation that escaped was lower than the normal background radiation (the implication is that it was therefore "safe"). Missing from these accounts is the fact that any release of radiation *adds* to the level of background radiation, thereby increasing the risk of radiation-induced cancers and mutations.

Examples of "abnormal releases" abound: With a half-life of 17 million years, iodine-129 enters the food chain and eventually concentrates in the human thyroid gland. According to a report issued by the Environmental Protection Agency in 1972, the iodine-129 removal system installed at the West Valley reprocessing facility did not perform according to dèsign. As a result, during the plant's operation (from 1966 to 1971), 45 percent of the total content of iodine-129 in the reprocessed fuel escaped into the nearby environment. At a distance of 5-6 miles from the plant, specific activity levels of iodine-129 were found to be 10,000 times greater than normal background radiation; 10 miles from the plant the levels were 10 times higher. In 1976, Vermont Yankee emptied 83,000 gallons of low-level waste water into the Connecticut River. In Florida, a leaking storage pool of spent fuel rod coolant has dumped thousands of gallons into the ocean because there is nowhere the radioactive fuel could be shipped so that repairs could be made. A recent explosion at Connecticut's Millstone I plant released excessive amounts of radiation into the environment.

Every nuclear power plant will eventually end up on the radioactive garbage heap, because a plant can operate for only twenty to thirty years before it becomes too radioactive to repair or maintain. When the time comes for a plant's demise, it must be shut down and "decommissioned": It must either be disassembled by remote control (because it is simply too radioactive to handle manually) and its constituent parts buried, or the entire plant must be buried under tons of earth or concrete to become a radioactive mausoleum for hundreds of thousands of years. In either case the remains must be guarded virtually forever.

A nuclear reactor constructed near Los Angeles is now undergoing the delicate process of disassembly by remote control. Built in the 1950s, this small plant cost $13 million. The price of demolition is estimated at $6 million and the project will take two years to complete. Authorities have not yet determined where to bury the plant's radioactive remains.

Larger reactors (1000 megawatt or greater) may in fact be impossible to decommission. Commonwealth Edison's Dresden plant in Morris, Illinois (at seventeen years old the oldest commercial reactor in the United States) has become too radioactive to repair. Since a new unit would cost more than $200 million, the utility is planning to clean the present plant for $35 million. The untried operation could impose serious health hazards on employees who must work in areas of high radiation.

Can we do anything to protect ourselves and future generations from the lethal legacy of nuclear sewage? At present the answer is no. Technologists have offered a number of ingenious proposals, ranging from solidification of high-level waste in glass containers and burial in salt formations, to lowering waste into ocean trenches, burying it under Antarctic ice, or launching rockets loaded with it into the sun. None of these techniques have been proven to be practical or safe.

Nuclear industry projections anticipate a total of 152 million gallons of high-level waste by the year 2000. The cost of preparing even our present load of 83 million gallons for geological disposal, however, is currently estimated at $2-$20 billion. Who will absorb these costs? At present it is not clear. The utilities want the American government (i.e., the taxpayer) to take on the wastes generated by nuclear technology. Since they do not account for the costs of decommissioning or waste disposal in their present rates, the utilities can easily present a case for "cheap" energy. Seen in its entirety, however, nuclear energy is far from cheap, and the hidden costs—to our well being—are enormous.

Succumbing to technological fervor, the U.S. government prematurely committed enormous economic resources, together with political and scientific reputations, to a half-baked technology that is neither cheap, clean, nor safe. The nation's public utilities should not have been permitted to proceed with nuclear energy production until they demonstrated that the public's health could be protected from the carcinogenic and mutagenic effects of its radioactive wastes. This was not done.

Industry engineers and physicists concede that the nuclear waste problem remains to be solved, but in their public pronouncements they urge us to trust them, to have faith in their abilities and in the inevitable advance of technology. I have no confidence in this line of reasoning. It is as if I were to reassure a patient suffering from terminal cancer by saying, "Don't worry, my medical training will enable me to discover a cure."

Nor can technology alone ever provide the answers we seek. For even if unbreakable, corrosion-resistant containers could be designed, any storage site on earth would have to be kept under constant surveillance by incorruptible guards, administered by moral politicians living in a stable, warless society, and left undisturbed by earthquakes, natural disasters, or other acts of God for no less than half a million years—a tall order which science cannot fill.

5

Plutonium

Plutonium is one of the most carcinogenic substances known. Named after Pluto, god of the underworld, it is so toxic that less than one-millionth of a gram (an invisible particle) is a carcinogenic dose. One pound, if uniformly distributed, could hypothetically induce lung cancer in every person on earth.* Found in

---

*Toxicity figures are for plutonium-239, the isotope used to fuel atomic bombs. Other isotopes are produced in nuclear reactors, including Pu238, Pu240, and Pu241. The mixture is 5.4 times more toxic than Pu-239 alone.

nature only in a remote region of Africa—and in minute amounts—plutonium is produced in a nuclear reactor from U-238 in quantities of 400-500 pounds annually! This alpha-emitter has a half-life of 24,400 years and, once created, remains poisonous for at least half a million years.

Plutonium is a chemically reactive metal which, if exposed to air, ignites spontaneously to produce respirable particles of plutonium dioxide, a compound also produced as a talcum-fine powder during fuel reprocessing. These particles can be transported by atmospheric currents and inhaled by people and animals. When lodged within the tiny airways of the lung, plutonium particles bombard surrounding tissue with alpha radiation. Smaller particles may break away from the larger aggregates of the compound to be absorbed through the lung and enter the bloodstream. Because plutonium has properties similar to those of iron, it is combined with the iron-transporting proteins in the blood and conveyed to iron storage cells in the liver and bone marrow. Here, too, it irradiates nearby cells, inducing liver and bone cancer, and leukemia.

Plutonium's ironlike properties also permit the element to cross the highly selective placental barrier and reach the developing fetus, possibly causing teratogenic damage and subsequent gross deformities in the newborn infant. Plutonium is concentrated by the testicles and ovaries, where inevitably it will cause genetic mutations which will be passed on to future generations.

In 1969 the second-largest industrial fire in United States history consumed 2 tons of plutonium at a military reactor site in Rocky Flats, Colorado. Miraculously, the fire was contained within the plant; nevertheless, plutonium oxide escaped and reached parts of Denver, 16 miles away. Radiation tests in the region demonstrated that thousands of acres of land, including a major water source, were contaminated. (Some of the soil contamination originated in 1,400 barrels of plutonium-contaminated oil stored above ground near the plant gates.) Hearings held by officials of the Colorado Department of Health in 1973 revealed that many local farm animals were being born with grotesque deformities.

The food chain concentrates plutonium many times over, most commonly in fish, birds, eggs, and milk; however, since plutonium molecules are large, they are not usually absorbed directly into the body through the gastrointestinal tract except by infants during the first four weeks of life (at which time their immature intestinal walls permit absorption). The extreme susceptibility of infants is compounded by the fact that plutonium concentrates in milk, whether from animals or humans.

Plutonium does not simply vanish at the death of a contaminated organism. If, for example, someone were to die of a lung cancer induced by plutonium and were then cremated, contaminated smoke might carry plutonium particles into someone else's lungs. When a contaminated animal dies, its polluted carcass may be eaten by other animals, or its poisoned dust may be scattered by the winds, to be inhaled by other creatures. Similarly, the same plutonium particles can go on concentrating in the testicles and ovaries of successive generations of human beings, conceivably causing repeated genetic damage for up to 500,000 years, while the damaged genes are themselves passed on from generation to generation.

Plutonium-241 has another deadly characteristic: It produces americium, a byproduct with a half-life of 460 years. Americium is even more potent than its parent: Because it is more soluble than plutonium, it is more readily absorbed into the food chain. In recent years, this deadly material has been used to power 20 million ionizing smoke detectors, which if damaged —by fire, say—would release this carcinogenic element into the air in powdered form, to be inhaled by unsuspecting people. Manufacturers are required to demand that used and defective detectors be returned to the factory, but they do not explain the urgency of complying with this directive. What will happen to these devices? Most likely, they will end up in local dumps, where the americium will probably migrate into the soil and future food supplies.

When, in 1941, the American physicists Edwin McMillan and Glenn Seaborg first identified plutonium-239, they also discovered that it was fissionable; in other words, it was raw material for atomic bombs. Four years later the U.S. military tested plutonium's fission power on Nagasaki.

Only 10–20 pounds of plutonium are required to make an atomic bomb. Since each 1,000-megawatt reactor produces 400–500 pounds of the element per year, any nation possessing a reactor could theoretically make 20 to 40 atomic bombs annually. Thus, even a small experimental facility can become an effective bomb factory. India proved this fact in 1974, when it used plutonium extracted from an experimental reactor bought from Canada to build and detonate the subcontinent's first homemade nuclear device.

Researchers at America's Oak Ridge National Laboratory have designed a simple reprocessing plant that would take four to six months to build from readily obtainable, inexpensive materials. The first 22 pounds of plutonium-239, reprocessed from spent fuel derived from nuclear power reactors, would be ready within one week. The plant would produce 220 pounds of plutonium metal per month—enough for about 20 atomic bombs.

Plutonium's role in atomic bomb production has made its value soar on the black market; it is vulnerable to theft by non-nuclear nations, terrorists, racketeers, and lunatics. Once an individual or group is in possession of plutonium, bomb fabrication is not very difficult. Using only declassified information, college students have succeeded in designing functional bombs. The designs call for metal fixtures bought at local hardware stores and 10–20 pounds of plutonium (toxic only if inhaled or ingested), an amount that can easily be concealed in a shopping bag.

Nuclear technologists look to plutonium as an eventual substitute for uranium-235 in nuclear reactor energy production. Experts have estimated that the world's supply of uranium-235 will be depleted by the year 2000. To eliminate the need for it, the industry has designed what is known as the "fast breeder reactor," which is fueled by a combination of plutonium and uranium-238. It is called a "breeder" because in the process of generating electricity, it creates more plutonium than it consumes. The average estimated doubling rate is 30–50 years; France's breeder reactor, the Super-Phoenix, is expected to take 60 years to duplicate its plutonium load.

The plutonium slated to fuel future breeders now lies in the thousands of spent fuel rods stockpiled in storage tanks throughout the world. Before plutonium can be used in a breeder, however, it must be separated from the hundreds of other waste fission products found in the spent rods. In "reprocessing," the rods are first cooled in spent-fuel pools for several months, to allow the radioactive materials with shorter half-lives to decay; the "hot" rods are then packed into strong lead containers, loaded onto trucks, and shipped over miles of highway to a reprocessing plant, where they are dissolved in vats of nitric acid. The plutonium and uranium are separated, purified, and removed, leaving behind the remaining high-level fission waste in solution. The purified plutonium and uranium are again stored in heavy protective containers, to be shipped to breeder reactor sites.

The U.S. military has used this reprocessing technique to obtain weapons-grade plutonium since the 1940s. Today, tons of extracted plutonium are routinely shipped along the nation's highways and railways, and flown into airports. In the year 2020, in an expanded U.S. plutonium economy, it is estimated that some 30,000 tons of plutonium will be produced and well over a hundred thousand rail and highway shipments will be made annually. A single accident could irradiate thousands of people.

The operation of a breeder reactor is more hazardous than that of an ordinary commercial reactor. Once out of control, a fission reaction in a breeder could cause not only a meltdown but also a full-fledged nuclear explosion. In addition, breeders are cooled with liquid sodium (rather than water), a substance that ignites spontaneously when exposed to air and is therefore highly dangerous in its own right. In 1966 a near-meltdown at the Enrico Fermi I breeder in Michigan threatened the lives of thousands of Detroit area citizens; following the incident, the reactor was shut down.

The American moratorium on the operation of commercial reprocessing plants and breeder reactors declared by President Carter in 1977 fails to recognize that such nuclear facilities are mere refinements: since anyone working in a small, properly outfitted laboratory can extract enough plutonium from spent fuel rods to build an atomic bomb, every commercial reactor breeds plutonium that could be used for nuclear weapons.

Recently, in a joint announcement made by the American Electric Power Research Institute (a research arm of the electric utility industry) and Britain's Atomic Energy Authority, scientists from both countries admitted for the first time that current nuclear reactors are producing vast quantities of waste that can be fabricated into bombs. More specifically, they acknowledged that as the radioactivity in spent fuel rods lessens over time, every spent fuel storage facility in the world becomes an increasingly accessible "plutonium mine." To deter Third World countries and terrorists from taking advantage of this situation, these scientists advocate a new method of reprocessing.

Called the "civex" method, it is supposedly more effective than the previous "purex" technique because, instead of individually separating and purifying the uranium and plutonium, it combines the two elements with other fission products to create an impure mixture that is too radioactive to handle safely. Civex's advocates are convinced that this new technique will discourage proliferation, but it is doubtful. What is to stop a nation from installing a conventional reprocessing plant? What evidence is there that the threat of radiation exposure is any deterrent at all to those intent on obtaining weapons-grade material?

The ability to create plutonium by means of the nuclear fission process is one of humanity's most diabolical powers. Once created, this isotope must be isolated from the environment virtually forever. However, some plutonium—perhaps as much as 2 percent or more—cannot be accounted for and presumably escapes into the ecosphere during reprocessing, transport and other industry activities. Seaborg, the isotope's discoverer, has estimated that 1.6 million pounds of plutonium may be produced by the year 2000. Thus, by that time, as much as 32,000 pounds of the substance may be dispersing through the soil, water, and atmosphere in densely populated regions of the globe. Dr. John Gofman has shown that even with 99.99 percent storage reliability, 160 pounds of plutonium would still be released: enough cancer doses for almost fifteen times the earth's present population. If the full 2 percent were to contaminate the environment, then, in Gofman's words, "assuredly we can give up on the future of humans."

Nor is plutonium pollution just a problem of the future. It affects us all right now. In 1975 a study carried out by the National Center for Atmospheric Research in Boulder, Colorado, revealed that more than 5 metric tons of plutonium were thinly dispersed over the earth as a result of nuclear bomb-testing, satellite reentries and burnups, effluents from nuclear reprocessing plants, accidental fires, explosions, spills, and leakages. As a result, most people in the Northern Hemisphere already carry a very small plutonium load in their reproductive organs. As plutonium contamination of populated areas worsens, that load will increase—with potentially devastating consequences for future offspring.

6

M. A. D.
(Mutually Assured Destruction)

The vision of "peaceful" nuclear power as a reliable energy source in the United States is fading fast. In 1965 the U.S. government predicted that 1,000 nuclear reactors would be operating in America by the year 2000. But new power plant orders have decreased from 20 in 1974 to none at all in 1977. Today, 65 reactors are in operation, and only 185 are projected by 1985.

Why is the domestic nuclear power industry not fulfilling the expectations of its proponents? The reasons are mostly economic: The price of uranium has quadrupled in the past four years, largely because multinational corporations have curtailed production to keep prices high. The cost of constructing a nuclear power plant stands at around $1.2 billion, and total plant construction time is now 10 years. Frequent shutdowns due to safety-related problems have cut the operating capacity of most plants to 45–55 percent. However, perhaps the major obstacle to expansion of nuclear energy has been the rapidly growing public opposition.

Because the dramatic decline in the U.S. market for

reactors has threatened the financial survival of the nuclear industry, multinational nuclear suppliers, especially Westinghouse and General Electric, are now heavily promoting overseas trade. Their most eager customers are developing nations, such as South Korea, Mexico, Spain, Taiwan, Yugoslavia, and Brazil. Many of these countries lack the capital needed to purchase a nuclear power plant, so American loans are arranged through the Import Export Bank. They often lack power-transmitting grids to distribute the electricity generated, but the desire to produce electricity is not always their primary motivation: often their ultimate goal in purchasing a nuclear reactor is to gain access to nuclear weapons-grade materials and to join the "nuclear club." India proved this point in 1974; Israel claims to have nuclear capabilities; experts suspect that South Africa may have atomic weapons; Idi Amin claims he will have an atomic bomb within two years; the Shah of Iran, who already commands one of the world's largest air forces, plans to have twenty reactors in operation in 1994; and Argentina, Brazil, Pakistan, South Korea, and Taiwan have the potential to develop weapons capabilities in the very near future.

This spread of nuclear power plants around the world—and the directly related proliferation of nuclear weapons—seriously threatens global peace and order. At this writing, the United States and the Soviet Union still maintain the balance of power, but the sale of each new reactor tips the scale toward a world of uncontrollable proliferation, in which regional nuclear conflicts could draw the superpowers into all-out nuclear war.

The nuclear industry knows that the reactors it sells produce material for weapons, but its major concern seems to be corporate profit, not morality or human survival. (General Electric is known to have conducted promotional conferences with Egypt and Israel on the same day.)

Nuclear suppliers have, however, voiced concern over the use of reactor by-products for military ends: Corporate representatives from Great Britain, the United States, France, West Germany, Japan, Sweden, and other countries agreed in 1978 that any country buying a nuclear reactor and using its plutonium to manufacture bombs would receive a "reprimand." Such a scolding would not, of course, preclude further sales to the country at fault.

The U.N. is keenly aware of the weapons potential involved with nuclear power. To minimize the diversion of nuclear materials toward weapons manufacture, it passed the 1968 Non-Proliferation Treaty (NPT), whose signators agreed not to utilize nuclear materials to build bombs, or to sell such materials to any other country for that purpose. But the NPT is impotent: The world's nations are not required to ratify it, and those which have can retract their ratification with ninety days' notice—during which time a nuclear weapon could be produced.

In 1956 the U.N. established the International Atomic Energy Agency (IAEA) to police the world's nuclear facilities and deter the conversion of fissionable material into weapons. Since 1968, the purpose of the IAEA has been to enforce the NPT, but it has been given few powers to carry out its responsibilities. Agency inspectors (all too few in number) are authorized only to inspect for the misappropriation of nuclear materials for use in bombs; they are not empowered to prevent a country from actually building one. Moreover, this purportedly neutral regulatory body is *promoting* reactor sales: in 1975 it recommended that Pakistan build twenty-four nuclear plants by the end of the century.

The American government is also conscious of the "diversion" problem. The Nuclear Non-Proliferation Act, approved by the U.S. Congress in 1978, attempts to restrict foreign purchasers of American nuclear materials from diverting such materials into nuclear weapons, and calls for universal ratification of the NPT. But the new law gives the President power to override any denial by the NRC of an export license.

In April 1978, for example, the NRC refused to approve the sale of enriched uranium to India because it had not signed the NPT or complied with IAEA safeguards, but President Carter promptly exercised his option and approved the deal.

U.S. government policy toward nonproliferation has been totally inconsistent. Before Jimmy Carter was elected to office, he asserted that nuclear power should be the last resort in America's quest for new sources of energy, and in his inaugural address and first State of the Union message he set the goal of "eliminating nuclear weapons from the face of the Earth." In keeping with this goal, he placed a moratorium on nuclear reprocessing and on the construction of breeder reactors. But in his proposed energy legislation, he shifted his position, calling nuclear power a safe, reliable source of energy, and allocating $1.7 billion for its development in his 1978 budget, compared to only $421 million for solar and geothermal research. The Carter Administration continues to promote and encourage nuclear reactor sales to developing countries, making reprocessing and breeder moratoriums irrelevant. Moreover, while candidate Carter attacked arms sales and opposed U.S. leaders "who try to justify this unsavory business on the cynical grounds that by rationing out the means of violence we can somehow control the world's violence," his administration has overseen a rise in U.S. arms exports of 17 percent, to a total of $13.2 billion in 1978, maintaining America's role as the world's chief arms supplier.

The sale of commercial nuclear technology to the world's developing nations is an extremely dangerous aspect of the suicidal arms race that, in 1978, will move the earth $400 billion closer to Armageddon. At a rate of over $1 billion a day, nation after nation is stockpiling weapons of unprecedented destructive power, preparing the way for global catastrophe. Entrenched and self-perpetuating, the arms industry reaps enormous profits, while the world's military bureaucracies grow in political influence.

Foreign arms sales is a booming business. From 1960 through 1977, the U.S. sent arms worth $71 billion to 161 countries, accounting for almost half of all the weapons sold abroad. The U.S., Russia, France, Britain, and China continue to dominate the postwar arms race and are responsible for 80 percent of all military expenditures and foreign sales. But the sharpest proportional increase in expenditures for armaments since 1960 has occurred among the developing nations (9 percent of the world total in 1960, 18 percent in 1977)—those least able to afford such spending. Their entry into the international arms market means that military power is being dispersed more widely over the globe than in any previous time in history. The wealthy nuclear nations dominate the poor Third World, where the majority of the earth's citizens live. The result is a war system which integrates nuclear weapons with conventional arms and shifts great-power confrontations to the battlefields of the Third World.

No matter where military spending occurs, the effects are the same. Arms expenditures not only enhance the threat of global war, but divert precious resources from urgent social needs, obstruct economic growth, fuel inflation, and raise unemployment.

In today's world, 1.5 billion people lack access to professional health services. Over 1.4 billion people have no safe drinking water. More than 500 million people suffer from malnutrition. But world governments spend twice as much on armaments as on health care.

Although 700 million of their adult citizens are illiterate and 500 million (more than half) of their children do not attend school, today's developing nations are importing the most sophisticated conventional arms at a rate of $6 billion a year.

In our modern arms economy, military research consumes the creative efforts of over 500,000 scientists and engineers worldwide and gets more public funds than all social needs combined. Over half the scientists in the U.S.A. are employed by the military-industrial complex. And despite the much-publicized "energy crisis," energy research and development in the U.S. still gets only one-sixth as much funding as weapons research.

In 1978 the developed nations will spend twenty times more for their military programs than for economic assistance to the poorer countries. In two days the world spends on arms the equivalent of a year's budget for the United Nations and its specialized agencies. At present levels of military spending, the average person can expect, over his or her lifetime, to give up three to four years' income to the arms race.

In the words of Ruth Leger Sivard, former chief of the economics division of the U.S. Arms Control and Disarmament Agency, "There is in this balance of global priorities an alarming air of unreality. It suggests two worlds operating independently of each other. The military world, which seems to dominate the power structure, has first call on money and other resources, creates and gets the most advanced technology, and is seemingly out of touch with those threats to the social order that have nothing to do with weapons. The other world, the reality around us, has a vast and growing number of people living in poverty, old people who need care, more and more children who are unable to attend school, more families who never see a doctor, have an adequate dwelling, or escape from the edge of starvation. The everyday world is a global community whose members are increasingly dependent on one another for scarce resources, clean air and water, mutual survival. Its basic problems are too real, too complex, for military solutions."

While the gulf between the rich and the poor continues to widen, the poorest nations of the world, many dominated by military dictatorships, continue to arm themselves not only with weapons—but also with the capacity to produce them.

By the end of 1976 nineteen countries had nuclear reactors, including fifteen non-nuclear weapons countries. By 1984 twenty-eight non-nuclear-armed nations are expected to have reactors. Their combined potential annual production of plutonium will amount to 30,000 kilograms—enough to produce 10 atom bombs a day.

In 1946 Albert Einstein, apprehensive about humanity's misuse of the power of the atom, expressed great concern for the future of mankind. Today's nuclear arsenal must exceed his worst nightmare: Between them, the United States and the Soviet Union, alone, have deployed some 50,000 nuclear bombs which stand ready to exterminate virtually all life on earth.

When compared to the threat of nuclear war, the nuclear power controversy shrinks to paltry dimensions. A reactor meltdown might kill as many as 50,000 people; a war fought with nuclear weapons would put an end to civilization as we know it.

Conventional weapons release the molecular energies of TNT, the chemical compound trinitrotoluene. Nuclear weapons contain the explosive force of the stars: their power can be millions of times greater than conventional bombs.

Only 10–20 pounds of uranium-235 or plutonium-239 are needed to fuel an atomic bomb. Like a nuclear reactor, such a bomb operates on the fission principle: Enough of the material is brought together to form a critical mass, resulting in a chain reaction; in one-millionth of a second all the nuclei in the mass decompose, liberating the explosive power of as much as 20,000 tons of TNT. The explosion of one of these bombs over a modern city can kill 100,000 people and lay waste to an area miles in diameter.

Atomic bombs will play a large role in nuclear war. Hydrogen bombs will also be important. A hydrogen bomb works on the fusion principle, the same process that fuels the sun. In such a bomb, the atoms in 1,000 pounds of lithium deuteride are joined two at a time to form atoms of helium. In the process, enormous concussive force and thermal energy are released. The high temperature needed to get the process going is provided by an atom bomb, which serves as a triggering mechanism, releasing more than 15 million degrees of heat. A thousand times more powerful than an atom bomb, one hydrogen bomb can kill millions of people within seconds.

By adding a 1,000-pound shell of uranium-238 to the deuterium and uranium-235 (or plutonium-239) in the average hydrogen bomb, the weapon's explosive power may be doubled or tripled at very little additional cost. The result is a fission-fusion-fission superbomb with the explosive power of over 20 million tons of TNT. In addition to the great force and heat it gives off, such a bomb creates an enormous number of fission products which cause radiation effects long after detonation.

The explosive force in 1,000,000 tons of TNT is called a megaton. During all of World War II, a total of 3 megatons were detonated. Today, some hydrogen bombs have the explosive power of 5–25 megatons. The detonation of a single weapon of this nature over any of the world's major cities would constitute a disaster unprecedented in human history.

Today, many missiles carrying one heavy warhead have been replaced by more accurate ones carrying three to ten lighter warheads; called MIRV's (multiple independently targetable reentry vehicles), these weapons are capable of breaking away from the main rocket and landing on separate targets with deadly accuracy.

The United States has 11,894 "strategic" warheads in its arsenal today; Russia has 4,396. "Strategic" weapons are those designed by the super-powers to travel intercontinental distances for use against each other; such weapons can be launched from underground silos, or by bombers or submarines. The missiles that deliver them take off from launchpads and enter outer space; they reenter the earth's atmosphere at twenty times the speed of sound, reaching their destinations, as much as 9,000 miles away, within 30 minutes. Alerted by its military satellites, the targeted country may respond in kind by launching a counterattack. Limited nuclear war is highly unlikely. Escalating to all-out nuclear warfare using these weapons, a full-scale nuclear confrontation could last about 30 to 60 minutes from beginning to end.

"Tactical" nuclear weapons are meant for "theater" use—that is, for short-distance fighting. Russia has 10,000 tactical nuclear weapons; the United States has 20,000, based in Europe and the countries surrounding the Soviet Union.

Tens of thousands of these nuclear bombs can be released in a matter of seconds—possibly by accident, as John F. Kennedy once warned. Over 100 near-accidents have been recorded in the past thirty years. On a number of occasions, U.S. nuclear-armed submarines on reconnaissance missions have collided with Soviet vessels; a Russian airplane carrying a nuclear weapon crashed in the Sea of Japan; a Soviet guided missile destroyer reportedly exploded and sank in the Black Sea; and an American aircraft is known to have accidentally dropped four plutonium bombs on Spain.*

Our future is vulnerable not only to human error, but also to the frailty of human emotions. A reckless national leader, or one under severe stress, could be disastrous. Several weeks before former President Richard Nixon resigned, concerned administration officials reportedly removed the mechanisms by which he could start a nuclear war. Premier Leonid Brezhnev has been treated with cortisone, a drug that occasionally induces acute psychosis.

The complex technology required by America's military and defense apparatus concentrates an enormous amount of power in the hands of a few common mortals. Spending long hours in cramped quarters, two men guard each Titan missile silo in the United States, knowing that at any moment they may receive orders to launch the missiles against the enemy. Each is armed with a pistol and is under orders to shoot the other if

---

*The U.S. dug up tons of the heavily contaminated soil and buried it in trenches in Barnwell, South Carolina, where the average monthly rainfall of over 4 inches threatens to leach the buried plutonium into the Savannah River.

he exhibits abnormal behavior. Since these missiles were first deployed, thirty of these men have been seriously psychologically disturbed.

Twenty-four hours a day, in eight-hour shifts, an airplane circles near Phoenix, Arizona. It carries two senior military men holding keys that must be inserted simultaneously into a technological device to initiate nuclear war. It is hard to believe, but the future of all life on Earth could be invested in those keys.

The truth is that there are probably only two or three years before the Arms Race will be out of control. Within two years the technologists at the Pentagon will have finished developing a system called Launch-on-Warning. That means when the reconnaissance satellite detects something in Russia—maybe it's a missile going off, maybe it's an accident, maybe it's nothing—it sends a message back to a computer and then to all the missiles in America which go off within *three minutes. And there's no human input or intervention!*

Then there are the cruise missiles. They are small strategic weapons, about 10 to 20 feet long. Because they're so small they can be easily hidden and can't be counted. Up to now Russia and America could count each other's strategic weapons by satellite. That's why we got SALT II—you don't have to trust each other. Without the cruise, America and Russia—for the first time—are essentially equivalent. The cruise missile means the end of Arms Control, possibly detente, and the end of the SALT talks.

There very nearly was a nuclear war on November 9, 1979. A fellow in the Pentagon plugged a war games tape into a supposedly failsafe computer and the computer took it for real. All the American early warning systems around the world went on alert for six minutes. Three squadrons of planes took off armed with nuclear weapons. At the seventh minute the Presidential 747 command post was readied for take-off. (They couldn't find the President. He was to be notified at the seventh minute.) If in 20 minutes it hadn't been stopped, we

64

wouldn't be here right now. And twice again, on June 3 and June 6, 1980, two computer errors nearly led us into a nuclear war. Remember, 20 minutes is currently the time limit for a retaliatory nuclear attack. This country is a sleeping giant!

What would happen if the world's nuclear arsenals were put to use?

Erupting with great suddenness, a nuclear war would probably be over within hours. Several hundred to several thousand nuclear bombs would explode over civilian and military targets in the United States (every American city with a population of 25,000 or more is targeted), and an equal or greater number of bombs would strike the principal targets in Europe, the Soviet Union, and China. Both major and minor population centers would be smashed flat. Each weapon's powerful shock wave would be accompanied by a searing fireball with a surface temperature greater than the sun's that would set firestorms raging over millions of acres. (Every 20-megaton bomb can set a firestorm raging over 3,000 acres. A 1,000-megaton device exploded in outer space could devastate an area the size of six western states.) The fires would sear the earth, consuming most plant and wild life. Some experts believe that the heat released might melt the polar ice caps, flooding much of the planet. Destruction of the earth's atmospheric ozone layer by the rapid production of nitrous oxide would result in increased exposure to cosmic and ultraviolet radiation.

People caught in shelters near the center of a blast would die immediately of concussive effects or asphyxiation brought on as a result of oxygen depletion during the firestorms. Exposure to immense amounts of high-energy gamma radiation, anyone who survived near the epicenter would likely die within two weeks of acute radiation illness.

Those who survived, in shelters or in remote rural areas, would reenter a totally devastated world, lacking

65

the life-support systems on which the human species depends. Food, air, and water would be poisonously radioactive. Physical suffering would be compounded by psychological stress: For many, the loss of family, friends, and the accustomed environment would bring on severe shock and mental breakdown.

In the aftermath, bacteria, viruses, and disease-bearing insects—which tend to be thousands of times more radio-resistant than human beings—would mutate, adapt, and multiply in extremely virulent forms. Human beings, their immune mechanisms severely depleted by exposure to excessive radiation, would be rendered susceptible to the infectious diseases that such organisms cause: plagues of typhoid, dysentery, polio, and other disorders would wipe out large numbers of people.

The long-term fallout effects in the countries bombed would give rise to other epidemics. Within five years, leukemia would be rampant. Within 15 to 50 years, solid cancers of the lung, breast, bowel, stomach, and thyroid would strike down survivors.

Exposure of the reproductive organs to the immense quantities of radiation released in the explosions would result in reproductive sterility in many. An increased incidence of spontaneous abortions and deformed offspring, and a massive increase of both dominant and recessive mutations, would also result. Rendered intensely radioactive, the planet Earth would eventually become inhabited by bands of roving humanoids—mutants barely recognizable as members of our species.

What would be left? Experts have projected two possible scenarios. According to one, hundreds of millions of people in the targeted countries would die, but some might survive. According to the second, the synergistic ecological effects of thermal and nuclear radiation, long-term fallout, and exposure to increased cosmic radiation would make it doubtful that anyone could live for very long. Destruction would most likely be absolute. There will be no sanctuary.

Is it not remarkable how we manage to live our lives in apparent normality, while, at every moment, human civilization and the existence of all forms of life on our planet are threatened with sudden annihilation? We seem to accept this situation calmly, as if it were to be expected. Clearly, nuclear warfare presents us with the specter of a disaster so terrible that many of us would simply prefer not to think about it. But soothing our anxiety by ignoring the constant danger of annihilation will not lessen that danger. On the contrary, such an approach improves the chances that eventually our worst fears will be realized.

The United States and the Soviet Union already have enough firepower in their arsenals to destroy every city on earth seven times over. Still, the arms race continues, the weapons multiply and become more specialized, and the likelihood of their utilization grows. Why? Because both countries, driven by fear and a mutual distrust bordering on the pathological, are locked into a suicidal strategy calling, in the words of the Pentagon, for "mutually assured destruction" (MAD) as the best deterrent to war. But "arms for peace" and "security through mass genocide" are strategies that defy logic and common sense. They epitomize our nuclear madness.

Nuclear disarmament is the first and foremost task of our time; it must be given absolute priority. It is increasingly urgent that we find a way to achieve this goal, for time is running out. Moreover, with nuclear reactors and thousands of containers of radioactive wastes vulnerable to attack around the world, all war—conventional or nuclear—is rendered obsolete.

Our environmental circumstances changed dramatically when the appearance of nuclear weapons forever altered the nature of war. If we are to survive, we must accept personal responsibility for war and peace. We cannot afford to delegate these responsibilities to generals, politicians, and bureaucrats who persist in the politics of confrontation and in outmoded ways of

thinking that have always caused—and never prevented
—wars. International disputes must now be settled by
reason—not with weapons.

If the 1978 United Nations special session on disarmament proved anything, it is that existing ap-
proaches to arms control are inadequate—and that it
is seemingly impossible to get governments to commit
themselves to genuine disarmament. It is imperative,
therefore, that a mass movement of concerned citizens
around the globe take up this cause and compel our
governments to make nuclear disarmament the central
issue of national and international politics. Joining together in an enterprise that transcends national bound-
aries, we in the free world must take the initiative.

Only if we abolish nuclear weapons and permanently
halt the nuclear power industry can we hope to survive.
To achieve these ends, it is vital that people be presented with the facts. Today more than ever, we need
what Einstein referred to as a "chain reaction of awareness": "To the village square," he wrote in 1946, "we
must carry the facts of atomic energy." Once presented,
the facts will speak for themselves.

Out of the growing number of organizations opposed
to nuclear power and nuclear arms must come a grass-
roots movement of unprecedented size and determina-
tion. Its momentum, alone, will determine whether we
and our children—and all future generations of human-
kind—will survive.

7

What You Can Do

For Gunvor Refetoff (1935–1978)
who epitomized the beauty of life—
and died of bone cancer.

A human being's strongest physiological instinct is for survival. How is it, then, that the politicians, scientists, and businessmen who order, design, and manufacture the instruments of death called atomic bombs and nuclear power plants have become disengaged from their most primitive instincts? I have seen these men of might and power exhibit a sense of goodness and love at death's door: when they themselves, or a close relative, are faced with death, they become soft, gentle, frightened human beings. Many of our national leaders seem to live in a schizoid world of, on the one hand, planned death by massive genocide and, on the other, a primitive fear of death when they are personally faced with its reality. This contradiction can be explained by the powerful defense mechanism of "death denial": we all survive by pretending we will never die. Males are particularly adept at the denial of unpleasant emotions. Perhaps it is this defense mechanism that sublimates the urge to survive and allow politicians to contemplate "first-strike capabilities" or "limited nuclear war"—in which the deaths of twenty million Americans or Russians are deemed "acceptable."

My experience with national political leaders has not inspired me with confidence. I find that they are generally ignorant of the major medical and scientific ramifications of their decisions. They are manipulated by powerful, well-financed industrial and military lobbies. Driven by power and the need for ego-gratification, they are, to a large degree, desensitized to reality. Their vision is limited to their meager two-to-four-year terms of office; the desire for reelection influences all their decisions. I have found, sadly, that a global view of reality and a sense of moral responsibility for humanity's future are very rare among political figures.

Even after Watergate, Vietnam, and CIA exposes, the American people still seem to trust their political leaders. When I speak at church meetings, describing the enormity of our nuclear madness, people approach me and ask, "The politicians don't know this, do they? Because they wouldn't let any of this happen if they did." I look them in the eye and tell them that their government is totally responsible for organizing this calamity.

But if we can't trust our representatives, whom can we trust? The answer is simple: No one but ourselves. We must educate ourselves about the medical, scientific and military realities, and then move powerfully as individuals accepting full responsibility for preserving our planet for our descendants. Using all our initiative and creativity, we must struggle to convert our democratic system into a society working for life rather than death.

"But," people often say, "it is impossible to change the system." I do not agree. I informed the Australian public about the medical dangers of fallout, and the federal government was finally forced to take France to the International Court of Justice. Three years later I pressured the government by teaching the nation's workers about the medical and military hazards associated with uranium mining. By September 1977 the Australian Court of Trade Unions (the executive body of the Australian Union movement) had passed a resolution declaring that unless the federal government agreed to fund a year-long nationwide debate and subsequent referendum on the wisdom and safety of uranium mining, no Australian worker would mine, transport, or load the stuff onto ships for export. The Australian Waterside Workers Federation voted unanimously to support the boycott; the Australian Railways Union refused to touch the material. In December 1977 the Australian Labor Party (which by then opposed the mining and selling of uranium on the open market, although two years earlier it had been in favor) announced that, if returned to office, it would ban the mining and treatment of uranium in Australia until adequate nuclear-waste safeguards were developed and until a satisfactory national debate had taken place. Nor would it allow the opening of any new mines. Moreover it promised, if elected, to cancel all the uranium contracts that the present Liberal Party government has signed with other countries.*

Few Americans are aware that in June 1977, 80,000 people marched in the streets of Australia's capitals, demanding that uranium be left in the ground: In Australia, despite the fact that huge profits would be reaped by overseas uranium sales, democracy has been mobilized to fight for human survival.

Nuclear power and nuclear war are primarily medical issues. Arguments about profits, jobs, and politics are reduced to irrelevancy when our children are threatened with epidemics of leukemia, cancer, and inherited disease—or sudden death, in the case of nuclear war. What will be the cost of hospitalizing all the people who contract these terminal diseases? The medical expenses incurred will far outweigh any economic benefits gained by this generation—to the detriment of all those that will come in the future. But of course no human life can be measured in dollars. Who would care to put

*Many of Australia's richest uranium deposits are found on sacred aboriginal tribal lands. Government efforts to further expropriate such lands continue a heartless process of cultural and religious persecution against these shy and innocent people, for whom the Australian continent has been home for millennia. Aboriginal "dream-time" myths describe a "rainbow snake" said to live on uranium-rich Mount Brockman. If disturbed, the snake would bring great disaster both to the local aboriginal and white populations, and also, it is believed, to the world at large.

71

a price on his or her own life? Each life is precious, unique, and invaluable—a truth brought home to me each time I see a baby born or a child suffer and die from leukemia or cystic fibrosis.

I am often asked what the medical profession is doing about the public health hazards posed by nuclear power and weapons production. I firmly believe that it should take a strong and unequivocal stand in opposition to the technologies of death. Unfortunately, my experience in the atmospheric-test campaign in Australia taught me that although most doctors readily conceded that radiation poses a growing public health hazard, few were willing to support the public stance that I had taken (most dismissed it as naive and doomed to failure) and fewer still were willing to give political meaning to their Hippocratic oath by speaking out themselves. I have found a similar reluctance among physicians in the United States, based in large part on a lack of information about the nuclear fuel cycle and the extent to which public health is threatened by the spread of nuclear power plants. Medical schools and journals do the general public a disservice by neglecting this major health issue.

When I have addressed the issue of nuclear power at medical meetings in America, however, the response has always been generally supportive. In 1975, for example, the New Hampshire Medical Association invited me to speak about the medical dangers of nuclear power at one of their monthly meetings. The doctors present understood the medical dangers of radiation, but they did not know the intricacies of the fuel cycle and the special radioactive health implications involved at each stage. They were generally unaware of the massive quantities of different radioactive isotopes produced as nuclear waste, and they really did not know that the storage of nuclear waste remains a serious, unsolved dilemma. After the lecture and subsequent discussion, these doctors were convinced of the gravity of the situation, and several who had posed the most searching and difficult questions approached

72

me. As they shook my hand, I noticed that they had tears in their eyes. They thanked me and wished me luck. Several weeks later, six wrote a letter to a major New Hampshire newspaper stressing the long-term medical dangers of nuclear power—provoking a stormy response from the nuclear industry. Because of the public controversy, many people became aware that nuclear power is *not* safe: after all, even their doctors saw it as a health hazard. We need more such controversies, engendered by doctors, nurses, and other health professionals dedicated to the practice of preventive medicine and the eradication of radiation's biological hazards from the environment.

It is currently believed that 80 pecent of all cancers arc caused by environmental factors. By definition, therefore, they are preventable. The U.S. government spends millions of dollars each year funding medical research into the cause and cure of this dreaded disease. At the same time, however, it spends billions funding the weapons and nuclear power industries—which propagate the diseases doctors are struggling to conquer. We in the medical profession must begin to practice what I call "political medicine," something we are not trained to do. Political medicine opposes industrial practices which contaminate the environment with disease-causing agents. In this way it attempts to attack the "front end" of the cancer cycle and prevent the disorder from occurring—rather than trying to cure malignancies after they are diagnosed, when it is often too late.

America's scientific community has a unique obligation to assess the morality of its work and to assist the public to understand the perils we face: in the event of nuclear holocaust, it is science that will have led us down the road to self-destruction. The first meltdown or nuclear-waste explosion will disprove, once and for all, the blithe assurances offered by industry experts regarding reactor safety and waste-disposal technology, but only after bringing tragedy into the lives of thousands of human beings.

The Industrial Age has enthroned science as its new religion; the scientific establishment has, in turn, promised to cure disease, prolong life, and master the environment. Thus, humanity now believes that it owns the earth; we have forgotten that we belong to it, and that if we do not obey the natural laws of life and survival, we will all cease to exist.

Unfortunately, my experience has taught me that we cannot rely upon our scientists to save us. For one thing, they do not preoccupy themselves with questions of morality. For another, science has become so specialized that even the best scientists are immersed in very narrow areas of research: most lack the time to view the broad results of their endeavor, let alone the willingness to accept responsibility for the awesome destructive capabilities science has developed. When confronted with the realities of our nuclear insanity, they are often either embarrassed or display a cynical fatalism, saying that humanity was not meant to survive anyway. Since about half of America's research scientists and engineers are employed by the military and related industries, they suffer from a profound conflict of interest: many simply prefer not to ponder the consequences of their work too deeply; after all, they have to feed and educate their children—a strange reaction, considering that, as a direct result of their research, their children may not live out their normal life span.

Many scientists *have* stood up to the nuclear establishment, but only at great cost to themselves and their families. Journalist Jack Anderson has observed that these "courageous scientists—Thomas Mancuso, John Gofman, Alice Stewart, George Kneale, Samuel Milham, Arthur Tamplin, Ernest Sternglass, and Irwin Bross—have come under malicious attack reminiscent of the campaign against Hollywood and Broadway liberals during the anti-communist hysteria. We have tried to tell the story of these scientists whose cautious warnings have been assaulted and belittled, whose personal reputations have been besmirched." Why has this happened? Because, he notes, "The stakes are enormously high. Both the federal government and the nuclear industry are committed to developing nuclear power. Too many unfavorable stories would jeopardize the industry's multibillion-dollar investment . . . Government officials have also staked their careers on the development of nuclear power. They would look foolish if their massive efforts had to be scrapped because they underestimated the dangers of low-level radiation. Not only would the billions spent on nuclear projects have to be written off, but additional billions might have to be paid in compensation to those whose health has been impaired." This intimidation ritual would be less popular with government if more scientists were to accept their moral responsibility to teach the public about the technological dangers to which science has exposed the world.

I spent one of the most important and inspiring evenings of my life in January 1976, talking with three men and their wives. The men were about to sacrifice their life's work and secure employment for the sake of a principle that involved the future of the human race. They were Dale Bridenbaugh, Gregg Minor, and Dick Hubbard, the three nuclear engineers about to resign from General Electric. As we sat together, discussing the ramifications of their decision upon their families, their lives, the nuclear industry, and the world at large, I could see the pain of uncertainty on their faces as they contemplated the future. Over the years, they had gradually realized that their highly paid and socially respectable jobs were an integral part of an entrenched multibillion-dollar industry which threatened future generations. Their wives were also worried about the impending resignations, and the possibility that their husbands would have difficulty finding stable employment. They realized that they would have to reduce their accustomed standard of living. But each of these women was totally committed to the decision; in fact, it was they who had first posed the unanswerable moral questions relating to the spread of nuclear power. These men and women demonstrated courage and self-sacrifice in the name of human survival. They stand as models that more members of the world's scientific and engineering communities should emulate.

How is it that the brilliant efforts of American scientists have been put to destructive uses? How did American culture become so embroiled in the death cycle? When Pearl Harbor was bombed, the Japanese declaration of war was delivered to the American Secretary of State half an hour after hostilities began. The Japanese admiral Yamamoto was devastated by this diplomatic breach of protocol, and said, "I fear we have awakened a sleeping giant and filled him with a great resolve." I think the American people were so shocked by the unprecedented devastation of Pearl Harbor that they resolved never to be vulnerable again. That is why America's politicians developed a nuclear arsenal after 1945, even though nuclear scientists pleaded that it not be developed. But the drive for invulnerability leads to total vulnerability. A valid concept of national security should ensure life and a healthy future for the human race. Instead, the Pentagon scenario of national security through mutually assured destruction assures our annihilation.

I am very worried by the fact that most Americans are not aware of the realities of their present-day existence. As I speak to thousands of citizens, I find that they generally know next to nothing about the medical effects of nuclear power and have entirely suppressed the atomic bomb anxiety that pervades the rest of the world. The Kennedy-Krushchev talks began to thaw the Cold War, but when Kennedy was killed, the world was devastated—not just because a popular president was slain, but because he had initiated a new era which sought to move away from nuclear brinksmanship. The international grief was compounded by fear for the future. As Lyndon Johnson took over the reins of government and enacted the Civil Rights program, however, somehow world attention was diverted from atomic bombs. Vietnam reared its ugly head, and Watergate became the overriding issue of the early '70s. During those years, it was a relief to think about "manageable" problems and forget the unthinkable. People became ostrichlike and pretended the nuclear threat had ceased to exist. Meanwhile, the Pentagon, always five years ahead (with Russia striving to keep up), quietly continued refining and building more and more atomic and hydrogen bombs, delivery systems, satellites, submarines, et cetera. In reality, nuclear madness had not disappeared: it multiplied.

Still, most Americans remain strangely silent, as if mesmerized into a feeling of safety and security. I find this self-delusion difficult to understand. On the one hand, I know several people, including two physicians, who have recently lived in Russia for a number of years. They report that almost every Russian with whom they made contact spoke spontaneously of a fear of the imminence of atomic war. Unlike Russia, which was invaded and lost twenty million people in World War II, this country has never suffered the total devastation of a massive military conflict, and I think this is the reason why the immediacy and danger of war is alien to American psychology. This society is geared to the joys of short-term satisfaction, with "happiness" projected as the ultimate goal of human existence. Death is denied by painting corpses to look like living flesh, by using expressions such as "passing away," or by arranging for people to die in impersonal hospitals away from the family. The tearing pain of grief is avoided at whatever cost. But death is a reality that must be faced, and war is an ever-present danger that must be confronted if we are to avoid it.

But what about the Russians? Every time the Pentagon needs more money, the Russian spectre is called up. The reality is that if both superpowers, together with the lesser powers, continue on this mad spiraling arms race, building more and more atomic bombs, sooner or later they will be used. We cannot trust in the sanity and stability of world leaders. (In fact, great power tends to attract disturbed individuals.) Recent history abounds with examples: Hitler, Mussolini, Stalin. Meanwhile, we are racing like lemmings toward mutually assured destruction. Someone must make the first move away from death and toward life. Do we really have anything to lose? We are doomed if we don't—but we may save the human race if we do. The elimination of nuclear weapons should be a national goal. I believe that the Russian people are so frightened of nuclear war that they would heave a momentous sigh of relief and would want their own leaders to follow America's moral initiative toward nuclear disarmament.

What is happening to our society? Even America's schools are being used by the nuclear industry for massive advertising campaigns: each year every high school in the U.S.A. is visited by a utilities expert, who subtly indoctrinates his listeners in the belief that nuclear power is "safe." It is my understanding that such advertising in institutions of learning is illegal; if it is not illegal in the United States, it should be. I have watched utilities representatives put on one-man-shows before auditoriums filled with high-school students. As props they use a simulated nuclear reactor and various other machines which use electrostatic energy to make the children's hair stand on end. They tell their audience that nuclear power is safe, clean, and efficient—and that plutonium is safe enough to hold in the palm of one's hand. On several occasions I have addressed students after an industry representative spoke; I described the real dangers posed by nuclear power. The children were obviously fascinated by the machines and the technology pertaining to the industry, but they became quietly sober after I had spoken. One representative told me, "I don't usually discuss morals when I talk to children about nuclear power. I'm not used to this." It is a disgrace that the nuclear industry should be allowed unlimited access to the gullible young, when it amounts to teaching children to accept and support nuclear power.

I spoke at many schools in Australia about uranium, and the young people there were very enthusiastic and receptive. Many joined anti-uranium groups and were particularly good at knocking on doors and talking to their neighbors.

My experience in this country has already taught me that established government institutions are hard to budge. In 1975 I wrote to each member of the U.S. Congress Joint Committee on Atomic Energy to ask if I could talk to the committee about the medical implications of nuclear power. My offer was never formally acknowledged, but I received some interesting replies from individual members, justifying nuclear power because the nuclear submarine program had been so "successful" (strange logic, in view of the fact that nuclear submarine workers at the Portsmouth, New Hampshire, naval yard are now dying of cancer at high rates). I was told subsequently by an administrative assistant that the committee had never heard testimony from an independent medical doctor about the medical implications of nuclear power, but only from members of the staff of the NRC and ERDA, so they were relatively ignorant of the basic radiobiological implications of nuclear energy. I might add that the Watergate investigation revealed that Gulf, Ashland Oil, and the Northrop Corporation, subsidiaries of which are leading suppliers of nuclear technology, were found guilty of making illegal "political contributions" to politicians in America and abroad, dispersing well over $10 million. The recipients of these illegal funds included key representatives and senators who were serving at the time on the committee. Clearly, illegal payments of this type make many state and federal legislators less than objective when voting on nuclear issues. Such bribery may partially explain how nuclear technology—although unsafe and uneconomic—could have been supported by so much favorable legislation over the years.

When contacted, the White House public liaison office assured me that this was an open administration —if you approached it the right way—and advised me to send a memo to Jimmy Carter. I sent a single-page document, briefly outlining the genetic, carcinogenic, teratogenic, and military properties of plutonium, and ended by saying, "I strongly urge your further investigation of this subject and I would like an opportunity to convince you of my concern." It was three weeks before I received a letter from the public liaison officer, giving me the name of a doctor employed by the Energy Research and Development Agency (ERDA) who, I was told, would be pleased to speak to me if I so desired. I didn't bother to make an appointment: ERDA is totally devoted to the expansion and development of nuclear power (it oversees the manufacture of atomic weapons, including the neutron bomb), and any doctor who works for that agency has already sold his soul to the devil.

The high-level bureaucrats serving in ERDA and on the Nuclear Regulatory Agency (NRC) are—and have always been—notoriously pronuclear. A 1976 Common Cause study revealed why industry preferences have received so much favorable treatment: Half of ERDA's top employees have been recruited from corporations with interests in energy development, and all nine executive positions have been filled by former employees of ERDA and NRC contractors; the NRC, meanwhile, has drawn more than half of its employees from corporations, laboratories, or universities under its supervision—including the U.S.'s "Big Five" reactor suppliers (Babcok and Wilcox, Combustion Engineering, General Atomic, General Electric, and Westinghouse) and other multinational corporations (such as

Rockwell International, DuPont, Bechtel, Allis-Chalmers, and General Dynamics) which profit from nuclear expansion and generous regulatory decisions. How can truly objective decisions regarding nuclear technology be made by agencies so rife with conflict of interest? They cannot.

The huge multinational corporations comprising the atomic industrial complex influence our elected representatives and appointed officials, through massive federal and state lobbying efforts which reflect their immense power and wealth. Financed by earnings reaped from a variety of technologies that are harmful to the environment and public health, such lobbying can subvert the democratic process by compromising the public interest in favor of the accumulation of ever more profit. As long as our democratic system prevails, however, the general public has an effective recourse in the form of the electoral ballot. The burden lies upon the electorate to become better informed about its genuine long-term interests, and then to make its demands known. Public education is the first step, to be followed in part by a grass-roots lobbying effort (in the form of a letter-writing campaign) and personal meetings with elected officials.

In 1976 I wrote to every federal and state politician in Australia, warning of the dangers of uranium mining. I enclosed a brief summary of the medical, military, and genetic implications of uranium mining and closed with a statement that this was the most important issue ever to face the human race, and that "they and their colleagues would go down in history either as great statesmen, or alternatively, as those politicians who made a disastrous mistake." Although most of the replies reflected party lines (to export or not to export), at least all these people were made more conscious of the medical hazards presented by uranium. Some asked for more detailed information; others contested that nuclear power is as safe but more practical than solar energy. Almost no one addressed the proliferation of nuclear weapons. Several months later I sent all these

81

federal politicians a copy of "The Plutonium Economy," a critical report prepared under the auspices of the American National Council of Churches, by a committee co-chaired by Margaret Mead and including several Nobel laureates. As a concerned citizen I felt it my duty to educate my political representatives.

We need to educate the politicians in America, by making sure they read about the biological effects of nuclear fission products and nuclear waste—and I mean *every* federal and state politician in the United States. It is imperative that our political representatives be educated regarding the long-term consequences of their nuclear-related decisions. Because such decisions exert their effects for millennia, they must not be influenced by considerations of short-term self-interest. The public must enable its leaders to understand and reflect popular opinion.

It is of vital importance to educate the workers of this country, as well, because they are the grass-roots members of our democracy and the true power behind this system. Because only 20 percent to 30 percent of America's workforce is unionized, reaching America's nonunionized workers, in particular, will require a massive effort, but that effort must be made. Contacts can be forged with factory operators and managers. Workers should be taught by knowledgeable, caring people. I urge America's labor unions to utilize their education committees to inform their members of the lethal hazards posed by nuclear power stations and weapons production. The irresponsibility of the nuclear industry to its own workers should be emphasized: Every potential employee of a nuclear facility, whether civilian or military, should be fully informed about the dangers to which he or she will be regularly exposed, and of the necessary precautions that must be taken in the workplace.

The argument is always raised that we need to build nuclear power plants and bombs to provide people with jobs. The truth is that the nuclear power and weapons industries are capital-intensive, labor-disintensive: that is, they provide relatively few jobs per dollar invested. The money needed to enrich uranium, build nuclear plants ($3 billion is needed for California's new Sun Desert facility), decommision reactors, and store wastes for half a million years would employ many more people in industries building solar panels, growing food, feeding the world's starving children, building mass transit systems, and rebuilding cities. The same is true for the weapons industry. The logic of the argument that it is important to build death industries to supply jobs which will eventually kill the people who hold those jobs—and their children—escapes me.

My success with the Australian labor movement prompted me, upon my arrival to the United States, to write George Meany. Expecting the attitudes of America's unions to be similar to those of Australia, I had hoped to forge a link with America's labor movement through Mr. Meany's good offices. To my distress, I received a reply from one of Mr. Meany's special assistants informing me in no uncertain terms that, because of the severity of America's energy crisis, the AFL-CIO supported the expansion of the nuclear power program and did not subscribe to the idea that radiation causes cancer. Further correspondence and other contacts underscored the degree to which the AFL-CIO is tied to industry-government policy.

Mr. Meany's argument is mistaken: The single most effective way of overcoming the world's energy crisis is through oil conservation in the United States, coupled with the development of alternative energies. At present, the American people, comprising only 6 percent of the earth's population, consume one-third of all the oil used in the world every day, *and consumption has been rising!* Daniel Yergin, a member of the Energy Research Project at the Harvard Business School, points out that "The amount of energy used per person in Sweden is 60 percent of the amount used per person in the U.S. In West Germany, the figure is 50 percent, in France less than 40 percent. This does not mean that we could instantly achieve the efficiency of those other countries in energy use. But these comparisons ... suggest that we could use a good deal less energy— 30 percent to 40 percent—*without cutting into our standard of living*. Such changes," he continues, "would call for new investment . . . But they would involve a good deal less investment and much shorter lead times than do oil or nuclear reactors."

My experience with Australia's unions confirms my belief that, when presented with the facts, workers will opt for health and safety. Seventy-five percent of Australia's workers are unionized, and at the outset of the anti-uranium mining campaign I wrote to each of South Australia's seventy-six unions (including the boiler makers, plumbers, pastry cooks, railway and metal workers) requesting an opportunity to address their memberships. Warning me that the need for jobs made it highly unlikely that I could convince them that uranium mining should be banned, they nevertheless agreed to hear me out. By September 1976 the Australian Council of Trade Unions had passed its fateful resolution.

Because of the contact I had made with the unionists in Darwin, I arranged a visit with the Trades and Labor Council there in order to have more immediate contact with the workers who would be most directly involved in opening and working the new Ranger mines in the Northern Territory. The Council was very receptive and has since become committed to a no-mining policy. The workers responded extremely well to my simple lecture on genetics and radiobiology.

On the same trip, I arranged with the Queensland Amalgamated Metal Workers Union to visit Mary Kathleen, a village in central Queensland that is the site of Australia's only working uranium mine. I was apprehensive as I flew across the dry, barren outback in a small, single-engine plane, because the miners at Mary Kathleen lived in a nice little town that enjoyed all the modern conveniences. They were deeply committed to mining uranium and had threatened to tar-and-feather the next person who tried to convince them that mining the ore was dangerous. Tempers were hot among the supporters of uranium mining in Australia, and I knew these people meant what they said. But I also know that they had to be spoken to by a physician, if they were to comprehend the full significance of uranium for themselves, their families, and future generations.

I was driven to the mine by several members of the Australian Amalgamated Metal Workers Union—strong, mature men in whose company I felt relatively safe. My first stop was company headquarters, where I spoke to the mine's manager. He was courteous but cold. Eventually he relaxed, and after answering some questions related to radiation-monitoring and workers' safety, he took me up to the mine face. Later we went down to the village of Mary Kathleen, where I was to speak to the workers. We stood in the town square, listening to numerous transistor radios forecasting the results of the Ranger Government Inquiry on Uranium Mining, a report that had been prepared by a three-man commission appointed to collect evidence from hundreds of Australians on the benefits and dangers of mining uranium ore. Both the federal government and the general public awaited the report with eager anticipation. Most of us felt that it would rule against uranium mining. The Mary Kathleen miners were apprehensive as the broadcast began, but when it was announced that the Ranger Inquiry had given a green light to uranium mining, miners jubilantly cheered. I felt nauseated, and a sense of impotence and despair descended upon me. Nevertheless, I summoned my energies to address the workers and their families about the medical dangers they faced.

Although many people were celebrating with mugs of beer and a lot of noise, they quieted down as I began speaking. Once again I talked about radon gas and lung cancer, radium and leukemia, stressing the fact that they had to be extremely careful to wash their hands and faces before eating. I went on to explain each step of the nuclear fuel cycle, and the serious dangers posed by nuclear waste (and nuclear war) to unborn children. They listened in silence, applauded at the end, then lined up to ask me questions. Several men told me that radiation had been detected in their regular urine tests, and wanted to know what that might mean. One of these men was only twenty-six years old and had a strong family history of cancer. I told him that if radiation was detected in his urine, it was probable that some radioactivity was already present in his body, and because of his probable inherited predisposition to cancer, he should leave the mine immediately. The men in general seemed very concerned; only one remained hostile to the end. They offered me a drink, and I think I would have been there all night, answering questions, if my union friends had not dragged me away.

I felt the trip had been successful. I had not been tarred and feathered. The reception had been polite, and the men learned of the many dangerous facets of their work, about which they had been totally ignorant. Subsequently the miners demanded that a health clinic be established at Mary Kathleen. Several resigned, and later a strike was held to demand improved conditions.

The Australian unions are among the most receptive and responsive people that I have talked to so far.

Nuclear workers throughout America are starting to worry about the effects of radiation exposure. Reports of higher-than-normal cancer rates at the Hanford, Washington nuclear installation led workers at Buchanan, New York's Indian Point Consolidated Edison station to begin expressing these fears. "I accepted a temporary assignment three years ago without knowing what it could possibly do to me," said one welder. "I hear top scientists saying now that there are no safe levels of radiation and I don't want to wind up as somebody's mistake." I find that the work force here tends to accept such dangers in a remarkably trusting manner. The nuclear submarine workers at Portsmouth, New Hampshire, are developing cancer at a very high rate, double that for representative men of the same age. I was invited to speak to a meeting of these workers, but only four men appeared. They told me that the navy had threatened them with the loss of their jobs if they came to hear me speak. I felt sorry for the men who didn't come, who feared more for their jobs than for their lives.

Media, the most effective way to reach the members of a democracy and the most powerful influence in America today, expose the masses to bland trivia and brainwashing. The subliminal effects of media propaganda and advertising teach people to desire what they don't need and to strive for materialistic pleasures. Communication and family relationships suffer as a result; people tend to be relatively shallow and spoiled, always desiring more of everything, but somehow unable or reluctant to comprehend the moral degradation of a world in which millions can be killed by the press of a button, a world in which two out of every three children are malnourished and starving. A long-term sense of responsibility toward the continuity of life is not evident in America. Life has become so easy, with everything ready-made or instantly served, that the true soul and center of the individual seems to have atrophied. People lack the resilience to face reality.

Television is the most important shaper of opinion in American society today. It is presently used to promote the activities and profits of the multinationals. It is supported and controlled by big business, and the vision of the American way of life it portrays has been carefully molded to comply with the profit motives of America's corporate leaders. Programming is developed to support and carry advertising; its standards often promote the low, banal, trivial, violent, and pornographic. The intellect, curiosity, responsibility, and self-reliance of the American people are rarely stimulated or acknowledged on most TV programs. How, therefore, can a mesmerized public be stimulated to learn about the true state of the world, and to become aroused and motivated to use democracy constructively, for survival?

In Australia, we were very successful in utilizing the media to inform the public—at no cost. All the exposure we received was free. Radio call-in shows, for instance, are ideal for voicing opinions and bringing provocative issues to public attention. They can also be used to advertise marches. We usually organized big ones once every six weeks, always obtaining a permit from the police department. We demonstrated on Saturday morning, during peak traffic time, when everyone went shopping. On Fridays we would use the call-in shows to advertise the march. We were often interviewed by local, popular commentators about some aspect of the uranium question, and at the end of the interview we would always tell the listeners that if they wanted to do something about this terrible problem they could join the march to be held the next day—always making sure to give its time and place.

At the conclusion of each march, we would have several prominent people give short, fiery speeches, and then announce the date of the next demonstration. Over a period of nine months, the number of participants at these marches grew from several hundred into the thousands. Banners above the crowd proclaimed "Geologists Against Uranium"—or "Teachers," "Railway Unions," "Housewives," "Clergy." Other signs read "Nuclear Power Equals Cancer."

The television and radio stations started covering our marches regularly, because they were becoming important political events. People would often be interviewed as they walked along, and their worries and concerns about uranium would be broadcast over the local and national networks. One march was led by a contingent of men dressed in pinstriped suits carrying umbrellas and a large placard saying, "Uranium Pushers"; behind them huddled a group of children with simulated deformities, the "By-products of Uranium." This imaginative approach appealed to the television cameras; it illustrated the medical implications of nuclear power simply and forcefully. The scene was broadcast on every television channel that evening.

Our marches yielded many practical results. First, they educated the people in the streets; second, they drew the media, thereby educating thousands of people sitting in their homes; third, they alerted politicians to the fact that many of their constituents were opposed to uranium mining, and that they had better learn more about the subject if they wanted to be reelected; and, finally, they produced a tremendous feeling of unity and solidarity among people from all classes of society. I always had the feeling that our marches exemplified the way people should relate to one another, as concerned human beings working together for survival.

We also organized a teach-in on the steps of Parliament House. We made banners proclaiming the medical side effects of uranium. We talked to people in the street and, if they showed concern, gave them information. Large bumper stickers were printed, reading "Uranium Is Thalidomide Forever." They were posted on cars and buildings all over town and soon were ubiquitous. We buried a time capsule containing a photo of a normal human baby under the foundations of a new highrise building, so that people could dig it up two thousand years hence to see what human beings once looked like.

We used every large gathering—whether anti-uranium or nonrelated—to solicit signatures for petitions and newspaper advertisements. We stood outside supermarkets. We canvassed churches, hospitals, schools, and universities. (I even canvassed the Australian Pediatric Association, collecting signatures from my colleagues during a cocktail hour.) The statement which these people signed read:

The Australian Government, under pressure from local and overseas interests, has decided to mine, use, enrich, and export uranium from Australia's considerable deposits. Power plants, fueled by uranium, produce vast quantities of highly radioactive nuclear wastes for which there is no satisfactory method of disposal. Inevitable contamination of the environment will lead to an increase in birth defects, leukemia, and other malignant disease. Nuclear power plants may present as great a threat to the survival of life on earth as does nuclear war. This vital issue is above profit or politics. We call upon the leaders of our country to reject the mining of uranium for use in Australia or overseas and to bring pressure to bear on other governments to do likewise.

Everyone who signed also donated $1, and after several weeks we had two to three thousand signatures and enough money to buy one third of a page in the state newspaper. At the bottom of the advertisement we added a line inviting anyone who agreed with the statement to send us their name and donation. Within weeks we had thousands more signatures—and enough money to repeat the ad in the national newspaper.

As more and more events took place, we were befriended by many reporters who had become convinced that uranium is dangerous. They covered all our events, even though the station managers were often allied with big business and tended to be pro-uranium.

Several loose-knit organizations co-ordinated our major efforts: CANE (Campaign Against Nuclear Energy), MAUM (Movement Against Uranium Mining), and FOE (Friends of the Earth). Although we met once a week to report on what we had all been doing, there were no rules and few agendas. Each individual was totally free to do what he or she considered necessary to further the cause. The organizations imposed no constraints, recognizing that we were all driven by a sense of urgency.

Since 1976 America's antinuclear movement has grown by leaps and bounds. Small local citizens' groups are springing up all over the country and are uniting to work together. Mobilization for Survival, a new national organization, comprises antinuclear and peace groups united to fight nuclear power, eliminate nuclear weapons, stop the arms race, and use the world's resources to fund human needs. I am very excited about these new movements.

One of the high points of this new effort occurred in 1977, when New England's Clamshell Alliance occupied the site of the Seabrook, New Hampshire, nuclear power plant: 1414 people were arrested and jailed in state armories. These people are so adamantly opposed to nuclear power that they accepted not only temporary jailing but, later, sentences ranging from one to four months. This event signalled the beginning of a tough new movement in which people are prepared to fight the system that condones, legalizes, and builds death-producing industries and weapons.

I spoke during the Seabrook occupation to a large rally of people gathered at a nearby beach. Later I was called in as an "expert witness" for Carter Wentworth, the first person to be formally tried for the Seabrook occupation. The judge ruled my evidence inadmissible, even though it concerned the medical dangers of nuclear power, and these dangers had convinced Carter to occupy the site. He was appealing on the grounds of a law of competing harms, which stipulates that if the danger from the occupation was less to society than the potential danger imposed by a nuclear power plant, the defendant must be ruled innocent. Without giving any reason why, the judge determined that this law was inapplicable. I realized that day that the spread of nuclear power could not be stopped here by appealing to the legal system; only by transforming

America's concerned citizens into the political majority could the antinuclear movement hope to attain its goals.

I have testified at hearings held on nuclear power plants in Long Island and Massachusetts. Each time I found myself talking to lawyers employed by the utilities, who know little or nothing about biology. The judges in these hearings are employed by the NRC. Thus, the litigation system surrounding nuclear reactors is often farcical. Subject to obvious conflict of interest, the arbitrators cannot be impartial. I would therefore advise people who are concerned about nuclear power to bypass the legal system, and not waste money and energy in an endeavor that will almost always end in defeat. Instead, mobilize in large numbers; march; demonstrate; educate and teach in schools, churches, political meetings—wherever people gather.

We are the curators of life on earth, standing at a crossroads in time. We must awake from our false sense of security and commit ourselves to using democracy constructively to save the human species, or our democratic heritage will atrophy and be lost.

The nuclear power plants encroaching on our suburbs make it no longer possible for Americans to bury their heads in the sand and pretend that the fissioned atom does not exist: The radioactive isotopes discharged into the environment by nuclear reactors and nuclear waste are identical to those released when an atomic bomb explodes. Moreover, the spread of commercial nuclear technology to other nations guarantees the uncontrollable proliferation of nuclear weapons. Obviously, something must be done to stop this spread and achieve total nuclear disarmament, but American and Soviet politicians seem unable and/or unwilling to take appropriate action. It is therefore up to us, the people of the world. The citizens of Australia are already mobilizing, setting a shining example that a society can effectively use its democracy for the good. Following its lead, we must all find the courage to take our destiny into our own hands.

The struggle by the antinuclear forces in the United States and other parts of the world has already begun to meet stiff resistance. In Australia, in June 1978, Prime Minister Malcolm Fraser's Liberal Government passed into law an Environmental Protection (Nuclear Activities) Act that could turn that country into a police state: empowering a government ministry to take any action considered necessary to control and eliminate hazards associated with "a situation resulting from nuclear activity," the Act gives the government virtually uncontrolled power to censor the press and detain antinuclear activists indefinitely, and without trial, whenever necessary to protect "nuclear activities." In the United States, meanwhile, some nuclear companies and utilities have already planted intelligence agents to spy on the growing opposition (a House Commerce subcommittee is investigating to see if such activities include illegal surveillance); the FBI has already begun to impugn the patriotism of antinuclear activists, alleging that their effort is an alien enemy attack on the United States. The truth is that this nation's only real enemies are the forces of disease and death.

Will we survive or will we destroy ourselves? What else matters, if we are wiped out this decade, this year, this week, this hour, or this minute? Nuclear technology is the crucial issue facing us today. To defeat that technology, we must begin now to shape world events.

The power of an aroused public is unbeatable. Vietnam and Watergate proved that. It must be demonstrated again. It is not yet too late, for while there is life there is hope. There is no cause for pessimism, for already I have seen great obstacles surmounted. Nor need we be afraid, for I have seen democracy work.

Each of us must accept total responsibility for the earth's survival. Ultimately, the future rests upon our commitment as individuals—as parents, providing a healthy and secure future for their children; as students, unwilling to accept a future of sickness and war; as citizens, believing that it is the people who should hold the balance of power in a democracy; as taxpayers, exhausted by an insane arms race and opposed to the waste of the earth's resources; as workers, farmers, professionals, artists, corporate employees, public servants, environmentalists, industrialists, rich and poor, black and white, red and yellow, men and women. In the face of nuclear technology, concern for human survival surpasses all social, political, and economic divisions. All of us—regardless of class, creed, or political affiliation—want the human race to survive. As members of the same species, we must work in harmony toward our common goal.

Epilogue: Three Mile Island

At four a.m. on March 28, 1979, the worst accident in the history of the U.S. nuclear industry began and, within several hours, the badly damaged radioactive core was thirty to sixty minutes from a meltdown. Although later engineering analysis doubted that a true "China Syndrome" could have taken place because of the hard rock foundation beneath the reactor, it is certainly well within the realm of possibility that a large fraction of the radioactive inventory could have been released into the atmosphere.

A normally operating 1000 megawatt reactor contains 15 billion curies of radiation, the equivalent of the long-lived isotopes released by the explosion of 1,000 Hiroshima bombs. When an atomic bomb explodes, much of the fallout is forced into the stratosphere and circulates west to east around the globe. Fallout is intermittent, occurring only with low pressure atmospheric conditions. However, in the case of a meltdown, any damage incurred to human population and property would depend upon the prevailing wind direction at the time of the release of the radioactive plume, and the plume would hover close to the earth depositing fallout continuously along its path. To understand the awful magnitude of destruction from a meltdown, the Government sponsored Rasmussen Report, now updated by the Union of Concerned Scientists, is very helpful. It states that in the *worst possible case* (a Class 9 Accident), if 10 million people were exposed; 3,300 people would die from severe radiation damage within several days; 10,000 to 100,000 people would develop acute radiation sickness within two to six weeks of initial exposure; 45,000 would become short of breath since the intensely radioactive gases produce lung damage; 240,000 others would develop acute hypothyroidism with symptoms of weight gain, lassitude, susceptibility to colds, impaired and slow mental functions, loss of appetite, constipation and absent menstruation; 350,000 males would become temporarily sterile as the gamma radiation would damage the sperm; 40,000 to 100,000 women would cease to menstruate, many permanently. In the fetal population, up to 100,000 babies would be born cretins with mental retardation because the radioactive iodine would destroy the thyroid gland; 1,500 others would develop microcephaly (small heads) since the developing central nervous system is highly susceptible to the deleterious effects of radiation. There would be 3,000 deaths in utero. Five to fifty years later, cancer would develop in various body organs of 270,000 people and there would be 28,800 cases of thyroid malignancy.

Economically, a meltdown would cost approximately 14 billion dollars in property damage, but even more horrifying is the fact that it could contaminate an area the size of Pennsylvania for hundreds to thousands of years making it uninhabitable.

As of 1980, 30 million Americans presently live within thirty miles of a nuclear reactor. How many could be evacuated?

At the time of Three Mile Island (TMI) the existence of an effective state by state evacuation plan was not a prerequisite for granting an operating license for a reactor. Under current regulations, individual states can submit emergency plans to the Nuclear Regulatory Commission (NRC) for approval, but at the time of the accident only a few states had NRC approved plans and Pennsylvania was not among them.

The size and location of the population to be evacuated would depend on the prevailing wind conditions, but the evacuation of a large population—New York City and surrounding areas, for instance, within hours after a meltdown—would be a frightening and utterly impossible scenario.

Even if such an evacuation were possible, physicians are totally unprepared to cope with such a large population of contaminated patients. Presently, our medical education does not include decontamination and treatment of radioactive patients; neither is the issue addressed in medical journals. Government regulations state that a patient should be hosed down to remove the isotopes from his skin and the contaminated water should then be drained. But it would be very dangerous for medical personnel to handle contaminated patients because they themselves could become contaminated. The sorrowful truth is that we cannot decontaminate radioactive lungs or other body organs, nor can we treat organs acutely damaged by radioactive exposure. We cannot cure sterility, and those males who might regain their fertility would have to be strongly advised not to reproduce since their sperm would almost certainly have sustained some genetic damage from radiation exposure. The medical community has made some progress in recent years in cancer treatment, but most forms of adult cancer are still incurable.

We know of only a few varyingly effective modes of

medical action to follow at the time of a meltdown. First of all, it is advisable that all people living within a hundred mile radius of a reactor have a supply of inert potassium iodide tablets in their medicine cabinets available for use in such an emergency. If a medically prescribed dose were taken thirty minutes to several hours before exposure, the nonradioactive iodine would be absorbed by the thyroid gland and subsequent uptake of radioactive iodine by the thyroid could be blocked. For exposed, unprotected patients who developed acute hypothyroidism, a thyroid extract could restore normal endocrine balance. A much less effective treatment for those who had no medication available could be to take a laxative immediately. By reducing transit time through the gut, absorption of the radioactive isotopes could be impeded. In short, we are hardly prepared to face such an emergency.

How did TMI happen at all?

It began with a mechanical failure and automatic shutdown of the main feedwater pumps in the secondary coolant system which closed some valves, thereby causing the water in the primary coolant system covering the radioactive core to quickly heat and expand. The pressurizer operator relief valve (PORV) in the primary system automatically opened as designed to do and started draining precious cooling water away from the core. When that happened, the reactor scrammed—control rods automatically dropped between the uranium fuel rods in the core, stopping the fission reaction. The core, however, remained exceedingly hot and the light on the operating panel failed to indicate that the valve was not shut but stuck open. This valve remained open for approximately two hours before the operators understood the situation. Thinking the core was covered with water, the operators turned off the water flow from the emergency cooling system causing the water to rapidly drain from the core; through the PORV while the emergency cooling system was closed tight.

Then, the one hundred tons of uranium core over-heated and the zirconium cladding of the rods reacted with water at 2,200° F, melted and exposed the cooling water to highly radioactive fission products and alpha emittors. The core was severely damaged and the hydrogen gas that collected in the containment vessel spontaneously exploded several hours after the accident began exposing the containment vessel to potentially dangerous explosive forces that could have weakened it. Believe it or not, this incredibly serious event was not recognized by either the operators, the utility or the NRC for several days. As more hydrogen continued to be generated over following days, Chairman Hendric of the NRC and others feared that oxygen released by radiolysis from water molecules would unite with the hydrogen bubble, explode and possibly rupture the containment vessel releasing large quantities of radiation; or else, a noncondensible hydrogen bubble would eventually uncover the core leading to a meltdown. Meanwhile, in order to reassure the American people that the reactor posed no danger, President and Mrs. Carter were taken into the operating room of the TMI unit 2 on the afternoon of April 1 at the height of the anxiety about this hydrogen bubble. This foolish exercise exposed the President to unnecessary danger.

Throughout the accident, the highly radioactive cooling water was being pumped through the PORV onto the floor of the reactor and from there into a tank in an adjacent auxiliary building. At this time, large quantities of radioactive gases were vented from this auxiliary tank from a leaking valve into the atmosphere, so intermittent plumes of radioactivity were dispersed from the reactor. The wind blew mainly to the northwest quadrant. The radiation was measured by various gamma counting devices. Beta and Alpha radiation were not measured, but it has been estimated that 2.4 to 13 million curies of noble gases—xenon and crypton—were released, and 13-17 curies of radioactive iodine escaped. Although noble gases do not combine chemically in the body, they are absorbed

98

by the lungs after inhalation. Ten times more fat soluble than water soluble, they tend to concentrate in the abdominal fat pad and the fat of the upper thighs. Xenon 133 and Crypton 85 are high energy gamma emittors like X-rays. Thus, the reproductive organs of people living near TMI could well have been exposed to gamma radiation, particularly if they were immersed in clouds of noble gases.

Because the monitoring device in the auxiliary building stack went off scale early in the accident (it was not designed to measure such large quantities of radiation), estimates of radiation release were extrapolated from radiation monitors some distance from the stack. Therefore, no hard data exists concerning the absolute quantities of the radiation release. Furthermore, because Alpha and Beta radiation was not routinely measured, it is impossible to precisely know which radioactive elements escaped. Noble gas measurements were not begun until April 5—eight days after the accident began. In other words, all calculations are only educated guesses from the available but inadequate data.

Official estimations from the government-sponsored Kemmeny Commission also predict that less than one case of cancer will occur from the radioactive releases in the exposed population during their lifetimes. However, using the Hanford-Mancuso data for cancer incidence, 60-70 deaths from cancer are a possible figure.

The facts are: Nobody knows precisely where the plumes blew, whether the radioactivity touched the ground or how it was dispersed. We do know, though, that the radioactive plume was monitored 250 miles away from the plant.

Dose calculations were made by averaging the radiation dose over the totally exposed population, but some people could well have been exposed to higher doses than others because of the uneven distribution of the radioactive gaseous plume and the fact that the population is not homogeneous. The dose to the adult thyroid of Iodine 131 was calculated to be

11.1 millirems, but the dose to the fetal thyroid would be ten to twenty times greater, and fetuses are many times more sensitive to the mutagenic effects of radiation than adults. Also, the carcinogenic effects of radioisotopes react synergistically with other carcinogens in the atmosphere to promote cancer. Therefore, depending upon the state of the environment, there very well could be a increase in various forms of cancer in the TMI area.

Dr. Gordon MacLeod, former Secretary of Health in Pennsylvania, was sworn in to his position twelve days before the accident. Out of town at the time of the accident, he was told about the radiation release by phone. He asked for someone in the State Health Department who knew all about the health effects of radiation release to phone him. There was no such person. He then asked for the liaison to the Bureau of Radiation Protection to call him. Again, no such person. He then requested that books on the subject be collected from the State Health Department Library so he could investigate them in the morning. There were no such books because there was no library. Subsequently, Dr. MacLeod initiated medical follow-up studies of the exposed population. He was also concerned about the medical consequences of the clean-up. In fact, whether we choose to believe it or not, the accident at TMI has just begun. It will take four to five years to complete.

The one million gallons of highly radioactive water that spilled onto the floor of the reactor buildings as well as the large volumes of radioactive gas and the mess of collapsed and fragmented hot fuel rods will all have to be removed from the reactor site. Not only is this operation expected to take years, but it will invariably involve more contamination for nuclear workers as well as the release of more radioactivity into the Harrisburg environment.

Dr. MacLeod requested that the Department of Health be intimately involved in this clean-up, but as this story becomes more and more surreal, he was fired, or as the official word came through the media, he was "requested to resign." Several people from the Pennsylvania Department of Health have since resigned and the only two departments now in charge of the operation are the Bureau of Radiation Protection and the Governor's office. There are absolutely no physicians supervising or monitoring the clean-up.

A number of possible health consequences of the nuclear power industry have been and still are largely ignored by the NRC. Their internal report, known as the Regovin Report, states, "the NRC has provided neither leadership nor management of the nation's safety program for commercial plants." In fact, early in the accident, former Chairman of the NRC Joseph Hendrie said, "We are operating almost totally in the blind, his (Governor Thornburgh's) information is ambiguous, mine is non-existent, and—I don't know—it's like a couple of blind men staggering around making decisions."

On another occasion, Harold Denton, who was the appointed spokesman for President Carter, said, "Yes, I think the important thing for evacuation to get ahead of the plume is to get a start, rather than sitting here to wait to die. Even if we can't minimize the individual dose, there might still be a chance to limit the population dose." But throughout the accident, as evacuation plans were being discussed by the NRC, the radioactive plume had already moved over the population.

When Governor Thornburgh asked Chairman Hendrie, "Is there anyone in the country who has experience with the health consequences of such a release?" he replied, "Ah—not in the sense that it's been studied and understood in any real way. There were back in the days when they were doing bomb testing. They managed to give groups of soldiers and occasionally a few civilians doses in the low rem range —a subject of discussion these days, but that's about the only comparable experience that occurs to me. You are talking now about a major release, not about the small ones that have occurred thus far."

101

The presidentially appointed Kemmeny Commission Report (October, 1979) and the Regovin Report (January 1980) both say that the state of the nuclear industry at the time of the accident was one of chaos. Accidents like TMI had almost happened twice before: once in 1974 at a Westinghouse reactor in Switzerland; and in 1977 at Toledo Edison's Davis Besse plant in Ohio. Both involved the failed PORV valve and misleading indications from the control panel which erroneously indicated the reactor coolant system was full of water.

A brief account of the Swiss accident was submitted to the NRC, but it did not prompt notification to operators that they might be misled by their instruments if a valve stuck open. The Davis Besse accident was intensely analyzed in the Regovin Report and then was filed away and never circulated.

Unfortunately, none of this is unique. The NRC receives many such reports, some trivial; some important, but in either case, the information is not systematically reviewed. For the most part, these reports are summarized in a few sentences for computer listing, distributed haphazardly to various staff offices and then simply filed away. Furthermore, there is absolutely no institutional mechanism within the NRC for developing solutions to potential dangers and insuring that such solutions are integrated into reactor operations through design changes, new procedures or improved training.

The Regovin Report states: "We have found in the NRC an organization that is not so much badly managed as it is not managed at all. In our opinion, the Commission is incapable, in its present configuration, of managing a comprehensive national safety program for existing nuclear power plants adequate to insure public health and safety."

There are five NRC Commissioners, working ineffectively together. Most of their meetings are spent discussing isolated safety issues, personnel, budget matters, administrative chores and export licensing—very little time is spent deliberating the crucial issues relating to reactor safety. This general inefficiency filters down to the NRC staff, where one of the most glaring deficiencies is a lack of any program requiring members to acquire experience in the design, construction and operation of nuclear reactors as well as radiation detection. In fact, Chairman Hendrie was the only NRC Commissioner with expertise in reactor engineering. Nor is the staff directly supervised on a daily basis by the Commission. They aren't even housed in the same state! The Commissioners and their staffs work in downtown Washington, D.C., while the NRC general staff are scattered among six office buildings in suburban Maryland. To make matters even worse, a strong we/they attitude has developed on both sides. To further illustrate what a potentially devastating mindset is operable there, before TMI, both the nuclear industry and the NRC had the attitude that such an accident was not *a credible event* and therefore *would never occur*.

The unfortunate truth is that nuclear operators are trained for only normal power operations and for the start-up and shut-down of the plant, not for the advent of accidents. The area of operating training has been a "backwater" with most utilities as well as the NRC.

The Regovin Report says that the problems revealed at TMI: inadequate training, unreasonably scanty manning sessions, lack of any requirements for minimum on-site technical supervisory competence are common to many and probably most power plants.

The point is that NRC inspectors spend a great deal of their time confirming utility personnel's bookkeeping procedures for maintenance and the logging in of any operating problems. One operator wrote, after experiencing a severe potential accident in the control room of TMI Unit 2 one year earlier, "You might do well to remember this is only the tip of the iceberg. Incidents like this are easy to get into and the best operators in the world can't compensate for multiple casualties which are complicated by mechanical and control failure. The President's Commissions found that the NRC failed to recognize that human beings who manage and operate reactors constitute an important safety system. And during the accident itself, the NRC was reluctant and did not assume control of the crippled plant. They only monitored and advised because the philosophy in the industry is, "the licensee is in charge even when they are incompetent."

The Regovin Report also found *a wide spectrum in the capability of the various nuclear utilities to operate existing plants in a safe fashion.*

Although current law places sole responsibility for the safe construction and operation of nuclear plants on the utilities, typically, the utilities possess less nuclear expertise than the architectural/engineering firms who design and build the reactors and even the NRC. After the licensing process is obtained by the firms and the NRC and the plant goes into service— the utility is on its own. Regovin thinks that some utilities will, in fact, be unable to afford the increased safety requirements, competent site management or first class trained operators necessary in the wake of TMI investigations.

But despite the most damning reports of the entire nuclear industry and the NRC, the Regovin Report and the Kemmeny Commission did not recommend the closing of any presently operating reactors. Why were they compromised? And must we wait for the inevitable meltdown before any further action is taken? If this country, and along with it the rest of the world, continues to rely more and more on nuclear power, a meltdown disaster is almost predictable, and when it does occur, disaster and chaos from the medical and psychological effects as well as the shutdown of electricity from all nuclear power plants will be the result.

For years now, the utilities and nuclear power industry have refused to listen to scientific logic and reasoning concerning the dangers of this technology.

In the light of past accidents and all the events surrounding TMI, perhaps it is time for emotion and for
passion and for commitment to stir our souls and our
hearts and our minds once again into action.

Bibliography

BOOKS

Alexander, Peter, *Atomic Radiation and Life*. New York, Penguin Books, 1965.

Aronow, Saul, Ervin, Frank R., M.D., and Sidel, Victor, W., M.D., eds., *The Fallen Sky: Medical Consequences of Thermonuclear War*. New York, Hill and Wang, 1963.

Asimov, Isaac, *A Short History of Chemistry*. New York, Doubleday, 1965.

Berger, John, *Nuclear Power: The Unviable Option*. Palo Alto, California, Ramparts Press, 1976.

Commoner, Barry, *Poverty of Power*. New York, Alfred Knopf, 1976.

Copeland, Lewis, and Lamm, Lawrence W., eds., *The World's Great Speeches*. New York, Dover Publications, 1973.

DeGroot, Lesley J., ed., et al., *Radiation-Associated Thyroid Carcinoma*. New York, Grune & Stratton, 1977.

Faulkner, Peter, ed., *The Silent Bomb: A Guide to the Nuclear Energy Controversy*. New York, Vintage Books, 1977.

Gofman, John W., and Tamplin, Arthur R., *Poisoned Power*. Emmaus, Pa., Rodale Press, 1971.

Gyorgy, Anna, et al., *No Nukes: Everyone's Guide to Nuclear Power*. Boston, South End Press, 1978.

Lewin, Leonard C., ed., *Report from Iron Mountain on the Possibility and Desirability of Peace*. New York, Dial Press, 1967.

Lifton, Robert Jay, *Death in Life*. New York, Random House, 1967.

Nader, Ralph and Abbotts, John, *The Menace of Atomic Energy*. New York, W. W. Norton & Co., Inc., 1977.

Nuclear Power, Issues and Choices. Report of the Nuclear Energy Policy Study Group. Ballinger Publishing Co., 1977.

Olson, McKinley C., *Unacceptable Risk*. New York, Bantam Books, 1976.

Patterson, Walter C., *Nuclear Power*. New York, Penguin Books, 1976.

Pauling, Linus, *No More War*. New York, Dodd, Mead and Co., 1958.

Pizzarello, Donald J., Ph.D., and Witcofski, Richard L., Ph.D.,

Basic Radiation Biology. Philadelphia, Lea and Febiger, 1975.

Russell, Bertrand, *The Autobiography of Bertrand Russell.* London, George Allen and Unwin Ltd., Vol. I–IV., 1971.

Stockholm Internation Peace Research Institute, *Weapons of Mass Destruction and the Environment.* London, Taylor and Francis Ltd., 1977.

Union of Concerned Scientists, *The Nuclear Fuel Cycle: A Survey of the Public Health, Environmental, and National Security Effects of Nuclear Power.* Cambridge, The MIT Press, 1975.

PERIODICALS

Abbotts, John, and McCarthy, Mary, "What's wrong with the Atomic Industry?" Public Interest Research Group (PIRG), July 1977.

Alfven, H., "Energy and Environment." The Bulletin of the Atomic Scientists, pp. 5–7, May 1972.

Anderson, Jack, "Colorado Plant Eyed as Radiation Source." Washington Post, March 25, 1978.

Anson, Robert Sam, "The Neutron Bomb." New Times, pp. 24–32, August 5, 1977.

Archer, U.E., Wagoner, J.K., and Lundin, F.E., "Lung Cancer Among Uranium Miners in the United States." Health Physics, Vol. 25, pp. 351–371, 1973.

"A-Tests May Have Exposed 300,000." Washington Post, February 11, 1978.

"A-Test Veterans In Area Should Call 295-0586." Washington Post, February 11, 1978.

"Atom-Job Transfers Tied To Drugs And Alcohol." UPI, The New York Times, August 8, 1977.

Bair, W.J., and Thompson, R.C., "Plutonium: Biomedical Research." Science, Vol. 183, pp. 715–722, February 1974.

Barnaby, Frank, "The Mounting Prospects of Nuclear War." A Report of the Stockholm International Peace Research Institute. The Bulletin of the Atomic Scientists, Vol. 33, pp. 10–21, June 1977.

Barnet, Richard, "A Time to Stop." Sojourners, Vol. 7, March 1978.

———. "Less Big Power Tension, Greater War Danger." New York Times, December 28, 1977.

Baverstock, K.F., and Vennart, J., "Emergency Reference Levels for Reactor Accidents: A Re-Examination of the Windscale Reactor Accident." Health Physics, Vol. 30, pp. 339–344, April 1976.

Beirwaltes, W.H., et. al., "Radioactive Iodine Concentration In The Fetal Human Thyroid Gland From Fallout." The

Journal of the American Medical Association, August 27, 1960, Vol. 173, pp. 1895–1902.

Benedict, Howard, "An Arms Race In Space." Boston Sunday Globe, March 19, 1978.

Bertell, Rosalie, Ph.D., G.N.S.H., "The Nuclear Worker and Ionizing Radiation." Banquet Address before Meeting of the American Industrial Hygiene Association, May 9, 1977.

Bjella, Lanceford C. Notes of testimony before Colorado Department of Health officials, Denver, Colorado.

Breitenstein, B.D., Jr., M.D., Norwood, W.D., M.D., and Newton, Jr., C.E. United States Transuranium Registry. Annual Report October 1, 1975 to October 1, 1976 To ERDA Division of Biomedical and Environmental Research. Hanford Environmental Health Foundation, Richland, Washington, December 1976.

Bross, Irwin, D.J., Ph.D., and Natarajan, N., M.S., "Leukemia from Low-Level Radiation—Identification of Susceptible Children." New England Journal of Medicine, July 20, 1972.

Burnham, David, "Nuclear Plant Got U.S. Contracts Despite Many Security Violations." New York Times, July 4, 1977.

———. "Panel Hints Nuclear Electricity May Be Costly." New York Times, April 11, 1978.

———. "U.S. Commission Blocks Shipment of Uranium for India Power Plants." New York Times, April 21, 1978.

———. "Congress Unit Says U.S. Tried to Balk California Nuclear Curbs." New York Times, January 16, 1978.

———. "A Student's Bomb Design Prompts Call for More Nuclear Safeguards." New York Times, March 23, 1978.

———. "Ex-C.I.A. Man Says Johnson Heard in '68 Israel Had A-Bombs." New York Times, March 2, 1978.

Burt, Richard, "U.S. Analysis Doubts There Can Be Victor In Major Atomic War." New York Times, January 6, 1978.

———. "Pentagon Reviewing Nuclear War Plans." New York Times, December 16, 1977.

———. "Neutron Bomb Study Irks Pentagon Aides." New York Times, February 1, 1978.

Cairnes, John, "The Cancer Problem." Scientific American, pp. 64–78, November 1975.

Campbell, E.E., Milligan, M.F., Moss, W.D., Schultz, H.F., and McInray, J., "Plutonium in Autopsy Tissue." Los Alamos Scientific Laboratory Report, L.A. 4875, 1973.

Clayton, Bruce Douglas, "Planning for the Day After Doomsday." The Bulletin of the Atomic Scientists, Vol. 33, pp. 49–53, September 1977.

Cobb, John C., M.D., M.P.H., ed., "Surprising Findings About Plutonium Dangers to Man Reported at the International Atomic Energy Meeting in San Francisco, California," December 25, 1975.

Cockburn, Andrew, "The Nuclear Disaster They Didn't Want To Tell You About." Esquire, Vol. 89, pp. 39–43, April 25, 1978.

Cohen, Bernard L., "The Hazards in Plutonium Dispersal." Institute for Energy Analysis, March 1975.

Comey, D.D., "The Legacy of Uranium Tailings." The Bulletin of the Atomic Scientists, pp. 43–45, September 1975.

Conrad, Robert A., M.D., et al., "A Twenty-Year Review of Medical Findings in a Marshallese Population Accidentally Exposed to Radioactive Fallout." Brookhaven National Laboratory, Associated Universities, Inc. USERDA.

Cooke, Robert, and Dietz, Jean, "Energy Future Lies In the Solar Cell." Boston Globe, April 29, 1978.

Cubie, Jim, "The Unacceptable Risks of Nuclear Energy: The Link Between Your Light Switch and the Bomb." Sojourners, Vol. 7, March 1978.

Cutler, S.J., Meyers, M.H., and Green, S.B., "Trends in Survival Rates In Patients with Cancer." New England Journal of Medicine, Vol. 293, pp. 122–124, 1975.

deVilliers, A.J., and Windish, J.P., "Lung Cancer in Flurospar Mining Community." British Journal of Industrial Medicine, 21, pp. 96–109, 1964.

Diethorn, W.S., and Stockho, W.L., "The Dose to Man From Atmospheric ^{85}Kr." Health Physics, Vol. 23, pp. 653–662, November 1972.

Dietz, Jean, "Scientists Unveil N-Waste Proposal." Boston Globe, March 4, 1978.

Eason, Charles F., M.D., "Medical Exposures of Radiation Workers—Should They Be Recorded?" Journal of Occupational Medicine, Vol. 16, March 1974.

Edsall, John T., "Toxicity of Plutonium and some other actinides." Bulletin of the Atomic Scientists, pp. 27–37, September 1976.

Eisenbud, M., "Radioactivity In The Environment: State of Radioactivity In The Environment." Pediatrics, Vol. 41, No. 1, Part II, January, 1968, pp. 174–193.

Fialka, John J., "Did Atom Agencies Squelch Report on Cancer Risk?" Washington Star, January 19, 1978.

"Fifteen Nations Agree on N-Safeguards." Globe Wire Services, Boston Evening Globe, January 12, 1978.

Ford, Daniel F., "Nuclear Power: Some Basic Economic Issues." Union of Concerned Scientists, April 28, 1975.

———. "A History of Federal Nuclear Safety Assessments: From WASH 2740 Through the Reactor Safety Study." Union of Concerned Scientists, 1977.

———. Kendall, Henry W., and Tye, Lawrence S., "Browns Ferry, The Regulatory Failure." Union of Concerned Scientists, June 10, 1976.

"Fourteen Cases of Cancer at Weapon Research Lab Studied." New York Times, January 25, 1978.

Fox, R.W., Kellener, G.G., and Kerr, C.B., "Ranger Uranium Inquiry, First Report." Australian Government Publishing Service, Camberra, October 28, 1976.

Gillette, Robert, "Transient Nuclear Workers: A Special Case for Standards." Science, Vol. 16, October 1974.

————. "Study on Nuclear Radiation Sparks Health Controversy." Los Angeles Times, December 3, 1977.

Glasstone, Samuel, ed., "The Effects of Nuclear Weapons." United States Department of Defense, U.S. Atomic Energy Commission, pp. 587–625, February 1964.

Gofman, John W., M.D., "The Fission-Product Equivalence Between Nuclear Reactors and Nuclear Weapons." Senate Congressional Record, Proceedings and Debates of the 92nd Congress, 1st Session, Vol. 117, July 8, 1971.

————. "The Cancer Hazard from Inhaled Plutonium." Committee for Nuclear Responsibility, CNR Report 1975–IR, Dublin, California, May 14, 1975.

————. "Estimated Production of Human Lung Cancers By Plutonium from Worldwide Fallout." Committee for Nuclear Responsibility, San Francisco, California, July 10, 1975.

————. "The Plutonium Controversy." Reprint Journal of American Medical Association, Vol. 236, July 19, 1976.

————. Statement on lung cancer hazards of Pu-239 and Americium-241. Pamphlet, Women Strike for Peace, Washington, D.C., February 21, 1978.

Gorman, J., "Wandering in the Nuclear Wasteland." The Sciences, pp. 6–10, November 1975.

Gottstein, Klaus, "Nuclear Energy for the Third World." The Bulletin of the Atomic Scientists, Vol. 33, pp. 44–48, June 1977.

Gwyne, Peter, "Plutonium: 'free' fuel or invitation to a catastrophe." Smithsonian.

Gyorgi, Anna, "Nuclear Waste Storage." New Age, June 1975.

"Hardsell on Nuclear Safety." Editorial, New York Times, March 2, 1978.

Hart, J.C., Ritchie, R.H., and Varnadore, Beverly S., eds., "Population Exposures." Proceedings of the 8th Midyear Topical Symposium of the Health Physics Society, Knoxville, Tennessee, October 21–24, 1974.

"Health Expert Says U.S. Should Reduce Radiation Exposure." New York Times, January 25, 1978.

"Hot Town." Environment section, Time, p. 50, December 20, 1971.

House, Karen Elliott, "U.S. is Facing Problem of How to

Dismantle Used Nuclear Reactors." Wall Street Journal, October 12, 1977.

Ibrahim, Youssef M., "U.S. Nuclear Industry Sees Bill a Threat to Exports." New York Times, February 15, 1978.

Ibser, H.W., "The Nuclear Energy Game: Genetic Roulette." The Progressive, January 1976.

Jacobs, Paul, "Precautions Are Being Taken By Those Who Know. An Inquiry Into the Power and Responsibilities of the AEC." The Atlantic, pp. 45–56, February 1971.

Johnson, E.R., and McBride, J.A., "The Plutonium Problem." INFO, Atomic Industrial Forum Public Affairs and Info Program. Presented at Workshop "The Nuclear Controversy in the U.S.A.," Lucerne, Switzerland, May 1974.

Kistiakowski, George B., "Can the Arms Race be Curbed?" Boston Sunday Globe, April 16, 1978.

Klurfeld, Jim, "A Very Private Public Man." Boston Sunday Globe, April 23, 1978.

Kneese, A.V., "The Faustian Bargain." Resources, pp. 1–5, September 1973.

Kochupillai, N., Verma, I.C., Grewai, M.S., Ramalinga Swami V., "Down's Syndrome and Related Abnormalities in an Area of High Background Radiation in Coastal Kerala." Nature, Vol. 262, July 1, 1976.

Kohn, Howard. "The Nuclear Industry's Terrible Power and How It Silenced Karen Silkwood." Rolling Stone, March 27, 1975.

————. "The Government's Quiet War on Scientists Who Know Too Much." Rolling Stone, pp. 42–44, March 23, 1978.

Krey, P.W., Bogen, D., and French, E., "Plutonium in Man and His Environment." Nature, pp. 263–265, July 21, 1962.

Kunz, E., Sevc, J., and Placek, V., "Lung Cancer in Uranium Miners and Long-Term Exposure to Radon Daughter Products." Health Institute of Uranium Industry, Institute of Industrial Hygiene in Uranium Industry.

Lamb, David, "Africa's Hunger for Weapons." Los Angeles Times reprinted in Boston Globe, March 21, 1978.

Langham, W.H., "Biological Implications of the Transuranium Elements for Man." Health Physics, Vol. 22, pp. 943–952, 1972.

Lash, Terry R., Bryson, John E., and Cotton, Richard, Citizens Guide: "The National Debate on the Handling of Radioactive Wastes from Nuclear Power Plants." Natural Resources Defense Council, Inc., November 1975.

Legator, Marvin S., and Hollander, Alexander, "Occupational Monitoring of Genetic Hazards." Annals of the New York Academy of Sciences, Vol. 269, December 31, 1975.

Lindsey, Robert, "Domestic Arms Race Pits Livermore vs. Los Alamos." New York Times, July 31, 1977.

Lisco, H., Finkel, M.P., and Brues, A.M., "Carcinogenic Properties of Radioactive Fission Products and of Plutonium." Radiology, Vol. 49, p. 361, 1947.

Loed, Vernon. "Pennsylvania Health Chief Leaves As He Began—Swiftly." Philadelphia Inquirer, November 1, 1979.

Lyons, Richard D., "Soviet Spy Satellite with Atomic Reactor Breaks Up In Canada." New York Times, January 25, 1978.

MacNeil/Lehrer Report. Transcript of "Danger: Radiation." Educational Broadcasting Corporation and GWETA, November 25, 1977.

Magno, Paul J., Reavey, Thomas C., and Apidianakis, John C., "Iodine-129 In the Environment Around a Nuclear Fuel Reprocessing Plant." (West Valley, N.Y.) US Environmental Protection Agency, Office of Radiation Programs, Field Operation Division, Washington, D.C., October 1972.

Mancuso, Thomas F., M.D., "Study of the Lifetime Health and Mortality Experience of Employees of ERDA Contractors." Department of Industrial Environmental Health Sciences, Graduate School of Public Health, University of Pittsburgh, Penn., September 30, 1977.

Mancuso, Thomas F., M.D., Stewart Alice, M.D., and Kneale, George, M.A., "Radiation Exposures of Hanford Workers Dying From Various Causes." Proceedings of Papers presented at Meeting of 10th Midyear Topical Symposium of the Health Physics Society, N.E., New York Chapter, October 11–13, 1976 at Saratoga Springs, New York.

Martell, Edward A., "Iodine-131 Fallout from Underground Tests II." Science, Vol. 148, June 25, 1965.

————. "Actinides in the Environment and Their Uptake By Man." National Center for Atmospheric Research (NCAR), Boulder, Colorado, May 1975.

————. "Tobacco Radioactivity and Cancer in Smokers." American Scientists, Vol. 63, July–August 1975.

————. "Cesium-137 From the Environment to Man: "Metabolism and Dose." National Council on Radiation Protection and Measurements, NCRP Report No. 52, Washington, D.C.

————. "Basic Considerations in the Assessment of the Cancer Risks and Standard for Internal Alpha Emitters." Statement at public hearing on Plutonium standards sponsored by USEPA, Denver, Colorado, January 10, 1975.

McGovern, George, "The Russians Are Coming—Again." The Progressive, Vol. 41, pp. 17–23, May 1977.

McGrory, Mary, "Nuclear Energy Use Looms As Campaign Issue for Carter." Boston Globe, March 2, 1978.

Middleton, Drew, "U.S. Military Study Adds Fuel to Debate on Arms Treaty." New York Times, January 11, 1978.

————. "Soviet Is Said to Top U.S. in Military Investment." Boston Globe, January 26, 1977.

Miettinen, Jorma K., "Enhanced Radiation Warfare." The Bulletin of the Atomic Scientists, Vol. 33, pp. 32–37, September 1977.

Miller, James Nathan, "The Burning Question of Browns Ferry." The Readers Digest, pp. 103–108, April 1976.

Morgan, Karl Z., Ph.D., "Reducing Medical Exposure to Ionizing Radiation." American Industrial Hygiene Association Journal, May 1975.

————. "Suggested Reduction of Permissible Exposure to Plutonium and other Transuranium Elements." American Industrial Hygiene Association Journal, August 1975.

————. "Yes, is the Answer to Question of R.H. Thomas and D.D. Busick Is It Really Necessary to Reduce Patient Exposure?" American Industrial Hygiene Association Journal, November 1976.

————. "The Dilemma of Present Nuclear Power Programs." Presented at Hearings Before the Energy Resources Conservation and Development Commission, Sacramento, California, February 1, 1977.

NAS Beir Report, "The Effects on Populations of Exposure to Low Levels of Ionizing Radiation." Report of the National Academy of Sciences, National Research Council Committee on the Biological Effects of Ionizing Radiation, Washington, D.C., November 1972.

Natarajan, N., and Bross, Irwin, D.J., "Preconception Radiation and Leukemia." Journal of Medicine, 1973.

Northrup, John, "U.S. Suppressing Radiation Cancer Data, Environmentalists Say." Birmingham Post-Herald, November 29, 1977.

Norwood, W.D., and Newton, Jr., C.E., "U.S. Transuranium Registry Study of Thirty Autopsies." Health Physics, Vol. 28, pp. 669–675, 1975.

"Nuclear Energy's Dilemma—Disposing of Hazardous Radioactive Waste Safely." Report to Congress by the Comptroller General of the United States, GAO-Government Accounting Office, September 9, 1977.

"Nuclear Plants Are Dying." Myers' Finance and Energy, No. 255, November 4, 1977.

"Nuclear Power Costs." Twenty-Third Report by the Committee on Government Operation together with Additional, Minority, and Dissenting Views. 95th Congress, 2d Session, House Report No. 95–1090. April 26, 1978. U.S. Government Printing Office, Washington, D.C.: 1978.

"Nuclear Power Growth 1974–2000. U.S. Atomic Energy

Commission, WASH 1139 (1974), ERDA-486, Vol. 1, July 1975.

"Nuclear Waste Disposal Costs (West Valley, N.Y.)." Hearings Before a Subcommittee of the Committee on Government Operations. House of Representatives, 95th Congress, 1st Session, March 8 and 10, 1977. U.S. Government Printing Office, Washington, D.C., 1977.

O'Farrell, T.P., and Gilbert, R.O., "Transport of Radioactive Materials by Jackrabbits on the Hanford Reservation." Health Physics, Vol. 29, pp. 9–15, July 1975.

O'Toole, Thomas, "U.S. Studying N-Plant Security." Washington Post, Reprinted in Boston Globe, January 15, 1976.

Oveharenro, E.P., "An Experimental Evaluation of the Effects of Transuranium Elements on Reproductive Ability." Health Physics, 1972.

"Papers From Reactor Study in 1965 To Update WASH-740," USAEC, Brookhaven National Laboratory. On file in U.S. Nuclear Regulatory Commission Public Document Room, USAEC Press Release R-252 and Attachments, released to the public, June 1973.

Patterson, Rachelle, "N-Workers Safe but Let's Make Sure—Rickover." Boston Globe, March 1, 1978.

Pincus, Walter, "House Panel Told That Exposure Limit for Radiation Is 10 Times Too High." Washington Post, February 9, 1978.

———. "GI's Win Some Illness Claims From A-Tests." Washington Post, February 5, 1978.

———. "Dispute Arises on Who Will Run U.S. Study of '57 A-Test Effect." Washington Post, January 6, 1978.

———. "The U.S. Errs; Bikini Island Still Isn't Safe." Washington Post, March 19, 1978.

———. "Thyroid Cases from '54 H-Test Increase." Washington Post, March 27, 1978.

———. "Indecision on Neutron Bomb." Washington Post, Reprint in Boston Globe, April 5, 1978.

Polhemus, Donald W., M.D., and Koch, Richard, M.D., "Leukemia and Medical Radiation." Pediatrics, March 1959.

Pollock, Richard, "The Price Anderson Act." Critical Mass Journal, Vol. 3, pp. 3–4, January 1978.

———. "Soviets Experience Nuclear Accident." Critical Mass Journal, January 1978.

"Preliminary Notification of Event or Universal Occurrence—PNO-79-67AE" Prepared for The Nuclear Regulatory Commission at the time of Three Mile Island accident.

"Prospects for Further Proliferation of Nuclear Weapons," Central Intelligence Agency Memorandum, DC1 N10 1945/74, September 4, 1974.

"Reactor Safety Study—An Assessment of Risks in U.S. Commercial Power Plants." U.S. Nuclear Regulatory Commission, Washington, D.C., WASH-1400 (NUREG 75-014)., October, 1975.

"Record Keeping Requirements Under the Occupational Safety and Health Act of 1970." U.S. Department of Labor, Occupational Safety and Health Administration, Revised 1975.

Regovin, Mitchell and Frampton, Jr., George T. "Three Mile Island, A Report To The Commissioners and To the Public," Nuclear Regulatory Commission Special Inquiry Group, Vol. I, January, 1980.

"Report of the President's Commission on the Accident at Three Mile Island, The Need for Change: The Legacy at Three Mile Island," Washington, D.C., (Library of Congress Catalogue Card Number 79-25694), October, 1979.

"Representative Warns Village of Hazard in Nuclear Waste Plant." (West Valley, N.Y.) New York Times, March 19, 1978.

Richards, Bill, "Army In Maze Finding Nuclear Test Participants." Washington Post, February 15, 1978.

Richmond, C.R., and Thomas, R.L., "Plutonium In Man And His Environment." Nature, pp. 263–265, July 21, 1962.

Rose, D.J., "Nuclear Electric Power." Science, pp. 351–359, April 19, 1974.

Rosenbaum, Ron, "The Subterranean World of the Bomb." Harper's, Vol. 256, pp. 85–105, March 1978.

Ryer, Flo H., "The New Health and Safety Act As It Relates To Occupational Radiation Exposure." Health Physics, 1975.

Sauve, Frances, "Council Requests Study of Smoke Detectors." Washington Post, February 23, 1978.

Schadewald, Bill, "the bull market ... Federal Government Spending by Function." Houston Business Journal, November 14, 1977.

Seldin, Charles, "Army Veteran of A-Bomb Test Dies of Leukemia." The Washington Post, February 10, 1978.

Severo, Richard, "Too Hot to Handle." New York Times Magazine, April 10, 1977.

Sikov, M.R., and Mahlum, D.D., "Plutonium In the Developing Animal." Health Physics, Vol. 22, pp. 707–712, 1972.

Sivard, Ruth Leger, "World Military and Social Expenditures 1977." WMSE Publications, 1977.

Smith, D.D., and Black, S.C., "Actinide Concentrations in Tissues from Cattle Grazing Near the Rocky Flats Plant." National Environmental Research Center Report, NERC-LV-539-36, pp. 1–33.

Smothers, Ronald, "Con Ed Welders Fear A-Plant Job, But Company Says Work or Quit." New York Times, March 24, 1978.

Solo, Pam, "Nuclear Crossroads at Rocky Flats." Sojourners, Vol. 7, March 1978.

115

"Soviets to US in '69: Let's Attack China." Washington Post, Reprint in Boston Globe, February 17, 1978.

Sternglass, Ernest J., Ph.D., "Strontium-90 Levels in the Milk and Diet Near Connecticut Nuclear Power Plants." October 27, 1977.

————. "Cancer Mortality Changes Around Nuclear Facilities in Connecticut." Testimony Presented at a Congressional Seminar on Low-Level Radiation, Washington, D.C., February 10, 1978.

Sullivan, Walter, "U.S. Space Mishaps In '64 and '70 Noted." New York Times, January 25, 1978.

"United States of America Nuclear Regulatory Commission, NRC/Response Center Discussion Related to Metropolitan Edison Company, Three Mile Island Station." This transcript was prepared from a tape recording.

"U.S. District Court Judge McMillan's Declaration, The Price Anderson Act Unconstitutional," Carolina Environmental Study Group, Charlotte, N.C., March 31, 1977.

Waldrop, Mitch, "The Technology Behind Nuclear Proliferation." C&EN, Washington, D.C., pp. 17–23, July 25, 1977.

Walker, Greg, "The Nuclear Playground." The Australian, No. 3830, November 9, 1976.

Wasserbach, Anna E., "Where to Throw Away a Radioactive Swab?" (letter to the editor) Woodstock Times, February 9, 1978.

Weighart, James, "The Dangers Aloft: A Matter of Relativity." Boston Globe, January 26, 1978.

Weinberg, A.M., "Social Institutions and Nuclear Energy." Science, pp. 1–18, July 7, 1972.

Weinraub, Bernard, "Study Backs U.S. Nuclear Posture." New York Times, January 10, 1978.

"West Valley and the Nuclear Waste Dilemma." 12th Report by Committee on Government Operations together with Additions and Dissenting Views, October 26, 1977, Union Calendar No. 394, 95th Congress, 1st Session, Report No. 95–755.

Wilford, John Noble, "Radiation Tests Set for Bikini Islands." New York Times, March 23, 1978.

"World Armaments, The Nuclear Threat." Stockholm International Peace Research Institute, 1977.

Yergin, Daniel, "The Real Meaning of the Energy Crunch." The New York Times Magazine, June 4, 1978.